TOKYO ZANGYO

ALSO AVAILABLE BY MICHAEL PRONKO

Memoirs on Tokyo Life

Beauty and Chaos: Slices and Morsels of Tokyo Life (2014)
Tokyo's Mystery Deepens: Essays on Tokyo (2014)
Motions and Moments: More Essays on Tokyo (2015)

The Detective Hiroshi Series

The Last Train (2017)
The Moving Blade (2018)
Tokyo Traffic (2020)

For more about the Detective Hiroshi series and Pronko's other writing: www.michaelpronko.com

Follow Michael on Twitter:
@pronkomichael

Michael's Facebook page:
www.facebook.com/pronkoauthor

TOKYO ZANGYO

by Michael Pronko

Raked Gravel Press 2021

RAKED
GRAVEL
PRESS

月に村雲、花に嵐

Tsuki ni muragumo, hana ni arashi

The moon will be covered by clouds,
flowers blown in a storm.

—Japanese saying

残業 Zangyo

Overtime work, often unpaid.

—Common Japanese word

Chapter 1

Shigeru Onizuka woke up shivering, naked, on the roof of his company building. His head spun from alcohol as he pulled himself up on the rooftop lunch table. He tottered but couldn't walk. His feet were tied. He hopped, once, twice, toppled onto the bench and slapped his arms and chest to warm himself, his head swollen and throbbing. His body shrank from the cold and shivered harder as he tried to piece together how he'd gotten there.

He'd had whiskey at the bar and more later, and almost nothing to eat. He must have blacked out. That had happened before—too much booze to remember how he got home—but he'd never woken up naked, tied up, and confused on the roof of the company where he'd spent his entire career.

And he had never heard voices before. They echoed inside his head.

On the far side of the roof, the smoking area shimmered like a mirage. On one of the trees that ringed the area in tall planters, he saw a light-gray *jinbei* wraparound shirt and tie-up shorts, hanging from the branches. He staggered toward the meager summer clothes, remembering—vaguely—having pulled them on earlier. A pair of tatami sandals was set below.

Squinting against the spotlights that outlined the roof, he tried to see if he was alone. The wind roared past his ear, speaking its own language. The spotlights cast stripes of dark and light across the roof. Beyond, in all directions, the lights of Tokyo shimmered and danced with each doddering step. The imposing buildings of Marunouchi's business district—the center of Japan's economic engine—swayed and blurred. He had to sober up.

Onizuka untied his ankles, his fingers stiff and sore from the cold. He stood, placing one bare foot on cold concrete after the next, and moved toward his *jinbei*, something at least to cover himself with. He shivered and slapped his skin again, almost there.

He snatched the *jinbei*, bashing his shin on the tree planter. He pulled on the shirt and tried to tie the flap, but after a couple of tries, he left it. He raised his leg to get into the shorts and tumbled over. He got up, but had to stoop down to yank them on. He slipped his feet into the soft tatami sandals, relieving the pain from the icy concrete.

The shirt and shorts did little against the harsh wind blowing crosswise twenty stories high. The *jinbei* was summer-wear and his limbs and his chest wouldn't stop shaking.

Where was his cellphone, money clip, and watch? He rubbed his wrists, raw from rope burns, remembering vaguely taking off the watch and putting it in the pocket of his wool pants. And where was his tailored suit and wool overcoat? He could feel his packet of Sobranie cigarettes in one pocket of the *jinbei*, a few still left.

He snatched at shards of memory, but nothing fitted into place. How did he get through the lobby? Did he come in through the parking lot? The service elevator? He remembered voices, women's voices, mocking, accusing, commanding. Where did they go?

A woman's voice whispered to him. "That way. Toward the lights."

Onizuka steadied himself with a tree branch as he peered around the glass divider into the smoking area.

"That way," the voice said again, clear and steady, a man's voice now, far away, muffled.

He spun towards the voice, and looked around the smoking area, but along the trees and inside the partitioned space there was nothing and no one, except himself.

He patted the pockets of the *jinbei* for his lighter, an expensive present. Had he been robbed? Holding the wall, he reached for one of the communal lighters in the smoking lounge. He held himself up on the shelf where people rested their laptops to work through cigarette breaks.

"Towards the lights. Over there," the man's voice whispered.

Onizuka spun toward the voice, but there was nothing there. He stood and turned and turned again, stopping in the direction of the national gardens and palace moat opposite to where the business district hummed, still lit up in late-night mode. The expanse of the palace grounds was dark.

It was his voice, though. They'd competed since the first day at the company, gambling on the other's tripping up and falling behind. But it had never happened—until now.

He twisted in the other direction and could see, dimly, hazily, lights on in buildings across the street. People must still be working. He twisted his wrist, feeling for his watch. He had no idea what time it could be, what day. It must be Monday morning. His appointment had been on Sunday, her busiest day.

"Toward the lights." He heard the voice as clear and sharp as the wind. It was a woman's voice now. The man's voice had changed somehow, as if coming from inside his own head. The woman's voice was there, too.

"Who's there?" Onizuka tried to summon his commanding tone as a *bucho* section chief in the top media company in Japan. He was used to giving orders, not receiving them. He called out again, but his voice cracked and slurred, weaker than wind, softer than the voices in his head.

He pulled out one of his Sobranie cigarettes and fumbled with the cheap, shared lighter. He flicked and flicked until it caught the black paper. The smoke cleared his head for a moment before confusion swallowed him again. He pulled the thin shirt around himself and scanned the roof for the voice.

He stared at the picnic tables, used mostly by the *OL office ladies* and new recruits who didn't bother lunching with managers, their promotion already stymied. He'd had those installed, and he sometimes ordered pizza for everyone when a contract was completed. He hated pizza.

"You know what you have to do, so do it." The voice came again, strong and demanding. He turned toward the lights and the new fence.

He realized who it was.

It was her.

He'd heard her voice for a year afterwards, but gradually it had faded and he could hear himself think again. Now, she was back.

From behind, a shove sent him tumbling onto his knees. He swayed on all fours for a minute. His body felt hollowed out and depleted. Hoisting himself upright, he held out his arms for balance as he clawed his feet back into the sandals.

"Go on. From the same spot," the voice insisted. Another shove sent him stumbling forward.

He wobbled away from the picnic tables and the smokers' area toward the spotlights along the Marunouchi side. A huge gash, which looked like an upside-down V, was cut into the protective fence that lined the roof. He didn't remember that V in the fence.

"You know the place. Right between those lights. Straight ahead."

"What place?" Onizuka croaked, accepting the voice.

"There. Straight ahead. The same place."

"I don't—"

"You know where. You know why."

The voice seemed closer, inside and outside his head, but he couldn't see anyone.

He turned to look at the cut-open V. It was where she had stood, just before. He'd been there many times, stood there smoking and thinking. He would look over the edge of the roof and down at the wide sidewalks of the Marunouchi district twenty floors below, empty now of traffic and pedestrians.

He'd lost another bet, the biggest one. He didn't need a voice to tell him that. He had a debt to pay, and he always paid his debts.

That was how he'd kept winning. Standing around smoking only postponed payment.

"Keep going. You know what to do." The voice was carried by the wind, mixing with it.

He might as well go. He heard more voices, a chorus now, his wrestling coach, that neighborhood policeman, his first boss at Senden, the guy he got betting tips from, all of them gone. The voices felt heavy and solid, joined together like arms pushing him, dragging him to the edge. He could no more resist the force of the voices than he could resist the force of gravity.

He staggered forward, all of them, all of it, behind him now.

He was so tired of the junior employees, the expenses, the bank transfers. He was tired of breaking in graduates from name schools, of drinking with contacts, golfing on Sundays. He was tired of the hassles with Human Resources, the endless meetings, reports, action plans, rule changes, mission statements, committees, presentations, the last train home.

He had never had a full night's sleep since he started work. He was emptied out daily and never refilled. Emi helped him live with it, distracted him from it. Gambling gave him the thrill he remembered from his youth. But all else, everyone else, was a drain.

He was tired of the grudging promotions, the observance of hierarchy, the constant niggling demand for loyalty. The company would suffer in foreign places by losing the roots of its Japanese-ness. He helped them expand overseas, but he should have, and could have, buried them with what he knew.

Taking the position overseas wasn't what he wanted. It was what he was ordered to do. That was his life, following orders, or guessing what the orders were and following through without even hearing them spoken.

He walked toward the fence and looked twenty floors down. The shape of the fence wire cut the city into small diamond sections. He patted his pockets for his cigarettes. He wanted one

13

more.

He thought of his wife and his sons, but they had never been close. They were casualties of his success. His oldest son was at a good company, and his wife had money from her family, and all the winnings he'd left her. His youngest son had shaken free.

He would miss Emi, though, and her ministrations. It was only with her that he'd felt anything at all. Even anticipating the result of a big bet was never as good. He could hear her, feel her around him, inside him, next to him, her heat warming him even on the roof.

He flick-flick-flicked the cheap plastic lighter and lit a last cigarette. He tried to stop shivering by wrapping his fingers through the fence. The wind felt colder at the edge and the lights brighter. He squinted as the strong light floated up like water from below and rose and fell into the distant sprawl and swell of the city. The fence was like one around a swimming pool, keeping him from entering.

He moved down the fence hand by hand until he came to the huge V, the only way to get to the light-water, to the city. The V in the fence was big enough to get through. He took another drag on his cigarette, held it up against the panoramic view below, almost done.

He stepped out of the sandals and positioned them neatly together, facing the edge, in the same place she had. His body shivered uncontrollably. His feet felt numb, making it hard to walk. He would swim instead.

He grabbed the fence with both hands and ducked through the cut-open V. He could see better there, the whole city before him.

It was easier than he thought.

He heard a shout behind him, but he tuned it out. He didn't need to pretend to listen anymore.

The voices faded as he stepped onto the outer ledge, balancing himself with a hand on the fence, listening to the wind.

He took a last puff and tossed the half-finished cigarette aside.

Tokyo flowed in all directions like an ocean of light. He was ready to dive in, to return. He'd swim over to Tokyo Station, its squat, quaint brick front waiting for him. He'd been through there twice a day since college, and loved the fierce power of the place. He'd swim to that energy, tap it, and from there, decide where to swim next.

He took a step forward, felt the edge with his toes, and breathed in deeply. He heard the fence rattling behind him and voices shouting, babbling.

He straightened his *jinbei*, sober enough at last to tie a knot to hold the shirt in place. Then he cleared his throat and dove into the light.

Chapter 2

Detective Hiroshi Shimizu reached for his buzzing cellphone, a victory of habit over fatigue. He flipped his legs over the edge of the bed and listened to explanations and directions, and then orders, from Detective Sakaguchi, head of homicide.

Half listening to Sakaguchi and half-asleep, Hiroshi looked at Ayana's long black hair draped over her pillow. Hiroshi ran his hand along the curve of her body from her shoulder to her hip, giving her butt a squeeze, soft enough to let her keep sleeping, firm enough to rouse her if she was half-awake. He loved the way she made love sleepy, humming, flushed, opening to it gradually.

She didn't stir, so better to let her sleep. She'd been working late at the archives every night the past couple of weeks, a massive reshelving project that left her exhausted. For weeks, she'd come home and flung herself on the sofa, skipping kendo practice. Neither of them had cooked for weeks. They'd ordered out or Hiroshi microwaved something.

Hiroshi eased himself up and struggled into some clothes as quietly as he could. In the kitchen, he dug into a bag of chocolate croissants. He stuffed one in his mouth, dropped an apple in his pocket and left the bag out for Ayana, the top rolled tight.

***

When he got out of the taxi across from Tokyo Station, Hiroshi followed the glow of the LED balloon lights that lit up the crime scene. He walked past two coffee shops, both disappointingly closed. Ahead, blocking all traffic, tarps were stretched across the street and sidewalks. He gave up on the coffee and headed toward the lights.

Hiroshi flipped his badge to the officer at the entrance and looked for Sakaguchi. He stood a head taller and much wider than everyone else on the force, so was always easy to find. Sakaguchi signed a form and started to limp toward Hiroshi. As a former sumo wrestler, Sakaguchi had always seemed immune to pain, and to fatigue. He'd grown up in the poor part of Osaka, where work was the backbone of the day and complaints were left unspoken.

"Your leg all right?" Hiroshi asked.

Sakaguchi stood rebalancing himself, letting the weight down slowly on his knee. "Doctor recommends surgery."

"Take time off," Hiroshi said.

"I would, but now there's this." Sakaguchi leaned over to reset his knee brace.

Hiroshi wondered where he'd found one big enough for his tree trunk of a leg. He knew Sakaguchi could only find clothes and shoes at the one super men's size shop in Tokyo.

Sakaguchi straightened up to take a clipboard from a young detective, scanned the form and signed it. Sakaguchi's injury occurred when he stepped wrong chasing a suspect. It compounded the injury that had sidelined him from sumo years ago, but which had led him to take the police exam in Tokyo. This injury, though, looked like it would result only in surgery.

Hiroshi looked at the medical examiners working on the sidewalk. Takamatsu, his *senpai* and erstwhile mentor, was kneeling over the body and surveying every mangled bit.

The body was a tangle of limbs, one leg crossed backward, the other underneath, one arm flopped to the side and the other, undamaged, angled eerily upward as if pushing to rise from the street. The rest of the body and head was clumped across the sidewalk like wet red clay. Takamatsu was inured to every grisly detail. At every murder scene, Hiroshi looked away, but Takamatsu looked closer. Takamatsu had been a family friend, Hiroshi wasn't sure of the exact connection, and had been the one to get him the position in homicide in charge of white-collar cases, overseas-related issues, and anything involving English. He was dragged into cases like this one, though, when he couldn't find a good enough excuse to work from his office.

"Gives you renewed respect for gravity." Sakaguchi looked up at the top of the building. "The windows don't open."

"Who called it in?" Hiroshi squinted against the lights.

"Some tourists from Indonesia."

"Ruined their vacation."

Sakaguchi said, "You want to get started on the roof? I'll send Takamatsu up when he's done down here."

Hiroshi headed through the markers next to splattered bits of the body. He didn't look down until he got to the entrance and hurried inside.

Above the lobby a huge sign announced the name of the company—Senden Central. Long, vertical banners stretched from ceiling to floor with city scenes of New York, London, and Singapore. Slogans cascaded down inside speech bubbles from the toothy smiles of female models: "Now Senden Infinity," "Going Global," "From Tokyo to the World," "Bringing People Together." The banners curved like bows tied over the well-wrapped image the company had of itself.

On a chair in the corner, a gray-haired security guard sat rubbing his head and staring at the floor. A young officer from the nearby police box held open the elevator door for Hiroshi and reached in to press the button for the roof.

The roof was bathed in LED balloon lights that solarized the bare trees and small shrubs planted in containers. Together with the picnic tables, the roof felt like a small park. Hiroshi pulled his too-thin wool jacket tight and turned up his collar against the cold, wet March wind. He followed the path of small plastic markers to the outer protective fence. It had been cut open and bent back.

His chest tightened with a shot of anxiety.

Growing up in Tokyo, he'd never given a thought to skyscrapers, but during his years studying in Boston he became used to lower architectural vistas. Linda, his Boston girlfriend who came back with him to Tokyo, loved taking photos from high up in Tokyo's tallest buildings, but all Hiroshi could think about was earthquakes and how to scramble back inside four solid walls close to earth. In the end, Linda scrambled back to Boston, and Hiroshi stayed in Tokyo, a city of walls close—and far—from earth.

"Can't help but think about it, can you?" Takamatsu asked.

Hiroshi jumped. "Don't sneak up on me like that."

"I always think about jumping." Takamatsu smiled. His Italian leather trench coat looked a lot warmer than the jacket Hiroshi had thrown on. Whatever the weather, Takamatsu dressed with an effortless correctness that covered up the time it took, probably because he spent most of his life dressed right—and dressed well—for investigating outside. He returned to his desk in the detective's room only when necessary. Hiroshi wore just enough to get from apartment to train, train to office, a place he preferred to crime scenes.

Crime scene specialists were looking at a pair of tatami slippers and discussing the best way to get prints off the fence, if they even could.

Watching them, Takamatsu said, "The fence looks like the kind they use for baseball backstops."

"Did he cut it open himself?" Hiroshi asked. He stared at the spot where the man had stood, making his last decision, the only one that really mattered.

"Doesn't seem like something a *bucho* department head would do himself." Takamatsu turned to a young woman in the crime scene crew. "No wire cutters anywhere?"

She didn't know, but hurried off to check.

"Of course there won't be any wire cutters." Takamatsu lit a cigarette and straightened his cuffs. "Whoever pushed him took them."

"Maybe he did it himself?"

"Maybe. Then there'll be wire cutters." As Takamatsu stooped down to look at the V, the smell and smoke of his cigarette vanished in the strong breeze. "He set his sandals together neatly. What most suicides do."

"I wonder why they didn't have a stronger fence?" Hiroshi shivered in the cold wind.

"It probably takes several suicides to be worth the budget. After one of those pop musicians jumped, every high school in the country put up fencing to stop copycats."

"A windfall for fence companies."

"*Roof* fencing companies. A Tokyo specialty." Takamatsu took out his portable ashtray and slipped the butt inside.

"How did he even get up here?" Hiroshi pulled his coat tighter and stared at the dawn light falling on the thick trees around the Imperial Palace beyond the glassed-in side of the roof.

Takamatsu said, "The guard said he hadn't seen anything, but they're looking at the security video now."

The young crime scene investigator came hurrying over, shaking her head—no, there were no wire fence cutters in evidence.

"And the guy was a department head?" Hiroshi asked.

"No doubt an asshole like all of them. Or an embezzler. You can't climb the ladder that high without making enemies...and without being a little corrupt."

"Aren't you jumping ahead of things?"

"That's our job." Takamatsu smiled. "Sakaguchi got you out of bed to start digging into his finances, and the company's. That'll save us interviewing a stream of boring company employees. I'd rather look through all the video footage than talk to even one of them."

"I'll remember you said that," Hiroshi said.

Detectives Osaki and Sugamo stood by the door, their bulky

figures casting wide shadows across the rooftop. Hiroshi trusted them about everything. They were the earthquake-proof foundation under every case, resisting every seismic shift. They'd worked in the department longer than he had, working their way up from beat cops just like Sakaguchi had. Hiroshi had been dropped in at the top, but the two detectives never displayed the least envy that Hiroshi could detect. They didn't have time for it. The crime scene crew, smaller than Osaki and Sugamo by half, reflexively stepped aside as they approached. They were almost as large as Sakaguchi.

"Where's Ueno?" Hiroshi asked.

Sugamo replied, "We've been letting him sleep in. Infection from the gunshot wound still. Late mornings and desk work until it heals."

Osaki said, "Takamatsu, you were right. It is that guy."

Takamatsu pulled out another cigarette, cupping his hand to light it in the breeze.

"What guy?" Hiroshi asked.

"What girl," Takamatsu corrected.

Osaki said, "That girl who worked a hundred hours of overtime in one month."

Sugamo shrugged. "We've had overtime like that."

"We're cops," Takamatsu said. "There's no overtime."

Osaki began to explain, "That girl who killed herself after posting on Twitter how she was harassed at work. It went viral and her mother sued the company."

"And won," Takamatsu added.

"Well, the boss who drove her to suicide was this guy," Osaki said.

"Which guy?" Hiroshi looked confused.

Sugamo pointed to the cut-open fence. "It was the exact same spot."

"Same spot?" Hiroshi asked.

"Where the girl jumped. The one who was overworked and

harassed to death. Wasn't any fencing then. They put that in after."

They all looked at the spot. Takamatsu pulled out another cigarette. He seemed to be smoking more than usual.

Sakaguchi came out of the door and the crime scene crew flocked to him, pestering him with forms to sign, and pointing at the carts loaded with evidence.

When he finished, Sakaguchi ambled toward Takamatsu and Hiroshi. Hiroshi winced at Sakaguchi's obvious pain each time his weight fell on his injured knee.

Before he could get to them, he was intercepted by two people, a tall, thin man in a suit and a tall young woman clutching a leather notepad and shivering in the cold. Hiroshi could not see her face well in the shadow of the lights but she kept her gaze fixed on him.

Sakaguchi waved Hiroshi closer and said, "This is the head of Senden's Human Resources Department, Nakata, and his assistant, Chizu, was it?"

The tall, polite man handed his *meishi* business card to the detectives with a curt bow.

Hiroshi said, "You're head of HR? Did you notice anything about the, um, deceased?" Hiroshi realized he didn't know the dead man's name.

Nakata gave a tight nod. "Onizuka. He was working as usual, getting ready to move to the London office where he would be in charge."

Hiroshi asked, "When was he leaving?"

"He was going to take over on April first, the start of the corporate year," Nakata answered. He wore a well-cut blue suit and was taller than Hiroshi, standing calmly, as if there were no wind sweeping across the rooftop.

Hiroshi said, "For most people, being posted abroad would be a step up in their career."

Nakata nodded in agreement.

"We'll need to see his personnel file, and we'd like to talk with the others in his section. Were other employees set to go abroad

23

with him?"

"If you need that information now, we can go inside. Or I can meet you later today or tomorrow if you—"

"Tomorrow...I mean later this afternoon, would be fine," Hiroshi said, wondering if it was.

"Please set up an appointment with my assistant, Chizu." He turned to the tall woman shivering in the cold. She stood as still as she could without a coat. She was tall, pretty and aloof. She handed Hiroshi her *meishi*. Nakata bowed before walking away, and Chizu pivoted and followed.

Hiroshi watched them walk away and looked up at the sky. The sun was just coming up and the sky looked huge without being blocked by imposing buildings, interiorized spaces, and the distracting rush of Tokyo life.

From the roof, it was easy to see the mixed colors of the sunrise—oranges, purples, soft yellows—brushed onto thin clouds. In the distance below, the grey buildings of the city rose up like endless stupas honoring the national religion of economics and the sub-sects of business, transportation, residence and shopping.

Sakaguchi rolled his head and stretched his huge body in resignation. "The chief's already called and told me he wants this quickly resolved. Senden is one of Japan's flagship companies."

Sugamo said, "We'll get onto the security footage."

"Cameras all over the building, no doubt," Osaki said.

Takamatsu looked at Hiroshi. "We need to tell the deceased *bucho*'s wife and talk with the girl's mother. One of the two might solve it for us."

"I'm loaded with cases and I've got meetings today with overseas bureaus that can't be rescheduled," Hiroshi said.

Sakaguchi dropped his bear paw of a hand on Hiroshi's shoulder. "Sugamo, you drive Takamatsu and Hiroshi. Maybe you can get Hiroshi back in time for his all-important meetings."

Chapter 3

Shigeru Onizuka's house was in the far west Tokyo suburb of Tachikawa. The homes were dropped into the center of lots whose size showed precisely how much salary the owner had. Wide roads with roundabouts, trees and streetside parks formed a flowing grid of wealth that made up for the commute into the center of the city. Onizuka's lot was large enough to distance the neighbors and have a spacious garden inside the enclosure, though no trees poked over the top of the solid, tile-topped wall.

Takamatsu pressed the call button in the gate of Onizuka's home. He had to lean halfway out the car window to reach the button, mussing his suit. Sugamo kept the car running. Hiroshi looked at his watch. "Maybe the new widow isn't home." But it was just past eight, when home deliveries started.

The blank camera eye on the button stared at the detectives.

Takamatsu held his tie back and pressed the call button again, his leather coat folded neatly on the seat beside him.

"We can come back later, or you can." Hiroshi drained the last of the take-out coffee he'd forced Sugamo to stop for. What he needed now was a couple shots of espresso in his office.

Sugamo looked in the rearview mirror. A black two-door Mercedes-Benz pulled up behind them.

"Wonder where she's been?" Takamatsu twisted for a better look.

The Benz pulled back and Sugamo backed into the street to let it by.

Instead of a woman, though, a square-headed young man leaned out. "Are you police?"

Takamatsu held up his badge.

"Follow me in," the young man said. The front gate slid open and the detectives followed the Benz up a short concrete drive that ended in a turnaround. The garden around the house was nothing more than smooth grass lawn, more field than garden. A single stone pagoda poked up, the only decor inside the surrounding wall of tan plaster and tiled top.

The young man hopped out of the Benz and stood waiting in a white shirt and black slacks. When Takamatsu and Hiroshi got out, he said, "I'm the son. Onizuka's son. Please come inside." He locked his Benz and flipped through a ring of keys to open the thick wooden door.

Takamatsu watched him closely as he slipped on his coat.

Hiroshi bowed. "We're here to let you know—"

"About my father? I heard already," he said, taking off his shoes in the entryway.

"And to offer our condolences," Hiroshi said.

The younger Onizuka bowed in thanks, paused, and motioned the detectives inside.

Hiroshi said, "We'd also like to talk with your mother."

He stopped in the hallway. "She hasn't answered her phone."

Hiroshi and Takamatsu followed him down a hallway. The home was a rectangular succession of stone, glass and wood. The living room was lined on two sides with windows looking out on the flat trimmed lawn. Below the windows ran a low shelf holding a single, dark vase. The room was either highly restrained or greatly ignored, and didn't feel lived in.

The son's small, sturdy frame had a quick, muscular way of moving. His sighs signaled concern. He pulled open one of the sliding windows to let in some air. The room felt overheated from direct sun. Takamatsu slipped off his leather trench coat and draped it over his arm.

"I'm Satoshi Onizuka, the first son." He motioned for them to sit.

"You have a brother?" Takamatsu asked.

"Yes, but he's not in Japan right now." Satoshi held out his *meishi* for the detectives. Takamatsu and Hiroshi handed him theirs.

"Please sit down. I'll get some tea."

"We just have a few questions," Hiroshi said, settling onto a leather upholstered chair.

Satoshi checked his cellphone. "I need some coffee. Are you sure you won't have some?"

Hiroshi said, "If you're making it for yourself."

Takamatsu waved his hand to say no and folded his jacket neatly over the back of the chair. Hiroshi looked out at the mowed lawn and plain wall, waiting politely.

They heard a car pull up in the drive, its door open and slam shut. Hiroshi and Takamatsu turned at the sound of the front door banging open. Down the hallway, a woman bustled in carrying a large purse and a shopping bag. Satoshi hurried toward her from a side door and started whispering.

Hiroshi and Takamatsu listened but couldn't hear what they said.

The woman dumped the bag into Satoshi's arms and flopped her purse on a shelf in the hall. She flounced into the living room and pushed back her long, straight hair with both hands.

Hiroshi stood up, trying to remember how old the *bucho* was. Sakaguchi had said he was sixty. But this woman seemed to be in her thirties. If the son was in his twenties, she must have had him quite young. Maybe it was her hoop earrings, tight skirt and stylish hair. It looked as if each single hair had been treated and trimmed separately.

She waved them to sit down and flopped into the wide leather sofa across from them. It whuffed as if it were new. "I'm Natsuko Onizuka. And you're the police."

Even across the room, Hiroshi could smell the booze. He saw Takamatsu lean back as he no doubt sniffed the same thing. Her face was flushed and she jostled herself into place, leaning back like they were all old friends. She was plastered.

Takamatsu spoke first. "We came to inform you..."

"I heard already. I got it out of the person who called," she said.

The detectives offered their condolences with a low bow. "I'm Hiroshi Shimizu and this is Detective Takamatsu. We have a few questions."

She crossed her legs and twisted her shoulders. Her compact face, angled chin and dimpled, padded cheeks were what most Japanese would call cute. Her eyes curved in neat brushstrokes to the far sides of her face, but inside, the whites were bloodshot and glassy.

Satoshi came in with three cups of coffee and a glass of water. He whispered something to his mother and she took the coffee with an irritated look. He set out another cup for Hiroshi and set the water in front of Takamatsu. Satoshi sat down beside his mother.

"You have another son?" Hiroshi asked.

"Yes." Natsuko turned to Satoshi. "Does he even know?"

Satoshi set his coffee cup down. "I called and left a message. He didn't call back yet."

Natsuko turned to the detectives. "He's backpacking somewhere in Southeast Asia. He's the only one who'll be pleased at the news."

Satoshi shook his head. "Mother, that's not true."

Hiroshi nodded. "They didn't get along?"

Natsuko laughed. "No one got along with my husband. This son suffered him. The other son left. Fled, I'd say."

"It sounds like your husband was hard to deal with," Hiroshi prodded.

Satoshi frowned. "He was gone most of the time working."

Natsuko put down her coffee. "He was gone *all* the time. He missed graduations, archery contests, chess matches. Barely came to the hospital for their births."

"So, you took care of the house?" Hiroshi prompted.

"I managed the household. Once the boys left, I was free to do what I want." She shook her head and drank more coffee. "Even freer now, I guess."

She sent Satoshi to get her purse.

"You've been married for..."

Natsuko pointed at Satoshi. "Twenty-three years. I was a young little *OL* office lady, naive as hell. Worked in another department. He was charming when he wanted something. When I got pregnant, I quit work and we married and moved in here." She gestured at the house as if it were nothing of importance.

Satoshi carried in her purse and she dug inside before taking out a pack of cigarettes and lighting a long, thin black one with gold foil around the filter.

Hiroshi could sense Takamatsu fidgeting beside him, but he resisted joining her. "When was the last time you talked to your husband?"

"I don't remember."

"Did you have any inkling of anything wrong?"

Natsuko pointed at Satoshi, "He talks to him more than I do."

Satoshi shook his head, unsure. "I talked to him, by phone, a few days ago. He sounded ready for the overseas expansion. It was just the usual conversation...how was work, did I have a girlfriend, nothing much."

Hiroshi turned back to Natsuko. "Were you going with him?"

"Overseas? No, no," Natsuko replied, blowing smoke toward the ceiling. "Visiting would be enough. He'd be working constantly there, too. That's all he ever cared about."

Hiroshi said, "He worked a lot?"

Satoshi said, "He was a workaholic. And a perfectionist. If things weren't going how he wanted, he made everyone follow his way. He wanted everything right, and he decided what was right."

"What kind of things?" Hiroshi asked.

Satoshi nodded, thinking. "School, sports, part-time jobs. He didn't want me joining a small company. All my life I followed his rules, met his expectations, his advice."

"And where are you working now?"

"A start-up IT company. First real decision I made in my life."

"Was he upset or acting strangely lately?" Takamatsu asked.

Natsuko smiled. "If he'd started acting normal, I would have been surprised."

"Would he have wanted to hurt himself? Commit suicide, I mean?" Hiroshi breathed through his mouth. Natsuko's alcohol breath was strong.

Natsuko shook her head, no. "He was too in love with himself to do that."

Satoshi said, "Since I was young, he told us how he was the hardest worker in Japan and why I should be like him. He was always sure of himself. He wasn't suicidal."

Takamatsu leaned forward. "So, nothing different lately of any kind?"

Natsuko looked at her empty cup. "He seemed busier, but he was always busy. Work consumed him. And now, I guess, it really has." She chuckled bitterly. "When I married him, I didn't know he'd only come home after midnight. At first, I'd get up to make dinner at one in the morning, turn on his bath. With the second son, I started leaving his dinner in the microwave. Some weeks, I'd hardly see him. He'd sleep a few hours, in the other room, change clothes and go back to work. I spent all day taking care of the boys. And now they're gone. And now he's gone."

Satoshi said, "I'll get you another coffee, Mom."

"The lawyers are coming soon," she said to her son, stabbing the cigarette out in her coffee cup.

Lawyers already, Hiroshi wondered.

Takamatsu breathed in. "Is there anything else you can tell us about him recently, anything related to work or finances or…"

Natsuko shrugged. "I've been thinking about that since the call woke me up."

"Who called, if I might ask?" Hiroshi thought the detectives would be the first.

"Someone from the company."

"Nakata from Human Resources?"

"Maybe." Natsuko nodded. "I just went back over everything, back to the first time we kissed, in a karaoke room. Recently, we lived separate lives, to be honest, so if there was something, I wouldn't know. He rarely came home for dinner, and when he did, he was hollowed out."

Hiroshi nodded. "And just one more question…who handled the finances for the family?"

She laughed bitterly and played with her coffee cup. "I did. I worked in accounting before I quit the company. Seems like a long time ago."

The doorbell rang.

"That must be the lawyers." Natsuko took her son's hand and rested it on her shoulder.

"Was there anyone who might have wanted to harm him?" Hiroshi asked, standing up.

Takamatsu took his coat from the back of the chair.

Satoshi shrugged and stood behind his mother. "He wasn't a likable person."

Chapter 4

It was less than an hour drive east to Kichijoji, where Sugamo pulled the car to a stop on a side street of one of the most lively and popular areas in western Tokyo, the streets filled every day with young and old shopping, living, and strolling. He peered at the GPS on the dash. "On the corner of the big street ahead."

Hiroshi said, "My GPS says it's the next street."

Sugamo pressed buttons on the dashboard GPS navigation.

Hiroshi put his cellphone away and started looking along the street. "There it is."

Hiroshi and Takamatsu got out of the car. After freezing on the roof and Takamatsu keeping the car window open to smoke, Hiroshi finally felt warmed by the late-morning sun. It had burned away the chill and quieted the wind.

The shop was located just outside the buzzing commercial area by Kichijoji Station, where the big store streets narrowed into calmer neighborhoods of three-story homes and prim apartment buildings.

Hiroshi said, "This used to be a funky, artsy area when I was at college. Now it's pricy and popular."

Takamatsu hummed deeply. "She must have gotten a good settlement when she sued Senden."

"What amount would cover your daughter?" Hiroshi asked.

Takamatsu, for once, didn't answer. They both stood on the corner observing the shop from across the street.

Buckets of fresh-cut flowers in easy-to-grab bunches lined the windows along the front and expensive flowers of bright yellow, orange with brown flecks, and rich blues and purples jostled in buckets on a metal rack. Chalkboard signs on either side of the open front door beckoned customers into the interior of fat-leafed house plants and refrigerated cases of even more expensive flowers. Elderly customers with rolling shopping baskets and housewives on battery-powered bikes stopped, while a young woman in a blue apron and blue cotton over-sleeves bustled around wrapping and tying everything with an easy smile.

A springy middle-aged woman in the same blue apron, her hair pulled back in a tight ponytail, chatted with customers while they tucked their flowers into their shopping bags before biking or strolling away

Takamatsu looked at Hiroshi, nodding for him to take the lead on this one.

Hiroshi crossed the street and walked over to speak to her. "Excuse me, but are you Toshiko Yamase, the mother of Mayu Yamase?"

The woman brushed her hair back and straightened her apron. She glanced at the badge Hiroshi held up and her face froze. She was an attractive woman with quick, darting eyes, and a soft youthful face turned blank in defense.

Hiroshi said, "Is there somewhere we could talk?"

She looked at him steadily before turning to glare at Takamatsu standing across the street. "I thought I was done with detectives."

The young woman in the blue apron stopped beside her with a tall bucket of water, as if ready to throw it on Hiroshi if she needed to.

"Suzuna, can you watch the store for a few minutes?" Toshiko said to her without taking her eyes off Hiroshi.

"Yes, of course," Suzuna said. She was in her twenties with dyed-blonde, braided hair wrapped in a thick swirl around her head. A row of piercings paraded along both ears and her round face was, like Toshiko's, taut and blank.

"We can ask the delivery guy to stop back this afternoon," Toshiko said.

"I'll tell him to come back after five," Suzuna responded.

Without another word, Toshiko turned into the shop and walked through the densely packed shelves of houseplants, watering pots and gardening tools. The shop was so full Hiroshi had to turn sideways to follow her.

The air inside smelled earthy and alive. Along one side, refrigerated cases held rows of long-stemmed flowers. On the other, a wide table held wrapping paper, ribbons and ties, and a cash register.

At the back of the shop, Toshiko pivoted and headed up a steep wooden staircase to the second floor. Hiroshi stared at her tight jeans ascending, but had to look away to find handholds on the bannister.

At the top of the stairs they entered a small room bright from a skylight. Bouquet baskets and gift boxes stood in neat stacks. In the center, a work table was littered with cut stems, twists of ribbon and cut-off plastic wrap.

Toshiko sidled through the crowded space and pivoted to climb a metal staircase even steeper than the stairs. On a narrow landing at the top, she set herself and shouldered open the door. Fresh, cool air flowed in. Hiroshi followed her onto the roof.

Stacks of different-sized clay pots circled the skylight. Down the middle, two knee-high beds of well-turned dirt lay ready for spring herbs and flowers. Beside the beds, planks on beer crates displayed two long rows of bonsai trees of all shapes and sizes. A small pile of autumn leaves lay unswept in the corner.

Toshiko sat in a chair at a metal table and folded her arms over her chest.

Hiroshi pulled out a chair and sat down.

"What happened to the other detective? The one with the mustache?" she asked, looking at the rows of bonsai.

"You mean Saito?"

She nodded.

"He retired," Hiroshi said.

"He didn't communicate well," Toshiko said.

"He was a relic," Hiroshi admitted. "I'll be more direct. Your daughter Mayu's former boss, Onizuka, died this morning."

Toshiko fidgeted in her chair, her jaw tight. "He should have killed himself three years ago."

Hiroshi cleared his throat. "We need to ask you a few questions."

Toshiko folded her arms over her work apron. "Let me ask a couple first. How did he die?"

"He fell,"

"Where?"

"Senden's main office in Marunouchi." Hiroshi didn't want to let her take control, but maybe backing off would let her stumble over her own questions.

Toshiko got up out of her chair and walked to the edge of the roof. She looked off in the distance at the rectangular flat rooftops and their tangles of old antennas, water tanks, and heating and air-conditioning units. A distant school building rose up with tall fencing around its roof.

Hiroshi stayed seated, but edged forward on the chair.

In a few minutes, Toshiko turned to him. "From the roof?"

Hiroshi nodded tightly.

She turned away again to look off at the hopscotch of rooftops. "Twenty stories. Same as Mayu. Only he wasn't harassed and overworked until suicide seemed the only way out, was he?"

Hiroshi waited for her to look back at him, but she didn't. He got up and walked closer. "We need to find out as much as we can as quickly as we can." Hiroshi could only see the side of her face, but tears had started running down her cheek.

She wiped her eyes and nose on her sleeve. "I didn't think I had any tears left."

"Yesterday, what time did the shop close?"

"Not this again." She dug in her pocket for tissues, but had to use her apron to wipe her face.

"I'm sorry. We're at the start of our investigation and have to know the basics."

Toshiko shook her head, resigned. "I worked until nine. It was Suzuna's birthday, so we went out for dinner."

"Where did you go?"

"An *izakaya* near here. The owner is one of our regular customers. He puts our flowers in his place."

"How long did you stay there?"

"Until eleven-thirty or so. They gave us a lot of free drinks. One of the cooks is kind of sweet on Suzuna."

"And then you went home?"

Toshiko nodded yes.

"Where do you live? Nearby?"

"In Mitaka, not far by bike."

"Apartment? House?"

"Apartment. I bought it with the settlement from the lawsuit against Senden. They gave more in return for a non-public apology. My lawyer convinced me to take the money instead of the open apology. Paid for with silence and secrecy."

"And where does Suzuna live?"

"She lives with me."

"What's your relationship exactly?"

"She was one of Mayu's best friends. They went to high school and college together, studied abroad together. She's like a second daughter to me."

"And where is Suzuna's family?"

Toshiko took a big breath. "They were visiting relatives in the northeast when the tsunami hit. There was no trace of them. One of her aunts came to live with her in Tokyo but they didn't get along. Mayu and I took Suzuna in after that."

"She lived with you?"

"Mayu and Suzuna were the same age, but Mayu was like her older sister, helping her with homework, deciding where they'd shop, saving money for Disneyland. Mayu had all three of us following her shopping lists, housework duties, exercise, bath and sleeping schedules. Mayu was a natural organizer. She kept organizing Suzuna even after they went to college."

"And your husband?"

"Ex-husband," Toshiko said. "I guess he's still in the Philippines."

"He's working there?"

"He's been there twenty years now. He came back for Mayu's funeral three years ago."

Hiroshi waited for her to continue.

"I didn't even know he was coming, but he was her father. I couldn't refuse."

"That was the last time you saw him?"

"Riding away in a police car."

"He was arrested?"

"Isn't there a record of this somewhere?"

"I'd like to hear it from you," Hiroshi said, wishing he'd read the files before coming.

Toshiko sighed. "Representatives from Senden came to the funeral. My husband went wild."

"He got angry?"

"He punched them out at the funeral."

"Was anyone hurt?"

"They weren't hurt enough. The police took my husband and let the corporate guys go. I had to get him out of jail."

"And then?"

"And then...he went back to the Philippines. There's been a few text messages, but that's it." Toshiko twisted her hands in her apron so hard it loosened. She undid the tie, pulled it tight again and retied the knot in back, wiped her face with her sleeve.

Hiroshi looked at the row of upturned dirt in the bed. "Was your husband violent before? When you were married?"

"He drank a lot. I guess in the Philippines too. He had punch-ups when he drank, but never with us. It was just one of those relationships that worked about two weekends a year. That's not enough."

"You were divorced formally?"

"Yes, when Mayu started college."

"Could you give us his address?"

"His company knows where he is. Isn't that in the police records?"

"And did Mayu have other friends?"

Toshiko nodded, looking away. "She had a boyfriend at the time. An American. He followed her back here from America."

"Do you have his address?"

"I don't know where he lives. Mayu never told me. He stopped by after the funeral a few times, but it was too painful to see him." Toshiko kneeled down to dig her hand into the flower bed and pull up two handfuls of dirt.

"He's still in Japan? Where does he work?"

"He doesn't, he's a musician, plays saxophone. Steve Titus. He plays at jazz clubs all over. Mayu used to go every time she could get away from work."

"And he was here at the time of Mayu's death?"

"At the funeral, he joined the fight, helped my husband. I got him out of jail, too, and kept him from getting kicked out of the country. Mayu seemed to really love him, though he doesn't speak much Japanese." Toshiko frowned and let the dirt trickle from her hands back into the flower bed. "I guess that would have been better than what I had. I see that now. I should have seen it when she told me."

"Anyone else from Mayu's circle of friends who—"

"Suzuna would know."

Hiroshi got up and said, "Thank you for your time. I'm sorry to upset you, but I thought you should know about Onizuka."

Toshiko nodded quietly and stood up, brushing the dirt off her hands. She wiped her face again, turned toward her bonsai trees. "Everything I worked for in my life was to give Mayu a chance at success. The right schools, English lessons, violin and piano. I stayed married longer than I should have. She got her dream job, a creative media company, the top in the country. She could use her English, work overseas…"

Hiroshi looked at the row of bonsai trees, their branches tied by wire. Most were bare at the end of winter, except for the miniature firs and tightly trimmed pines. Here and there, a few orange-brown leaves hung onto the branches, left unclipped for the winter or too stubborn to fall.

Toshiko said, "Onizuka was the one in i sin in main I wanted to see dead. But with him gone, I'm not sure who to hate from now on."

Chapter 5

As Hiroshi crossed the street outside the flower shop to where Takamatsu had been waiting and smoking, he called Akiko, his assistant, who managed everything in his office with frightening efficiency. "I think I can just make it back for the meetings…"

"They've all been canceled," Akiko exclaimed.

Hiroshi stopped in the middle of the crosswalk, pedestrians biking and walking around him, a car waiting patiently for him to move on.

"The chief called and told me to clear your schedule for the next few days. That's what I've been doing all morning," Akiko said.

"The chief told you to cancel *my* appointments?"

"I thought it was you canceling," Akiko said. "I should have double-checked with you. I can try to reschedule them…"

"I wanted to get what we have on those cryptocurrency cases to Interpol, so we could get their assistance."

"I'll get them set up again," Akiko said.

"Forget it." Hiroshi hung up and finished crossing the street. As soon as he got across, he called Akiko back. "Sorry."

"I'll see you tomorrow. I really didn't know," Akiko said.

"I should have called."

Hiroshi knew there was nothing more to say on that. He couldn't survive without her assistance, especially her research and good sense. This was the only time she'd done anything like that. Usually, she preceded him in preparation and organization. Hiroshi shrugged questioningly at Takamatsu. "Where's Sugamo?"

"I sent him home with the car," Takamatsu said.

"Why is everyone making decisions for me today? The chief canceled my appointments."

Takamatsu snickered. "Now you see why I can't stand the guy."

"You think the chief knows something we don't?"

"If he does, it'll be the first time." Takamatsu turned toward the train station. "Let's get something to eat. I'll tell Sakaguchi to meet us."

"He shouldn't be out walking around on his knee."

Takamatsu said, "He shouldn't be cooped up in the office. He's been working since three in the morning."

Hiroshi followed Takamatsu through the maze of small, casual drinking places that meandered toward Kichijoji Station. Each place fit a row of seats along a bar with a small kitchen and prep counter. Takamatsu always took the smallest streets when he could, and he seemed to know them all over Tokyo. Hiroshi ducked under the overhead signs and cross-braces.

They took the Chuo Line to Asagaya Station. Outside the station, Takamatsu headed into another maze of alleys with standing bars and yakitori shops. The shops were so narrow they seemed to have been split off from one another, as if walls were chucked down dividing them into halves and halves again.

"Why do you always take the most circuitous route through the smallest streets?" Hiroshi yelled up to Takamatsu.

Without turning around, Takamatsu pulled to a stop in front of the entryway of a four-story concrete building, the largest on the street, but divvied up into a dozen smaller shops. Takamatsu looked at Hiroshi. "Because these small *yokocho* streets remind me of my youth. Anything wrong with that?"

Hiroshi sighed and followed him into a small elevator.

On the third floor, they got out and ducked under a huge *sugidama* cedar ball suspended from the ceiling. Inside, the wait staff called out, "*Irasshaimase!*" Hiroshi toed off his shoes. A long row of refrigerated cases filled with 1.8-liter *isshobin* sake bottles glowed under the display lights.

"One from every prefecture," Takamatsu said. "And then

some."

The restaurant was still prepping for the first wave of diners, but Takamatsu's smooth, chatty manner made it hard to keep them waiting until opening time. The detectives put their shoes in the wooden shoebox, took the hand-carved key, and followed a waitress to a floor table at the back.

"I don't think Sakaguchi can sit on the tatami with his knee," Hiroshi said. "I don't want to have to help him up."

Takamatsu aha-ed and asked the waitress for another seat. She led them to a table with an in-floor drop that let everyone's legs hang below.

The waitress came back with steaming *oshibori* towels. Hiroshi dumped his face into the soothing warmth and felt instantly better. He folded the white towel neatly on the wood table. The walls of the *izakaya* were covered with the names of sake brands brushed on *washi* paper. The names read like poetry across the dark-wood walls, the sake names drawn from classic literature, Buddhist concepts, and clever plays-on-words.

The waitress left the day's specials on a whiteboard propped beside their table. Takamatsu ordered beer and perused the board.

When the two mugs of cold beer arrived, they clinked glasses and drank deeply.

Takamatsu pulled his cigarettes out. "The *bucho*'s wife seemed like a wild girl in her time, not some *ryosai kenbo*."

"No woman lives up to that 'good wife and wise mother' ideal. You're way out of date." Hiroshi drank another slug of beer.

Takamatsu pulled the ashtray over and lit a cigarette. "Yeah, but the next time you talk to them, tell them what great wives and mothers they are. They'll be flattered."

"The idea of women has changed. The idea of motherhood, too."

"Changed to what? Drinking in the morning?" Takamatsu laughed and held his beer mug out for another toast. "That's what we need you for, bring in all this fresh understanding of the new Japanese society."

"I thought it was my English and accounting skills."

"That was just a ruse." Takamatsu laughed and swallowed the last of his beer.

Hiroshi leaned back, feeling light-headed. He hadn't eaten anything since the croissant and apple before dawn.

Takamatsu waved the waitress over, eyed the handwritten specials menu and reeled off a list of dishes. She made a few suggestions, which Takamatsu took, and wrote everything down on small slips of paper she tucked inside the top pocket of her *happi* coat.

"Nice way with a pen and paper, that girl," Takamatsu said.

She came back with two white ceramic cups, chilled, and an arm's-length bottle of sake which she hoisted with one hand and upturned with her thumb over the top. "*Daiginjo* from Niigata." She thumbed off the top and poured out two perfect cups, stopping just when the sake reached the rim and leaving the bottle for them to study the label.

Hiroshi leaned over to sip, eyeing the blue circles at the bottom of the cup shimmering through the translucent liquid. Takamatsu brought the cup to his lips with steady hands, not spilling a drop. They gave each other a silent toast.

The waitress brought small bowls with little white shrimp, two slices of tofu, and a sprig of steamed green vegetable. Hiroshi tucked quickly into the appetizers. A plate of sashimi arrived in a round blue-green bowl. Atop a bed of ice, the red, white, and silver flesh of the fish and shellfish glistened. Dark-green *shiso* leaves, a mound of daikon, a plug of wasabi, and yellow *kogiku* flowers rounded out the spread.

Hiroshi poured soy sauce into dipping plates, mixed in wasabi and hovered his chopsticks, deciding which to go for first. The fish melted on his tongue, so fresh, he hardly needed to chew.

Takamatsu, showing no sign of hunger or fatigue, took another swallow of sake and leaned against the backrest. "She knew it was coming."

"Who knew what was coming?" Hiroshi asked.

"She didn't seem surprised or upset at her husband's death."

"The HR guy, Nakata, had already told her. And she was drunk."

"I wonder why she didn't take his money and leave him long ago?" Takamatsu mused, finally taking a bite of the sashimi.

"Money, the kids. The usual."

"What did the girl's mother tell you?"

"She took me to the roof." Hiroshi washed another sliver of *sashimi* down with more *daiginjo*. She hadn't said much. He should have pressed her for more details.

"Did she cry?"

"A little. Mostly she stared off at the horizon."

"Tears of revenge? Or tears of relief?" Takamatsu asked.

"Just tears." The sake was making him contemplate the ineffectual flow of the day. "We'll have to talk to the girl Suzuna and Mayu's other friends. And the father and the boyfriend."

"I send you out alone for once and you bring us more people to interview."

"Maybe the wire cutters will turn up."

"With fingerprints. That would be nice to get a suicide wrap on this and get back to other cases." Takamatsu waved the waitress over for another round of sake. "That they're missing is either sloppy police work or perhaps the killer's attention to detail."

"Or maybe the security camera footage will solve this and we won't have to interview everyone in the company." Hiroshi could feel the sake sinking in. He needed to eat more.

Takamatsu tapped his cigarette pack on the table. "Those companies are like cults. Everyone devotes their entire existence to the place. They won't open up even if we talk to them for hours."

The front door opened and the wait-staff hustled over to welcome Sakaguchi. He leaned against the wall to take off his shoes. He couldn't bend over to pick them up, so one of the waiters put them in the wooden shoebox for him and gave him the key. Hiroshi switched to Takamatsu's side, so Sakaguchi would have more room.

Sakaguchi eased himself onto the bench and ordered another plate of *sashimi* and more sake. "This damn knee. The brace barely fits around my leg. If I wrap it myself it takes an hour. And comes loose. If only I had my old sumo stable manager here, he'd wrap it perfectly."

The waitress brought out fresh cups and hoisted a new bottle of sake for all three of them. The bottle cradled in both hands, she poured them out perfectly to the lip of the cup.

They toasted.

The second *sashimi* plate arrived and Sakaguchi ordered fried fish.

Takamatsu said, "What did you find back in the safe confines of headquarters?"

"You first. I didn't eat all day." Sakaguchi plucked up his chopsticks.

Hiroshi explained everything they found, which was not much at all.

"What about this Onizuka?" Sakaguchi asked.

Hiroshi sighed. "Onizuka was unlikable, even his family said that. Enemies add up in the corporate world, Takamatsu just reminded me."

"How unlikable?" Sakaguchi asked.

Takamatsu shrugged. "I'm usually for murder, but this could be suicide. Seems like a mid-life, mid-career thing, pressures of his position, money problems, a bad affair, maybe he screwed something up at work. For someone who has built a career on pride and position, it doesn't take much to make leaping seem a solution."

"He could be making amends for the girl, Mayu, he bullied into suicide," Hiroshi said.

Takamatsu laughed. "A salaryman with a conscience? The only regret inside the corporate world is when profits don't go up."

Sakaguchi ate as he listened. "All this doesn't sound like much."

Hiroshi frowned. "Why is the chief insisting on us wrapping this up? He canceled my appointments."

"I heard from Akiko." Sakaguchi took another gulp. "The chief called me two dozen times about this today."

Takamatsu lit a cigarette and shook his head in disgust. "Same as always, some bureaucrat called him and laid on that old-boy-network pressure."

Sakaguchi put down his chopsticks. "Onizuka had a blood alcohol level of zero point three eight."

"That's coma level," Takamatsu said. "He would hardly have been conscious, much less able to walk up the stairs or cut the fence." Takamatsu put out his cigarette and rolled up his cuffs.

"What about the camera footage?" Hiroshi asked.

Sakaguchi set down his chopsticks. "There was nothing on any of the cameras."

The waitress set down a plate of grilled *saba*, flayed, the skin bubbling brown. She also set down a plate of *hirame karaage*, deep-fried flounder in golden bite-size pieces, and two plates of vegetable tempura stacked in a neat pyramid.

Takamatsu said, "Are you sharing any of that?"

"I ordered one tempura for you two," Sakaguchi said.

Takamatsu called the waitress over and ordered another grilled *saba*. Sakaguchi could finish one of the plump oily fish on his own, and the flounder too.

Hiroshi said, "How could there be nothing on video?"

Sakaguchi poured soy sauce on the grated daikon and stirred the dipping sauce for the tempura. "The tech guys said there were flashes of bright light, then black, and back to normal. They said the equipment was out of date, the backup faulty. But forty-two minutes showed nothing. Then the video worked normally again."

Hiroshi said, "But between the parking lot and the roof there were a lot of security cameras. It's not easy to get to the roof and back without being caught on one of them."

Sakaguchi said, "All those blanks were maybe just glitches."

"Or maybe not." Takamatsu hummed, holding his cup in the air. "Camera dysfunction is rarely that well-timed."

"You'd have to know where they were," Hiroshi said. "Or work efficiently."

"The tech guys said they'd slow it down, enhance it and check again. The chief came down and yelled at them about it. Twice," Sakaguchi growled.

"Anything from the autopsy?" Takamatsu asked.

Sakaguchi finished chewing before he answered. "By the time I got to the examination room, most of him had dripped into the collection buckets under the table."

Hiroshi set his chopsticks down.

The waitress brought another bottle of sake. "This is from the owner. He said you are always welcome here."

Takamatsu smiled. "See, the perks of right livelihood."

"Now, you're a Buddhist?"

Takamatsu ignored him and joked with the waitress.

She hoisted the bottle and poured three full cups. They bowed their thanks and toasted again.

Hiroshi said, "We should talk to the lawyer who handled the mother's lawsuit against the company."

Takamatsu smiled and waved his cigarette. "See, that's the fresh thinking we want from you. Interview everyone."

Sakaguchi said, "You're both going to Senden tomorrow. I had Akiko call and make an appointment. They were expecting you today."

"We should have gone." Hiroshi hummed and frowned.

"Better to let them reflect on their corporate sins until tomorrow." Takamatsu raised his glass again for a quick toast.

Hiroshi nodded. "Onizuka wouldn't have harassed only one woman over the years."

Sakaguchi nodded agreement as he chomped into another large bite of fish.

Takamatsu said, "And we need to go over his finances, don't we? Money is at the bottom of every crime, Hiroshi keeps telling me."

Hiroshi took another drink of sake. "You've been secretly listening to me?"

Chapter 6

At the door of his apartment, Hiroshi fumbled with his key, wondering what his own blood alcohol level was. At the *izakaya*, Takamatsu and Sakaguchi kept ordering food and sake, and Hiroshi followed along. He lost count of the cups of sake and took a taxi home.

When he got the door open he stepped inside, and the door slammed shut faster than he wanted.

"*O-kaeri-nasai*," Ayana mumbled.

"*Tadaima*," Hiroshi shouted, trying his best to sound sober.

He bumped against the wall as he peeled off his shoes and walked into the living room with as much balance as he could muster.

Ayana sat up from the sofa rubbing her face.

"Were you sleeping?" Hiroshi asked. He pulled off his coat and tossed it on a chair. "Is the reshelving all finished?"

"Reshelving the archives is never going to finish. Every day, there's some lost manuscript box, some numbering problem. Today, everyone was too exhausted to do more. We went out to that big French bistro."

"Did you have steak frites?"

"I did actually. And so did most of the others. We ate like we hadn't eaten all day."

"Like a sumo wrestler."

"Is that polite?" Ayana rolled over on her elbow.

"Well, the only sumo wrestler I know is Sakaguchi. And Sugamo. And both of them eat a lot. Don't know what to tell you." Hiroshi went to the sofa and squeezed Ayana's legs so she'd curl them back and he could sit beside her. He leaned in for a kiss.

"Are you drunk?" Ayana asked, recoiling.

"No," he said. "Are you?"

51

"I had a couple glasses of wine. What did you have?"

"Sake."

"How much?"

"Lost count."

Ayana pushed him aside and stood up. "You smell drunk."

Hiroshi flopped down where she'd been and rolled onto his back.

"Don't fall asleep there." Ayana walked to the kitchen and took the water filter pitcher out of the fridge. She poured a big glass and brought it to Hiroshi.

Hiroshi sat up and drained the glass in one go.

"Where did you go drinking?"

"An *izakaya* in Asagaya that Takamatsu knows. He knows places all over the city, wherever we are. We were talking about the case."

"Seems like you always have to lubricate yourselves pretty well to discuss the case. How do you get anything done sober all day?"

Hiroshi sighed and signaled for another glass of water.

Ayana poured another. "What time did you leave this morning?" she asked.

"Before sunrise."

"And you didn't eat all day?"

"That's why the sake hit me."

"It wasn't the number of glasses?"

"That, too."

Ayana took the glass from Hiroshi, watching him.

He drank the water, as he had the sake, dutifully. "Big guy in a huge ad agency dove off his company building. Turned to mush."

Ayana sat down on the edge of the sofa with the pitcher and glass. "I thought you were working on cryptocurrency? Nice, clean online numbers in your office?"

"Chief yanked me off of that. He's a fucking asshole." Hiroshi used the English.

"You've said that before. Which ad agency?"

"Media company, they're now called. Senden Central, Infinity, whatever."

"They're the biggest."

"You remember the girl who killed herself and her mother sued the company?"

Ayana nodded and poured more water.

"That's him."

"Him?"

"The guy who harassed and overworked her until she killed herself."

"So, he got what he deserved." Ayana went back to the kitchen and refilled the water pitcher and put it in the fridge.

"Nobody deserves a fall from a twenty-story building." Hiroshi pulled his legs around and sat up. "I still can't figure out why that girl wouldn't just quit. Why wouldn't she just leave?"

Ayana looked at Hiroshi. "Harassment isn't that kind of thing."

"Not what kind of thing?"

"If you quit, you're out of a good job for the rest of your life. You'll never get hired at a big company again. Then it's the single life and *hakken* temp work forever after. Or treadmill part-time service jobs. Or marriage to someone who's no longer a regular worker, too, because you can't marry too far up the hierarchy. Or—"

"But you chose marriage." Hiroshi hummed with drunken insight and wobbled to his feet, stretching.

Ayana leaned back. "What do you mean?"

"That's why you got married. To avoid a worse fate."

"That was part of it." Ayana stood staring at Hiroshi for a minute before she said anything more. "After university, I took a job at the export company bank, Marutobi Corporation. I was following expectations. A big company means success. I'd made it. You know the equation."

"You should have come to Boston."

"You should have invited me." Ayana looked away. The outside porch lights were off and the glass doors reflected their figures. "I figured you had an American girlfriend by then anyway."

Hiroshi started to protest, but stopped himself from pretending to deny it.

Ayana continued staring out the window. "My boss, well, if everyone in our department went out drinking, he made sure to seat me next to him. The younger women had to arrange everything, so I had to stay and settle the bill and he'd hang around, take the train in my direction, even though he lived way up in Saitama. Things like that."

Hiroshi looked confused. Why had he never heard this before? Why had he never asked about this before?

"I didn't want to quit. I thought I'd get a chance to do something, take on some responsibility once I got through the training phase. But after the first year, I could tell that none of the women were going to be promoted."

Hiroshi stepped over and took her in his arms. She twisted away and looked out the window, so he held her from the side.

"Then my boss started asking me to go with him to visit other companies. I thought, maybe I'll learn something I can use. But all I did was carry the laptop, open it up, and nod in agreement. Of course, my boss was just doing the face-to-face with clients, trying to maintain the relationship. I was supposed to sit there and smile at the right time. And after each company visit, he'd ask me to go out to eat and drink."

"You mean, just the two of you?" It made no sense to feel jealous about something that happened so long ago, but he did, and angry too.

"He was mentoring me with crumbs of advice, but he didn't know much. He did as he'd been taught to do. Nothing more to it."

"And you—"

"I got tired of fighting him off."

"How old was he?"

"Early forties I guess."

"Married?"

"Divorced with kids. I had to listen to all that too."

"So, you quit?"

"One of the people we met regularly at another company asked me out. So, I went."

"That was who you married?"

Ayana nodded. "We had to keep it secret at first. Dating a client would have been grounds for dismissal."

"But dating your boss would have been OK."

"No, but everyone would know and pretend they didn't. It got worse, so I started leaving work early. I called in sick a few times. All of that was seen as disrespect, disinterest, getting ready to quit. Which it was. My boss felt rejected and followed me. One day he saw me with *my* soon-to-be husband, one of *his* clients. The next day he reported me to Human Resources. I told HR what he'd been doing, but they saw it as a misunderstanding, part of working closely together. In a way they were right. It was the status quo."

Hiroshi nodded. "I didn't know any of this."

"You didn't ask, mister detective." Ayana walked over and leaned on the kitchen island, undid her hair and retied it into a high night-time ponytail. She rinsed the glass and set it on the drying rack.

"I dreamed of you coming to Boston."

Ayana leaned into him. "Senior year, in January, I got my passport. I bought a ticket to Boston. I read it was cold in Boston in February and March, so I bought a new coat. I thought I'd just go to Boston even though I didn't know how to find you. I figured I'd just wait at the gate to your school until you passed by, pretend it was an accident."

"Why didn't you?"

Ayana shook her head. "You hurt me so badly by just leaving in the middle of college without a word. Eto Sensei finally told me the truth about where you were, but even he didn't have your address. I thought it was my fault."

"I'm sorry."

"How could you just leave? And say nothing? You really hurt me."

"I didn't mean to. I didn't even know I had the capacity to hurt anyone. I only knew I could be hurt."

Ayana pushed him away and went to the window. "As it turned out, I probably should have toughed it out at the company. As soon as I got married, my husband lost interest in me. I couldn't figure it out. We bought this place but he got transferred to America and then to Paris. I was free to do what I liked. I went back to school, studied library science, and got back into kendo. That was the best part of the marriage, his indifference gave me freedom. Looking back, I guess I was never really in love. So, when I finally divorced him, I thought of that time as one long study trip. I disappointed my family twice. Failed at work, failed at marriage."

"You're not failing with me."

"Why didn't you write me after you went to Boston?"

Hiroshi didn't try to answer. He walked over and hugged her from behind, both of them looking out the window, seeing their own reflection and the balcony outside. Hiroshi knew there was nothing to do but hold her tight.

Ayana twisted around to face him, leaned back and started pounding him in the chest, gently at first, then harder.

Hiroshi let her pummel away until she slowed and stopped and rubbed her face against his chest.

"That was the first workout I've had in weeks," Ayana said, giving him one more slug in the chest. "You stink of alcohol."

Hiroshi turned her toward the bedroom, enveloping her from behind as they walked in sync, close, tired and reassured.

Chapter 7

The conference room on the top floor of headquarters was rarely used, but the chief called all the homicide detectives in for a briefing on Onizuka's death in Marunouchi and no other room was large enough to fit everyone. The tables faced the front in perfect hierarchical rows.

Hiroshi sat in the last row next to Takamatsu. His sake hangover felt like a huge steam iron on his head. His body felt bloated, feverish, and achy. He squinted at the front of the room, and then closed his eyes in foggy resignation.

Sugamo and Osaki sat right in front of Hiroshi, a human scrum to hide behind. Sakaguchi squirmed at the front next to the chief. It was early morning at the front of the room and twilight at the back.

After an hour of the chief's asking the same questions repeatedly and prattling about the importance of the first forty-eight hours of the investigation, Hiroshi whispered to Takamatsu, "He's keeping all of us from getting any work done."

Takamatsu fiddled with his lighter. "The tech guys will come through on the video footage soon enough."

"What if they don't?" Hiroshi growled, his throat scratchy and dry.

As the briefing stretched on, he sent text messages to Akiko. She, at least, was working in his office, where he should be. He asked her to get the information assembled to send to Interpol so he could restart the cryptocurrency cases he'd been working on until yesterday.

He was about to explain to her what to do about an investment scam case when the droning from the front of the room stopped and the chief shouted, "Hiroshi, are you listening?"

Hiroshi leaned to the side around the shoulders of Sugamo and

Osaki and looked toward the chief at the front of the room. Several detectives turned around and stared at Hiroshi with bored faces.

Hiroshi held up his cellphone and tried to look apologetic. "I keep getting calls about canceled meetings. Interpol wants to work with us here in Japan, but..."

A few coughs and a couple chuckles echoed through the room.

"Is that the cryptocurrency thing you're still working on?" the chief shouted.

Hiroshi nodded.

"You need to put that off until we get this Onizuka case finished. This guy was one of the leaders in the Japanese business world. Senden Central—"

"Senden Infinity," Hiroshi corrected him, and wished he hadn't.

The chief leaned across the front table. "Senden whatever. It's one of Japan's flagship companies. They are leading a wave of Japanese expansion overseas. To catch up with China. And what are you doing, Hiroshi? Chasing invisible numbers around the internet."

Hiroshi started to reply but Takamatsu cleared his throat to warn him to shut up.

"Today, and until this is solved, you're to focus on this top executive and nothing else. When this happens in the boardroom of one of Japan's top corporations, we need to stay focused, work quickly and finish quietly. That's how we support Japan and support the economy. Is that clear?" The chief stopped to let the silence resonate. "You all have your assignments."

Outside the conference room, Hiroshi and Takamatsu joined the rush of detectives keen on getting away from the chief. They squeezed into the first elevator down and got out in the sub-basement passageway that linked the main building with the annex building where Hiroshi's office was hidden away. Neither of them spoke until they got to the fire doors dividing the two buildings.

"The chief always wants to uphold the system," Hiroshi said.

"He's benefited from it from the beginning, so he supports anything that will get him more connections and move him up another rung on the ladder," Takamatsu said.

"How does this case help him?"

"He can't promote himself, can he? You'll see. He'll use it to his advantage."

They arrived at the office and Hiroshi felt glad once again to be far away from the main headquarters. Just the short underground walk was enough to gain headspace and refocus.

When Hiroshi first moved in, the isolation of his office let him work efficiently, making calls to overseas police departments without all the other detectives in the same room. The smell of cleaning supplies stored in the room before he took it over faded, and Hiroshi's office became a hideaway for Sakaguchi and Takamatsu, a place they could gather to talk over cases without the chief's interruption or the other detectives' banter. And of course, people liked to talk with Akiko, who was, in Hiroshi's estimation, the best member of the support staff in the entire headquarters.

When Hiroshi and Takamatsu started up the stairs up to Hiroshi's office, they heard the fire doors slam behind them and turned to see Sakaguchi plodding toward them. They waited to help him up the half-flight, but he waved them off and grabbed the handrail.

Akiko heard them coming, and when they got to the office, she had already cleared the files off the foldout futon chair so Sakaguchi could flop onto the chair with a loud whoosh.

Hiroshi beelined to the espresso machine, hoping some caffeine would jolt the hangover and clear his head. He could feel the veins pounding along the side of his skull.

Takamatsu smiled at Akiko, pulled off his jacket and hung it on the rack. "You missed the excitement. Hiroshi, lifeguard of Tokyo Bay, used his hero status from that case to argue with the chief."

This was the first time Takamatsu had mentioned being saved

from the freezing water in the bay on a particularly grisly case during the past winter. Hiroshi had saved Takamatsu's life, but Takamatsu was too grateful, or too proud, to speak about it until that burst of sarcasm.

Akiko was never bothered by any of Takamatsu's banter. "It's just good he didn't let you drown."

Takamatsu nodded for an espresso and straightened his cuffs. "We can all get back to real work when the video footage shows which resentful colleague helped Onizuka to the edge of the building."

"Is that what happened?" Akiko pulled a chair around for Takamatsu, but he stayed standing.

Sakaguchi shrugged. "It's as good a guess as any at this point."

"The girl's family seems more likely, doesn't it?" Hiroshi said. "I mean, the mother, the father, they must have been devastated."

"Or the American boyfriend," Takamatsu said. "This seems like the work of a younger person."

"Where do you get that?" Hiroshi asked.

Takamatsu shrugged. "From my gut. Where I get most things."

"I'll go get you some tea." Akiko patted Sakaguchi's shoulder as she hurried off to the vending machines down the hall.

Hiroshi handed Takamatsu a double espresso and set another on Akiko's desk.

Akiko came back with a can of tea for Sakaguchi and smiled at her steaming espresso. "I pulled together some things about the girl, Mayu Yamase."

"What did you find?"

"A lot of articles, how much overtime, how many harassment reports, it's all detailed. Seems like she stuck it out for a year after it got bad. I found her case mentioned in most of the articles about *karoshi*."

"How do you say *that* in English?" Takamatsu asked.

Hiroshi shook his head. "It doesn't happen there, or not in the same way. 'Death from overwork' comes closest."

"Americans would just quit, I guess," Takamatsu said.

"And rightly so," Akiko said. "Japanese hope *gaman* will get them through."

"That quality of self-denial is different in America too." Hiroshi swirled his coffee cup. "In Japan, it's the national curse."

"And blessing," Takamatsu said. "Without perseverance and tolerance, Japanese society wouldn't function."

"But it's always women who are supposed to have more *gaman*," Akiko said. "Enduring a meaningless, low-paying job that's killing you is no virtue."

Takamatsu looked at her. "You seem to be speaking from experience."

"I am." Akiko sipped her espresso and stared back at Takamatsu, who was a master of letting things go only to ask about them later. "I was brought up to be able to suffer in silence but I changed at my first job. I was strangling on the monotony. So, I quit and set off to study in America. The best choice I ever made. And maybe the first real choice."

Takamatsu smiled at her.

Sakaguchi swirled his can of hot tea. "The foreign sumo wrestlers didn't put up with bullying and baiting in the sumo stable. They weren't used to it like the Japanese wrestlers, who knew how to quietly bide their time."

Akiko read from her computer screen. "Mayu told people what was happening, but no one listened. The articles said that Onizuka had harassed other employees before her. Some of them gave testimony at the trial."

Hiroshi nodded at her. "Let's gather their names and start contacting them."

Takamatsu shook his head. "Let's do that later, if the video footage doesn't give us anything."

Akiko held up two folders stuffed with printouts. "Her case really drew attention. The mother won her lawsuit against Senden because the public, and the press, were on her side."

"And yet Onizuka kept working at the company." Hiroshi asked Akiko, "Did you find the name of the lawyer who handled Mayu Yamase's case against Senden?"

Akiko clicked on her keyboard. "Want me to make an appointment?"

"Let's leave the lawyers out of it," Takamatsu said. "We have the case transcripts."

"They always know more than what's on the record. A lot more. We can stop by on the way to our appointment with the HR people at Senden."

Akiko pulled up the number and called.

Hiroshi went for another espresso, picked up the bag of beans and examined it. "Did I buy decaf by mistake?"

Hiroshi said, "I want to look into Onizuka's finances, too."

"All right," Sakaguchi said.

Hiroshi was surprised he got his way so easily. "As for Onizuka's cashflow, let's look through credit card stuff first and then we can see whether he tapped into the company budget."

Takamatsu pulled his jacket on and straightened it. "And we need to talk to these two exemplary Japanese mothers again too. Second time around they usually change their stories."

Sakaguchi stood up and everyone moved to help him. "I've got paperwork."

"That takes real *gaman*," Takamatsu said. "Hiroshi, I've got a couple of things to check on, so I'll meet you in the parking lot in thirty minutes."

Takamatsu walked Sakaguchi back to the main building.

Hiroshi turned to Akiko. "We also need to find Mayu's estranged father. He works in the Philippines."

Akiko was one step ahead of him. "I already tracked him down, but his company in the Philippines said he wasn't there. On vacation, apparently."

"Vacation where?" Hiroshi asked.

"They didn't know."

"And this jazz saxophonist, Steve Titus, I want his full schedule."

"Aren't you too busy for jazz?" Akiko asked.

"That's Mayu's old boyfriend," Hiroshi said.

Akiko hummed as she searched on her computer. "He's playing at a club in Shinjuku tonight." She sent the map to Hiroshi's cellphone.

"I know where it is."

"Also, you might want to read these." She turned her computer screen toward Hiroshi, leaned back in her chair and shook her head.

Hiroshi scooted his chair over and frowned at the list of messages. "What's this?"

"Those are Mayu's tweets."

Hiroshi started reading. "What tweets?"

"The ones she sent right before she died. I asked the tech guys to scour Twitter for the rest." She leaned back so Hiroshi could read them.

"It's five in the morning and I haven't slept. My body's shaking in bed. I have to get ready in an hour. I'm so exhausted."

"I'm terrified every night when I come home because I know I have to leave again."

"My health is terrible. I've missed my period for two months, but I'm not pregnant. It's stress. I can't eat."

"My boss told me never to come to work looking bad again. He said to put on better makeup and a more feminine outfit."

"I think dying is better than not sleeping."

"My boss told me I'm not even a woman and it was like working with a man to work with me."

"I'm not even a person any more, just a drone, an ugly drone, according to my boss."

"I couldn't stop crying today at work alone in the bathroom stall."

"Everything I did today, the boss criticized."

"I had to redo all my work today. It took me all night again, and now it's morning."

Akiko shook her head. "And those are just the ones from the week before she jumped from the company roof." She looked up at Hiroshi. "On her twenty-sixth birthday."

Chapter 8

Sugamo looked at the GPS on the dashboard and squinted at the small blue address signs bolted on the outside walls of the buildings. The streets near the train station spoked out in all directions.

"I thought you said Mitaka?" Sugamo said.

"Mitaka Station," Hiroshi said. "But it's not Mitaka City. Maybe it's Musashino City?"

Sugamo said, "And I thought this was a rich area?"

"This is the part that's not rich yet," Takamatsu said.

Sugamo pulled over next to the fence running along the sidewalk. "It's got to be this building, but the numbers run around the other side."

"We'll find it easier on foot," Hiroshi said. He got out and started checking the addresses against his cellphone map.

Takamatsu got out and straightened his jacket, leaving his trench coat in the car. "What's the address?"

"One, seventeen, thirty-six," Hiroshi said, looking for a sign on one of the stores. Even numbers ran one way and odd numbers the other around the square *chome* block of buildings. They walked around the block twice before they found it.

The building was an old one with a tiled entryway lined by metal mailboxes, one bashed in, most with the bottom rusting, and the rest with small padlocks or stuffed with junk mail flyers. A stack of just-delivered packages tottered below the window of the guard's office. Hiroshi pressed the button for the elevator and they rode up to the click and grind of elevator gears.

At the lawyer's office, Hiroshi tapped on the frosted glass window, pulled open the door and shouted, "*Sumimasen*, excuse me, anyone here?" They stepped inside. The office comprised six desks inside a perimeter of metal filing cabinets with just enough room to push the chairs back to get out. It had a damp smell, despite the dingy windows being open a crack.

"*Sumimasen*," Hiroshi shouted a bit louder from the doorway.

A toilet flushed from somewhere down the hallway and a pudgy man with long curly hair stepped out of a door at the end of the hall. He finished wiping his hands on his handkerchief and said, "Ah, you're here."

He waved them inside the office to an area separated by shoulder-high dividers. In the middle was a laminated table chipped on the top and sides. Mismatched chairs cluttered the partitioned space.

"I'm Sekimoto," the pudgy man said. "Welcome to my consultation room."

Hiroshi and Takamatsu bowed and handed over their *meishi* name cards.

Sekimoto reached over to a small plastic tray at the side of the table and tossed two of his *meishi* on the table as he squeezed into a chair. His button-down shirt, threadbare at the collar, fitted tightly over his plump chest and belly. He pushed back curled strings of longish hair and took in the detectives. Hiroshi couldn't tell if the random stubble on his chin and cheeks was style or indifference.

Hiroshi held Sekimoto's *meishi* in his hands. "You handled the case for Toshiko Yamase against Senden Central."

"Senden Infinity," Sekimoto added. "Don't forget that 'Infinity.'"

"We need to know what you know about the case," Hiroshi said.

Sekimoto pointed in turn at four filing cabinets next to the consultation room. "How much time do you have?"

"All those?" Hiroshi asked.

Sekimoto nodded with a sly smirk.

Takamatsu said, "That's just it. We don't have time."

"You heard that the *bucho* Onizuka fell from the same spot as

Mayu jumped," Hiroshi said.

"I heard he died, but the newsfeed gave no details. I guess he was murdered?" Sekimoto leaned forward.

"You don't seem surprised," Hiroshi said.

"He was a serial bully, so it was only a matter of time."

"All bullies get punished eventually, you mean?" Takamatsu asked, putting his arms on the chipped tabletop. "I wish that were true."

Sekimoto chuckled. "Me, too. But his kind can only keep going so long."

"What's 'his kind'?" Hiroshi asked. "Bully? Harasser?"

"That and then some." Sekimoto shook his head. "Hard to know where to start. High school? College? Company? His night life?"

Takamatsu laughed. "He's the real deal, then?"

Sekimoto smiled. "He was. Let me start with high school. Here's the short list. Suspensions for bullying junior students, fights, shoplifting and a gambling circle. Other records were sealed, since he was a minor. You could look them up."

"Where did he go to high school?"

"Over in Edogawa-ku. Single mother. A gang. The usual."

"You got into the details."

"I had a good investigator."

"Could we talk to him?"

"He died last year. Car accident." Sekimoto frowned. "He was a great help. And clever as hell. He was an older single guy. His sister sent everything to be burned, as his will requested. I've got everything he gave me in one of those cabinets, though."

"What about college?" Hiroshi asked.

"Onizuka got into Waseda with a wrestling scholarship."

"Freestyle or Greco-Roman?"

"Greco-Roman. His high school made him choose—wrestling or reform school. Funny choice. He won championships all through college but stopped in his fourth year to focus on job-hunting."

"Did he work anyplace else other than Senden?"

Sekimoto shook his head. "He was old school. In the worst way. At Senden, he was the one who added the 'Infinity' by the way."

Hiroshi said, "He moved up quickly?"

"He was held back by a stream of complaints," Sekimoto said.

"You saw his personnel files?"

"No, I tracked the women down one by one, or rather, my investigator did. Some talked. Most said they had moved on already, that it was just a job."

"What about Mayu's case?"

Sekimoto nodded. "We had enough former employees willing to give evidence, but since the company was never compelled to turn over the records from Human Resources, it was just the women's voices against the largest media company in Japan."

Hiroshi held up his hand. "They kept the files secret in a trial like this?"

"I teamed up with another bigger law firm, but even so, we didn't have the connections with any of the ministries. They argued that if one company opened their records for this kind of trial, then every company would have to follow suit. The judges agreed." Sekimoto shrugged.

"But—"

"It doesn't make sense, I know. And was legally questionable. But the Ministry of Labor, who should have been filing the case in the first place, was unwilling to help." Sekimoto shrugged again. He was good at shrugging.

"Still, you won," Hiroshi said.

"It was my first big win, yes," Sekimoto said. "Mayu's mother, Toshiko, said she didn't want the money, she wanted a public apology. I had to explain to her that they weren't going to offer anything but a superficial apology, public or private. She finally took the money. I helped her set up the flower shop business, accounts, taxes, paperwork."

"Can you give us the names of the former employees who testified against Onizuka?"

Sekimoto took a big breath, thinking about that. "I can save you some time with that, sure, but I wish my investigator was around. He's the one who knew every little detail of Onizuka's life."

"Like his cashflow?" Hiroshi prompted.

Sekimoto smiled. "You're on the right track now."

Takamatsu said, "Let me guess, he was spending a lot more than he made."

"He ran tabs at some of the top hostess clubs in Ginza, Akasaka, and smaller clubs near where he grew up, Koiwa, Funabori, and Kinshicho. It took a long time to find all of them." Sekimoto leaned back in his chair. "You've been to his house, too, right?"

Hiroshi nodded.

"And his wife was a big shopper."

"How big?"

"The monthly interest payments on her credit cards alone were impressive."

"Anything about her drinking?"

"She was good at that too." Sekimoto nodded, his oily curls bouncing. "She was half his age, but the drinking made her look older." Then he added, "One of the tweets Mayu sent out before she committed suicide hinted at receipts for golf clubs, top-shelf liquor, luxury watches, that kind of thing. Presents maybe, bribes more likely."

"Did you find evidence of that?"

"Senden was less than cooperative, so no. At one point, they claimed there'd been a break-in at their record file storage facility."

Takamatsu laughed. "You'd think a company like that would at least be creative in their excuses."

"So you won the case even without that info?" Hiroshi asked.

"Onizuka's harassment was undeniable and Mayu's mother clearly deserved compensation for her daughter's death. Twenty women had quit the company because of Onizuka."

"And did you talk to anyone in the ministries who helped at all?" Hiroshi asked. "I thought they had a workplace harassment initiative."

"That initiative came as a *result* of this case. After it got media attention. Some Diet members got a workplace harassment bill through later, but the only punishment is name and shame. That might get a few apologies and resignations, but not much else. Companies like Senden feel complaints are a sign of a hard-driving, aggressive corporate style." Sekimoto leaned back and stretched. "That was basically Senden's defense. We work harder than any other company and some employees can't hack it. They were proud of their resignation rate, the highest in Japan."

"So, you must have done well with the settlement?" Hiroshi asked.

Sekimoto laughed. "We did well. But that's when the fun started for me. My long-term clients started switching to other law firms. A classmate at the Ministry of Labor stopped taking my calls. Even my bread-and-butter rent disputes, insurance claims, and inheritance cases started drying up. The law firm I teamed up with for the case deleted our shared files and won't answer my emails."

"So, you think Senden did all that?" Takamatsu asked.

"The 'Infinity' isn't for nothing." Sekimoto shrugged. "Thriving law business before and scraping by after. This is my second office downsizing. I can still afford two paralegals, but that's about it."

Hiroshi frowned. "How could Senden influence your client list?"

Sekimoto stretched his arms wide. "That's what big companies do—wield power."

"But didn't you get more harassment lawsuits? That win must

have helped—"

"It wised up companies and scared off clients. Companies are settling with clients and accusers before their names get dragged through the papers. The women quit sooner and demand compensation on their own. Frankly, I wish I'd never taken the case." Sekimoto gestured around the run-down office. "When I read Onizuka died, I wondered if he had somehow gotten crosswise with the company. He was a real pain."

Takamatsu hummed.

"You've been most helpful to us." Hiroshi stood up and Takamatsu followed. "Can you send what you have? Anything that might help us."

Sekimoto stood up. One button over his belly had popped open. "I'll have my paralegals put that together. We take breaks in shifts so someone's here to watch the place. We had a break-in not too long ago, middle of the day. Luckily, those second-hand file cabinets have good old locks. I can barely get them open with the key." He smiled.

Sekimoto walked them to the door. As Hiroshi and Takamatsu turned to bow, he said, "And if you ever need any legal work done, a problematic supervisor or section chief...."

Takamatsu responded with a wry smile. "The only harassment we get is our chief's incompetence."

Chapter 9

On the sidewalk, Takamatsu pulled out his cigarettes and lit one.

"No smoking here," Hiroshi said.

"Yeah, yeah, I know." Takamatsu blew out the first lungful. He held up his cigarette with his fingers splayed. "And this is all mental frustration, bad habit, death wish, repressed sexual urges."

"That's right," Hiroshi said.

"Same for this case," Takamatsu said.

"Unconscious motivation?" Hiroshi looked for Sugamo and the car.

"No, conscious. We're just not getting to it. The company failed, the bureaucrats failed, the legal system failed. The guy did what he wanted."

"Until yesterday." Hiroshi looked in both directions for the car.

Takamatsu held his cigarette away from people passing by.

Sugamo pulled around the corner, driving slowly through the street full of pedestrians. Takamatsu flicked his cigarette into the gutter. "No throwing trash, either, I know." He got in the car.

Hiroshi leaned in the window. "I'll check with Mayu's mother again. You said she'd change her story."

"Or at least cough up the telling detail."

"See you at Senden later."

Takamatsu nodded and Sugamo pulled away.

Hiroshi walked back to the big street that led to the station and hailed a taxi. It was only a short drive east to the flower shop through orderly rows of houses with neat front doors. The sidewalks were lined by painted railings and dotted with small plots for trees and shrubs. The residents set out tidy bags of trash and recyclables under crow-proof nets.

He got out near the flower shop, thinking about what the lawyer Sekimoto had told them and feeling as far as he could be

73

from the surety of his usual flow charts and spreadsheets. There, at least, he could find the underside right away, and the motivation was always clear—greed. On most financial scams, everything added up neatly from one angle, even while the other angles started to crumble.

A chalkboard sign hung on the shop door, with "Lunchtime, Back at 1:30" circled by pastel flowers chalked with cheery energy. Hiroshi peeked in the window. Toshiko, Mayu's mother, and Suzuna, Mayu's best friend, were sitting at the counter in the back of the shop eating lunch.

Seeing Hiroshi looking in, Suzuna got up to open the door.

Hiroshi stepped inside. "*O-jama shimasu.* Sorry to bother you during your lunch hour, but is this a good time?"

Toshiko waved him in. "As soon as lunch is over, we'll get too busy to talk. We missed so many lunches, we finally started putting up a sign. Would you like to join us?"

Hiroshi looked confused. "Um, I didn't—"

"Cup ramen OK? And this?" Toshiko took an *onigiri* rice ball from a small plastic container and slid it across the counter. It was handmade, the black *nori* sticking to the rice in lumps and sprinkled with *furikake* topping.

Hiroshi bowed in acquiescence. He loved handmade *onigiri*.

Suzuna walked to the stairs. "What flavor do you like?"

Hiroshi shrugged his shoulders. "I like everything. Whatever you have."

Her braids bounced down her back as she clomped upstairs. As Toshiko had said, Suzuna really was like a second daughter.

Hiroshi breathed in the shop's potent fragrance of cut stems, flower petals, and moist dirt.

Toshiko set her chopsticks down. "You want to ask me who I think killed Onizuka, right?"

"Um, yes, actually."

"Is curry OK?" Suzuna shouted from upstairs.

"That's my favorite!" Hiroshi shouted back. Behind the

counter on a shelf were framed photos of Mayu, in school uniforms, at graduations, in a *freshers* work outfit, with Suzuna in Disneyland and New York City. In every photo, Mayu stood smiling with a pleasant face and bright eyes. Only her hair style changed. Beside the photos, a bell rested on a cushion beside a small, squat Buddha statue.

Suzuna scrambled down the stairs, pulled the top off the ramen cup and poured in hot water. "It's miso and curry combined. Hope that's OK."

"We try a new addition each week. Last week, it was *natto*, kimchi, and cheese," Toshiko said.

Hiroshi made a face. "Cheese? On ramen?"

"Goes with a light soy sauce." Suzuna handed Hiroshi a pair of chopsticks and a steaming cup of ramen.

Hiroshi breathed in the salty, sour aroma. "What's this week's, um, addition?"

Suzuna held up a bottle of red sauce covered in Vietnamese script. "*Sriracha* sauce."

"That sounds better than cheese," Hiroshi said. He took the bottle and dropped a couple of splashes in his large, disposable cup.

Toshiko said, "We got tired of *umeboshi*, *wasabi*, pickles."

"Instant coffee was good," Suzuna said.

Hiroshi made a face. "You put instant coffee into your cup ramen?"

Toshiko and Suzuna giggled.

Toshiko spoke in a mock-serious voice. "Well, we were always making a cup of coffee in the middle of the day and getting called away, so it would get cold."

"You don't like coffee?" Suzuna asked.

Hiroshi cracked open his chopsticks. "I don't like anything in my ramen other than what *should* go in ramen." Hiroshi put his hands together with the chopsticks. "*Itadakimasu*."

The three of them slurped quietly.

Toshiko took a deep breath and forced a smile, her eyes

blinking. "I don't know anyone who would kill Onizuka, if that's why you're here today."

"It must have crossed your mind. You must have wondered who did it."

"Actually, I was up all night thinking about that."

Suzuna focused on her noodles, slurping and chewing without looking up.

Toshiko continued. "I imagined doing it a thousand times, in a thousand different ways. I was so angry. But after the trial, I started to feel differently. No less angry, just less vengeful. I realized my part in Mayu's life, what I did wrong. I guess I'm a slow learner. The flowers help. Suzuna helps." She smiled at Suzuna. "And maybe Onizuka's death will help too."

Suzuna smiled back at Toshiko, returned to her ramen and then spoke in a low voice. "Mayu said Onizuka was a really evil man. He tormented her. And a lot of other people, too."

Hiroshi was sweating from the noodles. He wiped his face and resettled himself on the stool. "Suzuna, could you give me the names of Mayu's other friends?"

Suzuna kept her eyes on the last bit of soup at the bottom of her cup. "I have them on my home computer."

"Not on your cellphone?" Hiroshi asked.

"It's easier to send later, if that's OK?" Suzuna dug out the last sliver of noodle with her chopsticks.

Toshiko fingered the leafy plant in front of her on the table. "Mayu and I slept in the same room after my husband moved to the Philippines for work, our futons side by side, talking until we fell asleep. She would scrub my back in the bath and I brushed her hair. She had beautiful hair. I wrote all that down and made my lawyer read it out loud. I wanted to be sure Onizuka and the others at Senden heard about Mayu's life."

"I hope they were listening," Hiroshi said.

"I'm not sure they were, but I wanted it on record." Toshiko looked out the window. "I went to a Catholic high school. On a scholarship. And then the sister school, a women's college. We read the Bible and sang hymns. I never took all that seriously, but losing Mayu was like something out of the Bible. I can't imagine revenge, but I can't forgive either. I still smell her and hear her laugh. We still follow the weekly schedule she made for us."

"Schedule?"

"She had us all so organized—exercise, shopping, cleaning, paying bills. She made a study schedule for Suzuna so she could pass the English tests and go with her to America."

"She just had the knack of order." Suzuna picked up the ramen containers and started to put everything in the trash, her eyes averted, readying things to re-open the shop.

Hiroshi finished the *onigiri* and Suzuna took the wrapper, stopped, turned and looked at Hiroshi. "I'm not sure how we can help you. I'm sorry, but Mayu's gone, and now that man is gone. Nothing else matters, does it?"

"Death always matters." Hiroshi looked at her until she turned away and dropped the trash in the bin beside the wrapping table.

A customer knocked on the glass and Hiroshi couldn't think of what else to even ask them. Toshiko and Suzuna seemed to be just what they were—mother and best friend. He left with a polite goodbye.

The meeting with Senden wasn't for two hours and he didn't want to go back to his office. He remembered a nearby jazz *kissaten* with a tube amp and vinyl collection. He hadn't been there for years and got turned around in the pedestrian alleys, but he finally found it and climbed the stairs. Loud jazz filled the dark, wood-lined space. He picked a seat by the window, ordered a cappuccino, ignored his messages, and drifted into the music.

What *did* matter on this case, or on any of them? On cryptocurrency cases, it all made sense up to the point where it didn't, where the connecting bridge was washed away and you couldn't get across. Many of the jazz greats said that in jazz there were no wrong notes, as long as you kept going, turning a wrong note right, pretending that's what you intended. Maybe that was the same with working a case.

When the waitress flipped the record, Hiroshi opened his eyes and looked out the window. On the pedestrian lane below, Suzuna walked by in a long wool coat.

Hiroshi got up and hurried to the register, wondering why she wasn't working.

He eased down the steep stairs, ran to the end of the lane and caught her heading into the nexus of small alleys Takamatsu had dragged him through the day before. Hiroshi hurried after her.

Inside the *yokocho* maze, he took the largest, straightest alley that emptied out on the street in front of the station, where Suzuna seemed to be heading. He kept sight of her loose wool coat and her blonde-dyed braids. She was carrying a large bouquet of flowers wrapped in brown paper with plastic and tinfoil at the end. Maybe she was making a delivery.

She took the escalator up to the ticket machine and up the next escalator to the platform. Hiroshi hurried onto the same train one car down. If he leaned back and stared down the center of the train, he could just see the dark orange and gray of her coat.

He stood quietly, checking on her at every stop, ready to get off when she did.

She stayed on until Kanda Station, where she changed to the Yamanote Line. The platform was narrow there, one of the older ones in the city, so he stood behind a vending machine until she got on, quickly hopping on just before the doors shut.

She got off at Nippori Station and headed up a steep slope into a quiet neighborhood with streets just wide enough for a single car at a time. She walked steadily and surely to where the street ended and a cobblestone walkway started. Was this Yanaka Cemetery? A signboard map of the burial areas said it was.

Suzuna turned into a cobblestone walkway between the neat squares of graves. Smooth stone blocks marked off each area, with stone lanterns, sculpted trees and chiseled grave markers inside each. Poking up behind were racks holding long wooden *sotoba* covered in brushed-on prayers in Japanese and Sanskrit. Ancient, craggy cherry trees hung over the walkways and graves, and here and there a few plum trees grew.

Hiroshi stopped to take a photo of a neat map of the plots in that part of the cemetery, the interlocking rectangles and parallelograms numbered precisely. He stayed angled behind a large, ornate mausoleum from where he could watch.

Suzuna unwrapped the bouquet she'd brought and set it in front of a gray stone marker. She put her hands together to pray. After raising her head, she went to get a broom and bucket and dipper from the communal area. She filled up the bucket with water and carried it back to the grave. She set it down and began sweeping away fallen leaves. When she finished she began laving water over the stones and brushing them down. With the last of the water, she filled up two vases attached to the stone on either side of the grave marker and arranged the flowers in them.

When she was satisfied with how it looked, she put her hands together again and her head down, her shoulders rising and falling inside the wool coat, breathing deeply or maybe sobbing.

Before she finished, two more women arrived. Both were draped in oversized sweatshirts, their heads tucked in their hoods. One was rather plump and the other short and wiry. They stepped up to join Suzuna on either side, putting their hands together to pray. All three stood close and held their heads down for a long time.

When they straightened up, they talked together while rearranging the flowers and resweeping the whole area. After tending the burial plot, they swept the steps again and returned the broom, bucket and dipper to the communal area, and walked off in separate paths out of the vast cemetery.

When Suzuna and the other two women were out of sight, Hiroshi walked to the grave, already knowing what would be carved on the stone: Mayu Ayase, 1991-2017.

Chapter 10

Takamatsu and Sugamo were waiting in the circle drive in front of Senden Central Infinity when Hiroshi got there. Takamatsu stripped off his trench coat as soon as they stepped inside the overheated lobby. To the right was the entrance to the museum of the history of advertising, featuring, of course, Senden Central and the company's newest incarnation, Senden Infinity.

"A museum advertising the history of advertising," Takamatsu said.

"And there's an ad for the museum." Hiroshi pointed to a banner hanging among the others.

"We're already going in circles and we're just in the lobby," Takamatsu said.

Hiroshi spoke to the receptionist at the desk by the elevators.

In a few minutes, a tall young woman dressed in a business suit walked out of the elevator straight to the detectives and bowed deeply.

"We met the other night? On the roof?" Chizu Kawamura said, and led them to the elevators.

"Oh, yes, of course," Hiroshi said. "It was a bit dark on the roof."

"And you were busy," Chizu said. She looked directly into Hiroshi's eyes, as if she had lived overseas and lost the Japanese custom of reserved eye contact. She also seemed to not know how attractive she was, unlike most Tokyo women who took every glance as compliment. She held the elevator door open for them and then pressed the button and folded her hands in front of her.

When they got out on the sixteenth floor, Chizu led them down a hallway to a conference room that looked over the broad Hibiya-dori Street and the green waters of the moat and thick stone walls that circled the Imperial Palace grounds. Beyond that was *shitamachi*, the lower town of eastern Tokyo, where Onizuka had grown up.

Chizu asked them to sit at the conference table, and then stepped out and left them alone. Hiroshi leaned back in the ergonomic chair and wondered if Akiko could somehow requisition chairs like these for his office.

Takamatsu fiddled with the connectivity panel poking up under a lid from the dark veneer tabletop. He ran his fingers over the inputs for video, audio, chargers, and network connectors. He flipped the top down with a loud clack that echoed in the empty room.

"You should have brought your laptop," Hiroshi said.

"Yeah, I always forget that." Takamatsu opened and shut the top as impatiently as he flipped his lighter, and just as loudly.

A young woman came in with tea and set out the small round cups with a soft-spoken *"Doozo."* She held the tray to her chest and bowed before departing the room. A blast of hot, dry air leaped out of the overhead heating unit. Sunlight angled in from the floor-to-ceiling windows, which further warmed the room.

The door clicked and a thin man with a flat, pale face came into the room. Following him was Nakata, the head of HR, who Hiroshi and Takamatsu had met on the roof the night before. The flat-faced man looked at both detectives closely as they stood up to greet him. He looked to be in his mid-sixties, with gray hair and a well-cut suit with a dark blue tie.

Nakata bowed and said, "This is our company president, Tanaka."

Hiroshi and Takamatsu bowed.

Tanaka said, "Thank you for your cooperation on this matter."

Hiroshi said, "Tanaka *shacho*, thank you for your help. We need a few files about Onizuka and then we can conclude this case as soon as possible."

Tanaka said, "I've requested the HR department," he gestured to Nakata and Chizu, standing in rank behind him, "to give you every assistance. We would like to put this tragic incident behind us. Our grand opening on the global stage is scheduled for this weekend. We have a press conference on Friday."

Hiroshi said, "With your full cooperation, we can expedite this. But cases have their own schedules. We will look into the files and keep Nakata-san up to date with our progress."

Tanaka looked at the detectives for a quiet minute.

Takamatsu straightened his cuffs and shifted his stance.

Hiroshi waited.

Tanaka finally spoke. "I've contacted the National Police Agency and the Ministry of Justice. We've already cooperated with the Ministry of Health, Labor and Welfare on other issues related to Onizuka. So, I'm sure you'll be able to conclude this investigation before this weekend."

Hiroshi nodded without saying anything more.

"Thank you for your understanding." Tanaka turned and said something to Nakata and looked back to the detectives with a brief nod before leaving.

Nakata and Chizu bowed to him as he left, then motioned for Hiroshi and Takamatsu to have a seat. Nakata sat straight with a breezy confidence, no doubt born from countless meetings, with his shoulders back and an imperious look.

"I've brought several files for you, which I think should get this incident resolved quickly." He turned to Chizu, who sat next to him with a stack of folders. She looked through them, checking the labels and handing them to Hiroshi.

Hiroshi opened the first folder and handed one to Takamatsu.

Nakata cleared his throat and set his hands on the table.

Hiroshi skimmed the files. "We need to get several pieces of information from you."

Nakata nodded. "I think it's all in there. Chizu will be able to follow up on any further requests that we can't answer today. She's my assistant in Human Resources and knows more than I do." A smile flickered across his face, meaning what, Hiroshi couldn't tell.

Hiroshi set the files down and looked up. "We'll need to see the actual HR file on Onizuka, not this edited one. We need specifics on how long he worked here, what sections, what positions, the essentials."

Chizu took notes on her tablet.

Hiroshi continued. "We need to know who filed claims against him for harassment, who transferred out of his section, who quit after working under him, and what disciplinary actions were taken against Onizuka. From what we know, he had a history of harassing his subordinates."

Nakata looked at Chizu, who showed him a page on her tablet computer. To Hiroshi, he said, "You must understand that a lot of that information is confidential, so we can't—"

"You must understand that this is a possible murder investigation and we need to rule out suspects as quickly as we can." Hiroshi watched both of them carefully. "Your company president just advised as much."

"We've certainly had enough negative publicity as it is," Nakata said, glancing at Chizu to be sure she was writing everything down.

"If we can't get all the information on Onizuka, our investigation could drag on for longer, possibly interfering with PR for your overseas expansion. We want this case closed as much as you do," Hiroshi said.

"More so," Takamatsu added, his hands clasped together on the smooth veneer of the table. "Could you tell us a bit about Onizuka based on your personal interactions as head of HR?"

Nakata cleared his throat. "If I can speak frankly, he was a difficult person. Many of his subordinates did not get along with him. But many loved his hard-driving work style, his loyalty, his successes. He was our best section chief in terms of productivity. Many of his co-workers, junior to him, attribute their own success to having learned the ropes from him."

Takamatsu smiled. "We'd like to send over some detectives this afternoon to talk with them. Can you set that up for us?"

"It's a bit short notice," Nakata said.

"So was Onizuka's fall from the top of your main building," Takamatsu replied.

Nakata looked at Chizu, who nodded and made a note.

Hiroshi said, "We need to talk with the other women who quit or asked to be moved from his section, or settled quietly and left the company."

Nakata said, "We're trapped by confidentiality agreements, but I'll see what I can do. You understand I'll need to contact the company lawyers first."

"His recent work focused on expanding overseas?" Hiroshi asked. He pulled a handkerchief out of his pocket to wipe the sweat from his brow. The heating, at least, worked well at Senden.

"He was lead on the overseas expansion project," Nakata said.

"That's a big project," Hiroshi said.

"Much of the groundwork was done little by little, but he was in charge of setting up the offices in New York and London," Nakata said.

"Can we get a list of what was done in that regard? Again, it helps us round out the picture of what he was doing."

Nakata nodded at Chizu and she wrote everything down. Nakata's cellphone buzzed in his jacket pocket, and he checked it. "I'm sorry, I have to take this." He stood up, nodding, and then bowed and stepped into the hallway.

Takamatsu growled deep in his throat.

Chizu pulled her cellphone out and held it toward Hiroshi. "Do you use LINE?"

"Yes," Hiroshi said.

"That's best for me, if it's all right with you?" She pressed her phone pad and held it out.

Hiroshi held out his phone for Chizu to capture his QR code.

"I'll LINE message you later," Chizu said, clicking on her phone to save his contact.

Nakata stepped back inside and Chizu quickly set her phone on the table.

Hiroshi said, "And we'll need access to your accounting section, too."

Nakata cocked his head and looked at Hiroshi. "Why is that?"

Hiroshi shrugged. "It's often the case that there are financial irregularities in cases such as this. So we just need to check on a few things."

"We don't just turn over our accounts to the police," Nakata said. "It could take weeks of meetings to get approval."

Hiroshi leaned back in his chair. "That's how long the investigation will continue, then."

Takamatsu leaned forward. "We can always route this through bureaucratic channels. But we're much more discreet than the ministries. You know how things leak out over there."

"The records for all of these things are not kept here," Nakata said. "We need to request those from our storage facilities. Some of the records go back a few years, if that's what you're asking for."

"That's what we're asking for. We need to see it all."

Nakata leaned back in his chair. "I'll have to get back to you later today."

"And while you're asking for permission, we need the name of the law firm that represented you in the lawsuit with Mayu Yamase. Were you the head of HR at that time?"

Nakata looked at Hiroshi. "The girl's death was a terrible tragedy—"

"Her name was Mayu. Mayu Yamase," Hiroshi said, raising his voice.

Takamatsu hummed a quick note of approval.

Hiroshi tapped the table. "We need to re-examine the case of Mayu Yamase. There are too many coincidences."

"Senden paid reparations to her mother, so we hoped that would put the tragedy behind us," Nakata said.

"It doesn't seem behind you yet," Takamatsu growled. "That's why we're here."

Nakata looked annoyed. "I was the head of HR at that time."

"If Mayu Yamase asked for a transfer, why was she not moved to another section? Was Mayu Yamase doing a poor job? Why was she denied a transfer?" Hiroshi asked.

"We weren't sure how bad the situation was," Nakata said, unruffled. "We've revamped our personnel and grievance policies since then."

Chizu had stopped writing everything down and stared at her tablet.

Nakata said, "The simple answer to your question is a lot of employees cannot handle the pressure. We have a unique, high-performance culture at Senden. We respect, and reward, hard work. The most driven section in our company was Onizuka's. Not everyone works well under pressure from their superiors, especially women."

"It's clear many don't," Hiroshi said, pushing back the chair to get up. "So, was Mayu Yamase one of the weak ones, in your scheme of things, or one of the strong ones who spoke up?"

Takamatsu tapped the connectivity panel which sprung open with a loud click. He stood up and cleared his throat, straightening his cuffs ready to leave.

Hiroshi let out a discouraged hum as he stood and stared at Nakata, who didn't move to get up. Chizu was frozen in place.

Hiroshi looked at the top of her head as he spoke. "We'll be waiting for those files. And if those don't help, we'll ask for more files, until something does help. Think of this as the start of our media campaign. We're reinforcing sentiments, presenting information, and increasing awareness. And if that doesn't work, we'll switch platforms. But I don't think you'll like the other platforms."

Without waiting for any response, Hiroshi and Takamatsu thanked them in sterile polite phrases and walked out.

Chapter 11

The jazz club was a square room with wood chairs facing the stage and narrow tables offering just enough space to set a drink. The place was half full and the band was cooking. Hiroshi took a seat in the back next to a huge photo of John Coltrane watching over the proceedings like a jazz saint.

After Senden's stonewalling, he and Akiko had dug through the company's details in his office. They'd set up appointments for the next day but made little headway. Takamatsu and Osaki had been called to sort out a suicide. Hiroshi had left his office in frustration and taxied to the club.

The quintet had an electric violinist, trumpeter and sax player on the front line, and a bassist and drummer whipping up thick rhythms. Hiroshi followed the trumpeter's solo, long, spare, and unhurried. The violinist took over, bursting with energy, with a pizzicato passage that sped to a dizzying pace before passing the soloing baton to Steve Titus, Mayu's American former boyfriend.

Steve took off mimicking the violin with nimble honks on his alto sax before sliding down the register for long, lean bebop lines. He kept dipping into the melody line for touch points while reeling off strong, fluid lines of his own. The ensemble wrapped it tighter and tighter before coming to an abrupt, breathless stop.

The audience demanded an encore.

Steve called for a rollicking Charles Mingus number and the evening romped to an end.

When the club started to clear out, Hiroshi walked up to the stage to talk with Steve. He was handsome, with dimples and a thin-trimmed beard. His dark hair was thick and tousled, as relaxed as his playing.

"Are you Steve Titus?" Hiroshi said in English.

"I am." He stopped cleaning the sax and swung a hand out to

shake. "Did you like the show?"

"It was both exploratory and satisfying. The perfect balance, in my opinion."

"Thanks, man, that's nice. Are you a musician?" Steve started wiping off the sax, working along all the parts carefully with the cloth.

"Just a fan. Who wrote that tune before the encore? Blues in a tricky time signature."

Steve smiled. "Except for the Mingus number, they were all mine." Steve eyed his reeds, wiping them with a cloth and filing them away. "I like to break out of four-beat."

"Have you recorded any of them?"

"Working on it. Hey, why is your English so good?" He ran the cloth over all of the keys, worrying over one pad that was sticky.

"I lived in Boston for a few years."

"I played there a few times. What do you do now?" Steve leaned over to nestle his saxophone into the velvet case and fold the cleaning cloth on top.

"I'm a forensic accountant in the homicide department. A detective." He let that hang in the air.

Steve put his reed case and neck strap away before he turned to face Hiroshi. "Are you taking me in? I want to tell someone before I disappear for three weeks again without even a phone call."

Hiroshi said, "I'll take you for a drink instead. I need to ask you about Mayu."

The violinist came over. She had long hair and eyes that twinkled even as she took in Hiroshi in the dim light of the club. She moved easily, her violin case bouncing on her hip from the shoulder strap.

Steve rolled his eyes at her in apology. "I'm going to go talk with this guy here. So, I'll meet you later."

She checked her cellphone and looked back at Steve. "I'll hit that jam session in Takadanobaba."

"I'll catch up with you there," Steve said.

"I got the pay and divided it with everyone. Here's yours." She handed him folded bills and walked off, glancing back once from the door.

"Girlfriend?" Hiroshi asked.

"Friend friend. She's a brilliant musician," Steve said. "OK, where to?"

"Coffee or whiskey?"

"Both if it's about Mayu."

They walked quietly out of the club and into the streets of Shinjuku. Most people were heading back to the subway or train. The late-night crowds who stayed up or worked all night had just started arriving.

Not far from the jazz club, Hiroshi stopped at a narrow three-story building. From three flights up, electric blues cascaded down the stairway. They trudged up the tight steps, careful not to bump the record sleeves hung along the walls.

Inside, a bar top took up most of the space and two rickety tables jutted against the far wall. Shelves of vinyl lined the back of the bar, where a bartender stood calmly wiping glasses. Two women sat at the far end of the bar deep in conversation.

Hiroshi headed to the tables and Steve pulled a chair over for his sax case and backpack.

Hiroshi went to the bar and ordered two shots of whiskey and two cups of coffee, then came back and sat down. "Maybe you heard, but Mayu's boss, the one who harassed her, died."

Steve sat back. "He...What?...When?"

"Yesterday."

"Yesterday? That was Mayu's birthday," Steve said, looking confused. "That's why you wanted to talk to me? I..."

"Where were you early yesterday morning?"

"I played a gig, and then met Yuna, the violinist." Steve looked down.

"You were with her all night?"

91

"After the gig, yes. We slept in late."

The bartender set the coffee on the bar top. The place was too small for him to get out so Hiroshi got up to carry it over.

Steve looked down at his coffee.

"Any—"

"Proof of my alibi? Just Yuna."

Hiroshi sipped his coffee. He could find her later to check. Her name was on the club's webpage.

"So, can you tell me a bit more about Mayu and yourself? You met her in America and followed her back here?"

Steve nodded. "She came to one of my shows at the student center. We had the midnight slot, so it was mostly stoners and jazz nuts, but we could play whatever we liked." Steve pointed at the speakers, Muddy Waters on vinyl. "I played in blues bands at first."

The bartender set out two shots of whiskey on the bar and Hiroshi got up to get them.

"So..." Hiroshi prompted.

Steve looked at the whiskey shots.

"*Kanpai*," Hiroshi said gently.

Steve slugged down his shot in one go.

Hiroshi downed his and shivered. It seemed to reignite the hangover that had eased by late afternoon.

Steve said, "The slow song in the last set, did you hear it?"

Hiroshi nodded.

"That was for her. I can't find a title. I'd have to write a hundred more songs to get down all my feelings about her."

"What about the violinist?"

"It'd be different songs for her."

Steve set the glass in front of him and looked at the record covers on the walls. Some of his tough-guy tension melted and he kept his eyes on the covers as he talked. "With Mayu, it was love at first sight. And that was weird, because I was so used to hooking up, casual, but with Mayu, it was like, well, it was enough just to look at her."

"You didn't...?"

"We did, but we also talked a lot. She came to all my gigs. We'd go to the library. I started studying. She was a serious student."

"And you were..."

"A musician, or my idea of one. She changed me. And I changed her. She told me she'd never danced before, so we went dancing. And she'd never traveled, so we took a road trip to Memphis, Nashville, New Orleans, Austin, all the music cities. I'd never been that close to anyone. It was—" Steve looked at the bar. "It was the best time I ever had in my life. She was so alive."

"What about Mayu's friend, Suzuna? She was there in America, too, right?"

"Does she know about this? Is she all right?"

"I spoke with her and she seemed fine. Mayu's mother, too."

"Mayu's mother always blamed me somehow. But I was the one telling Mayu to quit, trying to protect her." He tried to drain one more drop of whiskey, gave up and wrapped his hands around the coffee cup.

"So, when did you come to Japan?"

"I was behind in my credits, so we spent a year apart, nine months actually, until I could graduate. Mayu had to find a job. She paid for my ticket with her first paycheck. She had an English teaching job lined up for me, an apartment, and everything organized when I got here. In fact, she got me all my jazz gigs, printing handouts for my gigs, and translating everything for me. She was a detail person. The exact opposite of me."

"Did you see her often?"

"I wanted to move in together, but she wouldn't leave her mother. Plus, she was always working. I was getting more gigs, so she'd come before the last song. We'd go out to eat at midnight, to a love hotel, and then she'd catch the last train home or call her mother to say she had an all-nighter at work. Which she often did. And we'd do it all again the next day." Steve picked up his whiskey glass. "I need another. Let me get a round."

"I got it." Hiroshi took the glasses to the bar and waited while the bartender filled them up.

Hiroshi set the shot glasses down on the table and they both sipped slowly, the coffee getting cold.

"Can you tell me what happened at Mayu's funeral? You were arrested."

Steve looked at Hiroshi like he knew that question was coming. "Not my best moment. These guys came from the company, the company that killed Mayu. They had no right to be there." Steve finished his shot in a swallow. "Mayu's father showed up, drunk, and he just lunged at them. I never hit anyone in my life, always worried about my hands. All of a sudden, I was handcuffed and in the police car. Suzuna walked over and spit in the face of one of the company guys. I remember that. And then three long weeks in jail."

"They kept you for the maximum?"

"I'd gotten in a few punches myself. My hand was swollen, but they wouldn't give me ice or a bandage or anything. They barely interrogated me. I thought, well, all the greats in jazz history got busted, why shouldn't I?"

"Mayu's mother bailed you out."

"She did."

"And you had never met her father before?"

Steve shook his head.

"Did Mayu talk about her boss?"

"She talked about him constantly. It was like an illness, an addiction. She'd just get hysterical at times. Running away from me or curling up in a ball and weeping uncontrollably. I told her to talk to the company about the bastard. She did and it seemed like it was better, but then it got worse again right away. I kept telling her we could go back to the States. She'd say yes one day and then no the next. She was crying all the time. It was like she was alive like in America, and then she'd die again when she went to work."

"Why didn't she just leave with you?"

Steven leaned back in his chair. "I...well...one night, she came to my place but I wasn't there."

"Where were you?"

Steven looked at the wall over Hiroshi's shoulder. "I told her I was jamming all night. I did go to a lot of jam sessions, but I always told her. I...met...this woman. She came up to me after a gig. She was gorgeous." He shook his head. "Mayu came to my place and sent a text message asking where I was."

"Did she suspect you'd been with another woman?"

"If she did, she never let on. But I think she knew. I never did that after meeting Mayu, but this woman...well, anyway, I wasn't there for her."

"Did she change after that?"

Steve shut his eyes and continued. "I felt guilty as hell. But she started to leave work, spend more time with her mother, go out with Suzuna and her friends. That was cool. We'd been spending a lot of time together. Then, on her birthday, she sent me a message she was quitting. I was thrilled. At last, I thought. I kept texting her all night, waiting. I thought she was explaining it to her mother, or sleeping for once."

"That was the night she killed herself?" Hiroshi prompted.

Steve tried to get one last taste of whiskey from his empty glass and turned to his coffee. "I should have gone to her mother's house to check. Or to the company. I could've—"

Hiroshi waited.

Steve drank his coffee, staring at the wall, back to the past. "Mayu wanted to leave, but it was like she was trapped by everything—her mother, her idea of success, her job, the whole system in Japan. She was trapped by her own need to have order. The more she struggled, the more she sank into it. She could organize everything except her own escape."

Hiroshi's phone buzzed.

Steve looked away and shook his head, slugged down the rest of his coffee.

Hiroshi took the call and listened closely, stood up and waved at the bartender for the bill. "How do I get in touch with you? We need to talk more."

Steve held up his phone and Hiroshi snapped a photo of his phone number.

"I'll call you."

Steve nodded OK in tight, tense motions.

Hiroshi paid quickly and hurried out, leaving Steve staring at the empty record covers on the wall.

Chapter 12

Hiroshi grabbed a taxi outside the club and called Sakaguchi back.

"How did you find him?" Hiroshi asked.

"When will you get here?" Sakaguchi asked.

"Fifteen minutes, if we can get past the traffic around the station." He showed the driver his badge and told him to hurry.

He regretted the whiskey, but it was too late now. He called Ayana to tell her he would be late. He leaned back and watched the bright lights of Shinjuku turn to crustier, darker streets toward Nakano, trying to imagine what Mayu went through and what her family and friends and colleagues must have felt. Everyone struggles to go on after a death, but not everyone struggles for revenge. When he lost his parents during college, he learned the world can't be reset, but that didn't stop him thinking about it.

Everything about this case reminded Hiroshi of why he hated big Japanese companies—the vicious competition, the strict hierarchy, the indifference. You were either in, under control, or you were out, and ignored. Fear of scandal and maintaining the status quo determined most decisions, with profit determining the rest. The Japanese corporate system rewarded people like Onizuka, and used him to use other people. A workaholic culture kept big companies thriving. One small blip like Mayu, or even Onizuka, was not going to slow them down.

Nearly drowning in Tokyo Bay rescuing Takamatsu last winter had pushed him to rethink a lot of things. He decided to ask his uncle about going to work with him at a nice safe spot far from death and danger. He wrote and rewrote the email but never sent it. His uncle, Hiroshi's guardian after his parents died, had always expected his nephew to work for him at his firm, but that had always felt too easy. He'd hated the idea of a prefab job and a preset life—his uncle was always so certain about everything—so he ended up in the homicide department. The corporate world was turning out to be dangerous and erratic in its own strange ways, too.

***

The taxi pulled up to Nakano Station and Hiroshi directed the driver a few hundred meters down Nakano Dori where the Chuo Line sliced through towering rows of twenty-story buildings crammed with convenience stores, udon shops, eyeglass outlets, and cram schools. Their brightly lit interiors were the happy face of huge corporations, spilling colored light and offers of convenience onto the passersby outside.

Hiroshi followed the GPS on his phone until he was close to the hotel and started looking for the car. Osaki stepped out and waved him over.

He got in beside Sakaguchi. "I thought you were staying in headquarters because of your knee."

Sakaguchi shifted his brace around his leg. "Sitting in the car is about the same as sitting at my desk. At least I can be an extra pair of eyes. And avoid the chief. He's texting me every fifteen minutes about this."

"Where's Takamatsu and Sugamo?" Hiroshi asked.

"Other side of the hotel. Another entrance."

"How did you find out the guy's back in Tokyo?"

"Akiko figured it out. She kept calling his company in the Philippines, kept getting the runaround," Sakaguchi explained. "Finally, she got travel dates and a phone number. His photo was on file."

Sakaguchi sent it to Hiroshi's phone. He looked a bit like Mayu, and Hiroshi could see where she got her good looks from—both parents. Mayu's father had brushed-back hair, a strong jaw, wide shoulders and a serious stare. "How long ago was this photo?"

"After Mayu's funeral. You read the files about his arrest?"

"He broke someone's jaw, gave another a concussion, and was stopped from slamming another guy's head against a car." Hiroshi frowned. "I thought he was a company employee."

"And a street brawler. He ended up with a broken arm."

"Hit the wrong cop," Hiroshi said.

"Hit several, apparently."

"How long has he been back in Japan?"

"About a week, but we couldn't confirm it. The computerized immigration system at Narita and Haneda wasn't working."

"So, he's back here for Mayu's birthday, for Onizuka."

"Timing's right. Motive surely. But we don't know where Onizuka went the night he died, much less where Mayu's father went. Linking them up won't be easy." Sakaguchi took a call and massaged the muscles above his knee while he talked.

"He's inside?" Hiroshi asked.

Osaki looked in the rearview mirror. "We're waiting for him to come back. Could be a long wait."

"What's the plan if he shows up?" Hiroshi asked.

Sakaguchi hung up. "Be ready. That's the plan."

Hiroshi said, "I'd prefer to avoid another brawl."

Osaki hummed in agreement. "Let's hope he doesn't bolt."

Sakaguchi stretched his knee back and forth. "That's what did my knee in, chasing people lighter than me."

"Almost everyone weighs less than you do," Hiroshi said.

"That's what I mean." Sakaguchi pulled at his knee brace.

Osaki twisted in the seat. "Takamatsu and Sugamo are on the other side, so we can follow each other with the GPS tracker apps the chief got us."

Hiroshi snorted. "Takamatsu is using an app?"

"Sugamo uploaded it for him just now. But when you're moving fast, there's no time to—"

"Is that him?" Hiroshi asked.

Hiroshi got out and Osaki followed. They stepped over an iron railing between the street and the sidewalk. Yamase, Mayu's father, was moving toward the entrance to the hotel with his eyes on his cellphone, texting as he walked.

Sakaguchi must have alerted Takamatsu and Sugamo because Hiroshi saw them turn the corner and walk toward them, looking as inconspicuous as an ex-sumo wrestler and a cop in an Italian leather trench coat can look.

When Yamase looked up, he must have noticed them bearing down on him, but he didn't do anything different. When he got to the next turn, though, he bolted to the right down a pedestrian lane that led to the Nakano Sun Mall Broadway.

The four detectives took off after him down the small lane, dodging around after-work shoppers.

Yamase spun a rack of women's blouses across the narrow passage and all four detectives slowed to high step over it.

Takamatsu got tangled in the blouses and shoved the rack back against the front of the store. Shoppers skittered out of the way, yelling in surprise and confusion.

Sugamo and Osaki sprinted past Takamatsu. Hiroshi held up his badge running forward and shouted, "Police. Out of the way."

Yamase crossed the covered mall and kept going down the small lane on the other side.

Hiroshi slowed down on the slippery-smooth tiles underfoot and kept going down the lane ahead.

Yamase snatched a display of girls' necklaces and barrettes from the right and a tall display of iPhone accessories from the left. They crashed down and skittered over the pavement, blocking the path.

Sugamo and Osaki slowed down to keep their footing over the hurdles, got around the goods and past the people, and kept running. Takamatsu caught up with Hiroshi and they ran to a T-intersection where they looked for any sign of Yamase.

Hiroshi turned right since Sugamo and Osaki had gone left, and Takamatsu stayed straight ahead.

Hiroshi ran to the middle of the next lane and slowed to examine the doors of the small restaurants and drinking spots he'd passed. Beside him, the tinted glass doors of a discount seafood restaurant blocked the view inside. Hiroshi ducked under the *noren* and looked inside, but there were no customers, only the staff putting on their blue aprons and tying towels around their heads. They looked at him curiously.

Hiroshi backed out and went in the other direction, where Sugamo had gone.

At the next corner, he looked down the long, narrow lane at Sugamo catching his breath, with his hands on his knees. He looked back at Hiroshi with a face of irritation.

The only place to duck in was a small *snacku* bar with a heavy wood door. Hiroshi pulled it open. The smell of spilled whiskey met the whiskey in his system and joined with a whiff of mildew. Hiroshi gagged. An old woman sitting at the bar doing accounts turned, looking surprised, but Hiroshi didn't stay long enough to apologize.

He let the door shut, looked in both directions and hurried to the next crossing, looking in all four directions. Sugamo was standing at the next intersection. When he saw Hiroshi, he shrugged.

Hiroshi backtracked to a smaller lane that ran parallel to the main shopping street, another inconspicuous little space, one of thousands of small dead ends in Tokyo, where the buildings lined up in odd patterns.

It was home to two little bars, one on each side. Hiroshi pulled on the doors, but they were locked. He walked toward the dead end, and, as he got closer, he realized it wasn't a dead end, but turned to the left.

The back wall had posters taped to an old bulletin board. Below it, the *kanji* characters for "No parking," "No graffiti" and, "No pissing" were written in faded white paint on the wall.

Hiroshi walked to the end and looked left. A shoulder-width

passageway held a jumble of dusty, sun-faded liquor crates, tall ones for sake and short ones for beer. It looked like an abandoned storage area for a long-gone liquor delivery service for the area's restaurants and bars. An old wooden hand truck, one handle rotted, leaned against the wall. A single street light cover, rusted metal with no bulb, hung above a splintered signboard. Overhead, an old piece of sun-cracked plastic was wedged between the buildings as a makeshift roof.

Hiroshi turned to go. He started back to the entrance but stopped and silently texted the others to say where he was. The tracking app had stopped working, so he texted some vague directions and hoped they'd be able to find him.

He looked for something, anything, like a kendo practice sword. From a tangled pile of discarded cleaning stuff, he found a mop handle with a rusted metal frame at the end. He held it in both hands and sized it up. It'd probably break after one strike, but it was better than nothing. Hiroshi looked back at the entrance, hoping everyone would get there before he needed to use it.

He turned back to the cut-off at the end of the alley and set the mop pole, balanced himself, and pictured his *kendo* teacher's stance.

He walked toward the crates, peering into the dark.

Hiroshi reached forward to pull aside the old liquor crate from the top of the jumble. He still couldn't see anything so he pulled out his cellphone and clicked on his flashlight app. Deep shadows webbed through the old crates and discarded junk.

Hiroshi moved the light around the dark until he could make out a man crouched with his back against the filthy wall. There was nowhere for him to go.

"Are you Yamase? Mayu's father?" Hiroshi called out.

The cornered man pushed the crates aside and stood up, brushing the dust off his jacket.

"Yes, I am," he said, putting up his hands.

"Stay right there until everyone else gets here." Hiroshi held the mop handle up and ready.

Chapter 13

When they got Mayu's father, Kazuki Yamase, back to the station for interrogation, Sakaguchi sent Sugamo and Osaki home. They didn't even pretend to argue, tired from running. Fortunately Yamase had not put up any fight. They had surrounded him in the alley and walked him back to the car without incident. Sugamo and Osaki apologized to Takamatsu and Hiroshi before heading home to their families and sleep.

As they waited outside the interrogation rooms for Yamase to get through booking, they saw the chief coming down the hallway. Takamatsu skipped away to the official smoking area, but Hiroshi was too slow to escape, and Sakaguchi's knee gave him no hope of fleeing.

The chief walked up and put his hands on his hips. "We have the corpse of one of the most accomplished businessmen in Japan in the middle of the business district and we've wasted another day. Is this the guy who did it?" The chief looked a lot shorter without his Borsalino hat.

Hiroshi shrugged. "He didn't try too hard to escape, so either he's innocent or has a great alibi. Or both. Or he's bluffing."

"Let's find out." The chief followed Sakaguchi up the three steps to the next-door observation room.

Hiroshi was surprised by the chief's unusually terse response. Maybe he was tired, too.

Hiroshi waited in the hallway until Yamase was led in by two officers and seated in the interrogation room. Yamase walked slowly and steadily, glancing at Hiroshi before calmly sitting down and staring straight ahead.

Takamatsu wandered back reeking of tobacco. "Big insights from the chief?"

Hiroshi gave him a look of exasperation and the two of them

entered the interrogation room. They sat down across from Yamase and another officer stood by the door.

Hiroshi started. "You're Kazuki Yamase, the father of Mayu Yamase, divorced from Mayu's mother, Toshiko Yamase?"

Yamase nodded and brushed back his thick hair. He was tall with wide shoulders and looked at ease with himself, maybe too at ease.

"Could you please state your answers clearly and audibly. We're recording this," Takamatsu said.

Yes, that's who I am. Kazuki Yamase. Divorced. Exiled. Daughter harassed to death."

"And you work at World Construction in Manila?" Hiroshi looked from his notes to Yamase's eyes.

"Yes."

"And you've been residing in the Philippines for the last twenty years?"

"Yes."

"When did you arrive in Japan this time?"

"A week ago. That would be March fifteenth."

"Narita Airport?"

He nodded.

"Speak up," Takamatsu said.

"Yes."

Hiroshi continued. "And what's your purpose in coming back to Japan this time?"

"I'm a Japanese national. I can come back anytime I want."

"Why did you come back this time?"

"Things to do."

"Personal things or for work?"

Yamase stared back at Hiroshi. "Personal."

Takamatsu leaned forward. "It's OK to answer with more than one word. What exactly were your reasons for coming back?"

"I wanted to visit my daughter's grave on the third anniversary of her death," Yamase said.

"And did you go to her grave?"

He nodded.

Takamatsu gave him a look. "What did I just say?"

"I went there the last two days. The first day, my ex-wife was there, so I waited and went back later, but it was dark, so I went the next day to replace the flowers she left."

Hiroshi stared at him. "You took the flowers your wife left and put your own flowers there instead?"

Yamase nodded. "She did that to my flowers."

Hiroshi didn't know what to think about that. "And why did you want to avoid seeing your ex-wife?"

"Doesn't everybody?"

Takamatsu leaned forward. "Save your sarcasm. You might need it in prison. You know what we need to know, so let's not waste time like this."

Yamase leaned back in his chair. "I got here a week ago, stayed at that hotel in Nakano. I'm on vacation from my job in the Philippines."

"And where were you Sunday night? That would be early Monday morning," Hiroshi asked.

"I went drinking with friends from the main office Sunday night. I headed back to the hotel just after midnight, too tired for a *nijikai*, and I went to sleep."

Takamatsu said, "We'll give you one chance to correct anything in that timeline before we go to confirm it."

"Please do confirm it. Call the main office and ask for Suzuki. Name of the *izakaya* was Kanda Rojin, and I'm sure the hotel has surveillance cameras in the lobby and the hallways. I had breakfast around seven in the hotel coffee shop. Need me to repeat any of that for you?" Yamase looked at Takamatsu.

"It's being recorded." Takamatsu pointed at the camera on the wall behind him. "It's when we turn it off that you need to start worrying."

Hiroshi leaned forward. "What were the names of your friends?"

Yamase shook his head. "Actually, I was supposed to meet them, but they didn't show up."

"They showed up or they didn't? Can't be both?" Takamatsu leaned back.

"I came back to Nakano and had a few drinks at some British pub, and went to sleep. You can find that on the cameras, I'm sure."

"You want to correct anything else?" Takamatsu asked. "Maybe you carried your own camera with you to record where you were and when?"

Yamase breathed out loudly. "The main office guys didn't want to talk to me."

"Because you get in fights when you drink?"

"No, because I applied to return to Tokyo but they don't want to let me back."

"What else have you done since you've been here?" Hiroshi asked.

"Bank, shopping, that's it. Mayu's grave again."

"Why does that sound like bullshit to me?" Takamatsu said.

"We need a list of all the people you've spoken to since you've been back," Hiroshi said.

Yamase looked exasperated. He recounted his daily whereabouts in ordered detail, but there wasn't much more than what he had just said, the names of the colleagues who didn't show up, a visit with his brother, and that was it. Takamatsu didn't bother interrupting to clarify or derail him, so maybe he was starting to believe Yamase, or maybe Takamatsu had already decided Yamase was the one who helped Onizuka over the edge.

"Your wife seems to have received a good settlement from Senden for your daughter's death. How much did you get?"

Yamase snorted. "I got nothing."

"Why didn't you get any of the settlement? You're the father, right?" Hiroshi asked.

"You have my records, don't you? The arrest at Mayu's funeral for assaulting the people who killed her."

"That's hardly a reason."

Yamase slumped to the side. "The company said they'd pay out to Mayu's mother, but not to me, because I'd slugged their president at the funeral. It was that simple. They were going to throw out the whole lawsuit if I was on it."

Takamatsu chuckled. "Maybe you shouldn't punch people. Especially cops."

"The cops sided with the company stiffs, let them go, and broke my arm." Yamase held up his right hand. "It's still not right."

"Why didn't you file your own suit separately?" Hiroshi asked.

Yamase stared back at him. "If it was your daughter, you wouldn't have cared much about the money."

"What did you care about? Revenge?"

Yamase leaned back in his chair. "Who wouldn't think about that?"

"Your wife apparently."

Now Yamase chuckled. "She gets revenge her way. For every little thing. When I was transferred to the Philippines for a project, for a promotion, she wouldn't go with me, and wouldn't let Mayu go. Wouldn't even let her visit. To punish me for all the transgressions she kept in her mental accounting. She wanted Mayu to have every advantage in Tokyo: girls' school, cram schools, private tutors. I helped pay for everything and didn't really contest the divorce. I got no visitation rights. Rights always go to the mother in Japan. Fathers don't count. Her revenge. I'm not even sure revenge for what exactly. For not being perfect, I guess."

Hiroshi said, "So, you lost contact with Mayu?"

"No," he said. "She kept in touch. Secretly. I sent her money secretly too. We went through a series of different messaging services, LINE, What'sApp, whatever she found to hide from her mother. She was clever, Mayu. So, I could at least send her messages, photos, advice. I saved every message from her, every photo, every emoji."

"How did Mayu handle her mother's pressure?"

"I thought when she finally made it to America, she'd become more independent. Her mother was against her going to America. She was worried it would put her out of the running for jobs at the best companies," Yamase said, shaking his head. "My ex-wife dominated her, made all the big decisions for her, then left Mayu to organize it all. I was surprised Mayu even had a boyfriend, much less one who followed her all the way home from America. But Mayu was a beauty." Yamase stared at the corner of the room.

"I talked to him earlier this evening," Hiroshi said.

"Steve? He's still in Japan?" Yamase asked. "I liked him."

"You speak English? He didn't seem to speak much Japanese."

"In the Philippines almost everything I do is in English. Our company switched to English a few years ago."

"He said he only met you once," Hiroshi said.

Yamase looked surprised. "We talked many times. Maybe he was nervous talking to a cop?"

"Maybe," Hiroshi said. "Did you see him this time?"

"No. We aren't in touch anymore."

"So, you'll be heading back to the Philippines?"

"If you let me out of here."

"And what about Onizuka? Did you see him?" Takamatsu asked, putting out his cigarette in the ashtray.

Yamase stared silently at the table.

Hiroshi watched Yamase carefully. "You know he's dead?"

Yamase nodded. "I know that."

"How did you find out?"

Yamase considered what to say, working his jaw. "I hired a private detective to follow Onizuka. For the past year."

Takamatsu leaned back in his chair. "You may be spending a few nights here."

"While you investigate." Yamase took a big breath. "That's OK.

I want you to do the investigation right."

"What's the investigator's name?"

"His name's Shibutani."

"In Akabane?" Takamatsu asked.

"That's him," Yamase said. "Office is right by the station, east exit."

Hiroshi turned to Takamatsu. "You know him?"

Takamatsu smiled. "He's old school. You didn't waste your money with him."

Yamase nodded in agreement. "He can tell you everything when you talk to him. He found out a lot about Onizuka, like his mistress."

"Mistress?" Hiroshi was confused because he used the English word for mistress, not the common Japanese words for an affair or a paid companion.

Takamatsu smiled. "He liked it rough?"

Oh, that kind of mistress, Hiroshi realized.

"Her name is Mistress Emi. She works at a place called SMQism. A full-on dominatrix. Onizuka used to visit her once a week."

"Is that right?" Takamatsu's interest in the case seemed to revive itself. "What else did Shibutani find?"

"Onizuka spends, spent, money in hostess clubs all over the city."

"Which ones?"

"I don't know. Shibutani just found that out. You'll have to ask him. He also found out Onizuka had overseas bank accounts."

Hiroshi frowned. "He was going to be posted overseas."

Yamase smiled. "Shibutani said there was a lot more money in these accounts than what a regular salaryman would earn. A lot more."

Hiroshi could sense Takamatsu smiling beside him. "You'll stay in custody until we check all this out."

Chapter 14

Outside the interrogation room, Hiroshi saw the chief's back receding down the hallway. Every other fluorescent light had been turned off to save electricity, so the chief's retreating figure lightened and darkened until he turned at the end of the silent corridor.

Sakaguchi stepped down from the observation room as two uniformed cops walked Yamase out of the interrogation room. Yamase bowed slightly before he turned toward the holding cells down the opposite corridor.

"See? The more people you arrest, the more breaks you get." Takamatsu fiddled with his cigarettes. "Shibutani is a first-rate investigator and a stand-up guy."

"He'll work with us?" Sakaguchi asked.

"Definitely. I'll leave him a message and we'll catch him early in the morning."

"Yamase's alibi won't check out, you think?" Sakaguchi asked.

"What alibi?" Takamatsu said. "Drinks alone, more drinks alone, hotel? If he lied about that, he'll lie about something else."

Sakaguchi bent down to pull up his knee brace. "I've got to get off this leg."

Takamatsu said, "I've got to get off both. Let's get a drink."

Hiroshi avoided their stares by checking the time and messages on his cellphone.

Sakaguchi said, "Ramen."

Takamatsu nodded. "I know a place in Shinbashi that stays open late. Their *kotteri* and *tsukemen* are the best in Tokyo. Plus, they have *shochu*."

Sakaguchi bent both knees to squat and stretch. "Is it counter only?"

"They have big booths. I'll call ahead," Takamatsu said.

Hiroshi looked up from his cellphone. "Not me."

Sakaguchi said, "Well, then we'll have to go back to the detective's room to review what we have so far."

Takamatsu took out his lighter and flipped it around. "If we go there, the chief will probably come down, and..."

"All right, I got it," Hiroshi said.

As he followed Takamatsu and Sakaguchi out the side entrance of the station, he sent a text to Ayana apologizing for being late again. She hadn't answered any of his messages all day.

In the taxi, Takamatsu sat in the front and launched into a discussion with the driver who kept waving his white gloves to emphasize his points.

Hiroshi looked over at Sakaguchi. "You all right?"

Sakaguchi shook his head. "With this knee, everything seems to take twice the effort. The pain pills the doctor gave me aren't working. I told him to double the dose for my size, but..."

"Ramen and *shochu* will help." Hiroshi put his phone away and resigned himself.

Takamatsu and the driver were surprised to discover they both came from the Kiso Mountains of Nagano. They talked and laughed all the way to Shinbashi. When they got to the ramen place, the driver refused to take Takamatsu's money, so they argued loudly, laughing at each response in their country dialect.

"I got his taxi number. I'll send him the fare tomorrow," Takamatsu said. "He'll probably send it back."

The streets of Shinbashi were alive with a steady flow of human traffic, most of it toward the station for the last train. Hiroshi felt Sakaguchi's huge, heavy hand drop on his shoulder, and Hiroshi pushed closer to help take the weight off his knee.

Takamatsu led them down a street lined with drinking places, mahjong parlors, and hostess bars. A few Thai, Chinese and Indian joints sprouted up in between the Japanese *tachinomi* and *izakaya*. The lights and signs pulsed and flashed from sidewalk to roof, spilling flickering colors onto everyone and everything below. Touts stood cockily outside clubs trying hard to ease in a few more late-night customers.

At the end of the street, Takamatsu stubbed out his cigarette and pulled back a sliding door into the one place without a bright sign. He ducked under the dark-wood overhang and stepped inside. Sakaguchi had to turn sideways and bend down to get in.

Inside, the rich flavor of boiling ramen and meaty broth enfolded them. It was calming and mouth-watering, like entering a kitchen and a steamy bath at the same time.

Takamatsu talked to the *master*, a stocky man with a serious face. A neatly rolled towel was wrapped tight around his bald head and his white chef's apron was spotless, though he must have dished out hundreds of bowls of ramen that day.

Sakaguchi eased onto the bench of a large booth and Hiroshi slipped in opposite. The menu was affixed to the wall above a neat arrangement of oils, sauces, and spices in small metal containers.

Takamatsu passed on Hiroshi and Sakaguchi's orders to the chef, who hopped into action, setting beer out and dropping the noodles into basket strainers nestled in the waist-high boiling pot.

Takamatsu brought over two bottles of beer and sat down. He poured for everyone and they held their small toasting glasses up for a tired *kanpai*.

Sakaguchi downed his in one gulp and pulled one bottle over for himself to refill his glass. "So…?"

Hiroshi drained his beer and poured again for himself and Takamatsu. "The company was singularly unhelpful."

"Are they hiding something?" Sakaguchi asked.

Takamatsu nodded.

Hiroshi sighed. "But I wasn't sure what until I heard what Yamase said about Onizuka's overseas accounts."

Sakaguchi loosened his knee brace under the table. "So, this is an embezzlement and murder case now?"

"Those often go together," Hiroshi said. "We've got to get into the company records, but we'll need help to do that."

"Pressure that the chief can bring to bear," Takamatsu said. "If he so chooses."

The *master* put three glasses of iced *shochu* on the shelf by the prep area. Takamatsu got up to get them.

"You'd make a good waiter," Hiroshi said, finishing his beer.

"One of the hardest jobs there is," Takamatsu said, setting the glasses on the thick wood table.

All three sipped the ice-cold *shochu* and leaned back in the booth. There were only two other people in the place, one at either end of the counter, reading their cellphones while slurping noodles.

Sakaguchi said, "Hiroshi, are you sure you can find what we need if you get into the records? You keep telling me the real estate scams and money fraud cases take a long time to untangle and a company like that must have vast records."

Hiroshi hummed. "If Onizuka embezzled the money, they might have found it already and hidden the tracks."

"That puts us back to the human side, I guess." Takamatsu drained his *shochu* and rattled the ice cubes.

Hiroshi finished his glass and Takamatsu gathered them all for a refill. The *master* saw what he was doing and set the large brown bottle of *shochu* on the counter, waved with chopsticks for Takamatsu to take it.

Takamatsu smiled and carried it back to the table, pouring for everyone. The *master* rattled a bucket of square-cut ice cubes, and Takamatsu went back for it and a pair of ice tongs.

"And the mother?" Sakaguchi asked.

"Maybe she's a great actress, but her grief seemed real enough," Hiroshi said.

"Grief doesn't make her innocent," Sakaguchi said. "If anything—"

"A woman wouldn't set up this whole thing on the roof,"

Takamatsu said.

"Why not?" Hiroshi asked.

"The guy was loaded. What did you say his blood alcohol level was? Zero point three eight? Someone had to carry him up there."

Sakaguchi held up his glass. "This is better than those anti-inflammatory pills. My knee's feeling better already. So, what about the American boyfriend?"

Takamatsu said, "Arrested for assault at the funeral. No surprise, Americans—"

"Are more violent?" Hiroshi asked.

Takamatsu nodded. "Why don't you call your friends at Interpol or over in America about this guy?"

"He got in a fight at his girlfriend's funeral. Most Japanese would do the same. Mayu's father started the fight." Hiroshi swirled the ice cubes in his glass.

"He'll have a record in the States, I promise you. You want me to call over there for you?"

Hiroshi snickered at the thought of Takamatsu trying that in English. "All right, I'll check on his criminal record in the States."

Takamatsu nodded smugly. "And who sponsored him for his visa?"

"They have cultural visas," Hiroshi said.

"Requiring a sponsor. We need to check it out." Takamatsu pinched ice cubes and stacked them to the rims before topping off everyone's glass with more *shochu*.

Sakaguchi said, "You don't like him for this, Hiroshi?"

Hiroshi swirled the fresh ice and *shochu*. "Not the type."

Takamatsu raised his eyebrows. "I've dragged in every type over the years. Musicians, too. Men get jealous, angry, and want to square accounts. It's automatic."

"You look at emotions, not the evidence," Hiroshi said.

"Not everyone can run an investment scam, but anyone can commit murder," Takamatsu said.

"A few can do both." Hiroshi added more ice to his glass.

Sakaguchi drained his glass and thunked it on the table. "Even a man would have trouble on his own to haul him up there, take him to the edge, and deal with the cameras."

Takamatsu lit a cigarette, leaning back to blow the smoke high above the table. "That cut fence is what gets me. Who did that? And where are the wire cutters?"

Sakaguchi poured another round.

The two late-night noodle eaters left and the *master* went to the door, locked it and brought in the "Open" sign that hung on the outside of the door.

"The only ones who seemed to be truly bullshitting us were the company people."

Takamatsu hummed agreement. "Those top companies do anything to avoid a scandal. Even the hint of a scandal. Covering up everything is a natural reflex for them."

Hiroshi took another slug of *shochu*. "The lawyer sure felt they could do anything. They derailed his career."

"That was child's play. Just wait." Takamatsu tapped his glass on the tabletop.

Hiroshi felt a lot more drunk than he had intended to be, but the cold *shochu* was rice-y, smooth with little bite, and easy to swallow. He'd have one more and stop.

Sakaguchi swirled the ice cubes in his glass. "The tech guys might still turn up something from the video, but they have to figure out how it got blanked out. The lab guys are still undecided on suicide or murder."

"Nothing either way?"

"Too much both ways."

"How long was it out?" Takamatsu asked.

"The security video? Forty-some minutes."

"That's a long time."

Sakaguchi nodded. "It is, so let's work from the assumption that they're all lying to us."

Hiroshi swirled his glass and tried to count how many he'd

finished. "Maybe that investigator Shibutani has what we need. But let's still get access to the internal company files."

"Let's not forget the S&M mistress, what was her name, Mistress Emi?" Takamatsu laughed. "She's sure to know a few of Onizuka's secrets. From the inside out."

"Talk to Shibutani in the morning. He's way ahead of us with Onizuka," Sakaguchi said.

All three of them stopped talking when the *master* set the bowls of *tsukemen* on the counter and ducked under the counter top to carry over the small ceramic bowls with thick broth and nori splayed along the rim. He set them carefully, precisely, in front of each of them.

The *master* went back for the three large bowls of noodles. Rinsed and shaken dry, they were placed in three neat folds, like someone bowing on their knees. Then, he set out three flat brown plates of glistening slices of *chashu* pork, cuts of *menma* bamboo shoots, and butterflied, flavor-boiled eggs.

Without another word, the three detectives started plucking up the noodles, dunking them in the rich, oily broth and slurping them down, ending the day with at least one certainty.

Chapter 15

In the elevator to his apartment, Hiroshi tried to re-count his drinks—two whiskeys, then one, two, hmm, four, possibly five, glasses of *shochu*, and a little beer. Actually, a lot of beer, as Sakaguchi had ordered more and poured for him.

He didn't want to pull his cellphone out to check the time. He'd already dropped it once in the taxi home. He bumped the side of the elevator as he got out on his floor.

It was the *shochu* that had done him in. It was like cool water on the tongue and a sumo workout on the rest of his body. He had to remember that Takamatsu was always in control and Sakaguchi was about twice his weight. Hiroshi was the one who always got hammered.

Ayana had decided to get back to kendo practice, so she was probably sound asleep. What time was it? She wouldn't still be frisky this late, would she? Was he? He had no feeling in his body, and his mind bounced between hazy ideas and vague impulses.

Hiroshi fumbled with the key at the apartment door. He tried to keep quiet as the heavy door swung shut.

He toed the heel of his shoes, but the pair was new and the laces too tight. He sat down on the ledge of the *genkan* to pull them off and knocked over the umbrella stand. Umbrellas clattered to the tiles. He got his shoes off, straightened the umbrellas and heaved himself up to standing.

When he turned, Ayana was watching him, yawning, from the end of the entry hall. Her hair was mussed and she squinted at him in the low light.

"Are you drunk?" Ayana asked, her arms folded around herself.

Hiroshi said, "We were discussing the case."

"Did you eat anything?"

"Yes, *tsukemen*. Did you eat?"

"A long time ago. It's two in the morning," Ayana said.

"Well, you should get back to sleep," Hiroshi said, his shoulder bumping the wall.

Ayana pulled a face and came toward him, hooked her arm under his. "You can't even walk."

"I'm just tired."

"How did you get home?"

"Taxi."

"Did you remember to pay the driver this time?

Hiroshi put his arm around Ayana. "I'm fine."

"Yeah, you seem great," Ayana said, as they shuffled down the hall together. "You smell like alcohol."

"Shochu."

She sniffed his jacket. "Did you spill *tsukemen* on yourself?"

"Of course not," he said, even though he had spilled some of the sauce on his pants.

"You need a shower."

"Don't we have some of that *ukon no chikara*? That's the only thing that takes the edge off the hangover."

"Too late for that now." Ayana let Hiroshi flop onto the sofa.

"I'll sleep here," Hiroshi said, curling up with a pillow.

"Are you going to come home drunk every night?"

"Apparently I am," Hiroshi said. "I don't eat all day running around, and things come in that have to get done and Takamatsu and Sakaguchi can only talk about the case when all that's done, and whatever I say, I still have to work the case. It's not like working at an archive."

"That's for sure." Ayana got the small metal bottle of *ukon* hangover cure and set it in front of Hiroshi. She got ibuprofen and water and sat down on the coffee table holding them out in her hand. Hiroshi sat up and reached in turn for the turmeric vitamin drink, the ibuprofen, and the water, swallowing them one by one. He held the glass up for more water.

Ayana growled and went to get more.

"You think all that really works?" Ayana asked, setting the water down.

"Something has to."

"What about drinking less?"

"What about working less? This case is driving me crazy."

"The dead *bucho*?"

"Yeah," Hiroshi said, draining the water glass.

Ayana reached for him. "Come on, let me help you into the shower."

"I don't need a shower. I'll sleep here," Hiroshi said.

"Come on, don't be difficult." Ayana stood over him.

Hiroshi eyed her. She wasn't going away, so he flipped his legs around and struggled up. She put an arm under his to help him to the shower. In the bathroom, he started peeling off his shirt, but she had to help him out of his shirtsleeves and pants.

"Even your clothes stink of alcohol." Ayana carried them to the laundry hamper. She sniffed them. "You spilled something on them."

He got the water turned on, and Ayana stood there to be sure he didn't slip.

"Here's your toothbrush." Ayana handed it to him. "It's like having a child."

Hiroshi gargled the hot water pouring down on him, and spit and rinsed and gargled and started brushing again. "I thought you wanted a child?"

"Less so now."

"He was horrible." Hiroshi gargled and spit again.

"Who?"

"The dead *bucho*. What company did you work in?" Hiroshi asked, the toothpaste garbling his already-drunken words.

"I already told you. Right after college. With Kumiko."

"Kumiko?"

"From our seminar. You told me she was beautiful once. To

make me jealous."

"Oh, that Kumiko. Your best friend."

"She was jealous of you when I started walking home with you instead of her."

"You both worked at the same place?"

"Yeah, Marutobi Company. I told you."

"That's a big company. They do a bit of everything, don't they? Congratulations."

"We thought congratulations too, at first. We had cute little outfits, scarves, a company pin for our first year."

"Whatever happened to Kumiko? Are you still in touch?" Hiroshi shouted over the sound of the shower.

"No. She killed herself."

Hiroshi turned off the water. "What?"

Ayana shoved a towel at him and turned to look in the mirror.

Hiroshi toweled off, and when he finished, he saw Ayana was weeping. "You never told me that," he said.

"You never asked. She took care of me after you left. I was devastated you just left without a word. But she kept me going. And I couldn't do the same for her."

He felt sobered, and wrapped the towel around himself.

Ayana pulled a hand towel from the rack to wipe her eyes.

Hiroshi put his hand on her back and massaged her softly.

"Everything you tell me about this case makes me think of her," she said.

"Why did she... she always seemed so... so grounded, so sure of herself."

"Lots of little things picked away at her. Harassment, stress, a shitty boyfriend, a shitty boss. She got assigned to a bad section, with boring tasks. She hated the pressure to look right all the time. To look perfect. They gave us rules on make-up, hairstyle, jewelry, high heels, polite Japanese. It was worse than a girls' high school."

Hiroshi pulled Ayana to him.

"Kumiko hated it more than me. And when things fell apart with her boyfriend and her asshole boss started criticizing her... well, she just..."

"I'm sorry. I didn't know." Hiroshi tried to wipe her tears, but she batted his hand away. Hiroshi wished he could magically sober up.

"I'm sorry," Hiroshi said and put his arms around her. She pulled away and then relented.

"We'd been such close friends for so long and I just didn't see it. Her boss tried to fix her up with guys in the company. As if that was why she was hired, why we women were hired, to marry one of the guys in the company."

"You were in a different section from Kumiko?" Hiroshi started moving them toward the bedroom with his arm around her.

"I was in a better section, but every night we had to go drinking with our section, meet other companies for drinks, or work overtime. Kumiko was allergic to alcohol. She couldn't drink even a little bit. But everyone kept pouring her drinks. She had to fight them off, make excuses, apologize for not drinking."

"That sounds... I can't imagine."

"Kumiko really hated it. She should have gone to graduate school. Eto Sensei asked her to."

"I remember she was a great student."

"But she came from a poor family, a traditional one. Her family forced her to go to work. She supported them and her younger sister, who took her money and despised her for it. I was so worn out myself, I didn't notice how bad it was with Kumiko. She was a friend from the first year of college. The first day, actually." Ayana started crying again, harder.

Hiroshi walked her out of the bathroom and sat her on the bed. He pulled on some shorts from the closet and hung the towel over the closet door. It was like Ayana had soaked up all the pain of Kumiko and stored it in an archive inside herself all these years.

Hiroshi could only sit next to her and hold her close. "I'm sorry I didn't even know about this."

Ayana doubled over and cried for a long time, not even bothering with a tissue or a towel, just letting the tears fall onto her sweatpants and Hiroshi's shorts.

Hiroshi just held her.

When she caught her breath, Hiroshi reached for some tissues and pulled Ayana close as she dried her eyes and crumpled the tissues to shreds.

Ayana started beating her fist on Hiroshi's chest. "Can you not get drunk every day?"

Hiroshi took her hands. "OK, I won't."

"My father was a salaryman who came home drunk every night after work. Sundays he watched TV and drank beer. I don't want that for us."

"I don't want that either."

"You're going to feel terrible tomorrow." Ayana rubbed his chest, then hit him again.

"I feel bad just thinking about how bad I'm going to feel," Hiroshi said.

Ayana smiled finally. "I'm sorry. I don't know why I'm crying so much."

"It's all right."

Ayana took another wet breath and wiggled to the side to slip the covers down and bend herself inside. Hiroshi climbed under the futon cover and slipped one arm under her head and wrapped the other around her, pulling her close and realizing that somehow her tears were his own. She was crying for them both.

Chapter 16

When he woke up, Hiroshi found a pot of coffee, a bottle of ibuprofen and a huge omelette set out on the kitchen island. It was bit too neatly presented, so Hiroshi took it for the scolding it was. His head felt like his brain had been removed, worked over with a wood file, and plopped back inside his skull. He looked for his cellphone, but turning his head made his eyeballs feel yanked on their stems.

Ayana had, thankfully, turned it off and left it by the sofa, to further reprove him or let him sleep, he couldn't guess. Cooking an omelette and turning off his phone so he could sleep were a bit different than the little signs of affection during their first months living together, but he would have to think about that later when his brain worked better.

His cellphone messages told him Takamatsu and Sugamo were on their way to pick him up. Hiroshi texted back for them to wait outside his apartment. He cut the omelette in half, forked in a big bite, and let the coffee ease down the back of his throat. He went to the shower, turning it as hot as he could stand. He opened a window as he dressed to cool himself down, and went back to the kitchen to finish the rest of the omelette and the coffee.

When Hiroshi emerged from the front door of his apartment building, he held up his hand and squinted against the morning sun.

Takamatsu was leaning on the car, smoking. Seeing Hiroshi, he stubbed out his cigarette, gestured at the car in irritation, and plopped into the front seat. Sugamo nodded good morning, twisted around to check they were all in, and pulled off.

Hiroshi closed his eyes for the ride to Akabane and was glad no one spoke. At a crime scene once, a member of the forensic crew told Hiroshi the brain itself has no pain receptors, but if that was true, where did the pain come from? It came from last night's *shochu*.

*✸✶

Shibutani's private investigator's office was on the fifth floor of a small building with a Family Mart convenience store on the first floor across from the taxi and bus circle outside Akabane Station. Sugamo waited outside by the car while Hiroshi got into the small elevator with Takamatsu.

"You know this guy Shibutani?" Hiroshi asked.

"He tossed some work my way when I was on suspension. Divorce cases mostly," Takamatsu said. "I only met him one time, then talked on the phone. Everyone who quits the department, or is fired, goes to him for work."

The elevator bumped to a stop on the fifth floor. The narrow building housed only one office on each floor, and the one small sign said simply, "Shibutani."

Takamatsu knocked.

Hiroshi stood to the side by the fire exit, the only other door.

Takamatsu knocked again and tried the door, but it was locked.

"Call him?" Hiroshi asked.

"I did when I was waiting for you. No answer." Takamatsu kneeled down to look at the doorknob.

The fire door clicked behind them. Hiroshi gave it a light push and it swung open onto the fire escape. He stepped out and looked down, feeling nauseous, and dizzy at the height.

Still kneeling, Takamatsu pulled out his folding knife and slid it into the gap by the doorknob. He fiddled it up and down for a minute, to no effect. He could get a warrant in an hour but never one to wait, Takamatsu pulled out his folding baton and smashed in the window. He cleared out enough glass to reach in and twist the handle from inside.

The office was a chaotic jumble of paper and folders. File cabinet drawers gaped, crumpled paper littered the floor, folders were tossed everywhere, and cups and glasses had been smashed in the sink. The office fridge, tipped on its side, dribbled water.

Then they saw Shibutani, behind the large desk, tied to an upended chair, not moving.

Hiroshi and Takamatsu rushed over.

The investigator's head was bleeding onto the worn gray carpet tiles, most of it coagulated.

Takamatsu cut the plastic ties from his wrists, arms, and ankles and Hiroshi felt for breathing and a pulse.

"Weak, but there," Hiroshi said.

Takamatsu called for an ambulance and Hiroshi called Sugamo and told him to bring the ambulance crew up as soon as they arrived.

They stretched Shibutani out on the carpet tiles and Takamatsu put his handkerchief under the back of his bloodied head.

"How bad is the head wound?" Hiroshi leaned over to see.

"Every head wound looks bad. We should have come last night."

"He must have been tied up for a while. Look at the bruising on his wrists." Hiroshi took a wool throw blanket from the top of a filing cabinet, the one thing in place, and spread it out over Shibutani.

The sound of the elevator doors preceded Sugamo by a few seconds. At the sight of the mess, Sugamo pulled back, his eyes wide on his usually impassive face.

Takamatsu said, "Sugamo, wait downstairs and bring them up as soon as you can." It was the first time Hiroshi ever heard Takamatsu raise his voice to any of the younger detectives.

Hiroshi looked back and forth at the mess. "I don't know how they're going to get him down in that elevator."

"I called Osaki to come right away. And I'll call Sakaguchi, too." Sugamo hurried off to wait downstairs.

Even through the fog of his hangover, Hiroshi could tell Takamatsu was furious at himself. He tried to get Shibutani to say something, but got only a low moan and a phlegmy rattle.

Takamatsu stayed kneeling. He patted Shibutani's face and

asked him questions. He gave up and turned to Hiroshi.

"Just start looking underneath everything."

Hiroshi looked around the room. "Underneath?"

"He's old school. Anything important would be taped up under a drawer."

"Did he know what we were coming about?"

"I told him. We just got here too late."

"It could all be gone."

Shibutani coughed.

Takamatsu looked down in his face. "Shibutani, can you tell us where you hid it?"

Shibutani cleared his throat. "Re—" he managed, before his head lolled to the side.

Takamatsu monitored his pulse and breathing, checked the head wound again. They both watched the door, listening for the elevator.

Finally, the gears and motor clicked, and in a minute, the elevator door opened and two ambulance crew members hurried in. Takamatsu got out of the way and watched them check Shibutani.

After a quick discussion, one of the crew said, "We'll have to hold him vertical to get him down the elevator. These buildings are not designed for this. Can you give us a hand?"

Hiroshi and Takamatsu helped raise Shibutani to a sitting position. He was too weak to even keep an arm over their shoulders. The two ambulance crew pulled the chair around and they got Shibutani into it. They took a strap from the gurney to tie around his chest to hold him upright. The rollers worked, so they pushed him to the elevator. Takamatsu squeezed in to ride down with him.

Hiroshi didn't know what he was looking for and had no idea what "underneath" could mean in the middle of this chaos, but he started by the door. Whoever ransacked the place had probably worked through the same pattern already. He pulled on gloves.

Hiroshi opened and checked each drawer, underneath and to the sides. He overturned every stack of papers, every folder, felt all the surfaces and into the cracks. He was looking everywhere for whatever an old-school investigator might have hidden in a place he knew better than anyone and Hiroshi didn't know at all. It was pointless.

Takamatsu returned to the office with Sugamo right behind him. "I told him never to work alone. When I quit and go private, one of you is coming with me."

"What did he say when you talked with him yesterday?" Hiroshi asked.

"He said he had it, but he didn't say what 'it' was." Takamatsu lit a cigarette. He scratched his forehead, took off his trench coat and looked for a place to put it. He righted the coat rack and hung his coat there.

Takamatsu pointed around the perimeter of the room for Hiroshi and Sugamo, and headed for the desk.

Hiroshi and Sugamo worked the room from opposite directions. The cabinets were rusted at the edges and dust filled the backs of drawers. Crevices had cobwebs. But the materials were in pristine order.

Takamatsu got on his knees and started peering at the desk, tapping on it.

Sugamo said, "It looks like each cabinet holds one year and is ordered by date, then by kana *a, ka, sa, ta.*"

Hiroshi went over. "Let's assume Mayu's father hired Shibutani right after Mayu's death. Start there and look at *ya*, for Yamase first, and *o* for Onizuka second."

Takamatsu looked over. "Try going backward from the last syllable. Probably why they beat him so badly. They couldn't figure out his filing system."

"OK, try *se* for Yamase and *ka* for Onizuka." Hiroshi searched back and forth for those drawers.

Takamatsu took his pocket knife out and knelt down looking

over the desk without touching it. "He'll have a false bottom or a hollow wall in here somewhere." He pulled open the top drawer of the desk and worked counterclockwise through the other drawers, but there was nothing.

Hiroshi pulled open file cabinet drawers, flipped through folders, and shut them again.

Sugamo said, "He was busy the last few years. Lot of cases in here."

Takamatsu got up from the floor and stared at the desk, kicked it. He pulled out his pack of cigarettes, put them away, pulled out his pocket knife again, and got down on his back to slide under the desk. Something splintered and Takamatsu pulled out a panel of wood with a long, loud crackle.

"Flashlight," Takamatsu commanded.

Hiroshi opened his cellphone flashlight app. Holding it under the desk, he heard the sound of more wood splintering until Takamatsu wiggled out waving a thick plastic file.

"How did you figure that out?" Hiroshi asked.

Takamatsu spread the contents on the desk, smiled and lit a cigarette.

Sugamo frowned at the top page. "What are all these companies?"

Hiroshi said, "Companies with embezzlement histories. I think."

Takamatsu held up another file. "And the one at the bottom says, 'Onizuka, Senden.'"

A local cop pushed in the door, looking nervous in his neat uniform with his baton up and ready.

"We're all detectives," Hiroshi said, all of them holding up their badges.

The cop looked relieved, put down his baton, and called for backup.

Chapter 17

Hiroshi hurried up the stairs to the family restaurant across the bus and taxi rotary from Shibutani's office. Sugamo had frowned at Hiroshi taking what should have been entered as evidence, Shibutani's files on Onizuka, but Takamatsu just asked how long Hiroshi needed.

Inside the bland comfort of the family restaurant, Hiroshi ordered corn soup and iced espresso. Just saying the words to the waitress made him nauseated. He got up to get a glass of water at the self-service counter, but the water tasted like *shochu*.

Hiroshi opened the files Shibutani had compiled on Onizuka, a thick stack of account statements, transfer notices and pages of hand-drawn flow charts. He'd done his work checking Onizuka's bank accounts, stock accounts, tax forms, salary statements, along with those of his wife and son.

At the bottom of the pile was a running total of what Mayu's father had paid him. Two million yen plus a list of itemized expenses for each of the past three years. Hiroshi didn't know exactly how much Yamase made in the Philippines, but that was a chunk of cash for anyone.

In a separate black plastic folder, there were documents from the Philippines, written in Filipino and English. They had Yamase's name on them. He'd been arrested for two cases of assault and battery in the last two years, one in Manila and another in Cebu. Shibutani investigated his clients before taking on their cases, it seemed.

Hiroshi returned to Onizuka's accounts and wondered how much Mayu knew about them before she killed herself. Maybe she knew too much about her boss? Was that what Mayu's father wanted to find out? Was that what Shibutani found?

The waitress brought his soup and coffee and Hiroshi smiled

at her, though he was really smiling in anticipation of finding out what the rest of the Excel files, spreadsheets, and flow charts might reveal. He spooned in his soup and felt the sweet, milky corn coating his stomach, making him feel slightly better. The cold espresso also helped.

Hiroshi kept turning page after page. There were a couple of hundred pages all told. Onizuka also had extensive forex trading accounts and cryptocurrency accounts at several digital currency exchanges. Hiroshi wondered how Onizuka had time to oversee his subordinates. He was too busy moving money across the globe.

But where did the money come from? Some of the accounts Shibutani turned up were in Onizuka's name and others were in Senden's name. One number might be the employee ID number for Onizuka inside Senden, but he'd have to check. Maybe the HR woman, Chizu, would confirm it.

Hiroshi was about to LINE message her but saw something in one of the documents that made him set down his phone—his own family name. He stopped to think about that, checked it again, looked at his half-eaten corn soup and spooned more in, thinking.

He looked through his phone for the number and was about to call, but stopped himself, deciding to stop by his uncle's in person instead. There was no way around that now.

Hiroshi called Akiko instead. "Sugamo's going to bring some account files in. Be sure Sakaguchi gets these files in as evidence. And don't tell the chief anything about this, OK?" Hiroshi pulled out his cellphone and started taking photos as he talked.

"You've got to be back here in time to go with the chief to the Ministry of Health, Labor and Welfare at four," Akiko said.

"Yeah, I know. We'll start with the forex and digital money accounts. And then move on to the Cayman Islands and Panama accounts. Let's get those in order to send to Interpol. And don't tell the chief."

"You said that already."

Hiroshi kept turning pages one by one, taking a photo of each and forwarding them to Akiko.

Akiko sighed. "You really will be back by four, won't you? The chief's called three times already."

"And call Senden and tell them we need to see the roof again."

"When? After the ministries?"

"We need to see it at night."

"Need, need, need. Anything else you *need*?"

"We need everything at this point," Hiroshi said. "I need to get over this hangover."

Hiroshi finished the photos, sent them to Akiko, paid and went outside. It was going to be a lot longer day than the last two, and just as confusing. He didn't notice Sugamo and Takamatsu drive up until Sugamo honked.

As soon as he got in the car, Takamatsu turned around. "So?"

Hiroshi said, "Shibutani pieced most of it together. Onizuka had a lot more money floating around than we thought."

Takamatsu laughed. "You're telling me this case is about money too?"

"As always. And Mayu's father had a couple of priors in the Philippines."

"Where to?" Sugamo asked.

Hiroshi said, "We've got accountants to see."

"Another exciting afternoon." Takamatsu reached for his cigarettes and rolled down the window to smoke.

***

The first accountant's office was halfway between Yotsuya Station and Shinjuku. The ground floor was a pizza delivery place with delivery scooters lined up neatly along the sidewalk. The building was an old one retrofitted for earthquakes. Huge steel trusses crisscrossed the outside of the building down to concrete mooring blocks that took up half of the sidewalk. The seismic braces turned the building into a lattice of giant Xs.

Sugamo pulled up to let Hiroshi and Takamatsu out. Takamatsu didn't even ask him how he knew the place and why they were going. It was clear it was in the files Hiroshi had just gone through. Hiroshi wondered if Takamatsu was actually starting to trust him.

Hiroshi tapped the files and handed them to Sugamo. "Turn these in with the other evidence. Sakaguchi will sign it into the chain of custody."

Sugamo waited for them to get out and pulled off with a word.

Hiroshi watched Sugamo leave. "Was he pissed off about breaking evidence protocol?"

Takamatsu shrugged and tapped the delivery warmer of one of the three-wheeled pizza bikes. "What is it with this pizza thing? It's all over the place."

Hiroshi ignored him and headed into the open-air entrance. He checked the building's directory and pressed the button on the elevator.

On the eighth floor, Hiroshi knocked on the glass door, and pushed it open gently. The office contained a dozen tables under bare fluorescent lights and a row of unwashed windows that looked out on Shinjuku Dori, a wide street lined by the tediously functional ten- and twelve-story buildings of Yotsuya's business district.

The five women hunched over their desks barely looked up when Hiroshi and Takamatsu entered. Finally, a woman sitting at one of the desks near the front stood up and asked them what they wanted.

"We need to see Kato-*san*," Hiroshi said.

She turned to the back desk. "Kato-*san*," she called out in a slight voice.

Kato looked up from his computer and frowned at the

interruption before standing up. He was tall with a thin frame that looked all the thinner because he walked with a slight limp. He came around the desks, bowed slightly, and sniffled as he waited for the detectives to speak first.

"I'm Hiroshi Shimizu and this is Takamatsu. We're homicide detectives. We need to talk with you about your auditing work for Senden Central Infinity." He handed over his *meishi*.

Kato nodded, his face an oval of inscrutability. "I used to work for Senden, but not any longer. You should talk to the current auditors." He spoke in a low, calm voice.

Hiroshi said, "We talked with Shibutani."

Kato's face stayed blank.

Hiroshi said, "We need to double-check a few points."

Kato turned to the five employees, their heads down at their desks. "I'll be gone for about half an hour," he told them.

They looked up in unison, nodded and went back to work.

Kato sighed and sniffled. "Follow me. We can talk on the roof and I can smoke."

"Sounds good to me," Takamatsu said.

They followed Kato down the outside hallway and up a narrow stairwell. It switched back three times before opening onto the roof. In the sun, Kato stopped to sneeze. Kato sneezed again as he took out his cigarettes and headed toward a red bucket set next to three plastic chairs faded from sun and rain.

He stopped by the chairs, but didn't sit down. One of the seats was cracked. The bucket was filled with a thick stew of brown water and cigarette butts. It stank, so Hiroshi took a step back as Kato and Takamatsu lit up.

After they sighed with relief, Hiroshi said, "Kato, you did the auditing on Senden—"

"That was three years ago," Kato said. "And I was with a different firm then."

Hiroshi flipped through the photos of files in his cellphone. "Nishimura Auditing?"

Kato nodded, sniffling and snorting to clear his sinuses.

Hiroshi wanted to recommend some allergy medicine to him. "And now you work here?"

"After I worked for the firm that handled Senden, I leased this space and started out on my own. I had some inheritance from my mother."

Kato looked off at a distance over the low wall around the roof. The view of Shinjuku Gyoen Park and the Akasaka Palace grounds was unimpeded. Farther away, the skyscrapers of West Shinjuku thrust gray and rectangular into the plain afternoon sky.

Hiroshi said, "You were fired?"

Kato looked back at Hiroshi. "Call it what you want."

"What was it that Senden didn't like about your auditing?"

"Their internal financial guys are not so smart. I tried to tell them how to move their money out of Japan discreetly and safely—and legally—but they thought they knew best."

"Did they?" Hiroshi asked.

"They left a trail of crumbs anyone could follow."

"You helped them with tax shelters, too?"

Kato nodded, snuffling through his nostrils. He finally pulled out a tissue and blew his nose, coughed and snuffled again, and got back to smoking.

Hiroshi showed the photo of Onizuka's forex account to Kato. "You've seen these before?"

Kato's eyes stayed thin as he read. "Not this one, but one like it."

"And these?" Hiroshi scrolled through the photos of the other files Shibutani had gathered.

Kato hummed confirmation. "I saw most of those right before they fired me. If you find the originals, bring them back here and I'll check them for you."

Hiroshi said, "We might need you to do that. So, after that, Senden fired your firm?"

"No, Senden made my firm fire me. And not only that, they reported *me* to the JICPA and the public tax accountants board, too. I had to go defend myself."

"They didn't like your advice," Hiroshi said.

"No, they liked it a lot," Kato said. "They wanted me to take the fall if the Tax Agency caught up with them. I wouldn't do that." Kato coughed and looked at the tops of the park trees in the distance.

Hiroshi said, "How did they hide things at Senden?"

Kato breathed in and out more quietly. "Mostly they keep everything important on paper and misfile it."

"Misfile?"

"Like a misfiled book in a library, you can never find it unless you know where it is. Only one or two people know, but no one else."

"You have to know to know?" Takamatsu asked.

Kato coughed and snuffled and nodded.

Hiroshi took a breath and looked off in the distance. "And personnel files?"

"I guess it's the same. Their misfiling system gives some people inordinate power."

"Knowledge is power?" Hiroshi prompted.

"Hidden knowledge is more powerful," Kato said. "They run the company on it."

Takamatsu and Kato flicked their cigarettes into the red can of murky water and the butts went out with a swift fizzle.

Chapter 18

Outside the office, Takamatsu waved down a taxi. "I'm starting to like talking to people in offices. I can smoke and don't have chase anyone down dirty alleys."

"I'm not sure which is more depressing," Hiroshi said, getting into the taxi first.

"At least in the alley you end up with something for your effort," Takamatsu said.

Hiroshi gave the driver directions. "The next one's just another accounting firm. I'll handle it."

"All right. I'll check up on Mayu's father. After a night in jail, maybe he's concocted some new alibis."

"I'll meet you in Shibuya later?"

"Sugamo and I can pick you up at Kanda Station. How much time do you need?" Takamatsu pulled up his crisp cuffs and checked his gold watch.

"Give me an hour." Hiroshi got out in front of a newly built five-story building not far from Kanda Station and Takamatsu rode on in the taxi.

Inside the automatic glass doors, the outside entryway had a small alcove in the stone wall with a shiny silver panel for contacting the offices. Hiroshi pressed the right combination of buttons and explained who he was to the voice in the speaker.

The buzzer sounded and he pushed into the atrium. The elevator was already descending. Beside the elevator door, a large freestyle *ikebana* arrangement with tight-packed white flowers and split zigzags of bamboo seemed to reach out for him, the bud-laden twigs curling forward like beautiful claws.

On the fifth floor, Hiroshi was met by a neatly dressed woman with a deep bow. She led him down a quiet corridor of offices to a meeting room, bowed again and left him alone with the chairs and a wide, oval table. He'd only visited the office twice before.

In a few seconds, his uncle walked in.

His father's younger brother was as tall as Hiroshi's father, taller than Hiroshi too and grayer than he recalled. He had been a ladies' man when he was young, Hiroshi remembered his father saying, and he looked as if he still could be.

More likely, he worked most of the time. That was the only way to build up a consultancy firm that handled auditing, accounting, budgeting, personnel issues and government regulations. It was a small business considering its actual size, but large based on its contacts, which, according to what he'd just read in Shibutani's files, included Senden Central and its new overseas venture Senden Infinity.

His uncle flashed a curious smile as he shut the door and sat down across the table. "It's been a while. Do you want coffee or anything?"

Hiroshi sat down, took a breath and said, "I'm only here for a few minutes. I was in the neighborhood."

Hiroshi's uncle smiled. "What does my detective nephew need today?"

"Information about Senden Central."

"That's a good reason to be in the neighborhood." Hiroshi's uncle looked down at the shiny table. "Onizuka, right?"

Hiroshi shifted in his chair to stifle a wave of nausea from his hangover.

His uncle straightened his light-brown button-down shirt. "What do you want to know?"

"You did consulting work for the company."

"Accounting mostly. We had a contract, but it ended."

"It ended from your side or theirs?"

"It was mutual. I think they were just fishing to see what we'd do."

"Did it end because you didn't want to—"

"Because they didn't listen to our recommendations."

"Recommendations about...?"

"All aspects of their business. That's what consulting is."

"Is it?" Hiroshi said it with more sarcasm than he'd intended.

"You were so quiet when you were young. Agreeable."

Hiroshi thought of his mother and father's loud, angry arguments, and how quiet his father had been after her funeral. They'd barely spoken until he died not long after.

Hiroshi's uncle sighed. "So, Senden was going global, and they wanted to expand. They also wanted to know the full range of options about overseas taxation and foreign accounts."

"How to keep their foreign profits out of sight of Japanese officials."

"That's about it, yes."

"Do you still have the files from—"

"They took everything back, even sent someone to be sure the files were erased from our server. All that was in the initial contract, but they were determined to carry it out. We still consult on a few issues with them, but frankly, I was glad to be done with them."

Hiroshi looked at his uncle. "Because of how many irregularities there were?"

"Partially that, but also because they wanted to purchase a lot of overseas real estate and put more money into offshore accounts. We'd have been besieged."

"By government regulators?"

"The Tax Agency would be all over it, yes, but we could deal with that. It was more that company people share inside tips, so every company would want in on it. I wasn't going to be the go-to firm for that kind of work. There are a lot of lines I don't cross. You should know that already."

Hiroshi met his eyes. "I know that."

"Then why are you asking?"

Hiroshi couldn't remember his uncle ever speaking to him in an angry way before. He would have welcomed an argument or two when he was younger, but his uncle never gave him that chance. After Hiroshi's mother and father died, his uncle took over as guardian. Without much input from Hiroshi, his uncle had decided his nephew would study in the States, and he took charge of the money for him, covering tuition, and sending ample spending money. His aunt had sent care packages, Japanese noodles, *furikake* seasonings, and photos of his cousin. Hiroshi studied whatever he wanted in his courses, alongside what his uncle paid for—accounting. It was like a six year vacation with the occasional exam. He'd got the degree for his uncle and took the other classes, history mostly, for himself.

Hiroshi couldn't blame his uncle, but he couldn't warm to him, either.

"Your name, our name, was on a list an investigator had. He was tailing Onizuka and looking into a girl's suicide."

"Of course, our name would be in there somewhere, but I don't know anything about a girl's suicide."

"You know the case of Mayu Yamase? Her mother sued Senden and won."

"From the news."

"It was Onizuka who harassed and overworked the girl to the point of suicide," Hiroshi said. "Now he's died, on the anniversary of her death."

His uncle frowned and hummed. "Senden has a tough corporate culture. I'm surprised there's only one girl like her."

"Only one we know of."

They looked at each other.

Hiroshi said, "I thought all this is what you wanted me to get away from when you sent me overseas?"

Hiroshi's uncle cleared his throat and started drawing his finger along the top of the table. "I wanted you to get *to* something, supporting yourself with a practical skill, accounting, and a global skill, English. I didn't want you to be dependent on anyone, not even on me. Your father would have been furious to see you not making your own life choices."

"You cut off my choices," Hiroshi said, the words sticking in his dry throat. "You pressured me to work for you."

"That wasn't pressure, that was help. Your father and I were very different people, but we were still family. You were only twenty when you left. I set you up for the most practical career around."

"A bit too practical."

"Maybe, but it was the best I could do at the time. Your father was my older brother. I relied on him my whole life. When he died, I wasn't sure what to do."

"You didn't even ask me what I wanted."

He raised his finger from where it was pressing into the table and took a big breath. "You know, I miss your father too."

Hiroshi took a big breath. "I know."

"What else do you need to know about Senden?"

"Are they that corrupt?"

"They believe they can bend anything to their will with hard work. They called it thinking outside the box, but it was often outside the legal box." Hiroshi's uncle shrugged. "Their corporate culture relies on micromanaging every detail of the company efficiently and completely."

"How do they do that?"

"By working their asses off and expecting everyone to do the same. Even an outside firm like ours was expected to follow their lead. When our contract with them finished, everyone here breathed a sigh of relief. It was a nightmare to work with them. *That* was pressure."

The sun had started to angle in the windows and reflect off the surface of the table, making Hiroshi squint. "Who should I talk to at Senden?"

"Upper management is controlling and conservative. The young hires are well trained, and pliant. My impression was middle management were the ones who wanted to do things in the gray zone. But you won't get much out of them. They're too loyal."

Hiroshi leaned back and looked out the window at the building across the street. It looked about the same as the office where they sat, endless desks and rooms and overhead lighting.

Hiroshi's uncle pulled a packet of black Sobranie cigarettes out of his pocket. "I'm trying to cut down, but let's continue this in the smoking lounge."

"I've got to go. I should have called ahead," Hiroshi said.

"You don't need to call ahead. Even after two years." His uncle put the pack back in his pocket. "I think your cousin would like to see you. She had a baby, you know?"

"I got the birth announcement," Hiroshi said. "I meant to send something."

"You and she were always close when you were kids. You remember playing together?"

"Yeah, I do."

"I don't even know where you're living."

"Kagurazaka. I moved in with my old college girlfriend, the one I left when you sent me to Boston. We got back together."

"You're never going to forgive me for that, but it made you who you are. If you didn't get outside the Japanese system, you weren't going to have an easy time. And if you didn't come back, well, you'd have just become American. Nothing wrong with that."

"I wanted to study history."

"You're living it, aren't you?" his uncle said.

Hiroshi remembered his father ending half-critical, half-ironic comments with, "Aren't you?" in just the same tone of voice.

"I'll stop by and see the baby. She still living in Jiyugaoka?" Hiroshi asked.

"Here's her phone number." His uncle put his cellphone on the table for Hiroshi.

Hiroshi leaned forward and took a photo of the number.

"What's your address? I'll send you a case of wine." His uncle took his phone and got ready to copy the info.

"I haven't gotten into the Japanese gift-giving cycle. I can never remember—"

"One of my clients pays in good wine, investment grade, and there's too much to finish. You don't like wine? Everyone likes wine."

"All right." Hiroshi pushed his cellphone across the table with his address showing.

His uncle took a photo of the address and saved it in his phone. "And if you're going after Senden, you better go hard. They know everything and everyone. And they'd do anything to keep expanding what they have."

Chapter 19

From his uncle's office, Hiroshi walked back to Kanda Station, thinking his uncle looked more like his father than the last time he saw him. His uncle and his cousin were his only close relatives, so it wouldn't hurt to visit. He would take Ayana with him and buy a baby present of some kind.

Near the station, he went into a convenience store and got a bottle of tea and two *onigiri* rice balls. He stood outside, chewing the rice wrapped in *nori* with a smoked fish slice tucked inside as slowly as a novice monk. He washed it down with tea and felt the lingering low from the alcohol dissipate.

Sugamo pulled to the curb under the overhead train tracks. Hiroshi got in the back. Takamatsu looked back, smirking. "Ready for our appointment?"

"I hope Akiko can get a reimbursement. Or I'm out sixty thousand yen," Hiroshi said. "Plus we have to pay for the hotel."

"Be glad we won't be paying for any extras. That'd double the price." Takamatsu chuckled. "Straight is a lot cheaper. Must be all the equipment."

"Did Mayu's father say anything new?" Hiroshi asked.

Takamatsu said, "Same as last night. I'm starting to believe him. And that makes me doubt him all the more."

Sugamo looked at Hiroshi. "The chief said don't be late. Four sharp. Or I'm responsible."

Takamatsu lit a cigarette and Hiroshi closed his eyes for the crosstown drive.

Two streets away from Shibuya Station, there was nowhere nearby for Sugamo to park. It was almost easier to keep driving than to look for an underground parking lot.

Hiroshi and Takamatsu got out to walk through the canyon of buildings that had sprung up as part of one of the biggest urban renewal projects in Tokyo—the new Shibuya. Just-built, over-designed buildings towered over the lively area that once wore a more human face. With the taller, sleeker buildings, it was more crowded with people than ever.

The detectives turned into a stylish hotel whose lobby access was a long, glass-sided elevator direct to the third floor. The lobby was empty and smelled new. They headed past the check-in counter to the elevators and rode up to the tenth floor. In the narrow low-lit hallway, the cleaning crew had to pull a linen cart aside so they could sidle past.

Hiroshi checked the room number and knocked on the door.

"Enter, slave!" a woman's voice called from inside.

The door handle clicked and Hiroshi went in first.

Inside stood a tall woman in knee-high boots and a leather body suit. She smacked the floor with a whip. A large silver zipper stretched from the middle of her breasts down to and under her groin. "I'm Mistress Emi and you are in for an hour of pain and pleasure. Kneel, slave." She snapped the whip again.

Hiroshi muttered, "*Konnichiwa*." Hiroshi wasn't sure if "good afternoon" was the right way to greet a dominatrix, but he had to say something. He stared at the whip. Her arm was covered in a full-sleeve black koi tattoo that seemed to swim as she rolled up the whip. The elaborate curls of her dyed-blonde hair bounced as the moved.

Mistress Emi noticed Takamatsu, and in a less commanding voice, said, "You booked for one. Is he watching or participating? The rate is different."

Takamatsu pushed Hiroshi forward and Mistress Emi backed into the room.

Hiroshi pulled out his badge. "We're detectives."

"There's no discount." Mistress Emi curled the whip up and reached for the riding crop on the bed.

"We just want to talk. About one of your clients," Hiroshi said.

Mistress Emi said, "I assure all my clients ultimate pain,

pleasure, *and* privacy."

"The client we want to ask about won't mind. He's dead," Hiroshi said.

Emi sat down on the bedcover, pulled her half-face mask off and crossed her legs. A red, orange and indigo dragon circled her left thigh, a blue peacock covered her right. Hiroshi didn't know much about tattoos, but these were marvelous. She looked up at Hiroshi with a question on her face.

Takamatsu moved to the other side of the bed, at an angle, watching her carefully.

Hiroshi showed her a photo of Onizuka.

Mistress Emi stared at it with a blank face, then looked away, squeezing her eyes tightly shut. Her body deflated, and she crossed the dragon over the peacock and sank into the bed biting her lip.

"He fell from the roof of his office building. Twenty stories," Hiroshi said.

Takamatsu started scrolling through his cellphone and said, "You want to see the photos on the ground?"

She shook her head in tight refusal. "No."

"You don't watch the news?"

Mistress Emi shook her head.

"So, you didn't know about Onizuka?"

She shook her head and looked out the window, still shaking her head.

Hiroshi wondered if this was more stagecraft, or whether she really didn't know. "What's your real name?"

"Emi Yoshida. My ID's in there." She nodded at a large black sports bag from which the tips of bondage gear poked.

Hiroshi pulled a chair over and sat down. He could check her ID later.

Emi zipped off one leather boot and dropped it on the floor, unzipped the other and dropped it. She pulled her legs up on the bed and reached behind her for a pillow which she dropped in her lap. She pulled out a hair tie and put her long hair in a neat ponytail. With the pillow and ponytail, she looked smaller, and girlish.

"Could you tell us where you were that night? Sunday night, Monday morning." Hiroshi asked.

Emi reached for her cellphone from inside her sports bag. Her long fingernails glittered with nail art diamonds. "I had two appointments that night."

"What time with Onizuka?" Takamatsu asked.

"Neither were with him."

"We'll need to check that. Send the names here." He held out his phone with his address.

She glanced at Hiroshi's email address and sent the two names. The back of her phone was engraved with a dominatrix in a police-style cap.

"When was the last time you, um, met him?" Hiroshi asked.

"Not for a while."

"A while?"

"Two weeks."

"How often did you meet?"

"He was a regular customer." Emi pulled her legs tighter and kneaded the pillow.

"Once a week? Twice a month?"

"Once or twice a month. More at holidays. Sometimes he called out of the blue."

"Did you meet him at this hotel?"

"At a special BDSM love hotel on the other side of the station. They have a lot of gear there for rent. Saves me carrying everything around." Emi pointed at her heavy-looking sports bag.

"What's the name of the place?"

"Hotel Hard Hello. HHH."

"What kind of place is it?" Hiroshi asked.

"Clean and reliable. And discreet."

"How long did you know Onizuka?"

Emi pushed on the pillow in her lap. "He's one of my oldest customers, from when I started five years ago."

"What did he, um, like?" Hiroshi asked.

Emi pulled the pillow, rocking slightly. "Privacy is how I keep my prices high, along with practiced technique and a strong storyline."

"We can take you in to the station as an accessory, if you like?" Takamatsu said.

Emi turned and smiled at Takamatsu. "I'd rather not. I know too many people there."

Takamatsu chuckled.

Emi frowned and twisted the pillow. "Onizuka liked all forms of humiliation. He was OK with a high level of pain."

"What kind of humiliation?"

"I could try things out on him. Practice for other clients." Emi's phone rang, but she ignored it.

"And what about actual intercourse?" Takamatsu asked.

Emi nodded. "That was not always on his list, before or after, but unlike most of my clients who are wet leaves, he was vital once he got started. His body was tight, strong, kind of wiry."

"How much did he spend?" Hiroshi asked.

"He liked throwing money away. Liked it more than sex sometimes. Whatever I added on to his charge, he paid. He did the math in his head. Always made me laugh. I have to use the calculator on my phone."

"What did he pay for most? Anything special?" Hiroshi asked.

"Is that important?"

"That's why I asked."

Emi looked at both of them and shrugged. "He liked anal, but almost all of them do. He also liked sounding. That always brought the bill up."

"What's sounding?" Hiroshi asked.

Emi dug in her bag and pulled out a long silver-colored rod with a handle like a wine opener and a small smooth bulb at the end.

Hiroshi cleared his throat.

Emi smiled. "You never saw this before? It goes up the urethra, tickles everything inside. One of his favorites."

Hiroshi cleared his throat again. "How did he pay?"

"Cash." She dropped the toys back into her bag and stood up, shorter without her heels. "He said our sessions were like therapy. Sometimes my other clients say that too, but not every time like Onizuka." She stared at Hiroshi and glanced at Takamatsu. "Is he really dead?"

Hiroshi said, "Killed by the impact of the fall."

"Twenty stories down," Takamatsu said.

Emi went to the window. "He had this psychodrama in his head that kept pushing him forward."

A knock came at the door and a man's voice shouted, "Emi?"

Takamatsu took a step toward the door, his hand on his retractable baton.

Emi said, "That's C3PO. Could you let him in, detective? And be careful."

Takamatsu pulled out his friction lock baton, walked to the door and pulled it open.

A tall guy with broad shoulders in a black leather jacket, vest, and black jeans rushed in and squared off with Takamatsu.

Emi yelled out, "It's OK, C3PO, these are detectives."

Everyone looked at each other for a minute. Hiroshi wondered about his nickname, but the Star Wars tattoos across the tops of both hands and halfway up his neck were sufficient explanation. He looked Asian, or half-Asian, but not Japanese.

Emi explained. "If something doesn't go right, I call and he comes. There were two of you so I pressed the button. He got here a bit slow today." She frowned at him and he pulled the door closed and stood there with his arms folded.

Takamatsu put his baton away.

Hiroshi said, "Is your clientele primarily company executives?

I don't see them as being much trouble."

"It's hard to tell when they call out at peak moments whether what they say is true or not. High-ranked schools, big companies, pretty wives, big apartments, kids, the whole escalator life. It's made them passive. They'll accept almost anything."

"Is that why Onizuka drank so much?"

"Probably. They all do. But he could hold his liquor, never got sick, never cried."

"What did Onizuka shout in the middle of things?" Takamatsu asked.

"In the middle of it, he would say anything and everything." Emi shook her head. "I can't believe he's dead. How could that happen?"

"That's what we're trying to find out," Hiroshi said. "What did he say?"

"He shouted all kinds of things. Shouting is half the point. About his job, women, work, colleagues, anything really. To be honest, I never pay that much attention. Most of them lead boring lives. The only thing they do outside the norm is with me."

Hiroshi wondered how that worked, how it fitted into the balance sheet in their minds.

"Onizuka was more handsome than most, and when he was done, he always had something interesting to say about books, foreign countries, politics. He liked to take me to dinner and to the horse races. He always won. He was a very lucky gambler." Emi sat down on the bed and cocked her head. "He liked to call me different names, not just Emi. I'd whack his ass a few times to get him warmed up and then he'd pick a name, Tomoko or Rio, Haruka or Kaho."

"What name did he choose most often?"

"That was a bit confusing, because it was also his safe name— 'Mayu.'"

Hiroshi looked at Takamatsu.

"Mayu was the name he called out when the pain got too

much?" Takamatsu asked.

"And it was the name he wanted to call me most often. I had to listen to *how* he yelled it to know if he wanted out—or wanted more."

Chapter 20

Sugamo was waiting on a side street near the hotel, traffic pulling around the side of the car. "How was she?" Sugamo asked as Hiroshi and Takamatsu clambered in, scowling at the cars waiting impatiently in both directions. When traffic cleared, Sugamo started back to the station to get Hiroshi there in time for the chief.

"Amazing tattoos," Takamatsu said. "I haven't seen such great ones since I was on crowd control at the Sanja Matsuri. Skin is the ultimate canvas."

"You're getting a few tattoos then?" Hiroshi asked him.

"Against the police code or I would," Takamatsu said, cracking a window and lighting a cigarette. "Well, she was a treat."

"You believed her?" Hiroshi asked.

"I wanted to believe her." Takamatsu blew the smoke out the window. "Didn't you?"

Hiroshi wasn't sure and stared out the window. If any woman could have managed to get Onizuka up to the roof, it was her. Her answers seemed straightforward and her surprise genuine. Her job involved a lot of play-acting, so a few lies wouldn't be too hard to manage.

She wasn't the break in the case they wanted, but they could talk to her again after re-checking the roof. He'd taken all her contact info, so best to let her stew for half a day and then go after her again. By then, maybe the fence cutters would turn up. Maybe the video footage would reveal something. The money angle would connect but that would take time, even with the files in hand. Revenge seemed more likely. If Onizuka liked receiving pain, he must have liked dishing it out.

When they pulled into the station parking lot, Takamatsu turned around. "What time can you meet on the roof of Senden?"

155

"I'll call as soon as I can shake free." Hiroshi hopped out at the entrance, hurried down the hall to the chief's office and plastered on a smile as he stepped inside.

"You're on time," the chief said, looking at his watch.

Hiroshi waited while the chief slipped on his camel hair overcoat and adjusted his Borsalino fedora.

"I think we'll get some help from my contacts in the ministries," the chief said, brushing past Hiroshi as he marched out the door.

Hiroshi followed, stifling a sigh, and thinking that the Ministry of Health, Labor and Welfare should be the chief's duty. The ministries were full of over-confident and disinterested people, who knew everything and did nothing, the kind who wanted to go to Mistress Emi but were too ashamed to even try.

The chief's car was waiting at the side door of the station. The contrast with the worn-down cars they usually took was striking. The chief's car was plush. Hiroshi had never seen it before. He didn't know the driver, either.

Settling into the back seat, the chief said, "Department chiefs have their own car now. It's another office."

Hiroshi listened politely.

The chief said, "One of my classmates works at the Ministry of Health, Labor and Welfare. It's good to know the right people. This will save us a lot of time."

Hiroshi hummed with feigned enthusiasm, but if there was a chance of finding out who had filed grievances at Senden Central over the years, then it wasn't such a time drain.

Hiroshi got a text message on LINE from Chizu, the young woman who worked in the HR office at Senden. She wanted to meet. He wrote back that he could talk with her in a couple of hours, and he'd be stopping by Senden later anyway.

She wrote back, "Not at the office. Tomorrow. Around lunch."

Hiroshi responded, "Fine. Text me where." He wondered if she was all right. Was she in the same snares as Mayu had been? He'd find out tomorrow.

As he fingered the panel of switches on the car door, Hiroshi wondered how the chief could rise through the ranks but still know so little about investigations. "I think we need to ask them for any harassment claims against Senden, and Onizuka in particular. They can give us that at least."

"I'll let you explain," the chief said.

So that was why the chief demanded Hiroshi accompany him.

The ministry buildings sprawled along wide boulevards between the Imperial Palace, the Diet Building, and Hibiya Park, a nexus of power with the greatest of Tokyo luxuries—open land in the center of the city. The government buildings were spaced apart from each other, with open sky in between. The driver pulled up to the outside roadblock checkpoint and the chief leaned forward to show his credentials.

The twenty-some-story building looked like *genkouyoushi* copybooks school kids used to practice *kanji*, all squares and blanks. A large, flat stone surrounded by well-trimmed bushes and carved into a massive stone with the ministry name was set back at an angle. Past the stone marker by the door, a guard in white gloves checked the chief's badge and explained where the driver could park and how they could enter.

Inside, past security, a receptionist checked their names and pointed them to the elevators. The upstairs hallway was wide and empty. At the office reception desk, two secretaries stood and one escorted them to a meeting room. The slightly run-down room was empty except for a table and chairs, a white board, and dingy windows that didn't open.

Hiroshi read the half-erased traces of notes on the white board until three ministry officials entered. The oldest was a man in his fifties with a touch of gray hair dressed in a navy-blue suit, white shirt, and striped tie. The second official, ten years younger, dressed exactly the same. The third had a bit longer hair, looked another decade younger, and sported a looser cut suit. The older

157

two officials' eyes radiated impatience. The youngest kept his eyes on the table.

The head official, Suzuki, rushed through the introductions and Hiroshi wondered when the chief would say something, but he quickly had the feeling that the official didn't really know who the chief was, that they had never met before. Suzuki and the other two waited for the chief to speak first with the entrapped forbearance of people who attend meetings non-stop. The chief turned to Hiroshi.

Hiroshi sat up and cleared his throat. "We're investigating the death of Shigeru Onizuka, a *bucho* at Senden Central Infinity. Because it is possibly a homicide, we need access to all filings about Onizuka and Senden. You'll recall he was the *bucho* who harassed Mayu Yamase, the twenty-five-year-old girl who committed suicide on her birthday after a hundred hours of overtime—"

Suzuki interrupted with his hand and pointed to the two younger officials. "They handled the case and were instrumental in ensuring that the case concluded successfully."

Hiroshi looked at him. "Successfully?"

The chief's head ping-ponged between them without adding a word.

"Successful in sending the message that companies need to control overtime," Suzuki said.

"The overtime was a form of harassment." Hiroshi prodded.

"Technically, harassment is not a violation, though overtime is, of course." Suzuki glanced at his two subordinates, who nodded accordingly.

"The girl died." Hiroshi was glad that Takamatsu was not there. He would have exploded.

The older two officials glanced at their cellphones set neatly in front of them on the table.

Hiroshi took a breath. "We need to know who else filed grievances against Onizuka or the company, and whether you looked into the company's budgets and financial activity. We believe there may have been irregularities."

Suzuki turned to the official next in age and spoke in a low voice. The forty-something official said, "Approval will take time."

"That's what we don't have," Hiroshi said, forcing a smile.

"Can't you get that information from the company directly?" the second official suggested.

Hiroshi nodded politely. "We tried that, but they didn't cooperate. We suspect they are covering something up. Letting them know what we're looking for is likely to cause more evidence to be hidden."

Suzuki squinted at Hiroshi.

Hiroshi nodded politely before continuing. "Even with a history of workplace harassment, budgetary indiscretions, and a well-known suicide, the company remains uncooperative and evasive. So, whatever measures were taken in the past..."

"Evasive?" Suzuki looked irritated. "Isn't that what detectives do? Evade evasion? Why are you asking us to do your job?"

Who was doing whose work? Hiroshi wondered, but calmed himself before he spoke in the politest Japanese he could muster. "We would like to know what the ministry found on this company."

The middle official spoke up. "Our concern with the Mayu Yamase suicide case was to show the world that Japan is addressing its workplace problems. We showed Japan has reformed workplaces and is ready for the next stage of globalization."

Suzuki looked directly into Hiroshi's eyes. "Senden is set to become one of Japan's premier media and advertising firms with a global presence. Any subsidiary that allies with them will also have a global presence. What happens to them affects many corporations large and small, and that affects the entire Japanese economy."

Hiroshi paused for a moment to let their momentum slow. In *kendo*, the best time to counterattack was after a strong attack. "That is precisely why we are coming to you for help. We need to be sure we don't make any missteps at this crucial juncture."

The officials leaned back, a blue-suited wall, unyielding and inflexible.

Suzuki straightened his tie. "Our goal is to assist companies with the right policies, regulations, and action plans."

Hiroshi could not believe they were putting assistance above oversight, and avoiding any responsibility for enforcement. "We worry that some tabloid will pick up this story and work it until even more embarrassing facts emerge. The best way through this is to finish quickly, and correctly, and let Senden get back to business as usual."

Suzuki checked his cellphone and the middle official folded his notepad shut. Suzuki pushed back and stood up, straightening his already straight tie.

Hiroshi and the chief had no choice but to stand up, too. Hiroshi's polite Japanese was straining him to the breaking point. "The harassment, the suicide, and the death of Onizuka are connected. We suspect financial improprieties are connected, too."

Suzuki hummed and straightened his tie again. "In that case, the Ministry of Finance knows more about this than we do. We'll set up an appointment for you. It's just around the corner. In case you don't have a car."

Suzuki nodded to his number two, who picked up his cellphone and made a call.

He spoke for a few minutes, hung up and said, "You're all set. A classmate of mine works there."

Suzuki bowed to Hiroshi and the chief. The youngest official moved to hold the door open for them to leave.

The elevator was down the hall.

Hiroshi and the chief rode down in silence, the chief's face rigid, his jaw tight. He worked one hand around a tightly balled fist.

As they headed through the lobby to the front door, the chief said, "The higher up they are, the less they do."

After calling his driver, the chief stood silently at the curb, rocking on his heels and mumbling to himself.

Hiroshi stared in the distance, too frustrated to even check his cellphone for messages.

When the car pulled up, the chief smashed his fist into his hand. "So that's how they want to play it. They've been chewing my ass about this but don't want to help? All they want is for us to deliver a tidy report, so they can be rid of this, and rid of us."

Hiroshi said, "So, on to the Ministry of Finance?"

"We're not wasting time with them. They'll just pass us to another ministry. They barely listened to us here."

"I need to go to Marunouchi then," Hiroshi said.

"You get back to work and do it your way. Takamatsu too." The chief reset his Borsalino, got in and slammed the door.

Chapter 21

Takamatsu was waiting in the lobby of the Senden Central building flipping his lighter and staring at the banners that swept down from the ceiling. When Hiroshi came in, Takamatsu nodded to the lobby receptionist, who placed a call.

In a minute, a retirement-age man in a bright blue uniform and brimmed cap emerged from a door beside the elevators and ambled toward them. His mottled pink face was pleasant and fleshy. "I'm Imasato, in charge of security for Senden. I worked at the *koban* police box in Roppongi for twenty years before retiring here."

Takamatsu smiled. "Most people transfer out of there after a few years."

"Not the stubborn ones. Follow me." Imasato led them down the stairwell.

Hiroshi said, "We received the footage you sent, but it's not quite what we needed."

"It didn't reveal much, did it?" Imasato said. "We put in for a new system last year, but, you know, budget cuts. With the overseas expansion."

"Some of the areas, especially on the roof, seem to have time lapses?" Hiroshi said.

Imasato said, "A cost-cutting measure. Some cameras skip minutes."

"How many minutes?" Hiroshi asked.

"Three, five, eight, they're all different. A few are set for ten-minute intervals," Imasato said.

Takamatsu said, "Ten minutes can be a long time."

Hiroshi frowned. Ten minutes didn't seem that long.

They followed Imasato out of the stairwell and into a dimly lit room with a flickering, refocusing bank of gray images streamed in from corridors, elevators, emergency exits, reception desks, and the lobby. Green-tinged screens brought in the parking lot, fire escapes, and outside walls. Every centimeter of the Senden building was visible.

Hiroshi turned to Imasato. "Could you walk us through the path from the parking area to the roof? We need to know how the camera could not have captured Onizuka getting to the roof."

"I've been trying to piece that together too. Let me get my keys." Imasato opened a metal cabinet on the wall with several dozen sets of keys. He took a thick ring of keys and led them out of the room and down the hall.

Hiroshi said, "Where are the video files stored?"

Imasato opened the door to an underground tunnel. "HR gets them."

"HR?"

Imasato said, "That's how they want it. After that, the tech guys take all of the video files and compress them, or whatever they do, and after that, I'm not sure where they go."

Takamatsu frowned. "What's your guess?"

Imasato stopped, took a breath, and said, "I have no idea. A file storage security company comes twice a week. We can rewind the past twenty-four hours here, but that's all we ever have."

Hiroshi walked toward the large parking garage door and Takamatsu turned to survey the high ceiling of dusty, car exhaust-stained concrete.

Hiroshi walked up the sloped drive to the entrance, stopped and looked back. Every spot was marked by department and position, a parking hierarchy.

Takamatsu nodded at the corner and Hiroshi followed his gaze up to a surveillance camera that hung too high for anyone to reach without a ladder. "OK. Let's see the others."

Imasato led them into the hall and turned right and tapped on a large service elevator that stood across from an extra-tall, double-wide door out to the parking lot. "This door is kept locked except for large deliveries."

"Keys?" Takamatsu asked.

Imasato jingled his keychain. "We get a call and come and unlock it. Stand there. And relock it."

Takamatsu walked down the hall and dragged back a hard plastic chair. He kicked off his shoes and stood on it, reaching up toward the security camera in the corner. He put his face close to the camera, followed where it looked, and then checked all sides of the camera, touching it here and there.

Takamatsu got down, put the chair back, kicked at a cut of wood used as a doorstop and nodded to continue.

The three men took the elevator up using a security card to activate the button panel. The large service elevator was covered in scratches, dents and skids.

"When did you discover the fence being cut?" Takamatsu asked.

Imasato sighed. "We check the roof in person once every two hours. You couldn't see the fence on the video screens downstairs. You saw what shape they're in."

Imasato looked at the number panel for the floors. "We're strict with the checkpoints. There's a card reader at each one."

"Everyone has their own card?"

Imasato nodded. "That record is saved in our files, if you want it."

"Was there anything out of the ordinary that night?"

"No, but there should have been." Imasato held the door open for them to get out on the eighteenth floor. The hallway looked the same as the ground floor, beige paint and fluorescent light. A stairwell opened to the floors below. The railings didn't meet in the middle, so there was a clear fall to the bottom. Hiroshi edged away, closer to the wall.

Takamatsu stopped in front of the surveillance camera and looked around for something to stand on. Seeing nothing, he motioned for Hiroshi to hoist him up so he could see the camera.

Hiroshi glanced at the open shaft between the stairs and stayed where he was.

Takamatsu pointed at the camera on the wall. Hiroshi cupped his hands and squatted to hold Takamatsu's weight on his thigh. Takamatsu slipped off one shoe, put his foot in Hiroshi's hands and clambered up.

Takamatsu poked at the camera near the lens for a few seconds, Hiroshi balancing him like a circus acrobat. Finally, Takamatsu waved to be lowered down, his stocking foot landing on his shoe. He slipped it on. "Next."

Imasato started up the stairs. "Next are some stairs. The service elevator stops here. Only the main elevator goes all the way to the roof."

Hiroshi followed Imasato up the stairs, being careful not to look down. "How long does it take usually from the garage to the roof?"

Imasato thought about it. "With all the locks and key cards, fifteen minutes at most."

"How often do they change the locks and key cards?"

"Never, as far as I know."

"How long have you worked here?"

"Fifteen years."

"Who went up there first that night?"

"I did," Imasato said.

"And there was no sign of anyone?"

"It was quiet, cold, like always."

"You didn't even feel like someone was up there?"

Imasato stopped climbing. "Not even that, no."

"Did you see the cut in the fence?"

Imasato paused. "I didn't look over there, didn't think to look. The only thing I've ever seen is someone working overnight taking a cigarette break."

"Why don't you use the regular elevator?" Takamatsu asked.

"They don't want customers to see us in the daytime," Imasato said. "At night, we just go the same way out of habit. We have to tap the checkpoint here anyway. A couple of flights of stairs feels good after sitting in front of those monitors all day."

Takamatsu looked for a camera. Hiroshi couldn't see one.

Imasato walked them up the last few steep steps to the rooftop door, more of a hatchway, and put his hip and shoulder into it with a hard shove. It opened onto the roof on the opposite side from the smoker's lounge and the cut fence. Yellow crime scene tape flapped loudly in the wind.

Imasato buttoned his uniform and waited by the hatch door for the service entrance.

Takamatsu looked around and walked to the smoker's lounge. Above the cross beam that held the dividing wall was a camera. He walked back to the hatch door and started again, counting his steps. When he got right below the camera, he lit a cigarette.

Hiroshi wished he'd added another layer, a sweater or something, but the night wind made him feel sober and alert for the first time that day.

Takamatsu finished a few more puffs, the smoke disappearing in the wind, and then stood on the rim of a planter to get a closer look at the camera. He pulled out his pocket knife, scratched around the surface of the camera and hopped down. He dropped his knife into an evidence bag.

Hiroshi walked over.

Takamatsu held up his fingers to Hiroshi's face. Even squinting, Hiroshi couldn't see anything. Takamatsu pressed his finger onto the back of Hiroshi's hand. Hiroshi shrugged.

"It's sticky," Takamatsu said.

"Meaning...?"

"Tape."

Hiroshi thought about that and started to call Sakaguchi to get the crime scene crew back to the roof.

"Don't call Sakaguchi yet," Takamatsu whispered. "What are the crime scene guys going to look for? Glue? We don't want it cleaned up and we don't want to let them know. They'll destroy all the video files."

"They sent them to us." Hiroshi could feel the glue getting stickier as he rubbed it between his fingers.

"We need the originals. They sent us doctored files," Takamatsu said. "It's the only way."

Hiroshi put his phone away. The tape would explain the blackouts in the video they sent, but Hiroshi wasn't sure how anyone could block the high camera in the parking garage. And now could they get up to the cameras to put the tape without being seen? The tech guys had said the video flashed and went black.

Takamatsu walked to the cut-open V in the fence.

Hiroshi followed. Looking past the edge through the crime scene tape, he could see the opposite sidewalk and a bit of the street twenty floors below. Hiroshi took several steps back. It was impossible to not think about the tumble, time, and landing, Onizuka's body on the concrete below.

Takamatsu ground out his cigarette, ducked under the tape, poked his head out the V, and leaned forward to look at the black tar on the outer ledge, where it sloped down to a rain gutter, no fence or rail, and beyond only air and gravity.

Takamatsu peeled back the yellow tape and put a leg onto the outside ledge.

"What are you doing, you idiot?" Hiroshi said, grabbing Takamatsu's sleeve.

Takamatsu balanced himself, one leg out and one in. He pulled up his sleeve and rotated his arm to lock wrists with Hiroshi.

Takamatsu leaned down toward the edge of the building, stretching his fingers toward something Hiroshi couldn't see. Hiroshi pulled taut on Takamatsu's wrist while he stooped and wiggled his fingers to the very edge.

Hiroshi dug in his feet and pulled back to let Takamatsu ease toward it, the edge coming closer with each stretch until

Takamatsu's fingers snatched something from the gravel. Takamatsu shifted his weight. Hiroshi grabbed him above his elbow with his other hand and pulled him back in through the cut fence.

Takamatsu held up a cigarette butt.

Hiroshi looked at it and then at Takamatsu's face. He was smiling.

Takamatsu pulled an evidence envelope from his inner pocket and slipped in the butt. "I got my DNA all over it, but it's the same brand. Gold and black. Sobranie. There were some in the smoking lounge ashtray. Onizuka's wife smokes them, too."

Hiroshi hadn't noticed. "How did the crew miss this?"

"I only saw it because of the light reflecting on the foil." Takamatsu put the envelope in his pocket.

"His last cigarette?" Hiroshi recognized the brand but couldn't remember from where.

Takamatsu looked around the rooftop area and straightened his cuffs. "If all the video is missing, or taped over, it's got to be an inside job." Takamatsu lit another cigarette, blowing the smoke high into the night wind.

"Detectives?" Imasato called out.

Hiroshi and Takamatsu turned to see Chizu, the young HR assistant, shivering in a business jacket and skirt by the main door to the roof, looking in their direction. Even in the dark, Hiroshi could see the worry in her face.

Chapter 22

Takamatsu put out his cigarette. "You take this one," he growled to Hiroshi, both of them staring at Chizu shivering by the smoking lounge. "I'm going to get a ladder and check out the parking garage camera."

Takamatsu and Imasato walked back to the hatch door and disappeared inside. Chizu bowed to Takamatsu and walked toward Hiroshi.

"It's cold up here," Hiroshi said.

"The wind's blocked over there," Chizu said, pointing at the other corner where large, Plexiglass barriers lined the two sides of the roof opposite the crime scene.

Chizu was tall with shoulder length, neatly cut hair that the wind blew dancing around her face. She moved easily, hunching her shoulders like too-tall people do. Inside the protective barriers, the wind lost its icy sting. Chizu circled to face the door from the elevator and looked at Hiroshi. She had thick lips and high cheekbones, and her eyes weren't afraid of his. They were intelligent and searching.

"Thank you for answering my LINE message," Chizu said. "I'm sorry I didn't get back to you. I'm not always free to send messages."

"What did you want to talk about?" Hiroshi asked, letting his eyes rest on hers.

"I changed my mind."

"About talking with me? It's all right to—"

"No. About the topic. Before, I wanted to give you my understanding of what happened. But now I hear you're interested in seeing the files on Onizuka."

"Where did you hear that?"

"It doesn't matter."

171

"Actually, it does."

Chizu blinked. "A friend in the ministries."

Hiroshi wondered if that was the silent thirty-something official he and the chief met. If not, it was someone like him, with a younger, fresher view of how the government ministries and large companies interacted.

"There are a lot," Chizu said, keeping a close eye on the door.

"A lot of friends? Or a lot of files?"

Chizu smiled, making her even prettier, even in the dark.

"Files," she said.

Hiroshi tried to keep her talking, but she kept looking at the door. "You've seen all the files?"

"I had to file them," Chizu said. "Or refile them."

"Where are they?"

"I'll have to show you. Otherwise you'll never get to see them."

Hiroshi turned to look at the door. "Can you take me now?"

Chizu shook her head. "That's why I wanted to schedule tomorrow lunch. I have a dentist appointment, the only way to get away from work, but now you know what I wanted to tell you, so it's better not to risk it."

Risk what? Hiroshi wanted to ask, but instead he nodded reassuringly. "I wish you'd tell me more about what you know."

"I will. But not now. Not here." Chizu stopped herself and turned from the door to look out through the Plexiglass barrier toward the Imperial Palace grounds. It was dark in that direction, but you could make out trees and the moat, and a guard station in front of the old stone wall.

Chizu was young, but already had a larger comprehension of the world. It came through in her calm manner and direct stare, and in the wariness with which she answered, not resistant, but cautious. That's probably how Mayu was, too, grasping the deeper implications of what was being done around her, of what she was asked to do, and not sure how to resist it, much less change it.

A man's voice coming from behind startled Hiroshi.

Chizu spun around.

It was Nakata, the head of HR, striding toward them. He stopped close to Hiroshi with a curt bow. Chizu took a step back. Nakata seemed taller on the roof than in the conference room, but just as sure of himself.

"Chizu-*san*, are you filling in the detectives with everything they need to know?" Nakata asked. "We've got the press conference on Friday. I thought you were preparing for that? Lots of things left to do."

Chizu looked down and nodded. She was obviously not supposed to be there on the roof talking to detectives. She was supposed to be working. Hiroshi tried to think of something to say.

Nakata pointed in the dark. "You can see the very heart of Japan from here, the Emperor's Palace," Nakata said to Hiroshi. "That's part of why we like our main office here."

Hiroshi said, "That's just what I was asking about. Chizu was nice enough to give me an explanation and a brief history of Senden."

Nakata forced his smile a little wider. "She wrote her graduation thesis on Senden, didn't you?"

Chizu drew a breath. "Yes, about the history of advertising in Japan."

"That's one of the reasons we hired her," Nakata said. "Among her other many professional qualities. Well, Chizu-*san*, we're probably interrupting important detective work, and we have so much to do for Friday's announcement. Did you get the redecoration of the lobby finalized and the conference room set up?"

Chizu nodded and said, simply, "*Hai.*"

Hiroshi looked at him closely. "We've gathered a lot of evidence, so we're getting near to understanding what happened up here." In fact, they had a whole lot of nothing, not much more than glue on the cameras and a cigarette butt.

"Can you give me a rundown on what you have so far? Or maybe you were just telling Chizu-*san* about that?" Nakata looked back and forth with a disingenuously blank face.

"We didn't find much in the files you sent, and the video seems to be missing quite a few minutes. The blanked-out part is longer than we can account for. We also need to get into the HR files for Onizuka. I think we've requested all of that," Hiroshi said in polite Japanese.

Nakata took a step closer. "I spoke with the company president and other CEOs, and it will take a bit of time to get what you asked for. All of the documents and files you requested should be ready in a few days, right, Chizu-*san*?"

Chizu nodded rapidly.

"A few days?" Hiroshi said. "We're used to moving a bit more quickly on investigations."

Nakata looked at him. "I'm sorry, but there are important privacy issues. When you deal with the human side of a large, successful company like ours, you need to be especially sensitive to these issues."

"We're not used to too much sensitivity," Hiroshi said. "It never seems to accompany the facts."

Nakata said, "Well, I can tell you this much right now. Off the record. Numerous women complained about Onizuka over the years."

"We need to talk with all of them." Hiroshi said.

"We don't even know where many of them are now."

"I just need the names. We'll find them."

Nakata took another step closer, well within the distance reserved for two people to bow. "Most of them were just not willing to put up with his demanding leadership style and, admittedly, sexist views. He was difficult to work with and a bit of a maverick. But those are not crimes."

"Nobody said they were." Hiroshi looked at Nakata but he gave not the slightest hint from his stance or his face about what he was really thinking.

"We want to get this investigation concluded and find out what happened up here, no matter what it takes," Nakata said.

"It might take more than you think."

"There are complicating factors. The women who filed complaints asked other women to obtain files for them illegally. Then, they misfiled budget and personal files. We've had trouble relocating essential documents."

Hiroshi wanted to laugh at this evasion. "Internal sabotage?" It was just as the sniffling accountant Kato had told them. Nakata was probably the one hiding files so only he knew where they'd be.

"Mistakes are common and that can be corrected. But deliberate misfiling weakens the structure of the entire company. Some employees have no loyalty. Often women employees, I hate to admit." Nakata glanced at Chizu.

"You mean, men are better employees?" Hiroshi wanted to shake the guy, or set him up in a *kendo* match with Ayana to take him down a notch or two.

Nakata shook his head coolly. "Men devote their lives to the company. Women don't because their loyalties are always divided. We have to keep that in mind in all HR decisions."

Hiroshi caught Chizu's eyes boring into the wall behind him, her jaw as motionless as stone. He couldn't see her face well in the dark but enough to tell she was holding herself in check. If only he'd had five more minutes to talk with her before Nakata interrupted them. Hiroshi looked away at the lights of Tokyo spreading like fallen, cooling stars all the way to the horizon. Overhead, the skyglow that hung over Tokyo blocked the real stars.

Hiroshi said, "The chief of homicide and I stopped by the Ministry of Labor this afternoon. They were quite interested in learning of our difficulties getting hold of the materials we need."

Hiroshi knew that was far from true, but as Takamatsu always said, save the truth for the end of the case.

"The ministries?" Nakata tried to contain a smirk. "I can tell you one thing that Onizuka understood well. On the global stage, we Japanese have to work harder than everyone else. What we lack in creativity, innovation and critical thought, we make up for in patience, perseverance, and attention to detail. What we lack in global vision, we make up for in solid traditional values. The government is pressured by outside forces to make overtime a crime. Harassment is an unfortunate side effect of a hard-working corporate culture. It's my job to bring the best out in workers and keep the company on pace toward continued success."

Hiroshi saw Takamatsu walking toward them with his coat tails flying behind. He was smiling. He must have found something.

Hiroshi spoke to Nakata without looking at him, "If Senden was concerned about Japanese values, they would prioritize the inherent value of employees, not just their use value. Senden seems to have that backward. Losing workers shows a failure in personnel management."

Nakata glared back at him.

"We'll get Onizuka's death properly determined, with or without your help. We're used to doing it both ways." Hiroshi held Nakata's gaze and then walked away without another word, knowing it was now going to be harder without his help. He could hear Nakata clearing his throat and coughing in the cold, dry wind.

He worried about leaving Chizu there. There was something in Chizu's silence that left him uneasy. He turned back to see her standing beside Nakata in the shadow of a tree. Takamatsu would back him if he wanted to take her along for her own safety, but he would find out more when they talked the next day. It was only a few hours, actually.

Takamatsu waited by the main elevator. The guard Imasato held up his passkey and slid it in the reader to let the detectives ride down by themselves, bowing deeply as the doors closed.

Just before the lobby, Takamatsu said, "Seems there's two ways up to the roof, and two ways down."

"There's two of everything at this company," Hiroshi said. "One they want us to see and one they don't."

Chapter 23

It felt good to be off the roof and away from Senden. Hiroshi started walking south beside the elevated train tracks. Long commuter trains clanged along the tracks above, their heavy rumble broken only by the overhead screech of wheel on rail.

Hiroshi ignored the cross street under the tracks into Ginza, and kept going past German beer halls, Chinese dim sum joints, Korean barbecue places, and yakitori grills with savory smoke billowing into the street.

Takamatsu hung a step behind, smoking, giving Hiroshi space to think.

Hiroshi kept walking, but near Shinbashi Station he stopped stomping forward to take a call from Sakaguchi. Takamatsu pointed at the smoker's lounge and Hiroshi gave him a vague nod.

"Who?" Hiroshi shouted into his phone.

"I can't pronounce his name," Sakaguchi said. "'*Su-chi-bu Tai-ta-su*' is what it sounds like to me. He had your *meishi* in his wallet."

"Where is he?"

"He's been arrested."

"For what?"

"Drugs. Some beat cops snagged him at a club near Ueno. For marijuana."

"Are you there now?"

"They called and woke me up. I'd finally gotten to sleep."

"I'm with Takamatsu. We'll pick him up. Go back to sleep."

Takamatsu put out his cigarette, said something to a woman he'd been chatting with that made her smile, and came over. Hiroshi waved for a taxi and explained.

Takamatsu said, "I was going to say, let's get a drink. But I admit interrogations do go better sober."

***

The police had blocked off an alley not far from Okachimachi Station where Ueno's eight- and ten-story ferroconcrete buildings turned to two- and three-story wooden homes, ragtag drinking spots, and boarded-up shops. Utility poles strung with power lines, internet cables and leftover wires jutted out of the street at irregular intervals. A single police car blocked each corner, leaving just enough room to squeeze by.

Hiroshi and Takamatsu hopped out of the taxi on the corner of an intersection between the bigger and smaller buildings. Police officers and narcotics agents were going in and out of an eight-story building whose upper floors had large glass windows painted with the names and numbers of the restaurants and clubs inside. Local police, lab technicians, and narcotics agents bustled in all directions. They led handcuffed suspects out of the building through the one-at-a-time door. Emptying the building would take time.

Hiroshi stopped an agent in a black windbreaker and bulletproof vest who steered them to a square window-less bus parked on the larger street where suspects were being held. Hiroshi and Takamatsu showed their badges and the guard on duty called for the agent in charge, a stout man in a windbreaker with a pockmarked face and a black stocking cap.

"We got a call about a foreigner here. Can we see him?" Hiroshi said.

"Westerners are just trouble when it comes to this. Rights, forms, lawyers, they think they're owed something. You just want to talk with him?"

"For now. We'll let you process him," Hiroshi said.

"Thanks," the stout agent said. "That smaller bus is empty, so you can talk to him in there. When this bus fills up, though, we'll need to put people in there. The club was crowded and we're taking everyone in."

"His name's Steve Titus," Hiroshi said. "Jazz musician."

"Oh, that guy. He doesn't speak a word of Japanese. All the Chinese we arrest are fluent." He shouted for someone to get the American out of the big bus and take him to the smaller one.

When Steve Titus came out he locked eyes with Hiroshi, but didn't say a word.

Hiroshi and Takamatsu waved their badges at the two agents walking him from bus to bus. The agents handcuffed Steve to a railing that ran down the middle of the bus between two benches. When they pushed the back door closed, the overhead light darkened but stayed on. Sitting opposite Steve, Hiroshi let the gravity of his situation sink in. Takamatsu stared him down.

Finally, Hiroshi said, "Don't you know the drug laws in Japan?"

"Yeah, but man, it's all over the place anyway." Steve pulled on the handcuffs. "Do you know where my saxophone is?"

"At the moment, unless you want to be held for twenty-three days, you need to start talking."

"Don't I get a lawyer?"

"You might, or might not, and the lawyer might or might not speak English, or immigration might come and drive you to the airport where they stamp your passport never to return. And that's the best-case scenario." Hiroshi tapped the railing between them.

The bus rocked. Someone was thrown against the outside and loud voices shouted back and forth.

"Look, it's just marijuana," Steve said.

Hiroshi stared at him and shook his head as if he was not understanding. "Foreigner-imported drugs polluting the purity of this island nation. A police record for fighting at Mayu's funeral. And do you think the Japanese arrested with you tonight are going to take the blame when they have a *gaijin* scapegoat?"

The door opened and an agent handed them two bottles of tea. "Tea ceremony for our foreign guest," he said, and shut the door again.

Steve took the tea gratefully, but with his hands cuffed to the railing, he had to lean over to drink it. Just the same, after a big slug of tea, relief washed over his face.

Hiroshi said, "Someone may have killed Mayu's boss, and with this arrest, you are moving up on the list of suspects."

"I'm a suspect?" Steve fiddled the top back on the tea bottle.

"I think you know more than you told me yesterday."

Steve leaned forward and rapped the bottle on the railing. "Who cares if that guy was killed? He harassed Mayu. He called her at impossible hours, made her move his money, asked her to redo her work, which was always perfect."

"You're making yourself look more suspect by getting angry."

"I'm exhausted," Steve said. "I can't even think straight."

"Wait until they start interrogating you. You'll think even less straight. It's better to talk with me. Now."

Steve nodded OK and leaned back, exhaling, thinking.

Hiroshi lowered his voice. "I think Mayu knew what was going on inside Senden, and that's why she was being harassed. And I think you know what she said about that. What money was she moving for Onizuka?"

Steve squeezed the tea bottle, which crinkled loudly. "She'd start talking about it and then start weeping so hard she couldn't keep it straight. The more she told me, the more I begged her to quit or hire a lawyer, but she just wouldn't."

"Why wouldn't she?"

"I'd get her calmed down and she'd take a day off. They'd transfer her for a week, and she'd feel better, and then transfer her back. It was torture. Onizuka was harassing her because she was so competent, if that makes any sense."

Hiroshi nodded. "It does."

"From what Mayu said, lots of people hated Onizuka, even when they weren't the direct recipient of his harassment. She'd talked to them."

"Did Mayu report it?"

"I forced her to, and she did, finally. But that only made it worse. That company is fucked up."

"So, why did she keep trying to work so hard?"

"She was a perfectionist. She wanted to find all the complaint files. But more than that, she was addicted." Steve looked at his hands. "I didn't even get to see her the last two weeks of her life. She was working 24/7. She texted me from the toilet, the only free time and safe place she could manage." Steve's body heaved with grief and a whimper escaped from deep inside. He leaned forward, tilted his head to the side and drained the rest of the tea.

Hiroshi gave him his unopened bottle.

Steve bowed in thanks, opened it and drank deep. "Do you know where my saxophone is?"

"I'll check on that." Hiroshi nodded, but it was probably lost in the shuffle.

Steve said, "A lot of people would have been happy to kill Onizuka. I know I thought about it. Mayu woke up from dreams about killing him, sweating and shaking, promising to get it all noted, reported and corrected. She talked about it in a crazy sort of way."

Maybe Takamatsu was right. Steve had the best reason for revenge. Mayu's parents lost their past, but Steve lost his future.

"Do you think Mayu's father did this?" Hiroshi asked.

"No. But he wouldn't let it go. He hired investigators to dig into Onizuka's private life. Onizuka was a total sleaze-bag. He'd go gambling while Mayu did his work."

"What else did Mayu's father find? He said he'd talked to you many times."

Steve looked away. "Yes, I wasn't up front about that because I was worried about him, about what he'd do. He also knew that Mayu had discovered Onizuka was funneling money overseas, in and out of various accounts, under his name and the company's name, and through Mayu's personal accounts, too."

"What else did her father tell you?"

"How controlling Mayu's mother was. I never liked her much. She acted nice and understanding, but she was the one who talked Mayu out of quitting each time she broke down. If her mother had really supported her..."

"What about her friends? Suzuna, her best friend, what did she say?"

"Suzuna also begged Mayu to quit. She was the angriest of all when Mayu...when she, uh, killed herself. They were like sisters."

"How did you know Suzuna was angry?"

"Angry isn't the right word, more like determined. I always thought she was kind of a flake, but she formed a support group for women harassed at companies. Working is an addiction like any other, I guess."

"Like marijuana." Hiroshi stared at Steve.

Steve shook his head. "I was in the wrong place at the wrong time. I was just sitting in with that band."

"You saw Suzuna after Mayu's funeral?"

"If I needed anything, she helped...registering at the city office, finding an apartment, reading a contract."

"So you were close?"

"It hurt too much to be around each other. I was getting more gigs and some musicians kind of adopted me."

"Same ones you were busted with tonight?"

"I've been playing some rock gigs to make ends meet. It's a different crowd at clubs like this one."

The back door of the bus swung open and two agents had two more people to put inside.

"Looks like you had a good crowd for the music tonight," Hiroshi said. "The arrests keep coming."

Hiroshi and Takamatsu stoop-walked out of the bus.

"You're leaving me here?" Steve shouted. "No one even speaks English."

Hiroshi looked in at Steve. "We'll see you at the station. Sleep tight."

The agents handcuffed the two new arrests on the railing inside the bus and shoved the door closed.

The drug agents' lights were still spinning around, casting red and blue light over the small lane. People leaned out of overhead windows watching the scene. Some took photos. Local cops held gawkers at a distance.

Takamatsu lit up a cigarette and Hiroshi got pinged with a text. It was from Ueno, who must still be in the station, some papers in English.

Hiroshi scrolled through the PDFs. "Looks like this kid has prior arrests in the States."

Takamatsu smiled at Hiroshi. "Like I said."

"Drugs, possession of a weapon, driving while intoxicated."

"Those are hardly crimes in America, are they?" Takamatsu said.

Hiroshi put away his cellphone. "What's important from what Steve said is that Mayu was moving money for Onizuka."

"Back to the money, as always," Takamatsu said. "You always focus on the big connections, Hiroshi, with your international scams, money laundering, and global transfers, but a small focus might help here. What evidence do you have of Mayu moving money, other than her boyfriend's word? Did you even search Mayu's room?"

Hiroshi hadn't even thought of that. Her mother had moved after her death, but even if her old room was gone, there must be a trace of something among her things. Her mother would be the type to save everything.

Hiroshi said, "I'll take Akiko with me tomorrow."

Chapter 24

Toeing off his shoes in the *genkan*, Hiroshi called out, "*Tadaima*." He hoped Ayana would still be awake. Her shoes were there and the light was on, but there was no answer. The living room was dark and the kitchen lights set low. Usually, Ayana left them on high, even if she went to bed.

Hiroshi went to the refrigerator and pulled out the water jug and drank straight from the top.

"Hiroshi?" Ayana mumbled from the sofa.

He spluttered water over himself. "Didn't you hear me come in?"

"I dreamed you came home." Ayana wiggled up, brushed her hair back and pulled the blanket onto her lap.

Hiroshi walked over and sat down next to her.

Ayana sniffed. "You're not drunk."

"I was working."

"That's what you say when you come home drunk."

"Why didn't you go to bed?"

"I didn't shower yet."

"Did you eat?"

"I was too tired."

"You have to eat something." Hiroshi put his arms around her.

Ayana leaned into him. "We finished another floor of the archive today. I was exhausted, but I went to kendo practice. That was a mistake."

"Mistake?"

"I thought a good workout would reset me, but it just drained the last of my reserves. What time is it?"

"Is there some of that pasta left?"

"I was saving it for you."

"Take a shower." Hiroshi stood and pulled her up from the sofa, turned her around and pushed her toward the shower. "I'll

187

heat the pasta."

Ayana slogged down the hall.

Hiroshi took the pasta out, pesto with mozzarella, and popped it in the microwave. He took two small tomatoes and cut them in quarters, sprinkled them with sweet red vinegar and let them drain. When the pasta warmed, he took the bowl out and slipped the tomatoes around the edges.

A bottle of red wine rested on the counter, open. Ayana hadn't been too tired to polish off half the bottle. Now who was drunk? He eyed the bottle. The thought of a drink made him shiver queasily. He took the pasta into the shower.

"Pasta delivery!" Hiroshi shouted.

"Why are you bringing that in here?" Ayana shouted.

"I have my reasons." Hiroshi waved a forkful in the air.

Ayana pulled the frosted-glass door open and Hiroshi poked at the pasta with the fork as he eyed her. She leaned forward for a bite, her skin, deliciously wet, flushed shades of red and pink.

"How is it?" Hiroshi asked.

"A little watery," Ayana said, wiping her lips.

"Lean farther out."

"I'll be out in a minute!"

"Just one more bite." Hiroshi held out another forkful.

She pushed the shower head aside, twisted her hair back, and leaned forward with her eyes on Hiroshi's.

Hiroshi tucked one of the tomatoes into her mouth, and then another.

"OK. Let me finish my shower!"

"I don't think so," Hiroshi said. "Supper before bath. Every kid knows that."

"I already ate." Ayana took another forkful. "You're getting water all over." Ayana slid the door shut.

Hiroshi set down the half-empty bowl on the sink, pulled off his clothes, opened the door and slipped in behind her. "I need a shower, too." He wrapped his arms around her and started nibbling the back of her neck.

"Don't. My legs are barcly holding me up," Ayana said.

Hiroshi continued.

"It's too slippery in here."

Ayana wiggled to the side and let the full force of the water whack Hiroshi in the face.

He grabbed the nylon scrubbing cloth, loaded it with soap, and ran the hard, scratchy cloth over her body.

"I'm too tired to stand up in here," Ayana said, pressing her hands against the tile to hold herself up against the rough scrubbing.

Hiroshi hummed. "All that wine."

"All that work. All that kendo." She twisted aside. "Enough!"

Hiroshi soaped the cloth and scrubbed himself. They rinsed together and turned off the water. Ayana stepped out and handed him a towel from the rack. "We need new towels."

"We need showers together."

Hiroshi dried off, tossed the towel on the rack and pulled Ayana toward the bed.

"My hair is dripping wet."

Hiroshi took a towel and wrapped it around her head. He held her tight as they walked like a quadruped toward the bed.

***

Afterwards, they lay together, loose and tangled, and stared at the ceiling.

"I've got to dry my hair." Ayana wriggled off the bed and went to the bathroom.

Hiroshi scooted to the edge and followed her to brush his teeth. "I talked to my uncle today," he shouted over the noise of the hair dryer.

"I can't hear you," Ayana said. She clicked off the hair dryer and gave him a look.

"I said I talked to my uncle today."

Ayana looked at him. "Did I know you have an uncle?"

"My cousin had a baby."

"And you have a cousin?" Ayana shook her head, and then clicked the hair dryer back on.

Hiroshi started thinking of what Takamatsu said about the ways up to and down from the roof. He went into the bedroom and pulled on a T-shirt. He pulled the wet cover futon off and folded it on the floor. He yanked down blankets from the storage closet and spread them over the bed instead.

Ayana came in with her hair in a tied-up ponytail and pulled on a T-shirt and underwear. Hiroshi flopped onto the bed. They pulled the dry blankets over themselves and clung together in the dark.

"Let's move to Boston," Hiroshi said.

"What would I do there?"

"Teach kendo. Work in a library. Open a flower shop."

"What about you?"

"I'd take the license exam for accounting. I guess I'm trapped for life."

"You don't have a green card. And neither do I," Ayana said.

"We'll figure it out."

She pulled back and looked at his face. "What brought all this on?"

"This case."

"The dead *bucho* at the media company?"

"The Japanese system crushes people's souls."

"Is this a new insight?" Ayana asked.

"Who's going to miss one more terrible boss?"

"When I worked in my company, it was a self-contained universe. Inside, different rules applied. It took over your life, like a cult. All questions were already answered."

Hiroshi stared at the ceiling in the dark.

"It's nice to be with you sober for a change."

Hiroshi looked at her. "It's crushing me."

"What is?"

"Running around the city, finding nothing on top of nothing. Nothing's going to change. We might find the person who killed this asshole boss, but there'll just be another asshole boss to replace him. Senden is held up as one of Japan's great successes, upholding traditional values, leading Japan into the world economy, but even a suicide, a harassment trial, and a death at the same exact place doesn't faze them."

Ayana rubbed Hiroshi's chest and flipped her leg over his. "I think that's what was so hard. For me and for our classmate Kumiko, but worse for her. She couldn't find any footing outside the company system, couldn't find hope for a life outside. She was too resentful of the unfairness to stay in the company and too short of self-confidence to make it outside."

"She believed in the myth of the safe, secure, stable company life."

"She wanted to believe it, but couldn't."

"I'm glad you escaped." Hiroshi took her hand.

Ayana rolled onto her back. "You're an accountant who knows English in the homicide department. What are you going to do, restructure Japanese society?"

Hiroshi growled. "What galls me the most is the way they wrap it all in some myth of a hard-driving workplace. What they really do is run their companies like feudal estates. You can't keep that kind of power structure in place without losing a few peasants along the way."

Takamatsu accepted that things couldn't be changed. Sakaguchi focused on what he could do right. Maybe they understood better. Sunk into the idealism of numbers, he wanted the answers to come out correct at some point, the accounts to square, but maybe they never would. Other scams, and that cryptocurrency case, had really bugged him, but Senden kept spinning in his mind. Ayana said. "I found a book for you."

"A book?" Hiroshi massaged Ayana's hand, felt the strength from kendo and shelving, and the delicacy from...well, from her.

"From the archives. A history of labor in Japan."

"Labor?"

"We were reshelving the second floor, and there it was. All the archivists were reading through it together at lunch today. It had amazing photos of all kinds of jobs and workplaces in the past. You wouldn't believe."

"What'd it say?"

"After years of strikes and riots, some reforms were instituted in the Meiji period."

"That's a hundred years ago."

Ayana laughed. "Things take time in Japan. Back then, there were no unions, no protections, no health care like now. The book said that after the war, the company structure was what kept workers going. I looked up Senden. They were the first to build a company culture with group bonding and pledges of loyalty. They were the first to have workers hike together to the top of Mount Fuji, the first to use company badges, set up company housing, create a corporate identity," Ayana said.

"You mean employees don't just work there, their entire lives take place there, eating, drinking, marrying, celebrating, all inside the borders of the company."

"Like it or not, that's what saved the Japan after the war. It gave the country direction, a sense of belonging somewhere."

"It's what's killing the Japanese now." Hiroshi repositioned his pillow.

"I still think about Kumiko. We should go to her grave. I haven't been this year." Ayana pulled the covers over them and fluffed them in place. "Will you come with me?"

"Of course. And let's climb Mount Fuji," Hiroshi said.

"I'd like that," Ayana said. "High and low." She turned on her side and fell asleep immediately.

Hiroshi stayed awake for a long time thinking about the case, his thoughts jumping in too many directions at once, figuring out nothing.

Chapter 25

When Hiroshi got out of the car near the flower shop, the sun felt especially warm. A morning without a hangover, mental fog, or nausea was a delight and made him feel in control. He hoped it would last. He knew it wouldn't.

Sugamo, Akiko, and Takamatsu waited in the car.

Toshiko hurried out, dangling a set of keys and smiling politely. "Suzuna can look after the shop, but I need to be back before it gets busy. Is an hour enough?"

"It might take longer than that, I'm afraid," Hiroshi said.

"Well, I'll leave you there to look through everything." She sighed. "I better ride my bicycle and meet you there. It's the apartment building on the corner here." Toshiko showed Hiroshi on her cellphone map.

"We'll find it," Hiroshi said.

"I'll probably get there quicker than you." Toshiko got on her bicycle and Hiroshi and Akiko went back to the car.

Suzuna, in her working apron and sleeves with her blonde braids circled on top of her head, set down the buckets of water she carried and waved politely as they left.

Takamatsu was unusually quiet in the front seat, but Hiroshi didn't want to get him started.

After a few blocks, Takamatsu turned around and said, "You want me and Sugamo to go get started with Onizuka's widow? Meet up later?"

Hiroshi grinned. "I don't think we can trust you alone with a wealthy widow. Especially one who drinks in the daytime."

Takamatsu laughed.

Akiko squirmed in her seat.

Sugamo kept driving, turning and stopping in the narrow lanes.

Toshiko was right. The car was slower through the narrow neighborhood streets. The bicycle cut through back lanes without stopping, but the car lumbered through stoplights, school crossings, and local bus stops on every other corner where elderly passengers got on and off at their own, slow pace.

Hiroshi and Akiko got out in front of the apartment building on a busy corner of Mitaka, where Toshiko was waiting.

Takamatsu leaned out the window and said, "We'll see if Shibutani has recovered from his beating and can talk yet. Call us when you're done. We need to talk to Mistress Emi again too, so I'll get that arranged."

"We do?" Hiroshi asked.

"She contacted me." Takamatsu ducked inside as Sugamo pulled away.

Hiroshi shook his head and looked at Akiko, who said, "He probably contacted her."

Toshiko led them into her apartment building. The entry area was small and finished in polished marble, with shiny mailboxes on one side and a new elevator on the other. Hiroshi introduced Akiko.

Her apartment had a heavy door that Toshiko had to pull open using the weight of her body. Hiroshi and Akiko followed her inside, taking off their shoes and stepping onto the wood flooring. With a whoosh, the door sealed tight behind them.

Hiroshi thought the place large for just Toshiko and Suzuna. Four bedrooms and a living-dining-kitchen area of twenty-some tatami mats. The whole place was double the size of Ayana's apartment. Toshiko must have received a substantial settlement from the lawsuit against Senden.

"Your place is lovely," Akiko said.

Toshiko led them into the living area. In the corner was a large black lacquer *butsudan*. The home altar had its doors folded open. In front was a low shelf, a miniature version of those at temples, with a box of incense sticks, a pot with fine sand to hold the incense, and a bell on a purple, embroidered cushion. Inside the altar, a large photo of Mayu on a black and gold pedestal looked out with intense eyes. The photo was surrounded by flowers, a pyramid of oranges and stuffed animal mascots, maybe from her schools.

All of this was clean and carefully arranged, as if she had died the past year, not three years ago.

"Do you mind if we offer our condolences?" Hiroshi asked, sensing Toshiko was expecting them to. She lit one of the candles on the shelf for them to use.

Hiroshi knelt down on the square *zabuton* in front of the shiny gold interior of the altar. Akiko knelt beside him and Toshiko to the side. He turned on his knees and bowed to Toshiko, then twisted back to the altar.

A black and white photo of Mayu gazed back. Hiroshi took three sticks of incense from a small box and lit them from the candle before burying the ends in the ash-filled burner. The smell of sandalwood drifted up and around the room.

He took a small wooden stick and rang the brass bell on the cushion. The strike was loud and full, and filled the room, before lingering with a sustained tone. Hiroshi bowed his head deeply and then leaned back, lingering on Mayu's photo as the bell's pure tone decayed, remembering his mother's *butsudan*, and how he had knelt there on a cushion after her death, too numb to comprehend.

After a quiet minute on the *zabuton*, Hiroshi moved aside, bowing to Toshiko again, and scooting aside. Akiko followed Hiroshi.

When she climbed off the cushion, the three of them kneeled there in deep silence, legs folded below their bent bodies, the incense calling forth thoughts and memories and feelings that would go unsaid.

Toshiko stood up and said, "I have so many things to do at the shop. Why don't I just leave you two here to go through her things."

She led them down the hall. "Here's Suzuna's room. She keeps it so neat, and cleans up the rest of the apartment, too. Mayu did that, too. I feel guilty I don't do enough." At the end of the hall, she stopped at a closed door and took a breath. She opened the door and musty air flowed out.

The room was filled with moving boxes in neat stacks.

Toshiko glanced around, then looked at Hiroshi and Akiko. "I've unpacked a few things, but it was so painful to even move it from our old place. I didn't... I can't... well I'll sort through it one of these days. Everything of hers is in here."

Akiko said, "We'll be careful with everything and put it back in the same place."

Toshiko looked down, remaining in the hall. "I don't know what I was thinking to bring it all here."

Hiroshi said, "It'll help the investigation."

"What are you looking for exactly?" Toshiko asked.

"It's just procedure." Hiroshi looked around the room. Photos of Mayu were arranged along a desk and two stacks of clothing still on hangers lay folded on the bed.

Toshiko hesitated at the door, as if her daughter was somehow going to appear out of one of the boxes. "Call me and I'll come back to lock up."

Akiko said, "We'll call."

Toshiko bowed and left.

Hiroshi looked at the boxes in despair.

Akiko cleared her throat and dug into her bag. "I brought this." It was an orange box cutter.

"And tape?"

Akiko pulled out a roll of tape and set it by the photos of Mayu on the desk.

"And gloves?"

Akiko pulled out a box of latex gloves.

"I couldn't do anything without you. But I did bring these." Hiroshi pulled out a couple of small plastic evidence bags.

"You always carry those." Akiko cut open the first box and handed the box cutter to Hiroshi. The several dozen boxes, all the same size, made Hiroshi feel shrunken, like a kid in a room of blocks.

Hiroshi was not surprised at the cute knick-knacks, *omiyage* souvenirs, college logo goods, and stuffed animals, but he was startled by the sheer volume. After going through five boxes, he wondered when they'd discover something of use.

He slowed down when he got into a box with vinyl records, all jazz, no doubt from her boyfriend Steve—Mingus, Coltrane, Miles, Monk, Art Blakey, Stan Getz, Clifford Brown, Jimmy Smith, Ornette Coleman.

"Are you reading the back covers of *all* of those? We'll never get out of here," Akiko said, handing him the tape. "And what are we really looking for anyway?"

"Bank books. Anything with money transfers, credit cards, whatever."

"Well, unless she used the album covers to hide stuff…" Akiko ripped a loud, long strip of tape from the roll to close the box.

Hiroshi put the vinyl back, taped the box and moved it to the other side of the room. The next box held an amazing array of undershirts, T-shirts, and blouses that seemed incredibly small. All were folded perfectly.

"Can you take this box?" Hiroshi asked. "This is kind of obscene, rifling through a young woman's things."

"It's just gotten more obscene." Akiko held up a metal container that once held gift cookies or desserts. When Akiko shook it, it gave off a muffled rattle. She smiled as she held the cover aside.

"What's that?" Hiroshi took a step closer and looked inside.

The box held vibrators and dildos in varying sizes, shapes, and materials.

"Quite a collection," Akiko said. "A rabbit, a wand, one for outside and one for the deep spots. Probably trying to unwind from all the pressure at work."

"I thought she had a boyfriend?" Hiroshi said.

Akiko tilted her head to the side and stared at Hiroshi. "Maybe you need a primer on women's bodies?"

"Not right now," Hiroshi said, shaking his head at the array of cosmetics filling the box he had just opened. Beside them was a cataloged collection of photos of boy bands sold to teenagers in Harajuku.

Akiko taped up the box and cut open another

"This is interesting." Akiko pulled out a binder. "These are the rules for dressing at Senden. Five-centimeter heels, acceptable shades of eye shadow, the right style of business skirts, pants, tops, jackets. The body has to fit the corporate space according to these rules. Not easy. Of course, easier for men." Akiko flipped through the binder and put it back. "Reminds me of my two years in a company. I'm glad I took off for grad school in the States. I couldn't hack all that."

Hiroshi taped his box shut, stacked it on top of the others and sliced open a new one. Akiko shoved the box against the wall.

"Finally!" Hiroshi said. "Bankbook, ATM card, credit cards. This is it. And what's this?"

Akiko came over as Hiroshi opened a beige designer bag and pulled out a wrapped handful of ten-thousand-yen notes. He set it back and opened another bag, which was also full of cash. He set those back and looked at the bankbook. It was three years old, but the transfers in and out of her account were in large amounts, nothing less than a million yen, and many around ten million.

Akiko stooped down to fish out another set of passbooks from the bottom of the box. "And here's another stack." She held up the hand-sized bankbook with printed transactions from different banks, all the transfers in large amounts, and all neatly organized.

Hiroshi leaned over as Akiko flipped through them for the year before Mayu's death. Hiroshi stared at the numbers.

Akiko held the bankbooks up. "This is a little different from your usual investing scams."

"No, it's the same. Nothing adds up. Now, all we need to do is to check these against Onizuka's bank books."

"How are you going to get those?"

"I'm going to waltz into Onizuka's home and ask his widow for them." Hiroshi wondered if it would be that easy.

Chapter 26

"Where's Akiko?" Takamatsu asked, when Hiroshi got into the car. Sugamo looked back, curious.

"She's taking evidence back to headquarters. There might be prints on some of the bankbooks. We took photos of everything," Hiroshi explained, patting his cellphone.

Toshiko had returned to lock up, but Hiroshi and Akiko had simply said they would bring everything back. Toshiko looked surprised at the multiple bankbooks, as if she'd never seen them. Maybe she packed everything in a daze, or Suzuna had packed them.

"How was Shibutani?"

"Still sleeping. Nothing to do but wait."

"So, back to Onizuka's home?" Sugamo asked.

"Exactly," Hiroshi said. "Still nothing on the security cameras?"

"The glue looks promising," Takamatsu said. "Lab guys told me there were two kinds of residue."

"Two kinds? Glue and...?"

"Up there for different amounts of time. Glue doesn't decay much, but enough to tell," Takamatsu said.

Sugamo said, "Those lab guys seem to know every substance in the universe."

"They were taped over twice?" Hiroshi hummed. "We need to get the tech guys to look again at the footage from the night of Mayu's suicide."

Sugamo said, "Speaking of substances, Osaki and I went to that S&M hotel. More clothes than you'd think get discarded there, and not retrieved."

"For oh so many reasons." Takamatsu chuckled.

Sugamo continued, "We dug through the trash for Onizuka's clothes, found a tailored suit and wool overcoat with his DNA. So at least we know he was there, or his clothes were. But no watch or cellphone."

"The cellphone would have helped immensely," Hiroshi said.

"The phone records haven't turned up, either." Takamatsu took out a cigarette and cracked a window.

"Are they still working on the video footage?"

Takamatsu grunted. "Used to be we could get a day's work done without getting motion sickness from forwarding through one damn video after the next. Working a case on the street used to—"

"Those cameras stop a certain percentage of crimes and solve another percentage," Hiroshi said.

"And miss the whole point," Takamatsu said. "Still, I think I figured out how they got past the cameras."

"How who got past the cameras?" Hiroshi scrolled through the photos he'd taken of the bankbooks from Mayu's room.

"I don't know who yet, but the lab guys are testing out my theory on how. They'll call later."

They rode the rest of the way in silence.

***

Sugamo pressed the bell in the side wall of the front gate at Onizuka's home. Without any response, the gate rolled aside and they pulled to the turnaround at the end of the drive. The son's Mercedes-Benz was nowhere to be seen. Beyond the house, the smooth grass lawn, cut low, swept around the single pagoda with nothing else to break up the expanse. Hiroshi wondered if that was intentional, with some hidden meaning, or if it was just the indifference of people who had more money than taste.

Despite Takamatsu's description of the wife's appeal, Sugamo declined to come in. "I don't like drunk women."

Hiroshi and Takamatsu knocked on the door.

Takamatsu whispered, "Don't mention the S&M mistress."

Hiroshi whispered back. "Thanks for the tip."

"She probably knew anyway."

From inside, loud footsteps came stomping toward them, then a bash against something heavy and the quick crash of ceramic.

Takamatsu turned an ear to the door.

Silence followed.

Hiroshi put his ear to the door.

The door lock clicked, and Hiroshi snatched the handle, but too late. The lock clicked, and Hiroshi pulled, but it didn't budge.

It clicked again and Hiroshi yanked. Onizuka's wife came tumbling out into Hiroshi's arms. He steadied her with his hands on her shoulders and waited while she regained her balance and brushed her long, tangled hair into place. The smell of alcohol leached from her body. Her face was red beneath messy make-up.

"Oh, you two. Lots of unexpected visitors today. I was expecting my son," she said.

Hiroshi gave Takamatsu a look. She was loaded.

"Onizuka-*san*, are you OK?" Hiroshi asked, steadying her.

"Come on in and find out," she said, feigning sobriety and turning inside. "You're the detectives."

"You remember us? I'm Hiroshi Shimizu and this is Detective Takamatsu," Hiroshi said. A ceramic pot lay broken in the *genkan*.

"Call me Natsuko. Especially if you're going to be stopping by every day." She laughed as she stepped up onto the inner floor. She kicked the ceramic shards aside with her feet.

They followed her in to the living room where they'd sat before, the smell of alcohol drifting behind her like a perfume gone wrong.

Natsuko flopped onto the sofa. She had a glass of something brown and un-iced in front of her in a tumbler. Even drunk, she was strikingly attractive. A long model's body with lively, if glassy, eyes and thick hair. She looked at the detectives. "Did you find who killed my husband? Or did you decide he managed to do that himself?"

Hiroshi said, "We have a few more questions."

"Well sit down and fire away." Natsuko looked back and forth at them. It seemed like she'd slept on the sofa. Pillows and blankets were tossed around.

Hiroshi said, "Was your husband upset, depressed, or distracted recently?"

"He was always in various stages of distraction." She looked surprised to see the drink in front of her, but reached down and took a sip.

Takamatsu sighed and went to the kitchen.

Hiroshi tried to determine just how drunk Natsuko was. He could smell the booze coming from deep inside her.

Takamatsu came back with a large glass of water. "Onizuka-san—"

"I said call me Natsuko." She giggled. "I'm getting rid of Onizuka pretty soon. Soon as I can file the form at the city office."

Takamatsu said, "OK, Natsuko-san, could you get some water in yourself? And let me take this." Takamatsu, usually the one encouraging everyone to drink, took the glass of whiskey, or whatever it was, and whisked it off to the kitchen.

Hiroshi waited while she drank the water in big child-like gulps. "We asked this before, but was your husband having money troubles?"

Natsuko shook her head. "I think it was just the opposite. He kept saying he was tired of being frugal. A few months ago, he bought a car for both sons, though one is still abroad. The son, not the car. He got me a new car, too, but my son took the keys away. And took the car away, too."

Hiroshi nodded. "And do you know about his bank accounts? Was he—"

"They're all over there. In that top drawer." Natsuko pointed to an antique *tansu*. "I quit paying attention to all that when the boys' college tuition was done. I have my secret *hesokuri* account, like all good housewives, but he kept pressing money on me. I barely paid attention, though once or twice the credit card company called—"

Takamatsu took over. "Did your husband gamble or have other, well, expenses?"

She launched into a digression on overseas gambling junkets—roulette and blackjack in Macau and Las Vegas, horse racing in Melbourne, Dubai, and Louisville, being comped in casinos, a lifetime of top-tier gambling.

While Takamatsu kept her talking, Hiroshi went to the top drawer of the low, wide *tansu*. Bankbooks, deposit and withdrawal slips, *hanko* personal seals, a jar of change and money clips pinching folds of cash were scattered in the otherwise empty drawer. It looked like she tossed anything related to money inside. Probably loaded it up at tax time and gave the whole mess to her accountant. Hiroshi picked up the bankbooks and carried them to the chair across from Natsuko.

Natsuko smiled at him. "Did you find what you wanted? I'm so sick of the whole thing. As for the gambling, he said he stopped when he was promoted. If I'd known he was a gambler I would never have married him. My father gambled. Lost everything. I told my older son the whole story."

Takamatsu said, "How do you know he stopped?"

Natsuko smiled. "Well, he's not kicking the furniture. But I guess he just stopped kicking the furniture, but kept on gambling. He told me to change the passwords on all the accounts, which I did, but he just opened his own, I guess."

Takamatsu nodded soothingly. "Did you share accounts or keep separate ones?"

Natsuko nodded at Hiroshi. "You can see for yourself. All the bankbooks are there."

"Did you control all of the household finances?" Takamatsu asked.

"Long ago, I controlled all the payments and gave him a monthly *okozukai*. He liked it that way, he said. It kept him on a leash and he couldn't spend too much," she explained.

"About how much allowance did you give him?"

"Ninety-thousand yen. That's more than most men get, but he was a *bucho*, so he needed to take his subordinates out for drinks." She laughed, thinking about it. "But like most things with him, the allowance was a charade. He accessed our accounts all the time. Moved money around, spent what he liked. I quit looking."

Hiroshi said, "Do you think your husband had accounts overseas?"

Natsuko thought about that. "He probably did. But like I said, when the boys graduated, I quit paying attention." She started looking through the blankets and under the pillows on the sofa, then going back through them all, standing up and bending over, her butt pointed right at the two detectives.

Takamatsu suppressed a smile.

She really was drunk. Hiroshi shook his head. "What are you looking for?"

"My cellphone. It's either in my purse or it slipped between the cushions."

"Where's your purse?"

"There it is." Natsuko picked up her cellphone and started punching the buttons. She clicked and scrolled through. Her nails were long, squared at the ends, and two had broken off. Hiroshi wondered how she could type with them, but she did.

They waited as she checked and frowned, checked again.

"Did you find anything?" Hiroshi asked.

After considerable scrolling and inputting of numbers, she held the cellphone up to Hiroshi.

Hiroshi took it and looked at it carefully, scrolling up and down puzzling over the deposits, transfers, and withdrawals. "When was the last time you checked this account?"

Natsuko shrugged and Hiroshi looked at her carefully. She looked away, thinking. "Maybe last year."

"You haven't looked at it since then? Are you sure?" Hiroshi asked, not looking up, but scrolling further and further in the monthly statements.

"He took my password and used it, then I changed it and he never said a word. But he figured it out again, starting using it again. I changed it again. I thought he'd explode, but he didn't even notice. He'd moved on in all kinds of ways by then."

"There's a lot of money in here," Hiroshi said.

"What's a *lot*?" Natsuko looked around.

"Do you know where it came from?"

She started to get up. "I need a drink. Would you detectives like something?"

"Onizuka-*san*. Natsuko. I think you need to stop drinking. Do you want us to call one of your sons?"

Natsuko looked down at the table in front of her. "One is overseas and one is working. They're turning out just like their father, only split in two, each with one side of their father's personality." Tears started in her eyes, but didn't spill over her puffy lids as she blinked and looked away.

"I'll return these," Hiroshi said, holding up the bankbooks. "We just need to check them at the station. Is that all right?"

"Sure. Check 'em wherever you like." Natsuko waved OK, her hand dancing in the air. "All you'll find is numbers."

"Can't we call your son to come over? Or someone else?" Takamatsu asked.

"I just need to sleep. To start over. Sleep and start over." Natsuko pulled her feet up on the sofa, dragged a blanket over herself, and looked at them with big eyes. "Can you detectives see yourselves out?"

Hiroshi and Takamatsu looked at each other, wondering what to do. Takamatsu tapped his watch and shrugged.

Chapter 27

Hiroshi leaned back in his office chair and stretched. He'd been matching withdrawal, deposit, and transfer slips from Onizuka's and Mayu's accounts for hours and his eyes were starting to ache and his shoulders stiffen. Mayu was amazingly organized, but the mess from Onizuka canceled that out.

Akiko said, "Why don't you take a break? You skipped lunch."

"OK, let's order something, whatever you like." Hiroshi eyed the espresso machine, but stayed away. "I'm getting jittery."

"Ramen?"

"Sure, something light, *asari* or *shoyu*." He pulled his futon chair out and unfolded it to its horizontal shape.

"Get some blood in your head. You're going to need it before we can assemble all these bank transfers into a single flow chart." Akiko called a nearby shop to deliver two bowls of ramen.

Hiroshi stretched out on the futon chair and immediately his cellphone buzzed. He should have left it in a drawer out of earshot. It was his uncle. That was nice, but he didn't have time to chat. He'd call him back after the case was finished. Closing his eyes felt like heaven after eyeballing numbers on the screen all afternoon.

"Hiroshi?" Akiko called.

"Is the ramen here?" He'd fallen asleep.

"I think you better see this." Akiko leaned toward her computer screen.

Hiroshi pulled his legs over the side and forced himself to his feet. The ramen bowls, one empty, one still covered in plastic, sat on a tray by the espresso machine.

"Why didn't you wake me when the ramen came?"

"I tried," Akiko said. "Get over here."

He stretched as he stepped over and stood behind Akiko.

Streaming from Nihon TV was a press conference. Five chairs lined up in front of a long table behind which hung the Senden Central Infinity logo. Camera flashes popped in staccato bursts, bleaching the table and logo.

"Turn it up, can you?"

Akiko slid the volume control.

On the screen, Chizu, the HR assistant, came around in front of the table to set out name plates. She adjusted the gooseneck microphones and set papers in front of each spot along the table.

"Can you record this?" Hiroshi asked.

Akiko clicked the screen recording.

"How did you find this?"

"I set a feed for news about Senden."

Hiroshi stared at the screen. The camera pulled back to a large conference room with journalists seated in chairs and photographers jockeying for position.

On screen, the room came to a hush.

The company president, Tanaka, and three other executives in dark suits, including Nakata, head of HR, walked in solemnly, turned toward the audience, and bowed deeply, hands at their sides. The video lights brightened and cameras clicked rapidly. After a long pause with their heads down, the men sat down stiffly in their appointed chairs.

"Pull up NHK news and one other station, too, can you?" Hiroshi said.

"I've got the tech guys recording all of them," Akiko said.

Hiroshi looked at her for a second, wondering how he could have been so lucky.

Akiko looked at him, frowned at him looking at her, and returned to her screen.

The company president started to speak. "Today, we are regretful to call this press conference about one of our former colleagues, Shigeru Onizuka. As reported, he fell from the roof of our headquarters this past week and died. We pray for his soul and send our condolences to his family." They all bowed deeply again.

"We also have unfortunate news to report about Onizuka. We had long been aware of improprieties connected with our move to internationalize and expand our business to other countries. We must now deliver some very unfortunate revelations about this difficult transition to international status."

A hush fell over the room and the camera flashes stopped.

"It appears that, pending further investigation and auditing of last year's budget, the deceased, Onizuka, may have been involved in financial irregularities connected to the international expansion. We deeply regret this and apologize profoundly."

Cameras started clicking.

"For this indiscretion and oversight, there is no one to blame other than those here at this table. Our supervision and guidance was insufficient, and for that we take full responsibility. After a thorough review of these problems, and an exhaustive examination of the issues, we have reset our budgetary priorities and personnel policies so that this will never happen again. These changes will allow us to continue to offer the highest quality services to our clients. As president, I sincerely apologize for this mistake." All of the executives bowed deeply.

"And now our chief financial officer will read a statement." He turned to the executive at the far end.

Hiroshi said, "They're dumping this on Onizuka? How convenient. They'll apologize, someone will resign, and they'll shut us out from finding what really happened."

The chief financial officer of Senden picked up his prepared statement. "I was remiss in not discovering this issue earlier and rooting out the cause of this. Sadly, with the passing of Onizuka many issues came to light, and the reasons for his suicide—"

"Suicide?" Akiko shouted.

Hiroshi cleared his throat with an angry rumble.

The CFO continued. "Budgets for advertising were not totaled correctly, which impacted what we charged our clients. Refunds are forthcoming. In addition, budget payments were not processed in a timely way. We've corrected that. And finally, invoicing and collection of payments from overseas customers is now reformed, with new procedures to be followed precisely." He paused and looked at the room, his hands shaking slightly, and continued. "I will from this moment resign as CFO of Senden. I have worked here my entire career and am ashamed to have failed the company that took care of me so well "

The CFO stood up and bowed ninety degrees before sitting back down.

The president pulled his mic closer and said, "Now our head of Human Resources will make a statement."

Nakata, the head of HR, gave a curt nod and picked up the prepared statement in front of him. "As head of Human Resources, I oversaw an internal investigation which formed the foundation to update our policies so that we can handle personnel issues efficiently and discreetly." He pointed at a screen at the side of the hall. A Powerpoint slide projected onto the empty white space. "As you can see, we have reconfigured HR to reflect the current values of our newly reformed workplace. We have rewritten the handbook for workplace interactions to include the latest organizational research and best practices. Finally, on this slide you can see our latest figures on overtime. Because one of our former, sadly deceased, employees, Mayu Yamase—"

"Finally, they mentioned the poor girl," Akiko said, sitting on her hands and leaning forward.

Nakata continued uninterrupted. "—was found to have worked more than one hundred hours of overtime in the last month of her life. From today forward, we now have a system regulating overtime work and contact between employees outside of regular working hours. We name our new system in her honor, and informally call it 'The Mayu Rule.' These new principles and practices will ensure overtime is reduced, and when it occurs, receives compensation. These will all be implemented as of today and are to be inviolable upon condition of dismissal. That applies to all employees."

On the screen, the president stood up and all of the executives joined him, bowing to the assembled media. Hiroshi caught a glimpse of Chizu standing at the far side of the hall as the camera followed the executives retreating out a side door. Chizu collected the prepared statements before bowing to the room and following the executives out the door.

The TV station returned to the studio, where commentators sat around a semi-circular table and started summarizing and commentating on what had been said. The roundtable included a lawyer for a union group, a former Senden employee, a business professor, and a reporter who covers economics. The commentators started nodding and answering questions from the announcers.

"He didn't resign," Hiroshi said.

"Who?"

"Nakata. The head of HR. He's the one who ignored the complaints from Mayu. Nothing happened to him."

"And they said it was suicide? Where did that come from?" Akiko fidgeted in her chair.

Hiroshi folded his arm and leaned on his desk. "They're trying to get out ahead of whatever we find. This announcement will buffer whatever we find and deflate the scandal before it even happens."

Akiko pounded her fist on her desk. "But the accounts and transfers speak for themselves. Look at how it all lines up. And that's just what we found today."

"We still need to connect all that to the company. And we can't do that unless we can get a peek inside their files. With this announcement, they can contend that Onizuka went rogue. Contrive plausible deniability. Play it out in the press. They sacrificed those two, who are dead anyway, to keep the company above reproach."

"Can we connect it all?"

"We'll find a way."

"We also have these tweets." Akiko held out a printout.

Hiroshi took it and started reading. "This isn't from Mayu—"

"The tech guys are tracing who it's from. These tweets about Onizuka proliferated in the weeks after he died."

Hiroshi looked at the long list of tweets complaining about conditions, demanding changes, criticizing Onizuka, and berating Senden. "Why didn't you tell me about these before?"

"We were working on the bank transfers."

Hiroshi hummed, frustrated that he was so slow in pulling together what he should have realized before. "These tweets could only be from one source. We need to head back to Kichijoji."

"To the flower shop?" Akiko scrolled through her computer. "There's a meeting of the support group tonight. And I'll send you these new tweets, organized into groups."

Hiroshi called Takamatsu and told him to get Sugamo and a car and meet him at the front door right away.

He pulled on his coat and gave Akiko an apologetic frown. "Can you pull all of today's work into a single flow chart? We're going to need it."

"Aren't you going to eat your ramen?"

Hiroshi looked at the bowl, but stood over it reading a LINE message. When he finished, he hurried off without another word.

Chapter 28

Outside the station, Hiroshi read the LINE message from Chizu again and pulled his coat tight against the cold. The sun had set and the wind had stopped, but the cold came on harder. Takamatsu stepped out from the front door without a word and lit a cigarette, nodding to some detectives coming in. He seemed to know everyone and Hiroshi, with his office in the annex, felt like he knew almost no one.

"The woman from HR at Senden, Chizu, texted."

"Is that where we're going?"

"She called from the toilet, so she—"

"From the toilet?" Takamatsu nodded at detectives going home for the night.

"The only safe place in a company for women to call from. She wants to meet, but wasn't sure when."

Takamatsu blew his smoke up high into the air.

"She found out something about Mayu."

"But we're investigating what happened to Onizuka." Takamatsu put out his cigarette in the upright ashtray outside the station.

"Mayu had been filing complaints almost from the time she started working at Senden. The complaints would be considered and rejected. She'd get moved out of Onizuka's section, and then, she'd get moved back into Onizuka's section. She'd file, wait, transfer out, have it denied, and get moved back in."

"Does Chizu have the files in hand?" Takamatsu looked for Sugamo and the car.

"She wants to hand them over in person."

"We should have brought her in, for protection." Takamatsu fidgeted with his lighter. Sugamo pulled into the parking lot and eased toward them.

"Chizu is probably getting squeezed like Mayu. Why not bring her in?"

"It seemed like she wants to take us to the files but doesn't have them yet."

"We could go with her. Or get a warrant and raid the place, if she'll still show us."

"I thought you liked to leave people hanging as bait?"

"Not everyone." Takamatsu blew his smoke up high into the air. "Did all the bank transfers line up?"

"The money in and out of Mayu's account matched the same amount in and out of Onizuka's account." Hiroshi waved at Sugamo across the parking lot.

Sugamo flicked his headlights. Hiroshi and Takamatsu started walking to Sugamo through the busy, crowded lot.

"But you know where the money went, right?" Takamatsu asked.

"Chizu said she had something on tha, too. We're supposed to meet her in the middle of the night to look over the files."

"You better go alone on that one." Takamatsu chuckled. "She's a looker."

"There's nothing like that," Hiroshi said.

"There's always something like that. Lighten up a bit. This case is getting to you."

Hiroshi grunted, but Takamatsu was right. She was a looker, and the case was getting to him. "Chizu said there's a storage facility for all the files. Don't you remember what the accountant Kato said?"

Takamatsu cleared his throat. He didn't remember. Maybe the case was getting to him, too, if he forgot a conversation. He usually recalled every minute detail.

"Remember how Kato said they misfiled the important materials, so only a few people knew how to find them. I'm hoping Chizu is one of those people. If we raid the place, and Chizu stays silent, we'll find nothing."

"Do you think Mayu knew that filing system too?"

"She must have."

Takamatsu hummed. "Was Onizuka forcing Mayu to help him with embezzled funds or his own money?"

"Or both. Or neither. That's what we need to find out." Hiroshi looked out the window.

"I don't like these company things. Too many bad guys in good suits. No wonder those women get chewed up there." Takamatsu put out his cigarette.

Sugamo stopped the car. Hiroshi got in the back and Takamatsu in the front.

Sugamo pulled out of the lot and into traffic. "Where to?"

"A woman's support group, an S&M bar, and a storage facility," Hiroshi said.

"Won't need evidence bags then?" Sugamo said.

"Not the regular kind anyway," Takamatsu said. "Nothing's opened this case up yet, but maybe tonight's trifecta will."

Hiroshi looked out the window. "They're all we've got, but they each might take time."

"Another long night," Sugamo said. I've been pulling double shifts at home, my wife's working extra hours getting the budget done at her company."

"You can nap in the car outside," Takamatsu said.

"What's your wife do?" Hiroshi asked.

"Accounting, like you, but she's just *hakken*. As much work as a regular employee, but half the pay." Sugamo stopped at an intersection.

"Temp workers are supposed to—"

"Yeah, they're supposed to be paid the same, but they aren't. Not even close," Sugamo said. "My wife knows exactly how much the full-time, regular employees make because she prepares the payment slips for them." He honked the horn at a car that pulled across the intersection late. It was the first time Hiroshi had ever seen him impatient.

"She should—"

"She should have taken her job-hunting seriously as a student, but she didn't. She shouldn't have married a detective either. Now, with two kids, and my hours, she wishes she had more stability. Anyway, she's studying for the next level of accounting license." Sugamo looked at Hiroshi in the rearview mirror.

"I can give her some tips sometime," Hiroshi said.

"Thanks," Sugamo said. "Anyway I got some sleep after my kid fell asleep after school. They overwork the kids so they're cranky and sleepy every day."

"Preparation for company life," Takamatsu said.

"What did I miss all day?" Sugamo asked.

"Just the Senden press conference."

"Press theater, you mean?"

"They handle PR for themselves first and foremost."

"What did they say?"

Hiroshi added, "It was all apology, the universal solvent of Japanese society."

Takamatsu said, "If they wanted to really apologize, they would have *all* resigned."

Sugamo said, "How many did resign?"

"Just one." Hiroshi looked out the window. "Meanwhile, they made Onizuka appear to be a faithful employee, the embezzlement a mild mistake, and overtime a sign of conscientiousness. And then they presented the company as the premiere global corporation in Japan. Progressive regulations on overtime, new policies on harassment, a global vision based on foreign, and Japanese values both. It was a nicely wrapped package."

"I've never known you to be so sarcastic, Hiroshi." Takamatsu turned to him in the back seat.

"That's your influence," Hiroshi said.

Sugamo pulled through a large four-way intersection and headed for the on-ramp for the Shuto Expressway that would take them crosstown to Kichijoji. Sugamo drove faster than he usually did.

Hiroshi sighed and leaned against the glass. "After today, I can see how the Senden people are pros at PR. They can now keep us from digging into their accounts and into Onizuka's death. They can just say it's all taken care of, no need to help."

Takamatsu chuckled. "I was ready to toss this one back and forget about it. One dead salaryman, who cares? But it was the glue that did it for me."

"Did they find out more?" Sugamo asked.

Takamatsu flicked his cigarette out the window. "If there was a video record of Onizuka anywhere in there, and if the company had helped us from the beginning, maybe I'd let it go. But now, we've got to take this all the way inside. There was glue all over the cameras, some put there recently, some years ago."

Hiroshi twisted in his seat. "Is this new insight coming from your intuition, your anger,or from the facts?"

"Mostly from the lab guys. But I always follow my intuition. The facts fall into place after. Or at least before I write the report."

"But they don't always fit, do they?" Sugamo asked.

Takamatsu nodded. "Not always, no. I would like to have shoved Onizuka off the roof myself after hearing how he did things. But what you have to understand is that the last vestige of ancient feudal values resides in those corporations. If we were dealing with a more modern, more humanized institution, I'd say let them handle it internally, tell us the result. They should have disbanded the *zaibatsu* after the war."

"I thought they did." Sugamo kept a steady pace along the expressway. Evening traffic was heavy and everyone seemed to be heading west.

"The restructuring didn't much affect the vertical connections between companies. If anything, the horizontal relations between industries were tightened and strengthened. Every company's locked into every other one. That network *is* the economy." Takamatsu turned and looked at Hiroshi and then at Sugamo. "Isn't that right, Hiroshi?"

Hiroshi nodded. "A single company produced everything from sugar to machinery to insurance. They hired textile workers, factory workers, architects, doctors, an army of workers all working together in the same family. Everything they produce is stamped with the family's name, and everyone is part of the family. Senden's a perfect example. They control everything, or think they do."

Sugamo grunted. "It's like the historical dramas my wife watches on NHK. I can't keep the connections straight."

"It's impossible to keep them straight even when you know what they are," Takamatsu said.

Sugamo pulled the car to a stop in the heavy evening traffic, sighed and twisted to see how far the traffic jam stretched. "So, you're suggesting Onizuka was murdered because he posed a threat to the company's reputation?"

"If it ends up being that easy, I'll be happy," Takamatsu said. "I would have been happy to pin it on that American, but he couldn't have set all that up."

"The father could have, though," Hiroshi said.

"You want to have another go at him? We hardly even pressed him before." Takamatsu turned around again to look at Hiroshi. He turned back. "I believe the father, though."

"I bought his story too. And he told us a lot," Hiroshi said. "And we're supposed to be checking people off the list, but they seem to be staying on the list, and for more reasons."

Sugamo looked back at Hiroshi. "Even the dead guy himself is still a suspect."

Hiroshi got a text from Akiko of the tweets directed at Onizuka. There were even more than the ones Akiko found before.

Hiroshi texted Akiko. "You're a huge help."

"I know."

"Go home and get some sleep."

"And a long hot bath."

Hiroshi started explaining what Akiko had found. "The tech guys said these tweets all come from the same account, but the main point is that they become increasingly threatening."

"Threatening?" Sugamo asked.

Hiroshi kept scrolling and reading. "We have all the tweets allowed into court during the trial."

"When Mayu's mother sued the company?"

"Yes, and another list of tweets that were disallowed at trial."

"Disallowed? Why would they—"

"The company lawyers must have gone through and excluded them. Anyway, we can ask the lawyer again. The support group meeting, Overtime Anonymous, is at seven in the flower shop." Hiroshi's cellphone buzzed. Chizu texted where to meet later that night.

Takamatsu turned around. "Is that the HR girl? She's in the privacy of the toilet again?"

Hiroshi nodded. "Must be."

"Let's go get her. Where is she? I don't like her wandering around," Takamatsu said.

"Are you going to bring the S&M mistress in too? Worried about her?" Hiroshi asked.

"I'm worried about her in a different way, but she must know how to take care of herself. She'll meet us at a bar later tonight."

Hiroshi called Chizu back, but she didn't answer, and until they got to Kichijoji, she didn't text back, either.

Chapter 29

Sugamo pulled close to the flower shop in Kichijoji. On the smaller streets farther from the station there was little traffic and the streetlights caught the heads and backs of bicyclists whizzing by and pedestrians heading home or out to dinner.

Hiroshi got out across from the shop and planted his feet on the sidewalk, thinking. The flowers that spread along the sidewalk in the daytime had been taken inside, leaving a long row of windows on either side with dark-green houseplants blocking the view of the interior. A sign said "Closed," but light trickled out.

Takamatsu rolled the window down. "We'll wait in the car. You won't be long, will you? You're just asking them about the tweets?"

"If someone comes out, stop them," Hiroshi said. "Suzuna's got be the one who knew Mayu's secrets, and the others probably know some of them too."

Sugamo and Takamatsu nodded in silence and looked for a good place to park the car, and for Takamatsu to smoke.

Hiroshi knocked on the door, peering around the window shade. After a shuffle of chairs, muffled voices and soft steps, the door rattled open.

Suzuna smiled at him, her face half-shadowed behind the door. In a thick wool sweater and blonde braids, she looked more like a Swiss farm girl than a Japanese city girl, but maybe that was the idea.

"Are you looking for Toshiko, Mayu's mother? She's at home right now," Suzuna said.

"Actually, I was hoping to talk with you," Hiroshi said.

"Me?" Suzuna strained her face to smile. "Well, could we talk tomorrow?"

"Tonight is better." Hiroshi leaned toward her.

Suzuna looked into the shop and then back at Hiroshi. "We're having a meeting now. Could it wait?"

"Is this your support group meeting? Mayu's mother told me about it. Maybe I could pick up something from the other people, something that would help."

Suzuna looked back inside again, keeping the door half covering herself. "We mostly just complain."

"That's just what I'd like to hear. Mind if I take a little time from your meeting?" Hiroshi pushed forward and Suzuna stepped back.

From the counter where he'd eaten lunch two days before, Hiroshi saw the startled faces of the group of women staring at him, squinting curiously.

The rich smell of plants and earth, so powerful and pleasant in the day, was stronger at night. Suzuna locked the door and followed him back to the circle.

Hiroshi smiled at the women, all in their late twenties or early thirties. They seemed to be holding their breath. "I'm Detective Hiroshi and I'm just following up on Mayu. And Onizuka. Do you mind if I sit down and ask a few questions? It would help immensely with the investigation."

The women looked confused, but one stood up and offered him her chair. Hiroshi sat down and nodded politely. They averted their eyes. Only Suzuna looked at him, her face hard with concern.

One woman, slightly older-looking than the rest, said, "We were about finished for today."

One of the women had red eyes, a wet nose, and downcast eyes, clutching a wad of wet tissues. Hiroshi must have interrupted her story.

Suzuna said, "I guess everyone can—"

"I'd like everyone to stay, actually," Hiroshi said. "I think my questions concern all of you."

Suzuna looked at him more closely.

Hiroshi pulled out the printed list of tweets that Akiko had given him and placed it on the table.

The women, who had not introduced themselves, scanned it one by one and passed it on without reaction.

"Do any of you know who wrote these?" Hiroshi pulled the list up on his cellphone and read off the threats. "'Onizuka should be killed.' 'Beat the *bucho*.' 'Harass him.' 'Resign or die.' 'Resignation letter up his ass.' I'm sure all of these are just for fun and not unusual at most workplaces. But then again, Mayu and Onizuka dying at the same place is too much coincidence."

The women fidgeted in their chairs, but Hiroshi could read nothing from their faces.

Suzuna took a breath. "We wrote those as therapy."

"Therapy?"

"To express our feelings, let them out."

"Feelings?"

"They weren't serious."

"They're serious now. Onizuka's dead."

The women sat quietly staring at the table until Suzuna spoke. "Our support group is for survivors of corporate harassment. We call it 'Overtime Anonymous.' We've met with psychologists, therapists, doctors. They all said the same thing, find your voice. So, we did."

"Your voice?" Hiroshi put his cellphone away and they passed the list of tweets back to him. He let it sit on the table.

The woman sitting closest to Hiroshi, the one who had been crying, said, "I was terribly depressed when I quit my job. It was a big company like Senden. I sat in front of my computer for two months, barely eating, and then I tried to commit suicide. But I took the wrong pills." She laughed. "I had no way to free myself from the pressure and shame until I came here. I had failed in society's eyes, in my parents' eyes."

The woman next to her, a small girl in a Disney sweatshirt and with multiple piercings, said, "My name is Shio. My parents were so proud when I made it to the top ad agency in Japan. I started at the same time as Mayu, and I quit right after she...she...died. I tried to explain to my parents, but they couldn't understand what it was like to never go on a date, to pour beer for old male bosses at cheap *izakaya*, address envelopes all day, to never have my own life. I was dying there. This group saved me."

A big, plump woman on the other side of the table said, "My name is Masayo. When I was being harassed, I ignored it by shopping. The only thing that meant anything to me was buying clothes and shoes. I never even wore them. I would shop online, on the train, at lunch, in the bath. My apartment was so crammed with purchases I couldn't move. I had two dozen credit cards, all maxed out. It was financial suicide."

The other women looked down at the table in silence.

Suzuna said, "Our tweets were angry, but they weren't serious."

Masayo, the plump woman, said, "When I saw #hatemyboss, #bosshole, #buchoasshole, hashtags that Suzuna thought up in English, I started to understand. And I started to laugh again. I worked in Onizuka's section, too, for a while, and hated him. I was lucky to be transferred."

Shio said, "And did you see the tweets Onizuka sent out? He sent out dozens a day criticizing the work of Mayu and everyone else. Our tweets were nothing. We had to fight back."

Hiroshi wondered why the tech guys didn't find any of Onizuka's tweets.

"Didn't you report these issues to the HR department?" Hiroshi's phone kept buzzing, but he ignored it.

Masayo spoke up. "Of course we did. I learned later that many of my *senpai* had reported Onizuka for years, but the HR people only replied that Onizuka was so important to the company, which was a way of saying how unimportant we were. He was a horrible man. He called me 'fattie' every time he saw me."

The small girl in the Disney T-shirt, Shio, said, "He kept saying he wanted to make us stronger, but most of us didn't learn any practical skills at university. All we brought to the company was our willingness to work and our ability to think. And that's what Onizuka and the company tried to kill off."

The woman closest to Hiroshi, who'd been crying, said, "I'm sorry Onizuka is dead, but I'm not surprised. Mayu was stronger than all of us combined. Look what happened to her."

"And Onizuka gambled," Suzuna said.

Shio said, "He'd curse about his horse racing bets in the middle of the day, whether he won or lost."

"And bicycle, boat, and motorcycle races. He had Mayu do research on them for him," Suzuna said.

Shio said, "We all wanted to finish work so we could relax at night, but he wasted all day with his selfish activities and then forced us to work overtime." Her Disney T-shirt reminded Hiroshi that these women went from wide-eyed Disney fan to solemn corporate worker with no transition in between.

"Why didn't anything happen to him?" Hiroshi asked. He reached in his pocket and turned off his cellphone to stop the constant buzzing.

Masayo said, "He was called in again and again, but every time he wiggled out of it. He pointed to what his section accomplished, helping the company expand overseas, but he couldn't even speak English. Any meeting, phone call or email with foreigners, he needed one of us to interpret. Then he took all the credit. He could barely read an email in English, and he wanted to be posted to head the overseas office? It was infuriating."

Hiroshi cleared his throat and looked again around the group of women, all of them survivors of a system he couldn't begin to grasp. "So who do you think might have wanted to kill him?"

"Kill him?" Masayo said. "I thought the company announced it was suicide? Wasn't it?"

The women stared at him, nearly out of their chairs, their bodies become limp, as if deflating. They breathed heavily and started fondling their cellphones.

Hiroshi looked at each of them in turn. "We haven't concluded our investigations, but what do you think, was Onizuka the suicide type?"

Shio tapped the table. "Mayu would have known, but she's not here."

Suzuna mumbled to herself, her face as twisted as the thick blonde braids that fell like ropes on either side of her round face.

Masayo and Shio looked at her, waiting for her to say more, and the others looked back and forth at each other, the table and at Hiroshi, their faces as blank and cold as the refrigerated cases along the wall.

Hiroshi waited, looking from face to face.

A loud knock startled everyone.

Sugamo was peering in the window, waving for Hiroshi to come.

Hiroshi walked over and unlocked the door.

"Isn't your cellphone on?" Sugamo asked.

"I turned it off."

"Come on, we have to go."

Sugamo looked in the room at the women and then at Hiroshi. "Chief called from Shinbashi and needs us. Right away. Sakaguchi called, too."

Hiroshi walked back to the table. "I need to know everyone's full name, address, and phone number. Suzuna, can you send me that information here?" Hiroshi held his cellphone toward her.

Suzuna took her cellphone and without meeting his gaze, copied his information, and then, like someone used to taking orders, she started copying and pasting the information to send him, both thumbs working the touchpad.

Hiroshi watched her awkwardly making mistakes and undoing them, her hands trembling all the way up her shaking arms. Then he hurried off to follow the orders of his own boss.

Chapter 30

As soon as Hiroshi got in the car, Sugamo put the siren on.

"What does the chief want?"

Sugamo said, "Sakaguchi said he was sullen and angry all day. Hardly said a word to anyone."

"The ministry officials brushed him off," Hiroshi said.

Takamatsu flipped his lighter open and shut. "That's what I've been trying to do for years, but it doesn't work. He never goes away."

Sugamo said, "He's had Osaki staking out the company and the ministry people. Ueno's been coordinating it all from the station."

Takamatsu turned around to Hiroshi in the back seat. "Big revelations from those girls?"

"They're women... and no, I needed more time. They didn't like the idea of it being murder, though."

"You want to go back? I'll make some excuse for you."

"Maybe the chief's deal won't take long."

Hiroshi checked his messages, hoping Suzuna had sent the names and numbers of the women, but she hadn't. Sugamo got onto the expressway and headed east on the same expressway they'd just taken west to Kichijoji. Hiroshi texted Suzuna all the way to Shinbashi, but got no answer.

He sent another LINE message to Chizu, wondering why she hadn't answered or decided where and when they'd meet. Maybe Takamatsu had been right, they should have brought her in, not left her working at company headquarters.

Sugamo pulled off the toll road into the neat, symmetrical blocks of Ginza. He turned down a back lane housing hostess clubs and small snack bars on the top floors, upscale retail shops and fine restaurants on the ground floors. Soft light spilled on the hood from all directions. Pedestrians and delivery bikes streamed around them on both sides.

Hiroshi checked his cellphone GPS app. "Sakaguchi said, 'Artemis Orchard.' Two blocks down and one over."

Takamatsu said, "Looks like the chief has tracked them right into the heart of it. More business deals have been made in these clubs than in all the offices in Tokyo."

Sugamo turned right and right again, onto a back lane that looked just the same except for the names on the signs. He slowed, turned right and right again onto the previous street. Takamatsu and Hiroshi craned their necks for Artemis Orchard. The sign could be written in any script, English, *katakana*, *hiragana*, or maybe just an image.

"Let me out. I can't see from in here, the buildings are too close." Hiroshi got out and walked in a circle reading the overhead signs and checking building directories. Judging from the website photos, the club looked like an expensive and roomy place with refined hostesses and a discrete atmosphere. The GPS said it should be right there, but there were too many signs for all the small clubs tucked inside the ten- and twelve-story buildings.

Finally, there it was, a small silver sign on an otherwise business-oriented building.

Hiroshi waved for Sugamo to pull past and park. Even tight against the wall, the car took up nearly half the lane.

Takamatsu got out and lit a cigarette. "The chief is wasting our time. We should be talking to Mistress Emi. Or following your intuition and talking with those girls again." He blew his smoke out quickly, without his usual evident pleasure.

Hiroshi saw Sakaguchi's huge figure ambling toward them from the corner. He limped badly. Sugamo got out of the car and walked over to offer his shoulder. Sakaguchi dropped his arm over him as he walked.

"You've got to get off that knee." Hiroshi took Sakaguchi's arm and leaned him against the car.

Sakaguchi nodded. "As soon as this is over. The chief and Osaki will be in position in a minute. Maybe it won't take long."

"What's this all about? We're supposed to be on the other side of town," Hiroshi said.

"The chief has this all set up. Let's just do it and then we can get back to work," Sakaguchi said.

"He has what all set up?" Takamatsu asked.

"The ministry officials and the Senden HR people are upstairs," Sakaguchi said.

"So that's it," Hiroshi said. "The chief was furious that the ministry people brushed him off and now he wants revenge?"

"And he wants to pressure them for help from the inside."

Takamatsu took a last drag and flicked his cigarette into a small puddle of water next to a drain. "Well, if it's that, maybe it's worth it. Are we going in tough or soft?"

Sakaguchi said, "You're not going in at all. You're watching this door with me. Osaki and the chief are taking the door on the other side of the block." Sakaguchi stopped to check his cellphone. "Hiroshi and Sugamo are going in. The twelfth floor is the Artemis Orchard. The tenth floor is a private mahjong parlor where the ministry officials and businesspeople can play with the hostesses. The entrance is through the hostess club."

"So, the chief tracked them here to catch them playing mahjong." Takamatsu hummed and smiled.

Sakaguchi said, "And there's one more thing you're going to like."

Takamatsu smiled more broadly.

"The media should be here in about—" Sakaguchi checked his watch. "Fifteen minutes."

Takamatsu let out a chuckle. "I'm starting to like this a lot. But I'd like to be going in."

Sakaguchi said, "I need you here for the press and the local beat cops, and anyone who tries to run. A few more detectives will be here shortly, and I'll call the local cops when the press arrives. Hiroshi, if they decide to come down this way, call us."

"Am I supposed to tell them the press is waiting outside?" Hiroshi said.

"The chief wants you to do just that. Squeeze them," Sakaguchi said.

Hiroshi thought for a moment. "There's no press at the door on the other side of the block?"

"Right," Sakaguchi said. "So, whether you find them in the mahjong place or the hostess place, give them the choice to cooperate and hand over Senden's files or—"

"Or face the media. Salacious scandal, private gambling den, corporate bribery, gorgeous hostesses, the weeklies will have a field day." Takamatsu laughed. "Don't let them go until they call and have sent a delivery messenger to the station."

"Ueno is waiting there to receive the package, so keep them until it gets in his hands," Sakaguchi said.

"And take a few photos," Takamatsu said. "For insurance."

Sugamo patted his breast pocket. "I just got a new cellphone with a triple lens. Nice chance to try it out."

Hiroshi saw a satellite van pull in at the end of the lane with a broadcast antenna. "They're early. We better go."

Takamatsu laughed again. "This is the kind of scandal they come early to catch."

Another van, unmarked, but probably full of reporters and photographers, turned in after the satellite van. Sugamo and Hiroshi straightened their jackets and went into the elevator and pressed the button for the twelfth floor.

The bouncer who met them at the elevator door on the top floor was a bald, plump guy who didn't look tough, and wasn't. Sugamo forearmed him out of the way and held up his badge as he pushed past. Hiroshi followed in his wake.

They walked past the coat check and alcoves spotlighting small statues of Artemis and other Greek goddesses. A very surprised young waiter in a waistcoat and bowtie looked up from the bar that stretched along the left-hand side. The bartender put down his cocktail shaker and hurried around the counter fumbling with his cellphone. Hiroshi held up his badge, then put his finger over his mouth for the bartender to be quiet.

Sugamo nodded to the booths at the right. Hiroshi took the low circular sofas on the left. A series of square lights stretched to the dark rear of the club. A huge chandelier hung from the ceiling, throwing glints of light through the low-lit club.

Businessmen chatted around tables covered with ice buckets, liquor bottles, mixers and cocktail glasses. Hostesses in sleek low-backed dresses sat between the men, smoking and smiling and nodding. At one table, a man in a wide open-necked collar sat with a stunning brunette in a dark orange one-piece. Another hostess clapped her hands at whatever he'd just said and squirmed on the low sofa.

Hiroshi wasn't sure if Sugamo knew what Nakata and Suzuki looked like. He hadn't been to either Senden or the Ministry of Labor. So, he checked both sides. But table after table, none of the surprised, offended glances came from anyone looking remotely like Nakata or Suzuki.

Two bouncers, the bartender and two male waiters, all in tuxedo waistcoats, headed toward them. One of the bouncers, almost as large as Sugamo, said, "Why are you bothering our customers?"

Hiroshi could hear karaoke coming from somewhere, a different tune than the background music in the main room. "Where are the VIP rooms?"

The bouncers and waitstaff conferred in whispers. One of the waiters then peeled himself from the huddle and waved the detectives to follow him into a tight hallway with doors on each side. Hiroshi pulled open the first one, but there was only a circular sofa and a huge, blank karaoke screen.

In the next one, one hostess and one customer looked up at him with stupid, drunk expressions. The next room had an older man with two hostesses. He looked surprised but unconcerned. The fourth room had a very drunk man singing karaoke with a younger colleague and two hostesses, who applauded wildly at their reverb-echo voices.

Hiroshi turned to the waiter. "That's all the VIP rooms?"

"Everyone's a VIP here," he said, mimicking the club's set line.

"Where are the changing rooms," Sugamo asked.

The waiter made the mistake of shrugging.

Sugamo grabbed him by the lapels of his cheap half tux and slammed him against the wall. "Where do the girls change and do their makeup?"

The waiter was no fighter. "One floor down." He waved for them to follow. At the end of the VIP hallway, he pulled aside heavy curtains. Behind was a small area with a coatrack and a door. The waiter led them down a circular staircase to the floor below.

At the bottom, he pulled open the door to a narrow room lined on one side with mirrors and a counter filled with hair dryers, tissues, cream jars, spray cans, and cosmetic cases. It looked like the makeup room for a movie set. At the far end of the narrow room stood tall wooden lockers with women's names on them. The air smelled so strongly of perfume and hairspray that Hiroshi sneezed.

The waiter stopped at the lockers and held his hands out wide, signaling that was all there was.

"How do we get to the tenth floor? The mahjong room."

The waiter started to shrug but when Sugamo took a step toward him, he quickly pulled out a set of keys and jangled them. He led them to a ceiling-high curtain and pulled it back to reveal a concrete-walled area in front of a small elevator door. "The girls want to escape from customers sometimes," he explained.

The waiter slid the key into the slot and a small elevator quickly arrived. He put the key into the inside panel and all four of them rode down one floor. The bartender stood aside to let them out.

When the door opened, Hiroshi stepped into the most amazing mahjong room he'd ever seen.

Chapter 31

A dozen mahjong tables were spread through the cavernous room, but they weren't the usual functional green felt and laminated wood. Instead these were made of inlaid wood atop an angled base of black lacquered steel with gold accents. Atop each table, copper-topped tiles were stacked in walls and laid open on the black felt. Glass-domed lights on long silver rods hung down from an industrial-chic track that curved along the high ceiling and the exposed concrete walls were hung with Persian and Chinese carpets that dampened the clack of the tiles.

Hiroshi and Sugamo stepped out of the elevator and surveyed the room. Play stopped and the room dropped to a hush. The waitstaff, young men and women in prim waistcoats with drink trays, halted in place. The men in the high-backed chairs turned to stare, their placid faces in shadow outside the circles of light. The hostesses, sitting opposite the men, brushed back their well-styled hair and plucked their dress straps.

At one table, the automatic tile-washing mechanism had just started a new game. The under-table gears clicked and mixed the tiles into four new hands. The underneath panels raised level with the table top and four neat walls of tiles were delivered precisely in place. Dice rattled in the small, sealed globe and shook out the next number. When the dice stopped, the room plunged into silence.

Hiroshi surveyed the tables for the head of Senden's HR, Nakata. Just as the chief had suspected, he was seated across from the Ministry of Labor official, Suzuki, the one who had rebuffed the chief the day before. The two bare-shouldered, lusciously dressed hostesses would have made it hard for Hiroshi to concentrate on the mahjong. Maybe they were used to such distracting partners.

Hiroshi and Sugamo moved toward their table.

The hostesses playing with Nakata and Suzuki made a move to depart, but Hiroshi waved them back into their chairs. Sugamo snapped several photos before Nakata and Suzuki held up their hands and the women hid their faces beneath their long curls. Sugamo snapped a couple more and looked pleased with his new cellphone camera.

Hiroshi stopped next to their table and looked back and forth from Nakata to Suzuki and then at the women. "Who's winning?"

When they didn't answer, he leaned forward to look at their upraised tiles. "It's nice that government and business get along so well. It's too bad we detectives can't get such cooperation."

The women looked down at the table and Nakata and Suzuki remained frozen in place, looking at the black felt top and half-finished hand.

Hiroshi asked, "What do you play for? A hundred yen for a thousand points? A thousand for each ten thousand?

"We just play for fun," one of the women in a black double-strap dress said.

"I'll bet you do," Hiroshi said.

Sugamo stepped toward a table whose players had started to put on their suit jackets. He motioned for them to stay seated. The two men both sported punch perm hair, with neat, tight curls that clung to their skulls, marking them as old-school yakuza from Kansai. Hiroshi couldn't hear what Sugamo said, but they settled back in place. This had nothing to do with them, so they would likely wait it out. But Hiroshi wished that Takamatsu and Osaki had come up with them. If things went wrong, they wouldn't get up the elevator in time.

Nakata found his voice. "So, why are you here?"

"We requested files from Senden and help from the ministries. I just wanted to check on when the promised assistance will materialize." Hiroshi spoke in a low voice so the other tables couldn't hear.

Nakata shook his head in disbelief. "Like I told you, it takes time."

"We're out of time, so make the call," Hiroshi said more loudly than before.

"What call?" Nakata closed his eyes and opened them.

"The call to have the files sent."

"Now?"

Hiroshi nodded.

Nakata glared at him.

Hiroshi turned to Suzuki. "And Suzuki-*san*, we need the same from you. Whatever you have about Senden."

"Tomorrow," Suzuki said.

Hiroshi spread his hands wide. "By tomorrow, you two could be in the news."

"Nakata-*san* and I were classmates, from grade school through college. We get together for a little mahjong and a few drinks."

"Why play here in this secret parlor if you're just friends?"

"The media can get the wrong impression."

Hiroshi smiled. "Interesting you mention the media, because they are waiting downstairs. With one of those satellite vans."

Nakata and Suzuki squirmed, their faces rigid. They knew what a scandal this would be and how it would affect their careers. The weekly tabloids thrived on stories like this, true or not. They'd be dressed down and reassigned at work, knocked off their career track. Their wives might not be surprised at their actions, but would be ashamed at everyone knowing.

"Do these women usually win, or lose?" Hiroshi looked at them. They were stunning—tanned, made-up, buffed from workouts, and draped in designer dresses that showed off their bodies to perfection. "Could I get your names, ladies?"

They squinted at Hiroshi and looked at the waitstaff for help.

"OK, OK, we can do that later. We have photos anyway." Hiroshi hummed. "So Suzuki-san, we really do need to know what the government knows. Make the call now. You know what we want, everything related to Senden. And Nakata, you too."

Nakata leaned forward and plucked at his tiles. "You're going about this the wrong way."

"We tried the right way. It didn't work. Get those files sent to us by courier or take your chances with the media downstairs. They can wait all night and there's only two ways out of here."

Suzuki said, "There's no one in the office at this hour."

Hiroshi took his cellphone and called Sakaguchi. "The media can come up. We're on the tenth floor. It's an unregistered mahjong parlor, so—"

Nakata held up his hand and pulled out his cellphone. "This could take hours."

"So does mahjong," Hiroshi said.

Suzuki fumbled for his cellphone in the pocket of his jacket hanging on the back of his chair, the same navy blue as in the ministry office.

Hiroshi spoke to Sakaguchi on the phone. "Hold them off for a minute, can you? It looks like we're getting somewhere."

When Hiroshi hung up, he turned back to Nakata and Suzuki. "The media are all out back. You can go out the front door, hop in a taxi and you're gone. Just as soon as we get those files in hand. Here's the address." Hiroshi showed Nakata and Suzuki the address of the headquarters where Ueno was waiting for the late-night messenger bikes.

Nakata and Suzuki told their subordinates what to get and where to send it. Hiroshi waved Sugamo over to take a few more photos. A little more insurance couldn't hurt.

When he was done, Sugamo said, "This camera works really well. My wife got it on a discount family plan."

Sugamo and Hiroshi talked loudly about cellphone cameras, phone apps and the price of phone plans while they waited for the files to be sent to police headquarters.

The two hostesses squirmed in place. One asked the waiter for a glass of water and the other pulled her cigarette case out of a bejeweled handbag and lit a long black cigarette. A waiter rushed over with an ashtray.

Nakata and Suzuki sat quietly. There wasn't anything else to do.

Nakata got a call back, listened, and looked up at Hiroshi. "It's on its way."

"One of the detectives will call me when it gets there."

Suzuki got a call and nodded with a disgusted look on his face. He motioned for a refill on his whiskey *mizuwari*. A waitress hurried over with a fresh glass.

The room remained as it was, but some of the players started chatting with each other, checking their walls and moving their tiles. As with most things, Tokyoites didn't really care what was going on as long as they didn't have to get involved.

A waitress came over with a glass of water for Hiroshi and Sugamo. Seeing the glass, a wave of thirst and fatigue swept through Hiroshi. He gulped it down. In Sugamo's huge hand, the glass looked small, hardly more than a swallow. The waitress, who had been waiting, took their glasses back with a polite bow.

Nakata turned to Hiroshi with a "Now what?" look on his face.

Hiroshi looked at Suzuki, who checked his phone again and stared dully at the table.

"We just need to be sure it arrives," Hiroshi said.

The hostesses laughed bitterly and shook their heads. Hiroshi wondered how much humiliation this would cause Nakata and Suzuki, and whether they'd want revenge on the chief.

One of the hostesses at a rear table got up and whispered to Sugamo. He nodded OK. She hurried off to the toilet on her high heels. As soon as the other hostesses saw her, they raised their hands like schoolgirls, their smooth arms glowing under the lights. Sugamo looked at Hiroshi, who shrugged. They all stood up, straightened their designer dresses, and shuffled away, whispering to each other in irritated tones.

Hiroshi's phone rang. He listened and nodded. "There's one."

"What's the plan here?" Nakata asked.

"We let you go out the front door. And that's that," Hiroshi looked down at Nakata, who reached for his jacket. "Why don't you wait for your classmate here?"

When the next call came from Ueno that the package had arrived, Hiroshi listened closely, nodding affirmatively. When he hung up, he turned to Nakata and Suzuki and said, "That didn't take long. We'll ride down with you."

Suzuki and Nakata stood up trying to conceal their shame by acting calm and unconcerned. Hiroshi could tell, though, they were very concerned, but that would be the chief's problem to dispose of.

A waiter brought their overcoats.

Hiroshi and Sugamo followed Nakata and Suzuki to the front elevator. A waitress bowed as she held the door open for the four of them and reached in to press the ground floor.

As they descended, Suzuki said, "How do we know there's no media waiting for us?"

Hiroshi didn't answer and Sugamo scrolled through the photos he'd just taken.

Outside the club, Osaki and the chief were waiting. Nakata and Suzuki barely looked at them as they shuffled through the door, scanned the street, and dove into a waiting taxi. As it pulled away, the chief turned to see the satellite news van pull around the corner. He waved his arms in a sweeping gesture toward the taxi Nakata and Suzuki took. The van sped after them through the wide main street of Ginza.

"Oops," the chief said, watching them go.

Sakaguchi's car pulled around the corner, Takamatsu driving.

Takamatsu rolled down his window. "We've got to go. Mistress Emi is waiting."

The chief said, "Who do you need with you?"

Hiroshi said, "Osaki and Sugamo."

"Done," the chief said, adjusting his Borsalino. "Sakaguchi, come with me back to the station."

Sakaguchi said, "Chief, I can't drive with my knee."

The chief took off his hat, smiling for the first time Hiroshi could remember. "I'll drive. Ride in the back. Put your leg up. That was a good day's work."

Sugamo and Osaki played *janken* to decide who would drive. Sugamo won, paper over rock, so Osaki drove. As the four of them drove to the other side of Tokyo, Osaki asked, "What's with the chief?"

"Revenge does strange things to people," Takamatsu answered.

Chapter 32

Where they were going to meet Mistress Emi was on the fifth floor of a building filled with clubs and bars in Akasaka. The narrow sidewalks were lined by railings to keep people safely flowing past the mismatched buildings filled with small offices, stylish restaurants, and elegant drinking spots.

A car was just coming out of a parking lot with ten spots, so Osaki pulled in with a quick twist of the wheel and backed in place. The locking plate flipped up from below to keep the car from being driven off until the parking fee was paid at the ticket machine.

"You two wait downstairs," Takamatsu said. "I don't think Mistress Emi will be too much trouble. Unless you pay her to be."

Hiroshi and Takamatsu walked to the back of the open entry area and got in the elevator.

Hiroshi said, "Who would call their club 'The Pink Lash'?"

"Only someone with a pink lash," Takamatsu replied. "In the old days, in places like Shinjuku *ni-chome*, you never knew what kind of bar it was until you were already inside."

"Times change."

"Tastes don't."

On the door of the club, a braided leather pink and white whip curved from the top to the bottom of the door and halfway back up again.

The interior was dark and cozy, with the usual rows of liquor and glasses, and jars of *otsumami* roasted peas, dried squid, and *senbei* in screw-top jars. Tall standing tables took up the middle of the room and dark booths jutted from the front wall. The ceiling was high with black spray paint covering the exposed struts, pipes, air ducts, and beams.

Unlike other bars, four large chains dangled from a ceiling rack ending in thick red ropes tied out of the way. Angled down from the back corner was a life-size male dummy hanging from ankle and wrist cuffs. He was adorned with a head harness, nipple clamps, and a spiked chastity belt. Four pink whips snaked through support wires as if permanently lashing him.

Sneaking up from behind the detectives, Mistress Emi joined them in admiring the decoration. "What do you think? One of my clients is a designer for department store displays. I wanted to add a few more touches, but he advised not overdoing it. We get a lot of first-timers in here."

Hiroshi almost didn't recognize her dressed in a skin-tight purple leather sheath that stretched from her breasts to her thighs, leaving only the peacock's claws and the dragon's tail of her tattoos dancing above her knees as she moved. Dark eye shadow and peacock eyelashes framed her deep-set eyes.

"Mistress Emi," Takamatsu said with a bit of a flourish.

"I'm off duty, detectives. Just Emi. Welcome to my club. I have to do something with my earnings, don't I? Thought I'd create a welcoming space."

"Very welcoming indeed." Takamatsu smiled.

"And behind the bar is Dana. My best bartender and best third."

Dana was busy setting up, but waved politely.

Hiroshi took a second to get what she meant by "third."

"Anyway, sit down. What will you drink?"Emi led them to the booth below the male dummy swaying overhead in masochistic ecstasy.

Hiroshi said, "We're on duty."

"I just got some wonderful *shochu* from a client in the liquor business. He keeps me supplied, and I him."

"Sounds delicious," Takamatsu said.

Hiroshi felt nauseous at the very word *shochu*. "Just a beer."

Dana started the drinks as Hiroshi and Takamatsu settled across from Emi. She was not just sexy, but beautiful, with the kind of strong neck and worked-out shoulders he always found attractive. Her gestures were quick but her voice was slow and resonant.

"On the phone, you said someone's following you," Takamatsu prompted.

"Yes, that. Well, about six months ago, I got more appointments all of a sudden. Except many of them were no-shows. That had never happened before. It was weird."

"And you noticed someone following you to and from those appointments?"

"An older man a couple of times, and then this younger guy, plump as a beach ball, always dressed in leather."

"Did they follow you back to the club?"

"The younger guy came a couple of times when I wasn't here, Dana told me. He never talked to anyone, just sat and drank. But lots of customers are like that. They want to be here, but can't take the next step."

As if on cue, a group of young leather-clad customers came in.

Emi shouted "*Irasshaimase!*" before turning back to the detectives. "I'm not sure it's the same guy, but Dana's description made me think it was. People wear a lot of different outfits in here."

"They never followed you home?" Hiroshi asked.

Emi shook her head, her dyed-blonde hair bouncing over her shoulders. "I had a bad incident when I first started out, so I always take precautions going home. It was more when I got close to the hotels that I noticed. I started to take an extra bottle of pepper spray in my bag, and this." Emi reached between her breasts and pulled out a small pink plastic case.

"A stun gun?" Takamatsu said.

"Mini size, but high volts," Emi said, and slipped it back inside her bra. "I have these bras made to order. And this." She held out her necklace, a gold chain with a black stone on a gold backing.

"Sends a message to…who?" Takamatsu said.

"The guy you met at the hotel, C3PO. If he doesn't answer, it goes to another service. But he always answers," Emi said.

Dana brought over their drinks. Hiroshi wasn't sure where on the gender continuum to place Dana, but Dana's warm smile and gentle eyes were beyond gender.

Emi had a gin and tonic with berries and orange peel. "It's the little extras that really make drinks. And sex." She wrapped her hands around the glass and Hiroshi stared at her *shunga* fingernail art. Each nail had a different sexual position, done like a *ukiyoe* painting. Hiroshi wasn't sure where to look. He took his beer, Takamatsu his *shochu* and they clinked glasses.

Emi set her jaw. "I saw the press conference today. Almost everything they said was a lie."

"We know that," Takamatsu said. "But how do you know that?"

"Onizuka didn't kill himself. I know he didn't," Emi said, taking a long drink with a shiver. "This whole thing is starting to creep me out. I just want to get back to whacking butts."

Emi dug into her bra again, on the opposite side, and pulled out a USB flash drive. "He's on here."

"Who?"

"Onizuka. I videotaped him as part of the humiliation. I told him I'd send this to his company if he continued to be a bad boy, the usual storyline. Most clients love that. I would replay the previous session for him when he was tied up, force him to watch. It added to the shame."

Hiroshi took the USB flash drive. He wanted to call Sugamo to come get it, but he could send it to the station after they finished talking.

Emi said, "I edited myself out. If it got out that I'd violated client secrecy, I'd be out of business. I hope you understand."

More people came in, a large group of obvious newbies, salaryman types already drunk. Dana and Emi called out, "*Irasshaimase!*"

A woman in turquoise *zentai* body tights, her face uncovered, rushed in and ran over to Emi and apologized for being late. She was clearly a she, with a young, lithe figure, and nimble steps like a ballerina. Maybe she was a ballerina, since everyone in the bar seemed to have multiple identities, genders, and modes of attire. She pirouetted and glided toe-to-heel to the bar to start work.

"Young people are so irresponsible. Show up on time, right?" Emi shook her head. "And the name you asked me about, Mayu? It's all over these recordings."

The newbie group were in hysterics at the smorgasbord of BDSM sex toys, tools, and gear hanging on the walls of the club. Dana herded them to the corner, dragging over standing tables and taking their orders. Their prim salaryman suits and ties were disheveled and their faces pink and mottled. It was not their first stop of the night.

Emi continued, serious. "You can see on the video how Onizuka really loved anal. Once he got worked up, whatever I put in there was great with him. I had to buy new gear for his tastes, so over the years I started to understand Onizuka. He was trying to make up for the sins of the day with sins at night. But, well, here's what I should have told you the other day." Emi looked at the salarymen laughing more loudly than before. "What I didn't tell you...the night he died, Onizuka had an appointment with me."

"So, you lied to us when we talked before." Hiroshi looked at Takamatsu, criticizing him for believing her.

Emi looked at Hiroshi directly. "I did, yes, I'm sorry. I was so shocked about Onizuka, I didn't know what to think. Or what to say."

"What about the truth?" Hiroshi suggested.

Emi nodded, resolved, maybe, to do that.

"Go on," Takamatsu said. "Tell us about that night."

"It was the strangest session I ever had with him, and many of them were very strange. I was contacted by some women. About two weeks ago. They said they used to work with Onizuka and wanted to teach him a lesson. I thought maybe they were the ones following me, so I agreed to meet. I figured the women could give him what he always secretly desired—ultimate submission."

"How did they know you knew Onizuka?" Hiroshi asked.

"I wondered about that, and still don't know, but they knew who I was, and roughly what Onizuka and I did. They told me what they had in mind and I thought it sounded like something that Onizuka would love. In fact, I wondered if Onizuka had set it all up with them, since he loved elaborate scenarios and was good at cooking them up. It would be another level of humiliation."

Hiroshi drank the rest of his beer.

Takamatsu took a large sip from his *shochu* glass and leaned forward.

"That night, once I got him hog-tied and ball-gagged, I told him he was going to get a few surprises. He twisted like he does when he loves something. I jammed a bottle of vodka into his anus and let it soak in."

Takamatsu said, "I know of two cases where people died from alcohol enemas."

" The women asked me to do that. I don't like to use knockout drugs after a couple bad experiences," Emi said. "I googled it and followed the instructions, and he was a strong drinker, but, well, he ended up passing out. I woke him up, took the ball gag out, and he threw up. I cleaned him up and figured he'd be ready in time..."

"In time for what?" Takamatsu asked, pushing his glass aside.

Emi took the last swallow of her gin and tonic. "For the women. They arrived in masks and hoods, so all I could see were their eyes. They told me they'd pay me triple my usual session charge to hand him over. That wasn't my understanding. I thought they were going to play with him there at the bondage love hotel, take some photos, whatever. But they wanted to take him away. I mean, he couldn't even walk. I was getting worried, but I felt maybe it was all Onizuka's money, and maybe his plan, so what did it matter? He'd done crazier things and when he threw money around, he really let it fly. But I still felt unsure. The women were too straight, you know, and he was too drunk by then to answer, so I asked them if this was Onizuka's plan."

"What did they say?"

"They looked at each other, and one of them, quickly, maybe too quickly, said, yes, it was all Onizuka's idea, and he was begging them, paying them, and paying me, to do this for him. I balked, but they doubled the price. I pressed the call for C3PO and he came right away, but he just shrugged when I explained." Emi looked up at the dummy hanging from the ceiling. "I shouldn't have let them take him."

Chapter 33

Hiroshi wanted to believe Emi but wondered if she was being too confessional to trust? And why was she talking so much now, after talking so little before?

Takamatsu was quiet, thinking it through.

The ballerina-like girl in turquoise *zentai* tights brought over another round of drinks. Emi asked her, "Do you know where C3PO is?" She shook her head. "Tell Dana to call him again. That group of drunk salarymen is starting to take things off the wall."

The ballerina flittered off but before she got to the bar a rack of paddles crashed down from the wall. The salarymen let out a hurrah and collapsed into laughs and apologies. The younger ones tried to put them back, but each time they picked one up, they laughed at the reversed cut-out text in the leather—XOXO, BITCH, PIG—that would raise legible welts on bare, hard-whacked skin.

Emi slid out of the booth and strode to the bar. Dana handed her a multi-frond flogger and a riding crop, which she cracked on the bar top as she shouted at the salarymen. "Shut up. Now!"

The salarymen lowered their hysterics to a simmering giggle.

Emi swung the crop against the ass of the man on her right. It landed with a loud thwack that made him spin away shouting, "*Ittai*! That hurts!" He rubbed his butt, and his companions snickered, shocked and amused.

"Pick up those paddles and set them on the counter," Emi commanded the cowering semicircle of sobering men.

Two of the men picked up the paddles they'd knocked from the wall and set them on the counter in a neat pile, but they had divided into two groups—obstinate and obedient.

Dana came around the bar to whisper something to Emi. She turned her head to the corner booth. Emi forgot the salaryman and strode to the booth.

The salarymen fell into a shouting match among themselves. The guy whose butt had been whacked started yelling and pushed the chest of one of his colleagues. The colleague threw a wild punch, too drunk to land it.

Hiroshi looked at Takamatsu. They stood up. Takamatsu headed toward the shoving, pushing salarymen and Hiroshi called Osaki and Sugamo to come up right away.

Through the doorway walked C3PO. He was bigger and more muscular than Hiroshi remembered. He surveyed the scene and went to stand beside Emi, leaving the salarymen to Takamatsu.

Takamatsu grabbed the arm of the guy who threw the first punch, twisted him to the ground, arm bent into the air, and reached for handcuffs.

But Takamatsu didn't see the sucker punch that caught him in his solar plexus. Hiroshi saw him double over, coughing. He looked for something as long and hard as a kendo practice sword, but before he could find anything Osaki and Sugamo burst through the front door and hurried over to corral the salarymen in the corner.

Hiroshi looked back at Emi shouting at the guy in the booth, but he was sitting tight and didn't respond.

"This is the guy who's been following me," Emi said to Hiroshi when he stood next to her.

Hiroshi pulled out his badge. The man had a delicate plump face, somewhere between masculine and feminine, with longish hair. He was decked out in a leather jacket with large zippers over a round chest.

"Who are you?" Hiroshi demanded.

The guy looked down and didn't answer.

Before Hiroshi could ask again, the sound of escalating words and tussling turned their heads. Sugamo had two of the salarymen by their arms and Osaki had another over the bar with his arm behind him. Takamatsu was still trying to catch his breath.

Hiroshi took a step toward them, and when he did, the leather jacket guy shoved his way out of the booth and bolted for the door. Emi and C3PO grabbed at him, but he wiggled free before Emi could even swing her riding crop.

"Sugamo, help!" Hiroshi yelled as he took off out the door after the guy.

Sugamo dropped the two guys to the floor with a kick to the back of their knees and raced after Hiroshi.

Hiroshi spun down the narrow staircase, dodging liquor crates, beer kegs and boxes of canned goods. The cool air hit him as he made it out to the street. He stared in both directions along the narrow sidewalk.

Sugamo thudded out of the entryway and looked at Hiroshi. "What's he look like?"

"Short black leather jacket with a lot of zippers on it, longish hair."

Hiroshi noticed a small passageway between the buildings. "You got a flashlight?"

Sugamo handed him a small one. Hiroshi shone it down the narrow gap and saw someone at the other end climbing over an air-conditioning unit.

Seeing the flashlight's beam, the leather jacket guy pushed out of the passageway and disappeared along the street at the other end.

Sugamo took off around the late-night pedestrians. Hiroshi started down the gap, but it was too narrow, so he backed out and went the opposite way from Sugamo.

He sped to the next corner and spun to the right, colliding with a group of women. With a curt apology, he cut around them and kept going. The cross street had a steep slope and he dragged himself to the top and looked in both directions. Sugamo was coming toward him at a trot, shaking his head.

Hiroshi climbed on the curbside railing and scanned both

"Why are you here?"

Ota typed with agile thumbs on his cellphone keyboard and held it up. "I wanted to find who hurt Shibutani. I'm checking everyone we followed before. I think someone connected to Onizuka hurt Shibutani. So, I followed Mistress Emi. But it's not her."

Hiroshi started to say, "I think you're right," but pulled out his cellphone and typed it out.

Ota nodded. "So who was it?"

Hiroshi gave him a "I don't know" look and started to type more, but a call came from Takamatsu, who told him to get back to The Pink Lash.

Ota typed into his phone. "Was that Detective Takamatsu?"

Hiroshi nodded.

Ota typed, "Shibutani told me to contact him if I needed anything."

Hiroshi waved him along and the three of them headed back.

At the bar, sex gear, broken liquor bottles and smashed jars of snacks littered the floor. Four of the salarymen, shirts untucked and clothes rumpled, were tied by one hand to the ropes extending from chains in the ceiling. They looked ridiculously off balance stretched up sideways.

Takamatsu was calmly checking the IDs of the salarymen, their wallets piled on a table.

Emi flicked her riding crop on the buttocks of the guy who threw the first punch. Dangling from his wrist, he tried to spin away and shouted. Takamatsu told him to shut up.

Dana and C3PO and the waitress stood to the side surveying the damage.

Hiroshi stood next to Takamatsu. "Who are these guys?"

Takamatsu shook his head and tossed the wallet onto the pile next to their confiscated cellphones. "Who's this guy?" He pointed at Ota.

Hiroshi said, "Shibutani's assistant. He's deaf."

Takamatsu turned to Ota and signed something that Hiroshi couldn't understand. Ota smiled and they exchanged a few signed exchanges.

"One of my cousins back in the mountains was deaf. I can't remember much." Takamatsu sighed. "The local cops will be here in a minute."

Hiroshi's phone buzzed again. It was Toshiko again.

From behind the bar, Emi took a long single-tail whip, cracked it once on the floor, stepped back, gauged the distance and landed the whip on the ass of the first salaryman. He yelped in pain, unable to move with his arm tied overhead.

"This is against the law," he shouted, breathing hard.

Emi cracked the next in line hard on the ass. He jumped and spun by his arm.

"I'm going to file a complaint with the police," the first man whimpered.

"We are the police," Takamatsu assured him.

Emi gave the third one a sharp, stinging smack that made everyone wince. The single frond whip was obviously more painful than the crop. The men rubbed their butt cheeks with their free hands and started breathing fast and hard as Emi coiled the whip, considering another round.

The first guy spun angrily by his tied wrist. "You'll regret this."

Takamatsu walked over and got right in his face. "You'll be doing the regretting when I report this to your workplace. Your employer will be interested to know you're fighting, damaging property, hitting a police officer, and not paying your bill at a BDSM club." Takamatsu turned to Emi. "What do you usually charge for this?"

Emi smiled. "Ten thousand a lash."

Dana totaled it up with a pad and pen and held it out to Takamatsu.

Takamatsu turned to the *bucho*. "You've already bought fifty thousand yen's worth. Keep talking and she'll add more."

He twisted and yanked on the rope, seething in silence.

Takamatsu turned back to Emi. "And what's the damage for broken bottles and the disturbed gear?"

Dana and the waitress in the turquoise *zentai* helped total it up, counting the bottles and BDSM gear on the floor and adding it on.

Takamatsu walked over to the dangling salarymen. "Now, would you like them to send the itemized bill to your boss? Add it to your company's entertainment expenses? Or would one of you like to go to an ATM to get the cash to pay this bill right now?"

Three local cops arrived in uniform. They sucked air over their teeth at the sight of the damage and put their billy clubs back in their holders.

Dana came over with the total bill and showed it to the local cops, who nodded.

Takamatsu explained what happened. He pointed to the pile of wallets on the table. "These fine examples of Japan's corporate elite were just about to settle their bar tab. Can you make sure they do?"

The beat cops nodded with faint smiles, calling on a walkie-talkie for someone to bring the report forms and more backup.

Hiroshi stepped aside to take a call from Toshiko. When he heard why she was calling, he grabbed Takamatsu's arm and pulled him toward the door, whispering something and then shouting for Osaki and Sugamo to follow.

"What about Ota?" Sugamo asked.

"Bring him along," Takamatsu said, and explained to Ota in sign language.

Ota nodded and straightened his shoulders.

Chapter 34

"Why back to the roof?" Takamatsu asked Hiroshi as they raced down the steep, narrow stairs. Osaki and Sugamo's heavy footfalls were close behind. Ota trailed after them.

"It's the only place I can think of," Hiroshi said.

They ran to the small parking lot and hopped in. Sugamo paid and Osaki got in the driver's seat.

Hiroshi said, "Use the siren."

Hiroshi called Toshiko back for more details.

Her voice was hysterical. "Suzuna left a message. She said she was so sorry, but she couldn't go on."

Hiroshi asked, "Could you hear anything in the background where she was calling from?"

"It was very quiet. Windy maybe? I called the other women in her support group but she left them the same message," Toshiko said.

"Can you give me their contact numbers?"

"I'll send them to you right now, and I'll give them yours," Toshiko said.

Hiroshi stared out the window as they sped through the Tokyo streets. It was long past the second late-night rush hour and the streets felt hollowed out and empty.

Takamatsu said, "It's the friend of Mayu's? With the thick blonde braids?"

Hiroshi said, "I must have spooked her when I talked with the support group. I thought a little pressure would get them to talk."

"Looks like it got her to act," Takamatsu said.

When they pulled up in the parking lot of Senden Central, two security guards were waiting. They waved them in and ushered them into the elevator, everyone running at a steady clip.

Takamatsu looked up at the security camera in the corner as

they passed. "Where's your chief Imasato?"

"He's up on the roof," one of the guards answered. "But he's too old to be climbing out on the ledge."

When they got on the elevator, the guard pressed the button for the top floor of the service elevator, but Takamatsu put his hand out to hold the door. "Osaki, you better stay here. Watch the parking lot. No one in or out. Keep Ota with you."

Osaki stepped out of the elevator with a curt nod and gestured for Ota to stay with him.

The elevator doors opened onto the floor just below the roof and the guards hurried to the stairs. Takamatsu and Hiroshi looked up at the surveillance camera. A square of black tape covered the lens.

They hurried up the stairs and onto the roof. Near the edge of the roof stood Imasato, the old chief security guard, and another guard, both of them standing by the cut fence, facing the ledge.

Outside the fence, on the outer ledge, stood Suzuna, clutching the fence with both hands behind her, facing the edge, her body trembling. The office lights from the building opposite caught her blonde hair and wool sweater.

Hiroshi rushed over.

"Don't come any closer," Suzuna yelled. One loosened braid swung as she turned her wet red face toward them. She had taken off her shoes and placed them inside the cut-open fence. "Stay back."

Hiroshi edged closer, wanting to yell at the guards for not re-sealing the fence with something more than tape. But it wasn't their fault, it was his.

Suzuna crouched lower and her feet slipped on the pebbles under her socks.

Hiroshi stepped closer, trying to think what to say, edging toward the cut-open fence.

"I said, stay away," Suzuna sobbed. Her sweater swung open and her thick cotton dress clung to her legs in the wind.

Hiroshi held his hands out and stepped closer. "I didn't mean to scare you."

"It's all true, what you said." Suzuna tried to pull her sweater around herself with her free hand, but she was off balance and the wind blew it open. She was shivering in the wind, her body shaking with fear and cold.

"What's true?" Hiroshi asked in a calm voice, stepping closer.

"About killing Onizuka."

"I didn't say that."

"You meant that."

"Come inside and we can talk about that," Hiroshi said.

"I set it all up. It's all me. No one else had anything to do with it." Tears rolled down her cheeks and she pulled her sleeve back and forth over her nose and eyes. She rose up to peer over the edge.

"Why not come back and tell me how it happened?" Hiroshi said, trying to sound calm and reassuring. He wanted to make a grab for her, but that wasn't going to work if she was this hysterical. He'd have to calm her down. "Just give me your hand."

Takamatsu and Sugamo edged past Suzuna along the inside of the fence. Takamatsu had Sugamo hoist him up, seeing if he could get over to the other side.

Suzuna saw him and shouted, "Get down. Get him down!"

Takamatsu dropped back inside the fence.

Hiroshi said, "We can work this out."

"It was all my fault." Suzuna wiped her face. "I'm the one who didn't answer Mayu's phone calls. I killed her."

"You didn't kill her."

"She's dead, isn't she?"

"But it's not your fault."

"I'm the one who organized Onizuka. And he's dead, too."

Hiroshi ducked his head through the fence. "Suzuna, look at me."

Suzuna looked over the edge again and then leaned back

against the fence, her socks slipping.

"Don't look down there, look at me," Hiroshi commanded as calmly as he could.

Suzuna looked back to where Hiroshi was reaching outside the fence.

"I want to hear you tell me what happened. I believe you."

"I killed both of them."

"No, you didn't." He got his shoulder and arm through the V, but it was still too far to grab her.

Sugamo circled back closer to Hiroshi, edging close behind him to the left.

Suzuna said, "At the group meeting, you implied we were responsible for his death."

"That wasn't my meaning. I found out more, so I know what happened. I know the truth now. Emi told me what happened." Hiroshi stretched farther out through the open fence, but Suzuna shuffled several more steps away and started crying harder.

"The truth? No one wants to hear that. They just want to hear who's in charge, who has the power, who's rich, who follows orders." Sobs racked her body and she stooped and twisted, wiping her eyes.

He had no idea about the truth, but he had to tell her something. He wasn't really sure they had done anything when he questioned them, but it seemed a decent bluff to draw them out. He didn't count on Suzuna being that sensitive. And was Emi's story even true? Maybe true enough to lure Suzuna back in.

Hiroshi took small steps closer, ready to lunge for her. He could feel Sugamo grab the back of his belt and waistband, curling them tightly into his huge fist.

Suzuna wailed, squatting down with her socks slipping on the gravel.

Hiroshi knew he had to hurry. "Tell me about studying in America. I studied there, too."

"It was great at first when we came back and then everything turned terrible."

"But you have a great job now at the flower shop with Toshiko. I talked to her. She wants you to—"

"I have to pee." Suzuna started to bounce and scrunch her body.

"There's a toilet right by the smoking lounge. Come on back. It's too cold up here."

Suzuna spread her legs apart, reached under her skirt and crouched. A thin trickle of urine sprayed out and pooled on the pebbles of the ledge. She was beyond shame and propriety, wiping herself with a tissue and tossing it over the edge. It floated on the updraft, before disappearing. "I feel better now. I'm ready. I don't want to exist anymore."

"Suzuna!" a woman's voice called and Hiroshi turned to see the plump woman from the meeting in the flower shop. "Suzuna, please!" Osaki followed close behind her with another woman from the meeting, Shio, dressed in a Disney coat.

Hiroshi waved to Osaki to let them come closer. He put one foot outside the fence onto the ledge and shifted his weight. Sugamo clutched his waistband tighter and set himself with his hand around the fence.

Hiroshi reverted to a friendly tone again. "Suzuna, Masayo and Shio are here. So, come back inside and let's talk. Get back to the warmth."

"There's no warmth," Suzuna said.

Masayo stepped closer. "Suzuna, you promised that we'd be honest about everything. So let's be honest now. We have more work to do."

Shio said, "Suzuna, we'll explain everything. People will trust us. I promise."

Suzuna's fingers clawed the fence, opening and shutting through the links. She stretched her other hand out to test the air and Hiroshi tensed to make a leap for her, Sugamo ready for his lunge.

Hiroshi waved for Masayo and Shio to keep talking.

Masayo and Shio stepped closer and Shio put her hand on Suzuna's fingers through the fence. Almost whispering, Shio said, "Suzuna, in group, we pledged to never let Onizuka hurt another woman. That includes you."

Suzuna kept stretching one arm out and back as if testing the air.

The opening in the fence was not big enough for Hiroshi to slip through quickly, and even if he could, he wouldn't be fast enough. He was pretty sure he could get a handful of her dress or maybe her arm, and Sugamo could pull back, but he wasn't sure he could hold on.

Suzuna touched Shio's fingers. Masayo put her fingers on top of theirs, the three women touching. Suzuna's right hand stayed on theirs, but with her left, she touched her lips and set a kiss on their fingers.

After that, she stretched her left hand up in the air.

When she did, Hiroshi snatched her arm. Sugamo, still holding his waistband, let him lean forward.

Her sweater slipped along her arm and Hiroshi let go of the fence and stepped out to snatch her other arm, Sugamo letting him all the way outside the fence.

Suzuna wiggled and squatted down onto the pebbles.

Hiroshi reached down and got an arm around her waist, but she kept struggling.

Hiroshi braced his legs to pin Suzuna between himself and the fence. He could feel Sugamo's hand on his waistband so he could use his knees to corral her as he got his arm around her waist to ease her up.

She kept twisting like a child throwing a tantrum. Hiroshi had to grab the fence with one hand to keep from being pushed over the edge.

Kicking and squirming, she kept Hiroshi from getting a firm hold on her, but with each twist, he could move her closer to the opening where Takamatsu was reaching for them over the top of Sugamo.

Twist by hysterical twist, they reeled her in.

When Hiroshi got her close enough, Sugamo got a hand around her wrist and yanked. She looked up surprised, hurt maybe, but Sugamo yanked again holding her arm as tight as a vise.

Takamatsu latched onto Suzuna's other arm with Osaki holding him from behind.

Sugamo let go of Hiroshi's belt band, got a two-handed grip on Suzuna and slid her through the opening back to safety inside the fence.

Hiroshi's foot slipped on the pebbles, but Takamatsu got a hand around his wrist and Osaki snatched his waistband.

Resetting his balance, Hiroshi ducked inside.

He stood up and looked behind him at the edge of the roof.

Takamatsu nodded at Hiroshi's arm. It was dripping blood where he must have ripped it on a sharp edge of the cut fence.

Osaki wrapped a handkerchief around it and Hiroshi pressed on it to staunch the blood.

Sugamo called for an ambulance.

Masayo and Shio wrapped themselves around Suzuna and rocked her back and forth.

Takamatsu reached for his cigarettes.

Chapter 35

The security guards brought a medical kit and a stretcher with blankets. Masayo and Shio would not let go of Suzuna, so the guards gave them a blanket and let them wrap her up and sit down on a picnic bench. Sugamo and Osaki hovered close.

One of the guards brought a medical kit and poured disinfectant on Hiroshi's arm. Blood was still oozing from two points where the fence had bit into the flesh. He pressed on it hard for a few minutes and it started to slow.

Takamatsu finished his cigarette and came over to check on Hiroshi. "I'm getting tired of this roof."

"I'm getting tired of roofs in general," Hiroshi replied, still pressing his arm to stop the bleeding.

"We better talk to the girls while they're still upset." Takamatsu looked over at the three women clumped together.

Hiroshi let the security guard put a fresh compress on and slip an elastic net sleeve over to hold it in place. Then he stood up, stretched his arm and winced. It would have to do. He pulled his torn overcoat back on.

The ambulance crew arrived with a stretcher and hurried to Suzuna. Masayo and Shio talked her into lying down, and the crew checked her vitals and covered her in a blanket. She had stopped crying, but her face went blank, her eyes staring at nothing. She'd stopped responding even to Masayo and Shio, who held her hands in theirs.

Hiroshi told the ambulance crew, "She's to be on suicide watch. Take her to the police hospital in Nakano." Sugamo and Osaki did *janken* to see who would go with her. Osaki lost with scissors. "Osaki, call ahead and get it arranged. And leave a message for Sakaguchi."

Takamatsu said, "Be sure they let her sleep. She won't be any help until her shock wears off."

Osaki followed the ambulance crew transporting Suzuna.

Hiroshi and Takamatsu turned to Masayo and Shio.

Masayo said, "We were ready to tell you when you came to the flower shop, but you ran off."

"I was called to another side of the case," Hiroshi explained.

Masayo shook her head. "I want to follow Suzuna to the hospital, and be there when she wakes up. I can explain what happened here, what happened that night, I'll give a statement or whatever I'm supposed to do after I'm sure Suzuna's all right."

Takamatsu took out his cellphone to record it. "Better to explain it all now."

Masayo looked at Shio, sighed and resigned herself to explain. "We found each other online. We all had the same experience and formed a survivors' support group. We met once a month to share our experiences and then go out for a meal and karaoke."

Shio pulled her Disney character overcoat tight and said, "We could talk freely together. We had new friends, a new start, regular jobs. It was a relief."

Hiroshi pulled his coat against the wind. "So when did the idea for revenge come up?"

Shio looked out from her Disney hood.

"Suzuna brought us a plan. Mayu's plan. At first we laughed," Masayo said. "But the next time we talked in our group, it turned serious."

"Serious?" Hiroshi asked.

"I don't know where to start." Masayo looked at Shio. "Shio had been sending tweets, the ones you found, about Onizuka, and another manager at Senden. She'd also taken a lot of photos at drinking parties and karaoke. They were embarrassing, but nothing more than drunk salaryman photos. Well, we got an online response right away."

Shio's face came alive. "It turns out a lot of people, women especially, hate their bosses. The horrible stories and embarrassing photos poured in. We were deluged."

"What were the hashtags?" Hiroshi checked Takamatsu's phone to be sure it was recording. He didn't trust Takamatsu with technology.

Masayo said, "We used #hatemyboss, #bosshole, #buchoasshole. Suzuna thought them all up in English. We laughed a lot. Then, it took off. We made Facebook groups, curated videos on YouTube, posted on Instagram. It's mostly all still up there."

Shio smiled under the Disney character hood of her coat.

Masayo pointed at Shio. "Someone posted herself cutting her boss's tires. It got to be too much, so in group we decided we'd just do one more thing and quit."

"That's when you got in touch with Mistress Emi?"

Masayo nodded.

"How did you know about Mistress Emi?" Hiroshi asked.

Masayo frowned. "Being at work all day every day at a company, it's impossible to hide much. But it was Suzuna who knew. Mayu had told her long ago. So, Suzuna contacted Mistress Emi and she was up for it. She said it was a whole new level of humiliation. Said she'd been reading more psychology and incorporating it into her act."

Hiroshi thought about the psychology of it all. "But where did the plan come from?"

"That's the beautiful part. It was Mayu's plan," Masayo said. Shio smiled.

"Mayu's? But she—"

"Suzuna found one of Mayu's notebooks after she moved in with Toshiko and started working at the flower shop. Mayu had written all this down in tremendous detail. She was a very organized person."

"Like Mayu, we just wanted to humiliate him," Shio added.

"So, why did you bring him up on the roof?" Hiroshi asked.

Shio nodded. "That was the whole point. We were going to text everyone at Senden, tell them there was a morning meeting, and Onizuka would be there naked, with some bondage toys, tied up, hungover."

Masayo said, "And that's all we did."

Takamatsu said, "How did he end up dead?"

Masayo said, "We were more surprised than anyone when we heard. We had a special meeting, but no one had any idea what happened."

"When you left, was he sober enough to walk?" Hiroshi asked.

"He was tied up," Shio said. "There was no way to get out of that on his own."

Hiroshi couldn't remember any rope in the things they found on the roof. Maybe there was rope fiber somewhere they could trace, but none of the crime scene reports mentioned it. They'd have to go over the roof again. "What kind of rope?"

Masayo looked surprised. "Some kind of soft rope. Jute maybe?"

Takamatsu hummed. "So, you picked him up from Mistress Emi. How did you get him up here?"

"With six of us, he wasn't hard to move around. We practiced." Shio and Masayo crossed arms to make a four-handed seat to show Hiroshi. "Onizuka wasn't that heavy. Like a couple bags of potting soil."

"So, you're saying Mayu planned this?" Hiroshi looked at Takamatsu, who was trying to hold his cellphone steady to record everything.

Masayo choked up. "I wish she'd done all this instead of... of... killing herself. We almost lost Suzuna, too."

Shio rubbed Masaya's back. "We wanted Onizuka to die of shame, not to really die."

Hiroshi looked at Takamatsu who was fiddling with his lighter with one hand and holding the cellphone in the other to record them. Hiroshi frowned. "So, how did you get him past the security cameras."

Masayo smiled. "That was tricky, but Mayu had it figured out. She was a perfectionist."

Shio said, "We could never have done it without Mayu working out all the details years ago."

"And Suzuna just stumbled on the diary?"

Masayo nodded. "Mayu had told her, but Suzuna thought it was a joke. But when she found Mayu's diary, it was all in there, the whole plan, down to the kind of baseball hats to hide our faces."

"There's a kind of light, what's it called, Masayo?" Shio scratched her Disney hood.

Masayo said, "I think it's infrared LED, right?"

Shio bounced her head. "Yes, IR LED. We had to order it specially, but if you shine it into the lens, it makes the camera go white long enough to sneak up and put a piece of tape over it. Mayu had stolen keys a long time ago, and Suzuna found those taped inside the box with the diary. Her mother saved every scrap of hers and kept it in boxes."

Hiroshi thought of all the things he and Akiko had found in her room. He hadn't told Takamatsu the half of it.

Shio continued. "We took the tape off on the way down to cover ourselves, doing it all in reverse."

"What about the camera in the parking lot? It's too high to reach," Takamatsu said.

Masayo smiled. "That camera uses radio waves, so you can just buy a jammer. Actually, we figured out that part, but it was the easiest. The other parts took coordination and practice."

"So, what happened after you left Onizuka here?" Hiroshi pointed at the roof.

Masayo pointed at the bench by the smoking lounge. "We left him on the bench. We don't know what happened after that."

Shio said, "We wanted him to get fired because that's what Mayu wanted. We wanted to do that for her and move on. We figured he'd get fired, or if not, we'd have photos of him and could release those."

"Where are those photos?" Hiroshi asked.

Shio and Masayo looked embarrassed. "Suzuna keeps them in a cloud storage file. We'll have to wait until she wakes up."

Hiroshi pointed at the fence. "How did the fence get cut?"

Shio said, "We didn't do that."

"You didn't see it?"

Shio shook her head.

Masayo said, "We left him right here." She pointed down at the spot by a bench. "After we made it out, we started to worry he would freeze to death. He only had on a thin summer *jinbei*, and it was cold up there."

"And the alcohol," Shio added.

"So we called the company and gave them an anonymous tip to go find him."

"That ruined the plan for him being found in the morning," Shio said. "But we had photos."

"Who did you talk to at the company?" Hiroshi asked.

Masayo and Shio looked at each other. Shio said, "The security guard, I guess. It was late. I hung up quickly."

"How long did it take you to get up and back out?" Hiroshi asked.

Masayo smiled. "We did it faster than we planned, eighteen minutes."

Takamatsu turned off the recording. He'd heard enough and stepped aside to light a cigarette.

Hiroshi looked at Masayo and Shio, starting to believe them.

The blanked-out space on the security tape ran a total of forty-two minutes. The extra twenty-four minutes must have been extended by someone. Where did those extra minutes come from? Tech glitch? The video must have been blacked out twice. The only people with access would be the security guards or the HR people. It must be the latter. He looked around the roof, wondering if they needed to start from scratch and run through it all again.

Takamatsu was smoking, the guards were securing the fence, and Tokyo's lights felt far away.

His arm still bled a little and as he pressed on it again, he noticed Chizu, the tall assistant from Human Resources, standing by the elevator. She wore a long trench-coat and carried a soft briefcase and a big, full bag. She waved for Hiroshi to come over.

Hiroshi told Masayo and Shio to think of more details and left Sugamo to watch them. He walked over to Chizu. "Where have you been?"

"We need to hurry," Chizu said. "I was up here that night. I'll explain on the way, but now is our chance."

Chapter 36

Hiroshi whispered, "How did you know we were here?"

"I told the chief security guard Imasato to call me if anything happened," Chizu explained. "Is she all right?"

"She's in shock, but seems stable."

"We need to go now," she said turning for the door.

"Wait a minute." Hiroshi walked back to Sugamo. "Take these two with you to the hospital. You and Osaki take turns watching them together with Suzuna. Don't let them leave." He turned to Shio and Masayo. "You have two choices. Stay in the hospital with Sugamo and Suzuna, or we'll take you in to headquarters. Which is it?"

"We have to work in the morning," Shio said.

"Then, you're going to be very tired," Hiroshi answered.

Masayo looked at Shio and nodded her head. "We'll look after Suzuna in the hospital."

Hiroshi looked at Sugamo who nodded it was no problem to watch them there.

Hiroshi hurried over and got in the main elevator with Takamatsu and Chizu. She said nothing as they rode down to B2 level, accessible only by key.

They exited into the bottom level of the lower parking lot. The place stank of exhaust fumes and years-old mold. Old generators and air conditioners were piled to one side. On the other, a recycling area had been set up for *sodai gomi*, computer monitors, desks and office equipment, tossed in tangles of metal and plastic.

Chizu strode forward past bare concrete pillars, her low heels echoing in the emptiness. She turned back to be sure Hiroshi and Takamatsu were following, and kept going.

She led them up a short ramp that veered toward the main

parking lot above. Chizu turned to a large metal door she opened with a key. Dim lights turned on when they stepped inside a long underground tunnel. The door clunked shut behind them.

Chizu's heels echoed louder in the confined space. Hiroshi tried to remember which direction they were going. It seemed like they were going under the street. That meant these tunnels were probably connected to those that ran in all directions from Tokyo Station. Most had been converted to underground shopping malls, others for storage. Hiroshi guessed

At the end of the tunnel, Chizu stopped at a large door needing two keys. It had a heavy metal handle that she had to lean on to open. The high-ceilinged space inside had three more doors, each with a similar two-key bank vault system.

The one on the right opened to another, mustier hall, with dimmer lighting. At the end was a wide, squat door with a number dial and a key. She spun the numbers, inserted the key and let the detectives in first. Lights clicked on with an automatic sensor.

The room was filled with shelves that slid on tracks attached to the ceiling and floor. The shelves held boxes, files and folders, all carefully labeled. Hiroshi looked at the labels on the side of the shelves, numbers and letters and some *kanji* that might be connected to different departments inside Senden. Was this the central storage area for company files? Nakata had told them that all files were stored outside of Tokyo in special, secure facilities.

Chizu turned into an aisle so narrow she had to turn sideways. She stopped in the middle, checking labels, and pulled down two boxes. She carried them to the end of the aisle opposite Hiroshi and Takamatsu. She pushed a button and gears clunked into motion. The shelf slid over to open a new aisle.

She walked back toward Hiroshi and Takamatsu, checking labels. Chizu reached for an overhead box and Hiroshi shuffled quickly down the aisle to help her get it down.

At the end of the aisle, an old wooden table took up a low-ceilinged sitting area. She pointed for Hiroshi to put the box down and clicked on the light above the table. She looked down the aisle for Takamatsu and whispered, "Detective, please!"

When Takamatsu got there, Chizu pointed at the boxes and files. "Nakata called me earlier tonight. He told me to give you the wrong files. Which I did. But these are the real files."

"I thought they were stored outside Tokyo?" Hiroshi said.

"No, only here. They are labeled in a way that only a few people know." She opened her bag and pulled out what looked like a small printer. "Do you have a USB flash drive?"

Hiroshi shook his head.

"I figured not, so I brought one for you." She pulled out the flash drive and handed it to Hiroshi. She ducked under the table looking for an electric wall socket.

"What's this?" Takamatsu asked.

"A scanner," Chizu said. "I brought it for you." She finished setting up the scanner and turned to the first box they took down. "Let's get to work."

Hiroshi said, "What are we doing?"

"Most of the HR stuff is hidden as are the files for the overseas expansion, especially the budget. That's what you needed, right?" Chizu looked at him and turned on the scanner.

Hiroshi nodded. "So what's in here?"

"Onizuka was moving money that should have been used for purchases to different accounts, but the same banks. None of the higher-ups remember the account numbers, so he could sneak it by them. Senden's money went to accounts—both Senden's and Onizuka's—in London and New York, but also the Cayman Islands, Nevis, Belize."

"I don't get it," Hiroshi said. "It would all be traceable."

"At first it would be, but after, Onizuka could make it disappear. Where? That's your job. Nakata figured out what Onizuka was doing, but he didn't know how to undo it," Chizu said. "Nakata was furious with him."

"Nakata said all this to you?"

"Rumor had it that Onizuka and Nakata were longtime rivals. They started at Senden the same year."

Chizu stopped talking and listened. "Someone's here. Just the guard. I'll go tell him everything's fine. Do you know how to use this?" She patted the scanner.

"I'll figure it out," Hiroshi said.

Chizu hurried off down the rows of shelves.

Hiroshi waved Takamatsu over and told him to hand the files one at a time and keep them in order, one after another. They got into a rhythm—hand, place, scan, save, hand back. Hiroshi heard another row of shelves moving in the far distance. The shelves were heavy and the rows longer than in a big library. In a few minutes, Chizu returned with two more file boxes. They had barely made a dent in the first box.

"Why isn't all this stored on computer?" Hiroshi asked her.

"Some of this is, but they only trust paper. It's all they understand. Let me take over the scanning. It might be faster to take photos of these smaller files. But if you don't have the whole picture, it's not going to be worth anything."

"Takamatsu, use your cellphone to take shots of all these smaller file folders, can you?"

Takamatsu moved the smaller folders to the next table.

Hiroshi started handing papers to Chizu, who was much faster. She stopped every ten or twenty scans to save them.

"The complaints about Onizuka's harassment are in here, too?" Hiroshi asked.

"All of those formal complaints are here, but the way of writing them is so toned down it doesn't capture the full scope of what he was doing." Chizu kept working as she explained.

"Do you think Mayu knew what Onizuka was doing?"

Chizu frowned. "She had to have known. She kept trying to transfer out, but he wanted to keep her close so he could see what she was doing. The longer she was there, the more she'd know, and become implicated, and the more he could control her. Strangely, though, his performance reports about Mayu were glowing."

Hiroshi stopped. "He gave her high evaluations?"

"Some of the highest in the company. Strange, right?"

"And Mayu knew about those?"

"There are open evaluations and closed ones. But she must have known."

"And what about the other women who filed complaints?"

"Mostly, he praised them, too. Maybe it was part of how he kept them in line. He was quite a manipulator."

They worked quietly for a while.

Hiroshi tried to think why Mayu would kill herself if she was getting stellar reviews. Takamatsu looked like he was making progress. He'd taken off his trench coat and his jacket and Hiroshi could tell he was fidgeting for a cigarette.

Hiroshi said, "You want to change places?"

"I'm fine," Chizu said.

"How do you know the filing system if it's supposed to be non-transparent?"

"That secret to the system has been kept inside HR for years. I learned it from Masayo, the woman who was just on the roof to help take care of Suzuna."

"What about Mayu?"

"She probably knew this system, or I guess she did."

"Why are you doing this?"

"I'm leaving," Chizu said.

"Leaving?"

"Quitting." Chizu stopped and looked at the wall, taking a big breath.

"Did you tell them yet?"

"Not yet," Chizu said. "I'll give them two weeks notice, as required. But I have six weeks' unused vacation time."

"So who knew about Onizuka's embezzling? If you knew,

others must have also."

Chizu stopped and looked at Hiroshi. "Yes, they knew, but I guess he was blackmailing them."

"But he was the one doing it."

"Onizuka maybe threatened to expose the truth about the embezzlement and embarrass the entire company. That would be enough to keep everyone quiet until they could force him out. But if he was overseas by then, they'd have a hard time catching him."

"But they admitted it all publicly at the press conference." Hiroshi tried to process what she was telling him, wondering what he would find in the files.

"They had no choice once he died. They had to move on with the overseas expansion and hope to cover their tracks. And they seem to have done that."

"They want to control the narrative, even if it's bad?"

"They want to control everything." Chizu shrugged and kept scanning. "That press conference is later today and I'm in charge. So it doesn't look like I'll get any sleep before now and then."

Hiroshi kept refiling everything she handed him. "You said you were on the roof the night of Onizuka's death. What happened?"

Chizu kept her eyes on the scanning. "It took me time to get the courage to talk with you. I should have just left the company." She paused, sighed and started scanning again. "That night, Nakata got a call from the security guards. And he called me. I came back to work, went up to the roof, and found Nakata and two guards standing over Onizuka. He was tied up, but he could talk. I pulled my jacket off and put it over him, he was freezing."

"You weren't surprised?"

"Nothing Nakata did would surprise me. I only waited to be told how to cover things up."

"What did Nakata say?"

"He said to let him have a cigarette. Somehow, whoever had stolen his clothes had left him his cigarettes."

"And Nakata lit it for him?"

"Yes."

"And then?"

"Then, he told me to go to the office to get all of Onizuka's transfer papers," Chizu said. "The papers weren't in our office, so I had to come down here, to this storage room."

"How long did that take?"

"The papers weren't here. And there's no cellphone reception in here. So, after I looked everywhere I could think of, I gave up."

"After how long, roughly?"

"I must have searched for thirty minutes or so."

"And then?"

"And when I got cellphone reception again, Nakata told me to go home." A single tear dropped onto the paper she was holding. She wiped it off with the back of her hand. "I hated what Onizuka did, but I didn't want to see him die."

Chapter 37

Back in his office, Hiroshi hung up his coat and headed straight for the espresso machine, clicked it on, and loaded the hopper with fresh beans. He'd been bent over the scanner so long, his neck was sore. His arm was throbbing, though the bleeding had stopped.

Takamatsu followed him in, holding his cellphone with the photos of Senden's files they took with Chizu's help. "She could still get in trouble. We should have brought her with us."

"I don't think anyone will figure out what she did," Hiroshi said, turning on his computer. "She said she was leaving anyway."

"There's leaving and there's leaving," Takamatsu said. "Let's send someone to watch the door to her apartment building."

"She's the one who walked off after she let us out that back exit. She had to hurry because she'd be working all night on the press conference about the overseas opening. We can't send someone into the Senden building." Hiroshi looked at Takamatsu.

"We should have put a call button on her like the one Mistress Emi uses." Takamatsu started flipping his lighter. "Send her a message at least."

Hiroshi sent a LINE message to Chizu, and waited for the little mark to show she read it.

But she didn't.

"I'll send her another message later."

Takamatsu looked around the office. "So, let me help. What do you want me to do?"

"Can you read a spreadsheet?" Hiroshi asked.

"No."

"Make espresso?"

"No."

"Send photos of the files from your cellphone?"

"Akiko does that for me."

Hiroshi looked at Takamatsu. "Leave your phone on her desk and write down the passcode."

"She knows what it is."

"Then why not grab some sleep?"

"A few hours horizontal in the bunk room wouldn't hurt. Are we going after them today?"

"From what Chizu said, it should all be here, so we should hit them as soon as we can."

Takamatsu left his phone on Akiko's desk and headed for the door. "I'll stop by the lab and see if they found any rope fibers." Takamatsu paused at the door, drumming his fingers on the doorjamb. "Thanks," he said, and left.

Hiroshi made himself a double espresso and tried to remember if he had ever heard Takamatsu say thank you before. Or offer to help. Even after he fished Takamatsu out of the freezing cold water of Tokyo Bay, all he had done was joke about it. Maybe he was getting soft, or getting old.

Hiroshi took his espresso to his desk and pushed the USB with all the scanned files into his computer. He wondered how Chizu knew exactly which ones to give him, and he panicked for a moment, worried that she had tricked him. He'd need to compare the new files with the ones Nakata and Suzuki had arranged to be sent during the mahjong parlor raid.

One of the nurses from the police clinic came in. "Takamatsu sent me. For your arm."

And now this... well, something must be up with Takamatsu. Hiroshi got up and took off his shirt. It was bloody and torn. He put it in an old convenience store bag and dropped it in the trash. The nurse took off the bandage and disinfected his arm. The blood and fluid spilled into a steel basin she'd brought with her.

"Do I need stitches?"

The nurse looked it over. "The puncture is a bit deep, but it should close up on its own. You need to keep it clean." The nurse put on a fresh bandage and slipped a longer flex bandage over that.

"When was your last tetanus shot?"

"I have no idea."

"I'll check your records. Stop by the clinic to get a booster before you go home, will you?"

"I'm not going home for a long time."

"Neither am I." She sighed and gathered everything.

Hiroshi thanked the nurse and pulled a new shirt from his file drawer. He ripped off the plastic, buttoned the collar and slipped it on. He pulled a sweater from the coat rack and put it on. He wouldn't be able to look at all of the files before the start of the working day, but he could get through enough of them to be sure.

The files showed substantial accounts in several places. Nakata didn't have his name on anything, and neither did Onizuka, but some of the accounts were earmarked for overseas HR use. Hiroshi looked at all of the overseas accounts and each one had transfers in and out at irregular times.

Hiroshi could not see how the fund transfers to the overseas accounts could be easily tapped, so there must be some trace of that. He looked at the loans to other subsidiary firms, but they looked to be in order. He went back year by year until he found where Senden had started overseas branches. Those seemed in order, too.

Hiroshi checked the investment banks that had lent money to Senden for the overseas expansion, and it seemed they had secured loans with collateral that lacked any verifiable origin. He was only looking at one small part of the whole scheme, but by loaning and repurchasing various assets, it seemed like the accountants at Senden had been very good at hiding debt, or rather spreading it around.

All the transfers were lateral, a sort of accounting sleight of hand, now you see it, now you don't, a variation of the *tobashi* schemes that Japanese firms specialized in during the early

1990s, schemes which nearly caused the collapse of the Japanese economy. By hiding bad debt from the past while amassing capital to expand overseas, and assuming profits abroad could be folded in, and also assuming the exchange rate moved favorably, it might work.

Quite neat, Hiroshi thought.

But how did that tie in to Onizuka?

Hiroshi got up for another coffee. He was suddenly hungry. He sent a message to Akiko to pick something up on her way into the office.

Akiko sent a message back. She had just gotten up and would be there soon.

Hiroshi sent a message to Ayana apologizing for not apologizing sooner.

He opened the HR files, but his eyes refused to relay the information to his brain, or maybe it was his brain that couldn't receive what his eyes were sending. He put in eye drops and stood up to stretch, taking big oxygen-full breaths. Then he sat back down.

He sent a LINE message to Chizu again, but there was still no answer and no small notice that she read the last one.

Hiroshi turned back to the files. As soon as he did, he saw two names, Masayo Uchibori and Shio Fujii. Was that the same Masayo and Shio who were Suzuna's friends? They had filed complaints against Onizuka, too. The two photos that popped up did not look much like Masayo and Shio. Their faces were tight, with their hair pulled back by hairpins. They looked pinched in their black jackets and tight white shirts, more straight-jacket than workwear.

To clear his head, Hiroshi grabbed a change of underclothes from his file drawers and went down to the showers. The nurse had left a waterproof arm sleeve for the shower. He inflated it to cover his arm from fingers to armpit.

He was careful to be sure his computer was turned off and Takamatsu's phone locked in his drawer. He locked his office, too, which he almost never did.

The water restored him, giving him the illusion that he had actually slept and this was a morning like any other. As he toweled off, he felt immensely better. He deflated the sleeve and his arm was totally dry. He headed back to his office, walking slowly through the bland hallways of the station.

There were the matching figures from Mayu and Onizuka's accounts, the transfer of funds overseas, and no answer from Senden on any of the rest of it. The security guards didn't look like they were up to anything and the head security guard, Imasato, had Takamatsu's trust.

That might create a scandal if exposed, but it was hardly worth shoving anyone off a building. Nakata was there, but Chizu had only seen them talking. And then she met Nakata... or no, she said they only spoke by phone. And then she went home.

He was missing "the last mile," as one of his accounting teachers use to say all the time in America. But it might as well be a hundred miles.

When he got back, Akiko was standing outside the office.

"I thought you had a key?" Hiroshi said.

"No, why would I? It's never locked." Akiko held up a convenience store bag with fruit, yogurt, and a couple of *onigiri* rice balls.

"Thank you. I'm starving." Hiroshi unlocked the door and they went inside.

"Takamatsu's cellphone is first."

"Did something happen to Takamatsu?" Akiko asked, stricken.

"No, he's sleeping."

"Don't scare me like that. I thought he'd fallen into Tokyo Bay again."

"Still time for that, but he took hundreds of photos of files. Could you send them from his phone to your computer and try to keep them in order? As soon as you get that done, search them all for Onizuka," Hiroshi said. "You want a coffee?"

Akiko nodded and sat down to work.

Hiroshi made espresso for them both.

"There's got to be a connection to Onizuka's history of harassment, but I'm not sure what it is yet."

"Did you figure out how he got onto the roof?"

"He was carried there by a group of women."

"What?"

"They left him there tied up, naked, drunk and, apparently, photographed."

"And then?"

"And then, I don't know. We can't get him from being tied up on the roof to the cut fence and then to the edge where gravity took over."

"On the roof, but not off," Akiko said.

Hiroshi winced, thinking of the body on the pavement, and handed her the espresso.

They worked separately, Hiroshi on the financial files and Akiko on the human resource files.

After a couple of hours, Hiroshi stood up and stretched. "I think I got it, the last mile."

"The last what?"

"The last kilometer." Hiroshi stretched his neck, yawned and moved his arms around. "If I can only stay awake long enough to remember it all."

"Write it down?" Akiko said.

"No time. Check when the Senden Central Infinity press conference starts, can you?"

Akiko searched around and said, "It's in two and a half hours."

"That's enough time. And where is it?"

"In the conference room attached to the museum of advertising, inside Senden's main office."

"And it's open to the public?"

Akiko did another quick search. "Yes."

"Perfect," Hiroshi said, smiling and yawning and stretching all at once.

Chapter 38

They had to take three cars. The chief rode with Sakaguchi and Akiko in his swank chief's car. Osaki drove two more detectives and Sugamo drove Hiroshi, Takamatsu and a new detective. Takamatsu kept turning around to talk to her, breaking her in with a stream of light-hearted sarcasm and long-ago stories. Hiroshi and Sugamo ignored him, but the new detective had no choice but to listen.

"Do you know how to use your retractable baton?" Takamatsu asked, flicking his out so Sugamo had to put up a hand to keep it out of his face.

"I took the training, and I did kendo for many years," she replied.

"So did Hiroshi, but he can't remember to bring any protective device with him ever," Takamatsu said.

The rest of the ride was the young detective nodding politely and responding to Takamatsu with an endless chorus of "*So desu, ne.*"

The chief security guard at Senden, Imasato, met the three cars at the door of the parking lot, directed them to parking spots, and ushered them through a side door. He led them to a high-ceilinged hallway just outside the conference room from which were filtered the muffled sounds of a presentation.

Imasato poked his head around the door. Flashes of light from the cameras ricocheted out. He let the door shut with a soft whoosh. "Still running through the PowerPoint," Imasato said, shaking his head.

Hiroshi ran through what he was going to say, and how. He looked out the narrow floor-to-ceiling window and wondered if it would work or not. It was a gamble to bring everyone, to stage a confrontation in public. But if Onizuka, an inveterate gambler, could take a few risks, a detective could too.

Imasato peeked inside again and leaned back to whisper to Hiroshi. "They're asking for questions from the media now." He doffed his cap as they entered. A large screen hung over a platform at the front, directed out at the rows of seats filled with reporters, company employees, and a few investors and curiosity-seekers. Video crews took up the aisles.

On the front platform sat Nakata with company executives and the company president Hiroshi had met briefly three days before. Beside them stretched out a longer row of younger employees in loose fitting suits, colorful ties, and stylish hair cuts. Only one woman sat on the platform, in the last seat on the right.

One of the men was gesturing at the screen, answering a question with an enthusiastic smile. He rolled the PowerPoint back to a previous slide and started answering a question about the overseas venture.

Hiroshi looked for Chizu, but could not see her anywhere in the huge room. He sent her another LINE message, but she had not responded since they'd locked up the file storage room and hurried off in separate directions. Takamatsu was right, they should have brought Chizu in for her own protection.

Hiroshi walked toward the front of the room. Takamatsu and Akiko followed, the chief somewhere behind. Hiroshi stopped halfway toward the front, waiting until the press questions slowed. Akiko handed him the folder of documents they'd selected.

Hiroshi raised his hand.

The young guy with the PowerPoint clicker in hand pointed at Hiroshi.

Nakata, seeing Hiroshi, leaned forward in his chair. The president of the company whispered something and Nakata nodded.

An assistant wearing white gloves hurried over and handed Hiroshi a microphone with a deep bow. She bent down and hurried out of the way.

Hiroshi turned the microphone on and cleared his throat. All eyes, and cameras, in the room turned to him.

Hiroshi kept his eyes on Nakata. "I have a question about one of your employees, Onizuka, who was set to lead the transition overseas. We've found evidence that he did not commit suicide. So the murder investigation is still open. Do you have any comment on that?"

The room fell quiet.

The president, Nakata, and the other executives sat stone-faced.

Hiroshi waved the folder Akiko had made of the important money transfers and camera flashes bleached out the room. "So, can you answer a few other questions for us?"

The young salarymen and one woman looked confused. They stood looking at the president and Nakata for direction. The company president whispered in Nakata's ear.

Video cameras panned from Hiroshi to the platform, and back again, as the company president whispered again to Nakata, his hand over the microphone.

"We have a list of people we'd like to talk to, starting with you, Nakata-san. Our investigation has led us to conclude that Onizuka did not take his own life and that the company finances for the overseas move have been compromised. I have several questions."

The president spoke to Nakata again.

Nakata stood up with microphone in hand. "You will have to excuse us. The president has some pressing business." He bowed to the hall. The younger employees looked bewildered at having their carefully prepared press conference interrupted.

Nakata followed the president out of the room.

Imasato pulled open the door to the hall for Hiroshi, Akiko, and Takamatsu.

The president and Nakata were walking quickly away but

Sakaguchi, who had been sitting in a chair outside the conference hall, stood up from his chair and limped to the middle of the hallway. He stretched out his arms and stopped them.

At his orders, two of the young detectives raced around the president and Nakata to Sakaguchi's side. Two other detectives hurried over to either side of the two Senden leaders and stood politely in place blocking their exit.

Hiroshi walked up to them, with Takamatsu and Akiko right behind.

The high-ceilinged hallway had an echo and light streamed in the tall, narrow windows.

"You were on the roof that night," Hiroshi said to Nakata.

Nakata laughed. "What? I was nowhere near there."

"A witness and video put you there." Hiroshi was bluffing about the video, but Chizu had seen him.

"Onizuka jumped," Nakata explained to the president.

Hiroshi said, "You untied him. You walked him to the ledge. You cut the fence. You threatened him and talked him into it."

Nakata stared at Hiroshi.

The president cleared his throat.

"You threatened him and helped him to the edge."

"Why would I do that?" Nakata said. "I had enough problems already with the missing funds—"

"That was an embezzlement scheme, one that you initiated, but couldn't control. Onizuka was too clever for you. Once you lost control, you had to do something more."

"We've already taken full responsibility for Onizuka's actions. We've made reparations with our clients—"

"But that isn't it at all, is it?" Hiroshi let the silence settle in.

The president said, "What is all this? We've cooperated with you fully and this is the thanks we get? We have a busy schedule, detectives."

"It's going to get a lot busier," Hiroshi told him. "At first, I thought Onizuka really was the culprit moving funds, but only HR has the full account information. It was you, Nakata, who moved the money through Onizuka's accounts with Mayu's help. At least until she died. That's why you kept moving Mayu back into Onizuka's section."

Nakata stared at Hiroshi and turned to the president.

"Let him finish," the president told him.

"Onizuka was just moving his gambling winnings. He'd been particularly lucky, was always lucky, apparently, and wanted his winnings overseas out of sight of the tax office. That's a crime, but paying back taxes would solve it. It took me all morning to figure that one out."

"What files are you talking about?" Nakata asked.

Hiroshi said, "I've only encountered one similar piggyback scheme before, but you are good. You should have worked in the accounting section, not in Human Resources."

The president looked at Nakata. "Is any of this true?"

Akiko handed the president the folder they'd assembled. Hiroshi caught a glimpse of her pleased, subtle smile as she handed it over.

The president flipped through it while everyone stood waiting in the high, wide hallway.

The president closed the folder and glared at Nakata.

Nakata started to speak in a soft voice. "There was no way we could send Onizuka overseas. He had a destructive streak we could contain here, but not abroad." Nakata looked out the tall, narrow window.

Everyone waited for him to continue.

"We worked with him as long as we could, but he was given two choices, leaving the company or becoming a *madogiwazoku*, sitting by the window doing menial tasks, never promoted, but never fired, either. Most people would be happy for that easy ride until retirement. But not Onizuka. He cashed in years of favors to get himself posted overseas."

The president cleared his throat. "The decision to send

Onizuka overseas was made long ago."

Nakata bowed deeply to the president. "When I found Onizuka on the roof, all I thought was—another one of his messes to clean up. I couldn't get him to say how he got up there. I untied him—the knots were tight. I got him to sit on a bench. I didn't know what to do. We sat in the cold wind for a long time. He said he'd had enough. He asked me to help."

Hiroshi realized that Nakata had thought it all the way through. He missed covering some of his tracks, but not all of them. Nakata would have taken his time, knowing he could blank out the video record of the two of them talking on the roof, and then of his ascending the stairs, and of any footage on any other camera. All he had to do was make some excuse to the security guards, and send them away, off the roof, and grab the footage before they saw it.

But what he couldn't hide were the bank transfers.

"Where is Chizu?" Hiroshi asked.

Instead of answering, Nakata bolted past the detectives, who were too slow to grab him, and took off running down the hallway.

Chapter 39

Sakaguchi took two steps after Nakata, then doubled over. He'd stepped wrong on his knee. Hiroshi took off after Nakata down the hallway.

The younger detectives, unsure what to do, stood watching. Takamatsu told Sugamo to go to the front door and Osaki to pull the stop on one of the elevators and take the other to the roof with the young detectives.

Takamatsu found Hiroshi hunkered down behind a car just outside the parking lot door and frowned. Hiroshi waved him down out of sight. "Nakata was heading for that door on the other side of the lot."

"The one that goes into the underground storage area?"

"Where Chizu took us."

"There were a dozen tunnels in there."

"Each with a locked door."

"I'll call Imasato," Takamatsu said.

"Do you think he has the keys?"

"He better. Did you find Chizu?"

"She hasn't answered."

"Let's hope we get to her before Nakata does."

Hiroshi thought they might already be too late.

Imasato hurried out of the door with the keys and the three of them raced for the underground door at the end of the parking lot. Imasato lagged behind, out of breath. He fumbled with the key ring, found the right one and opened the heavy metal door.

Takamatsu grabbed the ring from him as the lights kicked on inside the empty hallway. Hiroshi and Takamatsu raced to the door at the far end.

Takamatsu held up the ring of twenty-some keys, eyeballing them one by one. Hiroshi waited until he picked the right one and the door swung open. The lights flipped on in an empty hallway with three doors.

Hiroshi slowed, trying to remember how Chizu had led them in there. It must be the far door, and in the next hallway, the one on the right, maybe. He wasn't sure.

Imasato loped down the hall after them. Hiroshi ran to the far door and Takamatsu skidded to a halt to try all the keys again.

He got it on the third try. Imasato caught up with a face red as a heart attack. "Here's the codes for the doors. It's one of these." Imasato handed Hiroshi a small pad with a column of combinations, written by hand. "I got these from the safety inspectors a few years ago. It's got to be one of these. Go on. I'll catch up."

Hiroshi and Takamatsu ran down the next hallway.

An alarm was tripped and the narrow hallway filled with a deafening siren and a flashing red light. Hiroshi cringed. Takamatsu nodded ahead to the doors at the end.

Hiroshi ran to the door halfway down with a combination wheel and large levered knobs like a safe. If it wasn't the one Chizu had taken them through before, they were already farther from Nakata, and probably Chizu, than when they started.

Takamatsu worked at getting the right key as Hiroshi put in the numbers. After several tries, the levers dropped. They pulled back the heavy door and smoke billowed out of the room. The siren and light kept on with distracting urgency.

Inside, the file storage room was dark and quiet. But it was the same one as before. He remembered the marker on the first aisle. He pulled out his cellphone flashlight and Takamatsu plucked out an LED penlight from his jacket. The endless stacks of folders looked the same, but it was hard to tell in the dark and smoke.

Imasato caught up with them and Takamatsu told him to hold the door open.

Hiroshi went one way and Takamatsu the other, looking down each of the aisles, but many of the racks were pressed tightly, efficiently, together. Hiroshi pressed one of the buttons at the end of the stack to get it to move, but it didn't budge. He tied his handkerchief over his face and worked his way to the end of the aisle, finding nothing.

From the other side of the stacks, he heard Takamatsu shout, and the sound of something heavy slamming. He almost ran to see, but instead kept going, making sure he wasn't missing anything before doubling back.

He heard Takamatsu shouting and the sound of boxes falling and metal racks banging against each other.

He turned toward Takamatsu's voice, but heard a shout of "Help!" closer by. The voice was hoarse and weak.

"Hello?" He searched in the dark, but couldn't see anything, and called back.

"Help!" the voice answered, a woman's voice. Metal shelves rattled. "I'm trapped. In here."

Hiroshi backtracked, peering down the aisles with his cellphone light. "Chizu?"

"Yes, it's me."

"Where are you?"

"I'm trapped between the shelves."

Hiroshi banged on a stack. "Is it this one?"

"You're close."

Hiroshi banged on another.

"That's it."

Hiroshi pressed the button trying to get the stacks to move, but he realized he'd have to go to the last one and move each stack one by one. He ran back and jammed the button on the last row but it didn't work. He shook the stack and pressed it again, and it slowly groaned to the side.

He moved down one by one pressing the buttons and leaning into the stacks to get them to move faster. The gears were slow. He moved down one more aisle, but that button failed to work.

"I still can't move," Chizu shouted.

Hiroshi yanked everything from the shelves in the open aisle, dropping them on the floor and removing the shelves so he could slide in and pull out more. He moved until he could see Chizu trapped between the stacks.

"Can you get up to this shelf?" He kept disassembling the shelves and dropping them on the floor behind him.

"My leg's trapped."

Hiroshi pulled on the stack, rocking it back and forth to loosen it, "On the count of three, pull your foot up."

"I got it!"

"I'll pull you out along this cleared row of shelves."

Chizu held out her arms, coughing and clearing her throat.

Hiroshi pulled her with one hand and pushed himself backwards with the other.

Chizu got to the opened aisle, and Hiroshi helped her down. They were both coughing. The smoke was getting worse and he could hear the shuffle of a struggle at the other end.

Chizu latched onto his hand as they stumbled over boxes and sidestepped files as they made their way toward the door.

When they got to the hallway, Hiroshi pushed Chizu into Imasato's arms and saw the hallway filled with detectives, firefighters, and company executives.

Hiroshi went back inside the smoke-filled storage room followed by the firefighters. The sound of fighting had stopped. Hiroshi held his light up, but the firefighters' lights clicked on and lit up the space.

Hiroshi hurried to the back as the firefighters searched for the source of the smoke.

At a corner at the back, Hiroshi found the source of the smoke—flames leaping from an avalanche of papers. Beside the pile, Nakata lay sprawled on the floor.

On the other side of the pile, Takamatsu was climbing onto his knees and shaking his head. He must have been knocked out. Hiroshi hurried over to help him up.

"He punches hard," Takamatsu said.

The firefighters sprayed foam on the stack of half-burned papers, but the smoke continued to thicken. Another pile of boxes and files smoldered at the far corner where the cinderblock walls met the concrete floor.

Hiroshi bent down and took Nakata's wrists, one over each shoulder and started dragging him to the door. He turned back to be sure Takamatsu was coming but he was bent over, coughing hard. Hiroshi waited for him and reset Nakata over his shoulders.

He met more firefighters coming in with bright head lights.

"It's over there," Takamatsu pointed. "Nakata was trying to burn files."

Hiroshi dropped Nakata on the floor in the hallway, and one of the new detectives slapped handcuffs on him as a firefighter put an oxygen mask over his face. His head rested against the wall and rolled back and forth, his eyes closed.

Takamatsu came through the doorway, his face bloodied and covered in dust and ash. He reached for his cigarettes, looked at them, and put them back. "Reminds me of when I first started. Bar fights and building fires."

Chizu was wrapped in a blanket and surrounded by detectives and emergency techs. "I told Nakata I was quitting. He asked me, politely, to find a few more files, bring them up from down here, my last assignment. Then, I don't know what happened. I woke up trapped, where you found me."

"When was that?"

"About four or five in the morning, after I'd finished everything for the press conference."

"You've been there since then?"

Chizu nodded. "He came back later, I guess. I couldn't see, but that's when I smelled smoke. He must have started burning the files I pulled down." Chizu wiped her face again.

"What did he have you pull?"

"I was so exhausted I couldn't even read. I didn't care

anymore. I told him I was leaving and that's all I could think about."

The president of Senden arrived with a small retinue of upper management. He went straight over to Nakata and stood over him where he was slumped again the wall.

Nakata stirred and his eyes focused.

Hiroshi leaned over to hear what he said.

Nakata took off his oxygen mask. He looked at everyone, taking in the scene. He leaned back, not bothering to stand, and started to speak. "I gave up smoking years ago, but I took one of Onizuka's after I found him on the roof. We sat there talking about the past. We started at the same time, competed for the same promotions, but the path gets narrower at the top. He was jealous of my HR spot and I was jealous of how much he got away with."

Nakata stopped to put the oxygen mask over his face again, his chest rising and falling. Then he continued. "Onizuka figured out the money I'd been sending through his section's accounts. Don't ask me how, but he did. I told him that money was going to cover deficits in branch offices, but he didn't believe me. Onizuka always knew everything. He must have known for a long time, but once I knew that he knew, everything changed. If he exposed the scheme, there'd be a scandal, and for once he wouldn't be the center of it—I would be."

"So what did you do?" Hiroshi asked, already knowing, in part.

"I helped him get the knots undone. He was freezing and I gave him my coat. He talked about how much he hated himself, hated a long list of people. He said he would be too humiliated if people knew about this. He said there'd be photos. He wasn't completely coherent. He just kept saying he'd had enough."

"Why didn't you call someone?"

"His scandal was our scandal. Senden always handles things inside."

"So...?" Hiroshi prompted.

Nakata took another lungful of oxygen. "He started begging me to help him over the fence. I thought about just walking away. I didn't think there was any way he could get over the fence."

"So, you went through the fence."

"There was a box of tools that had been left in the hallway, under a tarp. They'd been doing some repairs on the roof."

"We didn't see any box of tools when we searched the roof."

Hiroshi looked at Takamatsu.

"There were pliers, with a cutting edge." Nakata shrugged. "I don't know where they went. I put them back."

The president turned to his retinue and they nodded assent.

Hiroshi kept at Nakata. "So, what happened after that?"

"I clipped the fence, just like opening a zipper, and pulled it open until there was enough room for him to get out."

"He pulled it open or you did?" Hiroshi asked. "He would have been too drunk to stand."

"No, he could stand. And he could pull it open himself. But then he said he knew I was on the roof the night Mayu killed herself."

"Were you?"

Nakata nodded. "I tried to stop her."

"But you failed."

Nakata nodded again. "I'd asked Mayu to return to Onizuka's section to watch him. We'd always met on the roof when she found something. But that day she got hysterical. Something just went off inside her. She stood up screaming, at me, at everything. There was no fence there at that time. And before I could even react, she ran straight to the edge, took off her shoes, and jumped. It was all over in an instant. I ran after her, but—"

"But you didn't do anything, didn't tell anyone."

"Who would believe me?"

"How did Onizuka find out about that?"

Nakata shook his head. He didn't know.

Chizu stared at him in disgust and turned away.

Takamatsu told the four young detectives to take Nakata to

the car. He told them that Osaki and Sugamo would show them the booking procedures at the station.

They hopped to it with enthusiasm, pulling Nakata up from the floor.

The president spoke to the detectives. "Could we remove the handcuffs, please. There's still media with cameras hovering around the premises after the press conference."

Takamatsu gave Hiroshi an "I told you so" look.

Chapter 40

In the hallway, everyone watched Nakata being walked away. Hiroshi wondered how much of what Nakata said was true and how much was self-protective PR. But it hardly mattered. He'd never work in a company again, or work at all, even if his jail time was reduced by the mitigating factors he was no doubt working up in his head. His name would be reported and the story blown out of all proportion in some scandal-loving weekly. Nakata would become yet another sacrifice to the Senden system.

Takamatsu whispered to Hiroshi. "I told you about the wirecutters."

Hiroshi whispered back. "They were pliers."

"They'll have Nakata's prints all over them. I promise you." Takamatsu pulled his lighter out and flipped it around in his hand.

Hiroshi whispered, "You're right. They will."

Chizu came over, still wrapped in the blanket. "Thank you for saving me."

"You helped us immensely," Hiroshi told Chizu.

"Like I told you, I'm quitting. I got accepted into an MBA program in America. I moved most of my personal things out already, so I just need to go upstairs and get my coat and bag," Chizu said.

Takamatsu told one of the detectives to accompany her and then drive her home.

"Best of luck," Hiroshi said. "You'll do great."

Chizu smiled. It was the first time Hiroshi had seen her smile. "Did you piece all the files together?"

"There are still a few missing connections, but without you it might have taken years, or never gotten done at all."

"Do you need me to come in and give a statement?"

"Why don't you rest first?"

"I haven't slept in two days," she said, rubbing her neck. She bowed before turning on her precisely five-centimeter regulation high heels and walking away.

"And thank you," Takamatsu yelled after her.

That was the second time Hiroshi had heard Takamatsu say thank you—twice in one day.

Imasato led them back through the maze of underground passageways to the parking lot. Sakaguchi was already in the car. Akiko was standing by the car, waiting for them, and writing notes for the reports they'd have to file later.

"We could have used you," Takamatsu said.

"Not with this knee," Sakaguchi said. "I got Osaki and Sugamo off to the station with the young detectives."

Hiroshi started to get in the car but was startled to see his uncle standing by the tall windows with a young man. They both dressed in three-piece suits and held briefcases. Hiroshi walked over to them, feeling curious and very surprised.

"Uncle, what are you doing here?" Hiroshi asked.

Hiroshi's uncle smiled. "I had a short meeting to conclude a few items left over from my work with Senden."

Hiroshi said, "It's quite a coincidence."

"Not really, your secretary...is that her?" Hiroshi's uncle looked at Akiko, who smiled back. "She told us you'd be here. I heard more about your life from her than I have from you."

Akiko turned to Hiroshi. "I filled him in a little bit."

Hiroshi's uncle said, "And this is the son of one of my former colleagues. Like you, he's an accountant."

"Watanabe *desu*." He bowed deeply to Hiroshi, Takamatsu, and Akiko, holding out his *meishi* name card in both hands.

As Hiroshi rifled his pockets for his *meishi*, Hiroshi's uncle said, "He works for the National Tax Agency, in the corporate tax section."

"Is that right?" Hiroshi found one last remaining *meishi* in his wallet. It was wrinkled and had an embarrassing smudge of dirt around the edges, but it was the only one he had.

Watanabe said, "I work with your uncle from time to time."

Hiroshi's uncle said, "Watanabe knows his stuff. All I ever have to do is follow the threads he's already connected."

Watanabe held Hiroshi's *meishi* and looked him in the eyes. "I was wondering if we might meet sometime. I've been reviewing Senden's taxes for several years now."

Hiroshi's eyes lit up. "I'd be happy to meet."

"What about tomorrow for lunch?" Watanabe asked.

"I've hardly slept the last week. Would Monday be OK?"

Watanabe smiled. "That'd be fine."

Hiroshi didn't want to go with the others to the station, so he begged off by telling him he was going to talk to Toshiko.

Sakaguchi's knee hurt and Takamatsu was still coughing, so Akiko drove them back.

Hiroshi walked with his uncle and Watanabe to Tokyo Station, chatting about this and that, none of it about work or the case. Inside the old brick front of the station, they parted for different train lines with brisk bows.

Hiroshi went up to the Chuo Line platform. The escalator felt like a gift. He bought a heated can of coffee from the kiosk and waited one train to be first in line to get a seat. In three minutes, the next train pulled into the terminus, and he sat down at the end by the door and sipped the hot can of coffee.

He texted Ayana and asked what she had planned. He'd completely forgotten what she had told him that morning, or was it last night? Ayana texted back not to forget the time, as if she hadn't even read what he wrote. He couldn't dredge up what it was they were celebrating, but he wrote back that of course he remembered. Dress nice, Ayana texted back.

As the train headed across the city, Hiroshi finished the coffee and let himself doze in the morning sun warming the train car.

He wondered if Nakata had been telling the truth. It would

take a lot of time to prove the rerouting of funds, and he didn't want to get into it unless he could acquire the actual files through proper channels. That meant going through the ministries. Senden might not cooperate. It was better to hand everything on Senden over to Watanabe at the Tax Agency. Let taxes trip them up.

***

Hiroshi woke up as the train pulled into Kichijoji Station and walked north through the small boutique and specialty stores. They cheated on their taxes too, the small shops, but he felt sympathy with them. It was the 70-50-30 rule. Individuals paid 70 percent of what they owed, small businesses 50 percent and large corporations 30 percent. Maybe with people like Watanabe in the Tax Agency that would change, though nothing ever seemed to change quickly in Japan.

Mayu's mother, Toshiko, was in front of her flower shop washing the windows. Hiroshi watched her for a minute, wondering what to say.

Toshiko noticed him and he tried to act like he had not stopped to watch her first. She set down the bucket she'd been using.

Hiroshi said, "I wanted to stop by and ask about Suzuna."

"I saw her this morning, but she was sleeping." Toshiko looked down. "I'll try to get her moved to a closer hospital in Mitaka. So I can visit her at lunch and after work." She set the sponge and squeegee into the soapy bucket. She stripped off her rubber gloves and buried her face in the crook of her elbow and fought back tears. "I almost killed her too, didn't I?"

"You didn't kill anyone. Suzuna's still in shock. It takes time."

"I don't know how I'll ever thank you for saving her. I couldn't have survived a second loss."

"Suzuna will get better in time."

Shio came out from the small walkway that ran along the side of the shop. She carried two bags of dirt over her shoulder, each of which looked heavier than Shio herself. She bent over to flop the bags down. "Did you get everything sorted out at the company?" Shio asked Hiroshi.

"Did Sugamo and Osaki let you leave the hospital?"

"They made Masayo and me promise to give an official statement today. We're going to do that in the afternoon."

Toshiko said, "Shio told me a little about what happened." She looked at Shio. "I feel like I've got another daughter."

"You do." Shio smiled. "And Masayo, too."

"Ones I'll take care of this time."

Masayo came out from inside the shop and bowed deeply to Hiroshi. "Shio and I can come to the station anytime to give our statement."

"Let's do that Monday," Hiroshi said. They last thing he wanted to do was put these two women in jail, even temporarily. That wouldn't help get the story straight.

"What's going to happen to these two?" Toshiko asked.

"You have a good lawyer, the one who got you the settlement with Senden. Call him."

"We'll accept whatever happens," Masayo said. "I'm so sorry about all this. We'll help get things cleared up."

Shio said, "I've got dirt to move."

They both bowed deeply before skipping off. Hiroshi watched them go. There wasn't much more he could do for them. He'd talk with the judges and prosecutors, but their stories spoke for themselves.

"I hope they'll stay for good," Toshiko said. "Suzuna and I were just about to rent a small space in the station building for walk-by traffic. The space is only this wide." She stretched out her arms and looked back and forth.

"An arm's width is all you need," Hiroshi said. "Especially now that you've got more help."

"We can't store much there when the shutters are closed, and the refrigerator is teensy, but we'll get delivery tricycles to take things back and forth from here. There are more people than ever in Kichijoji these days," Toshiko said.

"I just wanted to let you know who was responsible for Onizuka's death, and Mayu's too, in a way."

Toshiko looked at him, ready.

"It was Nakata, the head of HR at Senden. We're not sure of all the details yet, but he was there."

"When Mayu jumped?"

"Yes. And with Onizuka."

Toshiko shook her head. "He pushed them?"

"He just said he was there. We'll see if that story holds up on further investigation. He has a lot of explaining to do and it might take some time to figure out what's true or not."

"At least it wasn't my ex-husband. Or Steve." Toshiko nodded in quick bounces, taking in the information. "Nakata was the last one to see Mayu alive?"

Hiroshi nodded.

Toshiko looked away. "Nakata was the one my husband knocked out at the funeral." She chuckled bitterly. "He was right about that anyway. Is he OK?"

"Your husband? He hired a private investigator who helped crack the case. We'll release him and I guess he'll go back to work in the Philippines."

"And what about Steve?"

"His cultural visa is still valid," Hiroshi said. "But it's hard to say since he was arrested in a marijuana bust."

"Marijuana isn't so serious. Mayu said she smoked it when she studied in America," Toshiko blurted out, then quickly covered her mouth.

"Don't tell anybody, but so did I," Hiroshi whispered.

Toshiko nodded. "And Suzuna?"

Hiroshi held up his hand. "There's a long list of crimes she, and the group, committed. Suzuna seemed in charge, but there are so many extenuating circumstances." Hiroshi wondered if Suzuna could get off without any serious charges. Maybe she couldn't escape everything.

"I'll get the lawyer on it. And our local Diet member's mother shops here, so I also spoke to her about Suzuna."

"Make sure the lawyer presents it as revenge. More of a game, with no intent to harm, just to embarrass. And have the lawyer contact Mistress Emi. The women know how to find her. And be sure they say they left Onizuka on the roof alive."

Toshiko said, "I got it. Thank you. I... I feel... well, I kept all my feelings submerged for so long, getting married and getting Mayu through the whole system. I was so stupid. I should have let my emotions guide me, tell me how to do things better. If I had..."

"I've got to go," Hiroshi said. "I've been up all night and barely slept this week."

Toshiko looked at him. "You work too much."

"Sometimes," Hiroshi said. "But not always." He turned to leave. "And by the way, the media will probably descend on you once the story gets out. Why not close up and take a vacation?"

"Vacation? I'm going to stay open. I'll be ready for the media this time. In fact, I welcome the chance to tell Mayu's story right."

Chapter 41

Too tired to go back home, where he'd certainly fall deep asleep and be unable to make up in time to meet Ayana, Hiroshi took the train back to the station. Akiko was at work in the office.

Hiroshi hung his overcoat on the rack and slumped in his chair. "Make copies of everything that Chizu gave us, and everything we had on Mayu's and Onizuka's bank accounts. I'm going to hand all of this to Watanabe. Let him get Senden." Hiroshi pushed himself up from his chair and headed for the espresso machine.

Akiko looked at him.

Hiroshi looked at her. "Watanabe and the Tax Agency can have this Senden case. They'll have more traction, and more teeth, than we could muster." He pressed the button for a double espresso.

When the grinder quieted, Akiko said, "OK."

"I forgot to get my tetanus booster. And I better get my bandage changed." Hiroshi gulped his coffee.

Akiko kept her eyes on the screen, making backup copies of the files.

Outside the clinic, Hiroshi ran into the chief. "What are you doing here?"

"Blood pressure pills," the chief said. "I kept losing them. So my wife made me leave them here. Then she calls me. Or the clinic calls me. I got too much on my mind to remember little things like this."

They stepped inside.

Hiroshi said, "So, are we going to move on the ministry? That Suzuki is in this thick."

The chief held his palm up. "You know, I've been thinking about that. As much as I'd like to ding Suzuki, I think we should wait. We already caught him gambling with an employee accused of criminal actions in a company he's supposed to be overseeing. So, why don't we just tell Suzuki we're still investigating, leave it open and let him sweat it out," the chief said.

"That sounds all right," Hiroshi said.

The chief swallowed his pill and took a little white cup of water from the nurse, the same one who'd come to his office earlier.

The chief crumpled his little cup. "That's what we need more of. Thinking ahead. Let's get on it."

The chief walked out and the nurse rolled her eyes.

"Double shift?" Hiroshi asked her.

"Someone called in sick." She got a tetanus booster out for Hiroshi and another nurse came over with a fresh bandage and arm sleeve. The bandage hurt coming off his arm, but Hiroshi was too tired to react.

When he got back to his office, Takamatsu was talking with Akiko about Steve's confession. "Akiko tells me you're passing up a chance to look through files full of numbers."

"I thought I'd bounce it to someone else for a change." Hiroshi frowned at Akiko, who smiled back at him.

"You must be tired. You might regret the chance to dig into this later—"

"I'm sure I won't," Hiroshi said. "Is that what you came to my office for?"

"I came to see Akiko, actually," Takamatsu said. "Like always. Oh, and Sakaguchi needs you. The American guy."

"Someone prepared the statement?" Hiroshi asked.

Takamatsu pointed at Akiko. "She listened to the tapes and put it together. She's a whiz."

Akiko took a lot of the load off. Hiroshi looked at her and she frowned at him again. He turned to Takamatsu. "How is the private eye, Shibutani?"

Takamatsu tapped his cigarette lighter in his hand. "I stopped by the hospital. He can talk, but he wouldn't say anything about what happened. That means he's fine. That generation, they keep things quiet. That guy Ota is handling the office for Shibutani while he recovers."

"He was a tough one, to get beaten up like that," Hiroshi said. "I hope Ota finds out who did it."

"Shibutani said Ota was clever, and thorough." Takamatsu hummed. "I'll see if I can help them somehow."

"You two must be exhausted," Akiko said to them.

Takamatsu smiled. "I got a few hours while our Americanized accountant here was busy piecing the numbers together. Anyway, I have a date tonight."

Hiroshi thought for a minute and then shook his head at Takamatsu. "Don't do that."

"Don't do what?" Akiko asked.

"You don't want to know," Hiroshi said.

Takamatsu laughed. "Just a little *background* research." He laughed louder.

Hiroshi said, "If you compromise this investigation, Sakaguchi will put you on suspension forever."

"What date?" Akiko asked.

"You don't want to know. Really you don't," Hiroshi said.

Takamatsu saluted with his lighter in hand and walked off.

***

Hiroshi found Sakaguchi in the hall outside the interrogation room with Steve inside.

"Glad to have this one over," Hiroshi said.

"Those company and government people are a pain. They always say how they sacrifice for the greater good of Japan, but they expect everyone else to sacrifice more to keep the system running to their advantage. They are born into it, educated for it, and believe in it like a religion. If you came from the poor section of Osaka like I did, you would have understood that from the beginning."

"You should take vacation time after the surgery."

"I will, but after that, I don't think I'll like being stuck with office work while I wait for it to heal. In sumo, you get right back out there. Ueno said it's driving him crazy."

"Ueno's walking better now, and it's good to slow down."

"I'll be out for the surgery from Thursday. Akiko got me set up to watch movies on a laptop." Sakaguchi handed him the papers for Steve to sign.

"I'll take care of this."

Sakaguchi nodded and hobbled off. Hiroshi felt like chasing after him and helping him, but let him go.

Steve looked a lot calmer, though puffy gray bags under his eyes told another story.

Inside the room, Hiroshi sat down across from him. "So, how did you like Japanese jail?"

Steve said, "It's like the opposite of jazz."

"Here's the form for you to sign." Hiroshi opened the folder on the table and pulled out a pen. It was all in Japanese.

Steve looked at it. "Don't I even get to know what I'm signing?"

"I'm not going to translate it word by word. But if you want that, you can go back to the cell and contact a lawyer and translator. That could take a week, maybe more."

Steve looked at it. "And if I sign it now, I walk out of here?"

Hiroshi said, "That's it."

Steve looked at the Japanese papers in front of him. He reached for the pen, signed and handed the pen back to Hiroshi. "So now what?" Steve asked.

"Now, you thank me," Hiroshi said.

"OK. Thank you." Steve managed a small bow of the head. "I need my saxophone."

"I'll walk you out."

At the registration desk, the clerk checked the papers and went inside the storage room to find Steve's saxophone. When Steve saw the case, he was visibly relieved.

"Don't you want to check it?" Hiroshi asked.

"I'm learning to trust, along with expressing thanks and apologizing all the time."

***

Hiroshi went back to his office to get his coat. He ransacked his brain for why Ayana was so insistent to go out. He had an hour before meeting her to figure it out. If not, he'd bluff his way through, or throw himself on her mercy and confess he had no idea.

Hiroshi got in a taxi outside the station. The late afternoon sun was turning everything a dark amber yellow, with shadows in between. At the first intersection from the station, Hiroshi saw Steve sitting on a bench at the corner, his saxophone case beside him, checking everything carefully. He didn't trust that much, apparently.

Hiroshi told the driver to pull over. He rolled the window down and shouted, "Steve, come on, let me give you a lift."

Steve looked up, surprised.

"Come on," Hiroshi shouted. "Get in."

Steve clicked his case shut, walked over to the taxi, and leaned in. "So, this is Japan. First the cops arrest you and then they give you a lift."

Hiroshi scooted over to make room. "C'mon, where are you headed?"

Steve got in. "Nippori."

"A gig?"

"Yeah, kind of."

"Which club?"

"Just by the station." Steve opened his case and started checking his sax again.

"Mayu bought it for you, didn't she?" Hiroshi asked.

Steve looked surprised. "How did you know?"

"Lucky guess. It looks expensive."

"American Selmer Mark VI. I have no idea where she found it." Steve took a big breath and caressed the keys before putting it back in place and clicking the case shut. "I don't know how those jazz and blues musicians could survive jail. I was in for a few days. It was clean. I didn't get beaten or called names. And yet, I'm completely wiped out."

They talked about jazz until the taxi driver asked where to stop by Nippori Station.

The taxi pulled over and Steve started to get out, but stopped halfway. "Why don't you come with me? If you have a few minutes."

Hiroshi checked his watch. He had time before he met Ayana. He paid the taxi driver and followed Steve upstairs onto a crossover to the other side of the station where a path sloped upwards along a concrete embankment.

At the top, Steve stopped for Hiroshi to catch his breath. "You OK?"

"I probably got less sleep than you last night." Hiroshi nodded to go on. His cellphone buzzed. It was a message from Ayana. "Shinjuku, west exit, seven sharp. Dress nice."

They walked past a few houses before the pavement turned to a stone pathway ringed by mossy earth. Hiroshi realized they were in Yanaka Cemetery.

Knee-high stone walls marked off the rectangular grave sites. Inside each area, polished stone markers rose to various heights like tall buildings in an earthbound neighborhood. Next to the central gravestones were five-tiered stupas, stone lanterns, flowering shrubs and Japanese maple trees. Cherry trees grew out of the common areas between the rows. With their leaves gone, the craggy branches spread out like a grandparents' fingers over the graves below.

Hiroshi realized where Steve was headed.

Steve stepped up two steps into the site where Hiroshi had followed Suzuna. The granite stone was buffed to a gleam and Mayu's name and dates, blacked inside the carved characters, stood out strongly.

Hiroshi put his hands together and bowed deeply.

Steve brushed away leaves and opened his case on the stone wall encompassing the small, immaculate lot. He twisted the saxophone neck into place and fiddled with the mouthpiece, all the time sucking on a reed. He slipped it into place, clamped it and gave a few puffs. He fingered the keys, reset the neck, loosened and tightened the reed, and reset the neck again.

Then, starting to play so softly that Hiroshi could hardly hear, Steve stood up, closed his eyes, faced Mayu's grave and started to play.

His melody flowed from long, full notes to shorter ones, modulating higher, moving lower, growing in strength, unlocking emotions. Steve's rhythm was slow and gentle, in no hurry, and his sound held soft attention to subtleties and semitones.

When Steve took a breath, Hiroshi could hear the clack of the tall, thin memorial boards held in racks as an offering. Covered in Buddhist scripture, each wooden board was a miniature stupa, layered from bottom to top in symbolic curves—earth, water, fire, wind, emptiness. Jostled by the wind, their clack-clack punctuated Steve's melody with counterpoint and odd rhythms.

An old woman stopped to listen, staring at Steve. Maybe the sax felt like a violation in her ancestral burial grounds. She watched and listened intently until three schoolgirls in white sailor uniforms came giggling by. They let their hard, heavy *randoseru* backpacks fall onto the stones, surprised to hear music along the route they took to school every day. They soon skipped away, giggling.

A group of mothers on pedal-assisted, new-generation *mama-chara* bicycles turned back to tell their pre-school children in the seats behind to listen, but they didn't stop.

And then a group of young people in their early twenties, everyone dressed in the same freshers' outfits, appeared. They stopped chatting when they got close and slowed their pace to listen, clumping together in the stiff black and white outfits all new employees wore for job interviews and initial training. They were probably coming from their soon-to-be company. The work year started in April.

They didn't listen long, and returned their attention to their new workmates, tuning out the song Steve was playing and losing themselves in their new working life as *shakaijin*, official members of society.

When Steve finished, he looked at the stone grave and let the sax loosen and hang from his neck strap.

Hiroshi was surprised to see the old woman still there listening from the stone pathway. She put her hands together, then smiled and waved at Steve.

Steve waved back, and she walked away.

"That was for Mayu," Steve said. "I just wrote it, inside. In my head."

"What are you going to call it?" Hiroshi asked.

Steve started putting his sax away. "*Zangyo*. 'Overtime' is the one word I'll never forget in Japanese."

Chapter 42

Ayana was waiting at the south exit of Shinjuku Station. Hiroshi saw her immediately in the crowd. She was really dressed up in a long skirt and a chic coat. She looked as beautiful as she always appeared to him.

Ayana watched him approach her through the chaotic trajectories of the crowd. Her frown deepened as he got closer.

He pulled her into a quick hug, but she pushed him back and held him at arm's length.

"What?" Hiroshi asked.

"I said dress nice."

Hiroshi looked down at himself. His jacket was wrinkled, his shirt untucked and he ran his hand over his face, brushing the stubble. He rubbed one shoe along the back of his pants, avoiding her eyes. "I—"

"You smell like smoke."

Hiroshi smelled his sleeve, suffused with smoke from the file storage room. He'd been too tired to notice.

Ayana took a breath. "And you didn't sleep all night and didn't go home and didn't follow my request for this special day."

"This case was—"

Ayana took a big breath.

Hiroshi closed his eyes, searching for some magical words to change her reaction, but he felt like his brain had shut down. "Where did you plan for us to eat?"

Ayana pointed at the tall skyscrapers of West Shinjuku, down the wide road a short walk from the station.

"A fancy restaurant?"

Ayana nodded.

"One of those up in a skyscraper hotel? Waiters in tuxedos, a cozy table by the window, champagne in a bucket, small dishes on big white plates, and dessert with our names on it?"

Ayana nodded. "I had to make the reservation two weeks ago."

"Panoramic windows, oceanic feeling gazing at the horizon?"

"Too bad you're not dressed for it."

"I'm not only not dressed for it, I'm barely awake for it." Hiroshi looked at the closest line of skyscrapers. They looked like massive stupa squared off, with none of the curving, complex meanings real stupa carried. They stretched blindly skyward in solid steel and stone, as if angry at the earth's gravity. The higher they were built, the emptier they became. It made Hiroshi dizzy. He looked away.

Ayana said, "Did you finish the case?"

"I'm taking two days off."

"We finished reshelving the archives."

"You must be—"

"I am, but today's an important anniversary."

Hiroshi smiled at Ayana, desperately ransacking his brain for what anniversary he had forgotten. When did they move in together? When had they gotten back together? It wasn't her birthday, or his. Was it the day of her divorce?

"OK, I give up. I haven't slept all night, and not much this past week."

Ayana smiled. "Want me to tell you?"

"You'll have to if we're ever going to eat."

"This is the day when we spent the night together on the beach in Kamakura." Ayana grabbed his arm, her face beaming.

Hiroshi remembered the night after their kendo tournament during the second year of college. It was the first time to be held tenderly, to spend the night together, to make love with anyone despite the sand and the cold on the beach, buried under their kendo gear after the contest. It was the most beautiful memory of his life. It was the day he started living.

"We didn't celebrate this last year. Did we?" Hiroshi asked.

"I came across some records of tournaments for the

intercollegiate kendo association at the archives. I got curious if ours was in there. It took a little time, but I found it. In fact, that tournament has a lineage back to the eighteenth century."

Hiroshi hugged Ayana. The swirl of people around them went ignored as Hiroshi kept tight hold of her. He could feel the stares of passing people. Hugs and clinches weren't uncommon late at night when lovers separated at stations to take trains far apart from one another. But hugging intensely before dinner with everyone sweeping past in one of the most public spots in the city was highly unusual.

Ayana patted his back and eased away. "OK, all right, already. Now I smell like smoke."

Hiroshi let her go. "I just can't go up into any high place. The case, well, I didn't tell you yet, but I had to rescue a woman who almost jumped. Twenty stories or so. So tonight, above the first floor, I wouldn't be good company."

Ayana touched his cheek.

"What if we go to the beach instead? If you really want to celebrate the anniversary. Recreate the past."

She smiled and nodded. "Sand, flies, sweaty gear. That's romance, I agree, but it's a bit far to get there right now."

"But we can do that sometime?"

"It depends on the beach." Ayana took a breath and pulled out her cellphone to call and cancel the reservations with an elaborate excuse. When she dropped her cellphone into her bag, she looked at Hiroshi. "That's canceled. So?"

"Are you disappointed?"

Ayana took his arm and turned him downhill. "With the reservation, yes. But it's still our anniversary. What do you want to do?"

"Let's walk home, find something to eat along the way."

They walked away from the south exit and turned north through the busy streets surrounding Shinjuku Station. People seemed jumpier closer to the big stations, as if some electric magnet was energizing them to move and gesticulate, talk louder, drink more, shop more desperately.

"Aren't you too tired?" Ayana asked, clutching his arm.

"No. A walk is just what I need. There's that tempura place you like."

"I'm overdressed for that."

"You're overdressed for most places between here and Kagurazaka and I'm underdressed for everywhere. I just want to get you inside someplace with good lighting so I can stare at you."

"I thought you always liked *tonkatsu* deep-fried pork cutlets when you're not with me, so what if I join you for once?"

"It's a bit heavy. What about ramen? I know a great place on the way home. They specialize in the 'two broth method.'"

Ayana laughed. "What's that?"

"They keep the two broths separate until the last minute, then pour them in together right before the noodles. It's special."

"What are the two broths?"

"Chicken feet is one and pork bones is the other, plus secret ingredients the chef would never divulge."

"I like the secret part."

They took each other's hands. Out of the busy part of Shinjuku, the streets became calmer, darker and quieter. It was more open but felt more intimate.

The quieter lanes closer by Tokyo Women's Medical University felt even more relaxed. A series of small temples dotted both sides of the street. Fewer cars buzzed by and the streets turned into neighborhoods.

"What about a place we don't know?" Ayana said. "Like that soba place over there."

"Let's just keep walking." Hiroshi pulled her closer. The night air felt warmer than the past few days, and the wind had stopped.

Ayana twisted free and skipped a few steps ahead. She turned to face Hiroshi, walking backwards and watching him.

He burst forward to catch up with her, pulled her close, and kissed her deeply.

They let go, gave each other a little squeeze, and slipped back shoulder to shoulder to keep walking.

"Is this really the day of that kendo contest?" Hiroshi couldn't quite believe it was.

"Why would I make that up? And anyway, it's better than typical anniversaries, birthdays or whatever, isn't it?"

Hiroshi felt deeply, strongly that it was much better.

They walked for a while in silence.

"It's nice to walk like this, without a plan. Like we did in college."

"That was walking without money. I had a lot of plans."

"It was nice back then. We couldn't plan anything more than what money we had in our pockets."

"Which allowed very few plans. Maybe that's the secret, to always have more time than money."

"Maybe the secret is just walking like this."

THE END

If you enjoyed this book, please consider taking a minute to write a review on your favorite book-related site. Reviews really help indie writers like myself.

And if you're interested in future releases and news and insights from Tokyo, sign up for my newsletter here:

https://www.michaelpronko.com/newsletter/

Special Thanks

Thanks to everyone who helped.

Allen Appel

Marco Mancini

Matt Kineen

Anne Brewer

Luis Carlet and Hifumi Okunuki of Tozen Union

Richard Sheehan

Nancy LaFever

And thanks also to my friends, family and students.

And always, thanks for all to my wife.

About the author

Michael Pronko is the author of three mystery novels and three collections of writings about Tokyo. He has written about Japanese culture, art, jazz, and politics for Newsweek Japan, The Japan Times, Artscape Japan, and other publications for over twenty years. He has appeared on NHK Public TV, Tokyo MXTV and Nippon Television. He also runs a website, Jazz in Japan, about the vibrant jazz scene in Japan.

Michael is a professor of American Literature and Culture at Meiji Gakuin University in Tokyo, teaching courses in contemporary American novels, film adaptations, and American art and music. When not teaching, writing or listening to jazz, he wanders Tokyo contemplating its intensity and figuring out the stories to come.

His award-winning collections of essays about life in Tokyo are available at online retailers and from his website, as are the Japanese language versions. His first three novels in the Detective Hiroshi series have won numerous awards.

***

For more on the Hiroshi series: www.michaelpronko.com
Follow Michael on Twitter: @pronkomichael
Michael's Facebook page: www.facebook.com/pronkoauthor
For more about jazz in Japan: www.jazzinjapan.com.

Awards for *The Last Train* (2017)

Winner Shelf Unbound Best Independently Published Book (2018)

Solo Medalist Winner New Apple E-Book Awards for Mystery (2017)

Winner Beverly Hills Book Awards for Crime Fiction (2017)

Winner Best Mystery Book Excellence Awards for Mystery (2017)

Winner Independent Press Award for Mystery and for Thriller (2018)

Global Award Reader Views (2017-2018)

Gold Award Literary Titan Book Award (2017)

Silver Honoree IRPA Benjamin Franklin Digital Awards (2017)

Silver Award Feathered Quill Awards (2018)

Silver Award Independent Publisher Book Awards (2018)

Reviews of *The Last Train* (2017)

"A flawless, dark, atmospheric mystery set in Tokyo. Our judges couldn't put this novel down." *Shelf Unbound Competition*

"For anyone who loves crime and cop novels, or Japanophiles in general, this is a terrific thriller." *Blue Ink Review*

"This exotic crime thriller is a lightning-fast chase to the finish line that'll leave hearts pounding and pages turning." *Best Thrillers*

"A well-paced and absorbing mystery, with quick action and a look at urban life, an utterly page-turning adventure." *Foreword Reviews*

"An absorbing investigation and memorable backdrop put this series launch on the right track." *Kirkus Reviews*

"Gripping and suspenseful, this fast-paced thriller unfolds on the streets of Tokyo, where a clever and cold-blooded killer exacts revenge." *Booklife Prize*

"Mystery readers will relish the progress of a detective torn between cultures, the reader of Japanese literature the depth of background." *Midwest Book Review*

"Tokyo comes to vivid life in this taut thriller, an unrelenting portrayal of a strong female character and the heart-pounding search to find her." *Publishers Daily Reviews*

"Nothing short of electrifying, a masterpiece that combines action with humor and suspense." *Readers' Favorite*

"A fast-paced thriller that skillfully exposes readers to the seedy urban side of Japan and leaves readers waiting for the next in the series." *Feathered Quill*

"Written from knowledge rather than research, he knows a lot more than he has any need to tell us brings the city gloriously to life." *The Bookbag*

"A heartfelt, thoughtful ode to a strange and beautiful city, in the way that so many classic detective novels are. Lyrically written with plenty of suspense." *Indie Reader*

Awards for The Moving Blade (2018)

Named One of Kirkus Reviews Best Indie Mysteries and Thrillers (2018)

Grand Prize Winner Chanticleer International Book Awards Global Thrillers (2018)

Winner Independent Press Award for Crime Fiction (2019)

Gold Award Literary Titan Book Award (2018)

Five Star Honoree B.R.A.G. Medallion (2018)

Gold Award Independent Publisher Awards for Mystery (2019)

Silver Medal Readers' Favorite for Thriller (2019)

Reviews of *The Moving Blade* (2018)

"An elegant balance of Japanese customs with an American-style hard-boiled procedural. A tight, rock-solid installment in a series that's only getting better." *Kirkus Reviews*

"A true page turner with main characters that come alive with intelligence, curiosity and imperfections." *Blue Ink Review*

"An homage to Tokyo and a savagely entertaining mystery that will grip readers and keep them guessing until the violent, octane-fueled finish." *SPR Review*

"One of the year's best thrillers. A string of grisly murders, high stakes geopolitics and the prose of a master craftsman elevate this crime thriller to rarefied air." *Best Thrillers*

"Full of East Asian and international politics and plenty of sociological commentary. Fun and thrilling throughout—an exciting modern mystery." *Foreword Clarion Reviews*

"This book made it to my favorites list before I even finished reading it. Suspense and intrigue from the very first chapter...and great writing." *Literary Titan*

"Ripe with surprising plot twists that take the reader into the deep underbelly of Tokyo. An intriguing story of murder, mystery, and maleficence." *US Review of Books*

"Detailed and compellingly plotted...for anyone with a fascination or even a curiosity about Japan, this is a great crime novel." *Crime Fiction Lover*

"A powerfully written crime novel; often stark and unsettling, the characters spring off the page." *The Wishing Shelf*

"A stellar novel with a unique storyline and setting, *The Moving Blade* is fresh and original." *BookLife Prize*

"The second in the Detective Hiroshi series is another cracker: real tension and a scenario which is (unfortunately) only too believable." *The Bookbag*

"More than most procedural crime novels...enriched by carefully drawn portraits of both political and cultural differences between Western and Eastern culture." *Chanticleer Book Reviews*

"The action-packed plot is not just a dramatic whodunit piece, but a slice of life piece inspecting Japanese heart and minds." *Midwest Book Review*

"Pronko brought this story to life so much that I found myself hoping that none of the negative aspects could possibly be true." *Reader Views*

Awards for *Tokyo Traffic* (2020)

Gold Award Literary Titan (2020)

Gold Medallian Book Readers Appreciation Group (B.R.A.G.) (2020)

Long-listed Shelf Unbound Best Indie Book (2020)

Reviewer's Choice Feathered Quill Book Awards (2020)

Winner Thriller Independent Press Award (2021)

Winner Thriller National Indie Excellence Awards 2021

Silver Medal Reader's Favorite Fiction Mystery Murder

Silver Winner Thriller and Suspense Foreword Indies 2020

First Runner-Up Eric Hoffer Award 2021

Reviews of *Tokyo Traffic* (2020)

"Pronko's immediate style puts you into the guts of the action but will pull at your heartstrings at the same time. The city of Tokyo shines brightly, with grit and glamour, and the author isn't afraid to tear the wrapper off of this dynamic city," Reader Views.

"A great page-turner with real tension towards the end and I hope that it won't be too long before we hear more about Hiroshi," *The Bookbag.*

"A dark and striking thriller with an indelible cast and setting," *Kirkus Reviews.*

"Starts fast and doesn't let up on its breakneck pace until bodies (both living and dead) are strewn all over the place," *Pacific Book Review.*

"With *Tokyo Traffic*, Pronko further establishes Hiroshi as one of the most distinctive and intrepid detectives in contemporary crime fiction," *Best Thrillers*.

"This is a classic thriller, the gritty atmosphere, the dark characters and a brave and slightly broken hero," *The Wishing Shelf*.

"Pronko develops characters that leap off the page. We want them to escape, we want them to get caught, we want them to solve the case," *Chanticleer Book Reviews*.

"Combining old-fashioned gumshoeing with modern-day social conventions, Pronko's tale is as much a Tokyo detective's diary as it is a gritty underworld whodunit," *US Review of Books*.

"Tokyo is described in all of its beauty and ugliness, where the sparkling world of music clubs, internet cafes and teen hangouts are tainted by a dismaying traffic of young people," *Advicesbooks*.

"Pronko's characters are fully developed, his dialogue is authentic, and his writing is clear and concise," *San Francisco Book Review*.

"It's clear the author knows Japan deep in his soul. Pronko is also a masterful storyteller. As the narrative's tension builds, readers will find themselves racing toward the inexorable moment when police, victims and villains collide," *Blue Ink Review*.

"A high-energy thriller set in the gruesome world of human trafficking and child pornography, TOKYO TRAFFIC keeps the adrenaline pumping until the very end," *IndieReader*.

"A story that winds through Tokyo's streets and Hiroshi's heart alike, drawing readers through a dangerous game that culminates in an unexpected, satisfying conclusion," *Midwest Book Review*.

"Taut and terse, this noir novel is executed to perfection," *Foreword Clarion Reviews.*

"Pronko creates the backdrop to this story as if it is a character all on its own and invites readers into this colorful world in an easy yet striking way. Thrilling crime fiction set in an exotic location," *Literary Titan.*

"I read and reviewed the first two in this series, and am happy to say that Tokyo Traffic is as good as the first two, if not better. It makes for uncomfortable reading at many points, but it's a necessary discomfort," *Crime Fiction Lover.*

"As both a love letter to Japan and a bold condemnation of certain human rights crises still alive and well in our modern world, Tokyo Traffic is a superlative addition to the Detective Hiroshi series," *SPR Review.*

"Rich in local colour and culture, the unfolding investigation into the dark underbelly of Tokyo life is fascinating, if disturbing," *Booksplainer.*

"This is a sophisticated, humane, and compelling take on the modern police procedural.

Fans will thrill to this mystery's lively characters, vivid descriptions of Tokyo, and unlikely heroics," *Booklife Review.*

"Adroitly takes readers on another outstanding Detective Hiroshi thrill ride into the streets of Tokyo, this time presenting a murderous case involving human trafficking that you don't want to miss," *Feathered Quill.*

"If there's a better crime series set in Japan, I've not yet read it," *Crime Thriller Hound.*

"Mystery readers who enjoy their detective pieces firmly rooted in reality will find Tokyo Traffic an excellent read," *California Bookwatch.*

"The worldbuilding is impeccable and I enjoyed the complex environment the protagonist navigates. Tokyo Traffic is filled with mystery and realism and I found myself rooting for the protagonist. It is fast-paced and emotionally rich," *Reader's Favorite.*